Country Roads

Also by Nancy Herkness

Take Me Home

Shower of Stars

A Bridge to Love

Music of the Night

Country Roads

Nancy Herkness

Montlake
Romance

Published by Montlake Romance
PO Box 400818
Las Vegas, NV 89140

ISBN-13: 9781477807699
ISBN-10: 1477807691
Library of Congress Control Number: 2013904922

To Maxine Kumin,

who made me feel like a real writer

Chapter 1

*J*ULIA CASTILLO HURLED THE LUG WRENCH INTO THE tall, dusty weeds by the side of Interstate 64. The odor of tar being cooked out of the asphalt by the midday sun made her cough. Wasn't it supposed to be cooler up here in the misty blue mountains of West Virginia? She kicked the flat tire on the rusty old Chevy Suburban. Twice.

If her uncle Carlos could see her now, he would frown and shake his head, since this just proved his conviction she wasn't safe out in the real world.

Thank God he wasn't here.

Before she could prevent herself, she focused her gaze on a nearby pine tree, checking for any waviness in her vision. "Stop it!" she muttered. She had driven all the way here without any sign of trouble despite the stress. She didn't need to start doubting herself just because she had a flat tire.

Julia raked her fingers through the tangled mass of her red hair, trying to think of what to do next. Her prepaid cell phone had run down its battery while searching for a signal en route. She'd left the one her uncle had given her in her studio, because she was pretty sure it was possible to track people through their cell phones. Or that might be one of those things you saw on television that wasn't true. Either way, she wasn't taking any chances, because she didn't want her uncle knowing where she was. As frustrated as she was with him, she preferred not to hurt him unnecessarily, and he would be very wounded by her current mission.

Squinting at the green-and-white sign at the top of the long uphill slope of the highway, she tried to read how many miles it was to Sanctuary. It was a single digit, but she couldn't tell if it was a three or an eight.

She could walk three, but not eight. Not in this heat.

The problem was her junk heap of an SUV had one door that wouldn't lock, and her paintings were too big to carry that far. She didn't care if thieves helped themselves to everything else in the car, but it would kill her to lose those paintings.

Scanning the landscape around her, she searched for a house or a store. All she could see was a river snaking under the bridge just behind her and a lot of green trees marching up the mountainsides. Four vehicles sped past her in loud rushes of hot, gritty air. She wasn't sure whether to be grateful not to have to worry about accepting help from a potentially murderous stranger or annoyed that chivalry seemed to be dead.

Another vehicle whooshed past, then flashed red brake lights and pulled over to the side of the highway well in front of her. Now that she had a possible rescuer, all the warnings about what happened to unprotected women with broken-down cars flashed through her brain. As the black, low-slung car reversed toward her, she wished she hadn't tossed the wrench; hefting it would have made her look a little threatening. Instead she had to settle for arranging her keys between her fingers so their ends stuck out as she made a fist, another tidbit she'd picked up from television.

The car's door swung open, and a man in a pale-blue shirt, red tie, and navy slacks emerged, unfolding his long legs as he stepped out onto the gravel.

"A tie seems pretty upstanding," she muttered, loosening her grip on the keys. "Serial killers probably don't wear ties on a regular basis."

She planted her feet wide apart and crossed her arms as the good Samaritan approached with a fluid, ground-eating stride. She guessed he was in his early thirties, and her artist's sensibility quivered with the urge to paint the planes and shadows of a face that was too strong for classic handsomeness but far more interesting. He had hair like an ancient Greek portrait: thick, dark waves you wanted to bury your fingers in. As he approached, his silver-gray eyes almost glowed in contrast against his olive skin. He would be a perfect model for one of those half-immortal, half-human offspring the Greek gods were always fathering. What were they called? Demigods.

His cool silvery gaze skimmed over her, making her aware of the dirt on the knees of her jeans from her futile attempt to change the tire. And the sweat that glued her white gauze peasant blouse to her shoulder blades. And who knew how crazed her long, curly hair looked after being blown around by the passing vehicles?

"Got a flat?" he said, stopping a few feet away as he shifted his survey to the limp pile of rubber nearly falling off the wheel rim.

She shook off her flight of whimsy. "That's an understatement," she said. "Could you call someone to come fix it? I'd be very grateful. My cell phone died."

She could have sworn he sighed. "If you have a spare, I'll put it on for you. No sense in paying for a tow if you don't have to."

He must have noticed the swaths of rust and multiple dents in her car and concluded she couldn't afford a tow truck. Which was true at the moment. She just needed to get to the Gallery at Sanctuary and things would improve. *She hoped.*

"My lug wrench is somewhere over there," she said, gesturing toward the weeds while a flush of embarrassment crept up her cheeks. "I think the nuts have rusted onto the bolts. I couldn't get them to budge, so the wrench seemed useless."

She had also been careful not to overexert herself, just as a precaution.

The corners of the demigod's mouth twitched slightly, but he said nothing as he squatted down to inspect the wheel. He picked up a rock and scraped at the rust on the lug nuts. She admired the stretch of blue cotton over a pair of distinctly godlike shoulders. Now she wanted to paint him in the nude.

"You may be right about that," he said, "but let me get my wrench and give it a try."

As he straightened to his full height, Julia felt a little frisson of nerves. He was a lot bigger than she was and still a total stranger. Maybe she should get back in her car and hope he didn't realize one lock didn't function.

"Be right back," he said, walking away before she bolted for the dubious safety of the SUV.

It was broad daylight, and plenty of vehicles whizzed past. Someone would notice if he grabbed her and dragged her off into the weeds, wouldn't they? She tightened her grip on her keys as he approached with a gleaming silver wrench in his hand.

"What's your name?" *If worse came to worst, at least she'd know who had killed her.*

"Sorry, ma'am, I should have introduced myself sooner. Paul Taggart." The sudden flash of his smile vaporized her fear as he held out his hand to her.

She had made a tactical error. She couldn't tell him her last name. "I'm Julia." His handshake was perfect: firm, warm, and not at all damp. He should be in politics with a smile and a handshake like that.

"I see." That clear gaze roamed over her face for a long moment before he released her hand and bent to fit the wrench onto one of the lug nuts. The muscles in his shoulders pulled at the shirt's fabric and he grunted with effort, but the nut didn't budge. He stood and braced his foot on the wrench, throwing his weight onto it. Still no movement. He turned to her with a shrug of regret as he pulled a slim phone out of his trouser pocket. "I'm afraid it's going to take more than human muscle to get this changed."

Damn! She was going to have to use her credit card. And then her uncle would be able to find out where she was.

She blew out a breath of frustration and examined Paul Taggart closely. His tie held the sheen of fine silk, and his trousers showed the drape of expensive wool. The vehicle parked in front of hers was some sort of sleek, powerful sports car. He looked like a man of substance. She screwed up her courage and did her best to project an air of honesty. "Er, I don't suppose you could float me a loan for the tow. I swear I'll pay you back. I just need to get to Sanctuary, and it's right up the road. Please." She injected a note of pleading into the last word.

He muttered something that sounded like, "How do they always find me?" She caught an undercurrent of resignation in his breezy tone as he said, "Sure. Happy to do it."

He didn't believe she would pay him back. Julia pressed her lips together so she wouldn't tell him to go to hell. She needed to get to the gallery. Then she'd show him she could return his loan.

If they liked the paintings.

Julia shoved the thought to the darkest recesses of her mind and pasted a grateful smile on her face. "Thank you so much."

"You're welcome. Let me call Bud to come get your car." She thought she saw a touch of guilt darken his eyes before he lowered his gaze to his cell.

"Bud?"

"He's the owner of the service station in Sanctuary. That's where you're headed, right?" He was already putting the phone to his ear.

"Are you from Sanctuary?"

He nodded. "Born and raised."

She wasn't sure how she felt about that. It would make it more satisfying to pay him back if she could see his face when she did it. On the other hand, she preferred to have the minimum number of people know she was in Sanctuary. The more she was seen, the more likely it was her uncle would find out she'd been there. She shrugged mentally. There was nothing she could do about it now.

Just then Paul spoke into the phone. He greeted whoever was on the other end of the call casually, yet it was clear he expected to have his request acted upon promptly. Her uncle worked the same way.

"The tow truck will be here in fifteen minutes," Paul Taggart said.

"Wow, that's quick." When it struck her that she was going to have to make conversation with him for those minutes, they suddenly stretched out to infinity.

"Why don't we go wait in my car, where it's quiet and air-conditioned?" he said.

She hesitated, fear tightening her spine. He didn't look like a rapist or a mass murderer, but neither had Ted Bundy. She flicked a glance at his car, discovering a slightly sinister cast in its dark, sleek lines. If she got in, he could lock all the doors and whisk her away to some isolated shack where she'd never be heard from again.

"You go ahead," she said, keeping her gaze on him as she edged toward the Suburban. "I need to rearrange a few things in my car so they don't shift when it gets towed."

She watched his shoulders lift and lower in another sigh before he fished a business card out of his shirt pocket and held it out to her. "Will this convince you it's safe to sit comfortably in my car?"

It was thick cream vellum with "Paul Taggart, Esquire" printed in block letters in the center. Below it was an address in

Sanctuary, West Virginia, as well as phone, fax, and e-mail information. Along the bottom, it read, "Admitted to the bar in: West Virginia, Virginia, Ohio, Kentucky, Maryland, Georgia." It was absurd, but the little piece of paper dispelled most of her nervousness. She slashed the card through the air like a miniature sword. "I guess this could inflict some really lethal paper cuts, if I needed to defend myself."

"At least you didn't make a crack about preferring a criminal to a lawyer," he said, gesturing for her to go ahead of him along the shoulder of the highway.

She felt like a mess next to his clean, pressed tailoring. She plucked at the back of her blouse, trying to peel it away from her skin before he saw how damp it was. She chuckled as she considered she had gone from worrying he was going to assault her to being concerned about what he thought of her appearance.

"Care to share the joke?" His voice came from close behind her and she swore she could feel the stir of his breath on her overheated skin. It was not an unpleasant sensation.

"Just laughing at myself." She tossed the comment over her shoulder and kept walking.

"I like that in a person."

They had reached the passenger side of his car, and he stretched his arm around her to open the door. As she slid onto the cool, smooth leather of the seat, she sighed with pleasure. Her trash heap's air-conditioning had died a hundred miles ago.

"It will get even better when I turn the engine back on." Startled, she looked up to find him leaning down so his face was nearly level with hers. She had to stop herself from lifting a hand to trace the strong bone structure.

"Watch your elbow," he said, closing the door as soon as she tucked her arm into her side.

He walked around the car's long hood, his stride claiming the space around him with the confidence of a man who controls his world. She envied him that. Her world had been taken out of her control since that terrible day she'd fallen off Papi's horse when she was six. And that was more than twenty years ago.

The driver's door opened, and he swung himself into the seat with a hand hooked on the roof. Inserting his long legs under the steering wheel, he punched the ignition on, bringing the engine to life with a roar of horsepower.

"Isn't this car kind of uncomfortable for someone as tall as you?"

"Do you ever wear high heels?"

Baffled, she nodded. "Sometimes."

"Are they comfortable?"

"Not particularly."

"So why do you wear them?" he asked.

"Because they look good. Okay, I get your point." His self-deprecation relaxed her just a bit.

He adjusted something on the climate-control panel and a waft of cool air brushed her face.

"Ah, that feels wonderful." She twisted the heavy mass of her hair up on top of her head and held it there so the delicious chill could reach her neck.

"So," he said, as he slewed sideways in the seat to settle his back against the door, his arm draped over the steering wheel. "What brings you to Sanctuary?"

Paul was just making conversation, but her eyes went wide and she hissed in a breath, dropping the bundle of vivid red hair back down over the smooth, exposed skin of her neck and shoulders.

"Er, business," she said, looking down at her fingers as she locked them together in her lap.

That caught his interest. The truth was he had tried hard to drive right by when he saw her standing beside the road. He was wearing his one and only Armani suit, bought on sale on a trip to Washington, DC, when he had taken the bar exam for Maryland. He had worn it for luck to the meeting at the Laurels, and he really didn't want to ruin it while changing a tire.

But he had never been able to ignore a damsel in distress, as his friend Tim always ribbed him. So he'd resigned himself to getting dirty, only to have his rescued damsel cadge a loan, give him the evil eye when he offered her the comfort of his car, and now look like he had accused her of scheming to rob a bank.

"If you'd rather not tell me, that's fine. It's your business," he said, but he suddenly wanted to know what sort of dealings this redheaded sprite, driving the worst piece of automotive junk he'd ever seen, could possibly have in Sanctuary.

"It's not that." She looked up at him, her green eyes clouded with guilt. "I'm kind of trying to keep it a secret that I'm here."

"Your secret is safe with me, but a lot of folks are going to notice that car being towed into town."

He watched the rise and fall of her breasts under the thin white material of her blouse.

"Yeah, I made a mistake buying that disaster, but it was the only thing big enough to hold my paintings."

"Paintings?"

She opened her mouth and closed it again as panic flickered in her eyes.

"Don't join the CIA," he said, trying to inject a little humor to ease her tension. "If you got caught by the enemy, you wouldn't make it through the first question of an interrogation."

"What? Oh." Her smile was shaky. "I've never tried to do something like this before."

"I don't know what 'this' is." He held up his hand as the smile fled from her face. "And you don't need to tell me, but I suggest you come up with a cover story before Bud's truck gets here."

"Why?"

"Well, people around here are naturally friendly, and they're likely to ask you the same thing I did. They might be offended if you refuse to answer them."

"Are you? Offended, I mean?"

"No, but I'm a lawyer, so I've developed a thick skin."

"I'm sorry if I was rude. I'm just nervous."

He followed the path of her hands as she rubbed them up and down the denim curving over her thighs. "I never would have guessed."

"You're being sarcastic." That seemed to reassure rather than upset her. Her hands stilled.

"Just some friendly teasing to lighten the mood." He tried to guess the source of her discomfort. His job brought him a fair amount of experience with handling skittish clients, but he didn't know enough about the sprite to speculate. The closest he could come was that she had stolen some valuable paintings and wanted to fence them, although why she had chosen Sanctuary for her activities was beyond him. It wasn't a hotbed for high-priced art sales. In fact, his little hometown wasn't a hotbed for much of anything.

She gazed straight ahead through the windshield for a long moment before turning back to him. "Do you know the Gallery at Sanctuary?"

A twitch of pain hit him in the chest. He knew the gallery all too well. The one woman in the world he had wanted to marry owned it, and she was the wife of his best friend. "An old friend of mine runs it. Claire Arbuckle."

Julia looked stricken. "I'm trying to find someone named Claire Parker."

"Parker was her maiden name. She's married to Tim Arbuckle now."

"Oh, thank goodness! I thought I might have come to the wrong place." The tension tightening her shoulders released. "So you know her? Do you know if she's working today?"

"I don't know for sure, but it's Thursday, so she's probably there. The weekenders start coming in, and they have the money to spend on art."

She pondered this for a minute before she turned those bright-green eyes back toward him. "Do you think Bud could just tow my car to the gallery?"

His new companion fascinated him; she managed to combine astonishing naïveté with a steely focus on her secret purpose. "He'll tow it anywhere you want, but how are you going to get the tire changed there?"

"I won't need that old heap anymore." Her gaze dropped back to her hands. "I hope."

"Maybe you should tell me what your business is. You can hire me as your lawyer so you'll have attorney-client confidentiality."

"You didn't look too thrilled about lending me money for the tow, but now you think I have the funds for a lawyer?" She slid him a sideways smile that sparkled with mischief.

"My curiosity has gotten the better of my good sense." And that smile had further undermined any shreds of detachment he was hanging onto. "Besides, I'm behind on my pro bono hours."

"That means you're doing it for free, right?"

He nodded.

"I guess I can afford a free lawyer. You're hired," she said, holding out her hand. As with the first time they'd shaken hands, he was surprised by the strength of her grip. She was such a slip of a thing; he didn't expect to feel such muscle in those slim fingers. "Where should I start?"

"How about your full name? I need to put it on the contract." That killed the imp dancing in her eyes, and he felt a pang of regret when she dropped her gaze to her lap again.

"Is that covered by the confidentiality too?"

"Sure. I'll call you Madame X in public." He wanted to coax the glow back into her face.

Instead she kept her eyes on her hands. "My name's Julia Castillo."

Chapter 2

*A*FTER A LONG MOMENT OF SILENCE, JULIA LIFTED HER head to find him staring at her as though she were some strange specimen from outer space. "The *painter* Julia Castillo?" Paul said, astonishment ringing in his voice.

"You've heard of me?" Julia asked. Then the reason struck her. "Oh right, you know Claire Parker, er, Arbuckle."

"Your paintings are worth hundreds of thousands of dollars and you're driving that rust bucket?" His gaze narrowed. "But you haven't produced any new work in, what, two years. Is that the problem? You've run through all your money?"

Now she was staring at him as disbelief smacked into her. "What do you mean I haven't done anything in two years?" She'd been painting nonstop until a week ago.

He straightened away from his lounging pose against the door, his eyes lit by an interest focused entirely on her. She had been intimidated by his height before, but now she was more worried about his mind. She sensed it would be impossible to hide anything from this man. Shifting sideways in her seat, she tried to put a little more distance between them.

"Claire has one of your paintings from back when she worked in New York. She says it's a masterpiece, and she wishes she had more to sell to her clients. But she hasn't been able to get her hands on anything new in a couple of years, despite the high demand for your work."

Julia forgot her concerns about Paul Taggart as shock punched her in the gut. Her uncle had told her people didn't like the changes in her style, so her new work wasn't selling. He kept trying to persuade her to go back to the way she used to paint. He didn't understand she couldn't.

When he'd seen her most recent set of paintings, he had told her he wouldn't even offer them to a gallery because they would ruin her reputation. Then he'd gently questioned her about how well she was sleeping, whether she was upset about something, and her diet. She knew he was just concerned about her health, but she hated the implication that her brain might be malfunctioning in a way that affected her work.

She'd spent a horrible night crying, pacing, and doubting herself before she decided to make a last-ditch effort to protect her art. So she had headed for Sanctuary because Claire Parker had been the first art dealer to buy her paintings, back when Claire worked at a big gallery in New York City.

"I take it those paintings in the back of your car are not the only new ones you've done in the last two years?"

Paul Taggart's deep voice cut through the agitation of her thoughts. "No, I've been working steadily." In fact, she had been excited about the direction her work was taking despite her uncle's criticism and implications. She could almost feel the power flowing from her inner vision through the brush and onto the canvas. It was a darker vision, full of risk, but it came from deep within her. That's what had given her the courage to strike out for Sanctuary on her own.

"But your agent hasn't been selling any of it?"

She shook her head. "He says people don't like it because it's different from my previous paintings."

"It sounds like we need to do a little investigation of your agent."

"I don't think so."

"Julia, he's either incompetent or hiding something from you. There's a huge demand for your work. Even I know that and I'm not part of the art world."

"He's my uncle, almost like a father to me." She felt tears well in her eyes and turned away so he wouldn't see them. "Why would he do this?"

Paul's voice was gentle. "It's a sad fact that I see in my line of work all the time. Family members aren't always honest with each other, especially when it involves large sums of money."

She shook her head, knowing in her bones her uncle wouldn't steal from her. "It wouldn't be about money." She blinked against the tears still threatening. "I just don't understand."

Long, warm fingers closed over the white-knuckled fist she had clenched on her thigh. His touch was firm enough to offer strength but light enough to be comforting. She turned back to him to say thank you, but the words evaporated as she met his eyes. In them she saw compassion and sympathy and something else that sent a shiver of awareness rippling through her body. The feel of his palm against her hand took on a sudden charge of sensuality. She felt exhilarated, not threatened.

The blast of a horn shattered the strange mood. A big flatbed truck with flashing yellow lights pulled onto the shoulder in front of Paul's car. He released her hand and swung open his door, saying, "The cavalry has arrived."

It took Julia a moment to pull herself back to the dusty roadside. She must have imagined the moment of connection, because her rescuer seemed unaffected by it. He had shifted back to the problem of her car without a moment's pause.

She got out of the car and joined the two men as they walked back toward her SUV.

"Bud, this is Julia," Paul said. "Julia, Bud Skaggs."

Bud wiped his hand on his coveralls before holding it out. "I hear you're headed for Sanctuary but fell a mite short. We'll get you there one way or the other."

"Thanks, I appreciate that." Julia liked the small, wiry man immediately. He had grizzled hair and skin like wrinkled leather. The three of them stood looking down at the flat tire.

Bud shook his head and raised his gaze to Julia. "I'm thinking you might want to trade the whole vehicle in for a newer model."

"Could you just take it to the gallery for right now? I'll figure out what to do with it after that."

"If that's what you want, it's fine with me," Bud said agreeably. "Paul, if you move your Corvette, I'll get this nice lady's SUV loaded up on the truck."

Julia put every ounce of the gratitude she felt into the look she gave Paul. "Thank you so much for everything. I'll send whatever I owe you to the address on your business card."

"Are you firing me so soon?" he said, lifting a dark slash of an eyebrow. "I think I should at least get to see these paintings and hear what Claire has to say about them."

"Are you an art lover?"

"No, but I have a weakness for a good mystery. I want to know if your uncle is right or wrong about your new style."

"He's wrong," she said, lifting her chin.

"I'm the last person to have an opinion on art, so don't look daggers at me," Paul protested, but the corners of his mouth were twitching.

"Hey, Paul, you going to move that 'Vette or am I going to drive over it?" Bud called out from the window of his truck.

"I'm on my way," Paul said over his shoulder before he turned back to her. "You might want to ride with me since the cab of Bud's truck isn't usually in any kind of condition to carry passengers."

As he strode away without waiting for her answer, Julia thrust her hands in her jeans pockets and watched him fold himself into his low-slung sports car. He pulled around the tow truck and stopped while Bud backed up to her Suburban and began hooking various chains to it.

Julia stood on the side of the road, the wind from the passing cars whipping her hair across her face, wondering how everything had gotten so complicated.

"Don't look so worried." Paul had walked up beside her. "We'll get it all straightened out."

"I'll bet you're a very successful lawyer," she said, glancing up at him. "You have that air of trustworthiness down pat."

"Maybe because I *am* trustworthy."

She wanted to believe him, because right now she was feeling very alone. No matter how much she and her uncle had disagreed over her work, she had trusted him. Now she had no one... except Paul Taggart. She could feel her lips start to tremble, and she pressed them together hard.

"Hey," he said, bending down so he could see her face. "Seriously. Everything will be all right."

Tears welled up in her eyes, and suddenly his arms were around her. His shirt held the scent of starch and a citrusy soap. It had been a long time since she'd found herself pressed against a male body, and she caught herself drawing more than mere comfort from his touch.

A grinding of metal on metal made her jump and pull away. Bud was winching her car onto the tilted flatbed. She swiped the back of her hand across her eyes.

Paul still held her shoulders in a gentle grip. "Are you going to be okay?"

"Just a moment of weakness. I appreciate the hug."

"Any time you need it. And I mean that."

She examined his face. His gray eyes were dark with concern, and he gave her shoulders a little squeeze before he released them.

Maybe he really did mean it.

Chapter 3

I CAN'T BELIEVE IT!" THE BEAUTIFUL DARK-HAIRED woman in the pink high heels took Julia's outstretched hand in both of hers and stared. "I've found Julia Castillo."

"Actually, I found her," Paul said. "Julia, this is Claire Parker Arbuckle. Julia's gone to a lot of trouble to get to you, Claire."

Claire shook her head once, sharply, and gave Julia a warm smile. "My apologies. I've been hoping to see more of your work for so long I can't believe my good fortune."

"And you owe it to me," Paul said.

"Actually, I did most of the driving," Julia said in a dry tone. "Paul just brought me the last few miles." And he looked at Claire as though she were a memory that made him sad and happy at the same time. She was trying to figure out what it might mean when Bud walked in carrying one of her paintings.

"Where shall I put this?" the older man asked.

"Right here," Claire said, pulling forward an empty easel from a corner of the back room where they'd found her. Her eyes lit up as Bud carefully propped up the plastic-wrapped canvas. "I feel like it's Christmas in June."

Terror clawed at Julia's gut. Now that she had the audience she had traveled so far to find, she wanted to turn and run. The confidence she had felt in the new paintings evaporated in the face of Claire's anticipation. She stared at the easel, but it showed no distortion around its edges. Somehow she was handling the stress.

"I'm being a terrible hostess," Claire said, turning away from the canvas. She waved to a couple of Lucite-and-metal chairs. "Have a seat. Can I get you something to drink?"

As the moment of panic receded, Julia couldn't decide if she was relieved or frustrated to have Claire's verdict postponed. Her throat was so tight she was certain she wouldn't be able to swallow anything. "No, thank you, I'm fine." She perched on the edge of a chair while Paul lounged in the other one, his long legs stretched out and crossed at the ankles, his fingers beating a quiet tattoo on the desktop beside him.

Claire sat back down in the desk chair she'd been occupying when they walked in. In her slim beige linen skirt and pink silk blouse, she looked like she should be strolling down Fifth Avenue. Leaning forward, she looked at Julia with a touch of bemusement. "Tell me why you drove all the way here in an unreliable car."

Julia had no idea how to couch her story in more positive terms, so she went with the bald truth. "I want your opinion on the paintings I brought."

Claire's eyebrows rose. "My opinion?"

"Yes. They're different from what I used to do, and I want to know what you think of them." She couldn't bring herself to tell this stunning, sophisticated woman her uncle-cum-agent hated them so much he wouldn't even show them to a dealer.

"I'm honored, but why me? Why the Gallery at Sanctuary?" Claire waved her hand at the storage room with its stark white walls, wide-plank floor, and racks of artwork. "As much as I love it here, it's not the epicenter of the art world."

"You were the first person to show my work in New York City. My uncle and I were so excited when you took those paintings of mine five years ago. Then he told me you'd moved to a gallery in Sanctuary, West Virginia." Julia locked eyes with Claire, willing her to understand how important this was. "It seemed like the right choice."

Claire's gaze was still puzzled as she scanned Julia's face. Paul's drumming ceased when he entered the conversation. "Julia's agent—who's also her uncle—wasn't sure about the market for these paintings, so Julia decided to consult with an expert. Knowing your interest in her work, she came to you."

Julia threw him a grateful look as he glossed over the whole car disaster and put her quest in blandly commercial terms. Of course, he probably didn't realize how gut-wrenchingly important Claire's judgment of her work was to her. "Exactly," she said, nodding emphatically.

Claire still looked as though she wanted to ask more questions, but after a quick exchange of glances with Paul, she smiled and stood up. "Well then, let's take a look."

Unable to sit still as her fate was being decided, Julia shoved up out of her chair, and Paul came to his feet beside her. Together they walked closer to the easel.

Claire took a pair of scissors from the desk and carefully cut the tape holding the plastic covering in place. She put down the scissors and peeled the plastic down from the surface of the canvas.

The terror roared back to life, clogging Julia's throat with the conviction her new work was garbage. Blackness crept along the edges of her vision as memory transported her back to the day of her first public portfolio review at art college. The professor was notorious for his scathing criticism, and Julia had wanted so badly to do well. As he walked up to critique the first painting, Julia had blacked out, regaining consciousness to find the teacher and her classmates staring down at her as she lay on the floor, their expressions ranging from concern to downright fear.

Trying to stave off the panic, she reached out and grabbed Paul's hand. He looked startled, but he wrapped his fingers around hers and tucked her hand in against his elbow.

Julia closed her eyes. She focused on the pressure of Paul's fingers over her hand, the solidity of his rib cage against her forearm, and the steady beat of his pulse where his wrist touched hers.

When she had beaten the fear down, she opened her eyes to see Claire standing in front of the painting with her hand to her mouth. Both the woman and the painting were clear and well-defined.

If Julia was going to have a seizure, this would be the moment, but no aura darkened her vision or heaved at her stomach. She swallowed and tried to speak, but all that came out was a croak.

Paul's fingers tightened on hers. "Claire, you're torturing Julia. What do you think of the painting?"

"What? Oh yes." Claire's hand dropped as she turned. Julia struggled to draw in air. "It's extraordinary. Such a huge leap forward from what you'd been doing before. It's got so much more power and intensity."

"You like it?" Julia had to gasp for breath as she spoke.

"I think *like* is too mild a word for what you're doing here. I'm blown away."

"Oh, thank God!" She sagged so hard against Paul, he dropped her hand to wrap his arm around her waist.

"You need to sit down," he said, shifting his grasp as he grabbed the rolling desk chair and eased her down onto it.

"Let me get a bottle of water," Claire said, starting toward the door.

"No, no, I'm fine," Julia said. "I just need to breathe for a minute."

As oxygen flowed into her lungs, a tear of sheer relief zigzagged down her cheek. She let her head fall back, muttering to herself, "I knew it was good. I knew it."

Someone touched her knee, and she tipped her head forward again to find Paul kneeling in front of her, his brows drawn together in a frown of concern. "Are you all right?"

"I'm better than all right. When you're barraged with criticism all the time, you begin to doubt your own judgment. You can't imagine the relief of knowing I wasn't crazy or blind."

Claire was unwrapping the next painting Bud had carried in. "This one is as good as the first!" she said, leaning it against the wall and walking away to gaze at it. "Maybe better."

Paul was still hovering in front of Julia. Reckless in her newly restored confidence, she asked, "What do *you* think of them?"

His eyebrows shot upward in surprise. "Me? I told you I'm not an art expert."

"Neither are most of the people who buy art," Julia pointed out.

He gave her a searching look and pushed off the floor, towering over her as he straightened to his full height. He moved in front of the easel, and she felt nerves squeezing her throat closed again. As he said, it shouldn't matter what he thought. After all, Claire was the expert, and she was bubbling over with excitement. But Julia wanted his approval too. She wasn't sure why. She just did.

She surged out of the chair, sending it rolling into the desk with a bang. "Oh gosh, I'm sorry," she said as Claire started. Paul didn't seem to notice. He stood stock-still, his arms crossed over his chest.

Julia tiptoed around so she could see his expression and wished she hadn't. He looked as though someone had walloped him in the belly when he least expected it.

"You don't like it," she whispered, the jubilation draining out of her.

It took him a moment to focus on her. "You painted this?" He shook his head in wonderment. "It's so…so big and wild and you're so…so, I don't know." He made a gesture toward her.

Claire came to his rescue. "So small and fragile-looking. To be painting with such emotional power."

"Right," he said. "I can't make the connection."

Julia turned to the painting, trying to understand what he meant. It was one of the pictures she called *Night Mares*, a massive black horse with glowing eyes galloping through a riot of colors and shapes.

"I have to admit, I'm sort of stunned myself," Claire said, coming to stand beside Paul.

"I guess I can't afford this, but I sure as hell would like to own it," he said.

"You would?" Julia asked, his enthusiasm warming her.

"Paul, when did you become an art lover?" Claire asked.

"When I found something I liked."

"It's yours," Julia said.

Both of them looked at her as though she'd lost her mind. "I'm much obliged, but I can't accept this," Paul said. "I know what your paintings are worth."

"It wouldn't be worth anything if you hadn't rescued me from the side of Interstate 64." Julia grimaced at the memory of all those cars whizzing past her. "I want you to have it for being kind to a total stranger. There should be a reward for that."

Claire's dark eyes sparkled with laughter. "Oh God, please don't make him worse. We call it D-I-D syndrome. Paul has a compulsion to save damsels in distress."

He chuckled, but Julia noticed he was tapping his fingers against the side of his thigh.

"Well, I'm a very grateful damsel, and I want you to have the painting."

"It's out of proportion to my contribution."

He wasn't taking her offer seriously, she could tell. "Well, then consider it your retainer since you're my lawyer now." She felt an overwhelming desire to know her painting was hanging somewhere Paul Taggart would see it every day.

His face relaxed into a smile. "It would take me the rest of my career to work this off."

"So you'll accept it?"

"No, ma'am. When it comes to the law, I only accept cash." His tone was light, but she heard the rock-hard refusal beneath. His pride wouldn't allow him to accept something he thought was too valuable.

Claire had been standing halfway between the two of them, simply watching, but now she interjected, "I could give you an advance against sales, if cash is a problem."

"You could?" Julia felt uncertain again. Her uncle handled all her financial affairs, an arrangement she'd never minded until the last few days, when she'd needed money to buy the car without letting him know about it.

"We do it all the time for our established artists. And you certainly qualify as established."

"Well, if you do it for other artists, I guess it's all right then," Julia said, although she felt uneasy about taking money she hadn't earned. "All I really need is enough to pay Mr. Skaggs for the tow and fixing the flat."

"You're not really going to drive that piece of garbage again, are you?" Paul broke in.

"I guess I could rent a car." She'd never done it before, since she almost never drove. It was another of those everyday tasks she had no idea how to perform.

He sighed. "Where do you live?"

Julia could see Claire's shoulders shaking with silent laughter as Paul tried to rescue her again.

She looked him straight in the eye. "You're not driving me back to North Carolina."

A look of relief crossed his face when she mentioned her home state. She wondered if he would have offered to drive her to Florida or Texas.

Claire took her hand away from her mouth to wipe her eyes. "You might as well resign yourself, Julia. Paul will not rest until he has delivered you safely back to your castle."

"This is the problem with people who've known you since high school," he said. "I have no intention of driving Julia back to North Carolina. I was going to suggest hiring Gordy Wickline to do it, paid for by your advance."

"Excuse me, I'm not a package," Julia said. "I can hire my own transportation." As she said it, she remembered she had to confront her uncle when she got home. She would have to confess to going behind his back to prove him wrong. He would be angry and hurt, a combination that stabbed a knife of dread into her heart. "I may not go straight home."

Bud propped another canvas against the wall and unslung a ratty duffel bag from his shoulder. "Well, that's the last of the paintings, and here's your overnight bag. Come on over to the station whenever you decide what to do with your car."

"Thanks. I think I want to junk it. Just let me know what I owe you for everything."

"Nothing at all. I can tell everyone I met a famous artist. And I can probably get enough parts off the car to make a profit." He winked.

Julia resolved to take him a gift as soon as she could find something appropriate. She'd ask Paul for suggestions. "I appreciate it, but I'm really not famous."

"Didn't you paint that picture Mrs. Arbuckle keeps in her special room?"

Claire spoke as Julia turned to her with a question in her eyes. "Yes, she did."

"That's famous enough for me." He nodded to them and walked out.

"I'll show you," Claire said, waving her toward the door.

They walked a few steps farther up the gallery's corridor and stopped in front of a door with a keypad beside it. Claire punched in a combination and swung the door open. Julia stepped into the room to see one of her early landscapes with horses hanging in solitary splendor on the opposite wall. It was lit perfectly, and she was surprised at how much she still liked it. Sometimes it was painful to revisit her older pictures; they were so immature. In this one she had managed to capture the light in a way that made it interesting, even if the subject was conventional.

She slid a sideways glance at Paul to see how he reacted to this painting. He was examining it with a detached expression. There was nothing of the stunned astonishment her other painting had evoked.

"I've always loved this painting," Claire said, her gaze locked on it as she walked forward.

"The light's good," Julia said. "I managed to get that right. And the chestnut's posture gives some interest to the composition."

"But you've left this particular style behind," Claire said with an understanding smile.

Julia was beginning to really like her. She nodded. "It was the best I could do at the time."

"Most painters would kill to do one-quarter as well," Claire said.

"I'm with Julia," Paul said. "This one's really good, but I like the new ones. They grab you by the throat and won't let go."

She beamed at him. He might not be an expert, but he got her new work. She opened her mouth to express her gratitude when her stomach growled so loudly both her companions turned to look at her. She pressed her hand against her abdomen, trying to muffle any further complaints. "Sorry. I didn't eat lunch today."

Carlos would be distraught if he knew her breakfast had consisted of a package of crackers from a vending machine and several gulps of water from the rest stop's drinking fountain. And the crackers were only possible because she'd found some stray change on the floor of her car. She'd spent all her cash to buy the rusty SUV, so there wasn't anything left over for food.

"Let me order you a sandwich," Claire said, reaching toward the telephone on the desk.

"No, I'll take her to lunch," Paul said.

"Don't you have clients to see? It *is* a workday." Julia couldn't resist a little dig, since he wouldn't accept her gift.

A half smile tilted his mouth. "No, my afternoon is completely open."

"So the meeting went well?" Claire asked. "They're going to fund the Pro Bono Project?"

"Yup." Satisfaction lit his eyes. "With a minimum of arm twisting."

"I'm so glad," Claire said, touching his hand briefly. "You deserve it."

"There are still a lot of details to be worked out."

"I'm sure, but you can take pride in knowing they were excited enough to travel all the way down here from New York."

"I'm pretty sure the golf courses at the Laurels were the main draw." His fingertips were oscillating against his thigh again.

"When did you become so modest?" Claire asked.

"Right about the time Julia here looked at me as though I were a serial killer."

Julia had been feeling left out as the two friends discussed something that clearly meant a lot to Paul. Now she happily leaped back into the conversation. "I was just being cautious," she protested.

"It's something about his eyes, isn't it?" Claire said. "He's got that scary laser focus."

Paul held up a hand to forestall further analysis of his potential as a mass murderer. "I think it's time to get some food into

Ms. Castillo. We'll leave you here to contemplate all the commissions you're going to collect from selling her paintings."

A sudden realization wrenched Julia's gaze around to Claire. "Wait! You never mentioned whether you could sell the paintings or not. You just said *you* thought they were good."

Claire's gaze slid away toward the paintings. "I can sell them, but all that intensity may not appeal to my usual clients. I'm going to have to reach out to a different audience, one I haven't been in touch with for a while."

"So they're not going to be as marketable as my earlier ones." Julia felt the weight of her uncle's judgment land on her shoulders like a lead shawl.

"That's not what I meant," Claire said, coming over to take Julia's hands and squeeze them encouragingly. "You've done your job. You've made superb art. Now you have to let me do my job, which is to find the right buyers for it."

"You don't have to sugarcoat the truth for me," Julia said, squaring her shoulders as she gently pulled her hands away. "If they aren't good enough to sell, just tell me."

"They're more than good enough to sell." Paul's voice was firm. "I want one, and I've never bought an original artwork in my entire life."

Claire's eyes lit up. "If you're planning to stay here in Sanctuary for a while, I have an idea. It's a little risky, but it might make a big splash in the art world."

"What kind of idea?" Julia wasn't big on making splashes. Most of her life had been structured to avoid anything that might create unnecessary tension for her.

Claire shook her head. "I need to work out the details before I tell you." She started toward the door. "Let me give you your advance, so you can buy lunch."

"It's my treat," Paul said.

Before she could protest, he put his hand in the small of Julia's back and propelled her firmly toward the door. Her shirt was so thin, it felt as though his palm was touching her bare skin. Little shivers of heat radiated out from his hand to skitter across her back.

Or maybe she was light-headed from hunger.

Chapter 4

$\mathcal{J}$ULIA TOOK THREE STEPS ONTO THE LIBRARY CAFÉ'S open-air dining terrace and halted, gazing with delight at the town of Sanctuary spread out below them. "It's like one of those perfect Victorian towns they set up around model railroads."

"We try to keep it nice," Paul said.

As they stood just outside the French doors, waiting to be seated, she glanced up to see him scanning the view with a proprietary air. "You look at it as though you own it," she teased.

A shadow crossed his face. "Sometimes I feel more like it owns me."

"What do you mean?"

"I was mayor of Sanctuary for two terms, and some folks think I still am."

"Best mayor we ever had." A white-haired woman wearing a yellow apron embroidered with an open book beside a piece of cake walked up with two menus tucked under her arm.

"Can you tell Mrs. Bostic was my number-one supporter?" Paul's smile was genuine as he leaned down to give her a peck on the cheek.

"Get on with you," the café hostess said. "I may have told all my friends to vote for you, but I was just doing what was best for the town. Sunshine or shade for your table?"

"Sunshine," Julia said, just as Paul said, "Shade."

"I figured you might burn with that fair skin and red hair," Paul said, as they followed Mrs. Bostic to a green metal café table set under a yellow-and-white striped umbrella.

Pleasure blossomed in her chest because he had noticed something about her, even if he should have asked where she wanted to sit. "Sometimes it's worth the burn to feel the sunbeams on your skin."

He pulled out the wicker chair. "It's not good for you, though." He sat down across from her, leaving the menu closed on the table as Mrs. Bostic pulled out an order pad. "I recommend the chicken salad sandwich and the sweet potato fries. And the pecan pie, if you have a sweet tooth," Paul said.

Julia had declared her independence when she loaded her paintings in the Suburban to set out for Sanctuary, and she wasn't about to give it up now. She opened the menu, scanned through it, and grimaced. He had ordered exactly what she would have chosen. She slapped the folder shut on the table. "And an iced tea, please."

"You see. I let you choose your own beverage." His pale eyes held an understanding glint.

Mrs. Bostic scooped up the menus. "I'll have your drinks here in a jiffy."

Julia waited until the woman was several steps away. "Are you always so bossy?"

"No, I just know what's best for everyone."

That reminded Julia of what her uncle had said when he told her he wouldn't offer her new paintings to the gallery: *I'm doing what's best for your career.* The pain of his rejection seared through her again. He had been like a father to her since her parents moved away. She turned in the direction of the view but saw nothing of its beauties.

"That was meant to be a joke." Paul's wry voice broke into her reverie.

She jumped and turned back to him. "I know. I was thinking about something else."

"Nothing good, from your expression." He was spinning a spoon back and forth through the fingers of his right hand.

"Are you nervous?"

"No. Should I be?" The spoon continued to twirl as though it had a life of its own.

"Well, it's just that you're fiddling with that spoon." She gestured toward his hand.

Frowning, he looked down and placed the spoon on the table, lining it up with the knife beside it.

"You didn't even realize you were doing it, did you?"

He shrugged. "It's a habit I should have broken by now." He unfolded his napkin onto his lap. "So, shall I drop you at Claire's house after lunch? She ought to be home by then."

"At Claire's house?"

"She invited you to spend the night with her."

"She did?"

"As we were leaving the gallery."

"I was distracted." By his hand warming her skin through the gauze of her blouse. Her eyes were drawn to his long, elegant fingers now lying still on the table.

"What's the verdict, now that you know about the invitation?"

Julia gnawed at her lip. Her original plan had been to head back to her home immediately after hearing what Claire had to say about the paintings. She had worked hard to cover her tracks, because she hadn't wanted Carlos to know she didn't trust his opinion of her work. Now she needed to regroup.

On one hand, it was exhilarating to be free of the protective cocoon her uncle had built around her. A cocoon she no longer needed, according to her doctors. On the other, she was ignorant of the way the art world worked. Her instincts told her to trust Claire, but then, she had trusted Carlos too. The thought of making what Claire termed "a big splash" held as much terror as excitement.

She looked at the man across the table from her, his gray eyes sharp with intelligence. Maybe she *should* stay here and hire him in all seriousness to help her through the situation. God knew, she was having a hard time thinking clearly for herself.

"I'm starting to feel like a bug pinned to a board," Paul said, lifting an eyebrow.

"I guess you've never had your portrait painted." She stalled as she considered her crazy idea. "That's how an artist looks at a subject."

"The town budget doesn't run to portraits of past mayors."

She chuckled halfheartedly as Mrs. Bostic returned with their drinks in tall glasses sweating with moisture. "You'd make a good subject, you know. You have a strong bone structure."

"Tall, dark, and handsome. That's me." He said it as though it was a line he'd used before but didn't really believe. She began to grasp his smooth patter covered a withdrawal from the conversation.

"Better than that. Tall, dark, and intriguing." She spoke without thinking because she was still focused on her inner debate.

But she had snagged his attention again. His gaze settled on her and sharpened. "So you want to know me better?"

"It's professional," she sidestepped lamely. "As a painter, I find you interesting."

It was true as far as it went.

He laughed and shook his head. "That's a first."

The white flash of his teeth against his olive skin and the husky maleness of his laugh tipped the scales of her decision. She would stay here for a few days. Since she would have to tell Carlos she had been here, she no longer needed to cover her tracks and could use her credit card. A change of scene might be good for her. And it would allow her to postpone the painful confrontation with her uncle a little longer.

"Let me guess. You're wondering what to say to your uncle when you get home," Paul said.

"How did you know?"

"Let's just say I wouldn't put you on the witness stand if you were guilty."

She frowned. "I've never needed to hide anything before." Most of her life, she had let her parents and then her uncle enfold her in their protective care while she focused on exploring her ability to create art. Except for her stint at art school in Greensboro, she'd never lived more than five miles from the house she grew up in, nestled in the mountains of western North Carolina. Even at school, she'd been so focused on excelling and so embarrassed by her public seizure that she'd isolated herself from her fellow students for the two years she stayed there.

She glanced back at the view. Sanctuary wasn't exactly a bustling metropolis, but it was filled with places and people she'd never seen before. And Paul Taggart lived in it.

"Talk to me, Julia. I'm your lawyer, so you can tell me what's going on behind those big green eyes." His long fingers circled his glass and he took a sip of the cola in it.

"I've decided to stay here for a couple of days, but not at Claire's. I can pay for my own hotel. And I want you to give me some legal advice about the problem with my uncle. For real this time, not pro bono."

His eyebrows rose. "So you're taking the advance?"

"I have a credit card. I just didn't want to use it."

"You didn't want your uncle to know where you had gone."

She nodded.

"Here you go. The best chicken salad in West by gosh Virginia." Mrs. Bostic slid their plates onto the woven placemats.

"You know, Paul got this library built when he was mayor. You wouldn't be sitting here enjoying the view without a whole lot of time, effort, and persuasion on his part."

Julia swiveled to take in the large brick building behind her. It was gracefully designed to hug its hilltop setting, yet it had the presence a repository of knowledge should. "That's quite an accomplishment."

"All I did was organize a lot of good, hardworking folks," Paul said, his fingers drumming on the tabletop. She liked the fact he didn't want to take the credit.

"So you're new in town?" the hostess asked Julia.

"I just arrived today." She took a deep breath before holding out her hand and saying, "I'm Julia Castillo."

"She's one of Claire's artists," Paul said.

"Well, I'll be. You painted that pretty picture of the horses over to the gallery. My daughter likes it so much, she goes to see it at least once a week." The woman pumped Julia's hand.

"Really? That's nice to hear." She meant it. She realized the isolation she lived in had protected her from the worry of criticism, but it had also deprived her of the pleasure of people's appreciation.

"Yup. She says it's so peaceful she just wants to lay down on the grass with the horses and forget all her troubles," Mrs. Bostic continued.

Fear clenched a fist around Julia's throat. Mrs. Bostic's daughter would hate her new work; there was nothing peaceful about it. Julia forced herself to take a deep breath and rolled her shoulders, trying to work the tension out.

The older lady leaned down to murmur something in Paul's ear. Smiling, he shifted his gaze to Julia, saying, "I don't think she'd mind at all."

"Would you autograph my order pad for my daughter? She'd be mighty pleased. Her name's Sherry."

Julia felt a nip of surprise. "Wow, this is the first time I've ever been asked for my autograph." She took the pad Mrs. Bostic held out, trying to think of something to say. Just writing her name seemed sort of arrogant, but her mind was blank about what to add to it. Evidently, she wasn't good at this kind of interaction. She tapped the pen against her cheek for several seconds before she gave up and did a quick sketch of a horse's head, signing her name under it. "I hope that's okay."

The woman flipped the pad around and crowed with delight. "Her very own horse picture by a famous artist. She'll be chuffed."

"You may have set a dangerous precedent," Paul said, as the hostess showed the pad to another diner. "Your fans will be demanding sketches with every autograph."

Julia had to look away quickly as Mrs. Bostic's audience turned around to stare at her. The warmth of gratification warred with a flutter of nerves as she found herself an object of attention. "That's fine with me. I'm better at drawing than writing."

To ward off her self-consciousness, she bit into the sandwich. The burst of flavor on her hunger-sensitized palate made her close her eyes to savor the taste. She opened them to find Paul lounging back in his chair, a slight smile playing around the corners of his mouth. "Aren't you going to eat?" she asked.

"It's more fun to watch you enjoy the experience."

She took another bite, trying to ignore the weight of his gaze. "It's rude to watch someone else chew."

He chuckled and picked up his own sandwich, sinking those dazzling white teeth into it. She couldn't help watching the strong column of his throat as he swallowed. An image of herself pressing her lips against the skin of his neck bloomed in her mind and she choked.

"Slow down," he said, pushing her iced tea toward her. "You don't need to devour it all in one bite."

She coughed even harder as a flush climbed up from her chest to her cheeks. She hated having a redhead's complexion.

Concern banished the smile from his face, and he shoved his chair back and started to stand. She waved her hand and croaked, "I'll be okay. Just swallowed wrong." Seizing her glass, she doused the flare of heat with several gulps of iced tea. Composing herself, she went back to their previous topic. "Do you have a recommendation on where I could stay in Sanctuary?"

Paul polished off the last of his drink and pulled out his cell phone. "You could probably afford to stay at the Laurels, but since you don't have a car right now, how about someplace closer? There's a nice country inn at the other end of town."

"If you recommend it, I'm sure I'll like it." She hated to admit it, but making so many decisions had exhausted her.

"You're very trusting all of a sudden."

"Well, you haven't murdered me yet."

He laughed and tapped at his phone's screen. She listened as he bantered with whoever answered. Her fingers itched for a pencil to sketch the sharp edge of his cheekbones and the slash of his brows over those luminous eyes. She hadn't lied about his bone structure: his face was a study in angles. She thought about carving it out of stone, but there was such a fierce intelligence animating it, she decided stone was too heavy a medium.

"You've got the Robert E. Lee suite," he said.

"Didn't West Virginia fight on the Union side?"

"Yes, but his horse was born near here, which is why it's called the Traveller Inn. They even have his training saddle on display."

Mrs. Bostic appeared with two whopping slices of pecan pie. "Dessert's on me. I still can't believe I have a picture by a famous artist on my order pad." She shook her head as she walked away.

Julia picked up her fork and gave him a cocky grin. "I think I could get used to being a celebrity."

Chapter 5

*I*T'S VERY…QUAINT," JULIA SAID, TURNING SLOWLY AS
she took in the Robert E. Lee suite.

The wavy glass of the Civil War–era windowpanes gave
soft edges to the blocks of sunlight on the faded Oriental rug.
An overstuffed sofa with rolled arms upholstered in indigo
brocade stood in front of a fireplace ornamented with fluted
columns painted robin's-egg blue. Through the connecting
door she could see a four-poster bed covered by a handmade
quilt splashed with yellow, peach, and green. She knew most
people would find the suite inviting, but the fussy details and
haphazard colors made her long for the streamlined moder-
nity of her studio.

"I'll put this in the bedroom," Paul said, hefting her battered
duffel bag, which they'd collected from the gallery. "The bathroom is a little old-fashioned but it's functional."

"Does it have a shower? That's all I care about right now."
She felt like she'd been on a four-day camping trip in a desert.
Following Paul, she stuck her head into the bathroom to see
if the innkeepers provided toiletries and sighed with bliss-
ful anticipation when she saw the L'Occitane labels on the
little bottles sitting by the antique marble sink. Her duffel
hadn't been intended for an overnight stay; she had planned
to change her clothes in a restroom before going to the gallery
to meet Claire.

As something pinged, she turned to find Paul frowning down at his cell phone. "Do you need to call someone back?" she asked. "I feel bad about taking up so much of your time today."

"No, it'll just take me a couple of seconds to answer this." His fingers flew over the touch screen before he looked up at her. "Claire texted too. She says to bring you to her house for dinner, and she won't take no for an answer."

"I'd love to, but I can't ask you to drive me any more places." A certain tension in his stance made her add the last caveat. The recent text seemed to have disturbed him.

His shoulders relaxed. "I wouldn't miss it for all the barbecue sauce in Texas. They're getting takeout from the Aerie."

"Wait! I read about the Aerie before I came here. Doesn't it have its own helipad so people can fly in to eat there? A place like that does takeout?"

"Only for Claire's husband. Tim's the local vet, and he saved Adam Bosch's German shepherd after the dog was attacked by a bear. Adam owns the Aerie, and he's very attached to his pet."

Julia wanted to laugh out loud at the whimsy of it. She couldn't wait to explore this brand-new place with its quirky residents, like the restaurateur who loved his dog to the point of cooking gourmet takeout for his vet. Carlos didn't understand how much she needed fresh experiences. "God, I should have done this years ago."

"Done what?"

"Run away from home." A realization speared through her and jerked her gaze up to Paul. "I need to tell my uncle where I am before he sends out a search party."

Paul held out his phone. She just looked at it as she chewed on her lip. She had no idea how to explain her abrupt flight without stirring up a hornet's nest of recriminations. However misguided her uncle's actions might have been, he had acted out of concern. She knew she was going to upset him no matter what she said, but she wanted to deliver the bad news as tactfully as possible. Tact was not her long suit.

"Tell him you needed a change of scene," Paul said. "You can blame it on your artistic temperament."

Anger flared. She was tired of people assuming her creativity made her flaky. Her health issue had nothing to do with her work; it was a physiological malfunction of her brain, nothing more or less. She glared at him. "I don't have an artistic temperament. I'm very easy to get along with." She snatched the cell out of his hand.

"So I see."

"I *used* to be easy to get along with. Until I met you."

"Yeah, I bring out the worst in people."

"Not according to Mrs. Bostic." She grimaced down at the phone in her hand before she punched in her uncle's number. Taking a deep breath and putting the phone to her ear, she walked into the living room and stood at a window looking out over the inn's garden. As the phone rang, she traced the curving brick walkway through the brightly hued blossoms, hoping the peaceful beauty of the scene would relax the tightness in her neck.

"Who is this?" Her uncle's voice with its faint accent boomed through the phone.

Julia winced. "It's Julia, Tío."

"Julia!" A string of rapid-fire Spanish bombarded her. She could follow the gist of what he said, which was that he was frantic with worry, was about to call the police, why hadn't she told him she was leaving, was she losing her mind, and where was she anyway?

"I'm in Sanctuary, West Virginia," she said when he paused for breath. That was the easiest question to answer.

"Where?"

"Sanctuary, West Virginia," she repeated. "I brought my paintings to show Claire Parker."

"You did what? I was trying to protect you from people seeing those...*dios mío*, Julia, how did you get there? You did not drive!"

"Yes, I did. I bought a car." She squared her shoulders. "I needed to come, to find out what someone else thought of my *Night Mares*."

Silence. Then in a heavy voice he said, "You did not trust my judgment."

"It was important to me," she said, hating the note of pleading she heard in her own voice. "If I don't have my art, what do I have?"

"Your life, Julia! Which you will not have if you go careening around in a car all alone. You know what could happen."

"Yes, I know, but I've been fine for two years since I stopped taking the medicine." She hunched her shoulders and murmured into the phone, not wanting Paul to hear.

"Do you have your medication with you?"

"No." She was practically whispering. "I threw it all away."

Her uncle exploded into Spanish again, ending with the demand that she fly home immediately.

"I thought I'd stay here a few days."

"Julia, *mi querida*, you have the courage of a lioness, but you are taking great chances. I will come tomorrow to get you."

As she tried to find a kind way to tell him not to come, she felt herself being herded back into the loving cage her family had built around her.

Paul leaned his shoulder against the doorframe and studied the woman bathed in the sunshine slanting through the glass. Her waving hair glinted with brilliant golds and reds while the light turned the thin fabric of her blouse almost transparent. She was silhouetted against the window so he could see the slope of her shoulders, the defined slimness of her arms, and the sensual curve of her waist and hip. Pure lust slugged him in the gut, and he straightened away from the door. This was a complication he hadn't expected, especially considering he could see the tension holding her back ramrod straight and squeezing her free hand in and out of a fist. Julia was obviously drawing on every ounce of her strength to get through a difficult discussion, and all he could think about was working his hands up under her blouse to touch the creamy skin tantalizing him through the gauze.

That would give new meaning to the attorney-client relationship. In his opinion she didn't really need a lawyer, she just needed some clearheaded perspective on dealing with a family member. He could offer her that without crossing any ethical boundaries.

He considered retreating into the hallway to put some distance between them, but figured she might need moral support. He also wanted to get a better idea of what the situation between her and her uncle was like.

So he forced himself to concentrate on her voice rather than her body as she justified her absence to Carlos, her tone becoming more and more tentative and apologetic. Her shoulders began to slump inward, and he could tell her resolve was weakening. She stammered out something before turning to look at him. Paul gave her the calm, supportive smile he used to encourage faltering witnesses in court, and he saw her spine straighten as she turned back to the window.

"No, Tío," she said, her voice clear and firm. "I'll call you in a couple of days to let you know when I'm coming home. Goodbye. *Te quiero.*"

She stood staring ahead for a long moment before she turned away from the window and gave him a wavering smile.

"It went pretty well," she said, her voice hitching midsentence. "He was giving me another half an hour before he called the police."

Paul tried to project humorous sympathy. "So he bought into the artistic well needing to be refilled?"

"More or less, since he already thinks I'm having a nervous breakdown because I'm painting such ugly pictures."

He could see the shimmer of pain in her eyes and wanted to curse her uncle for his cruelty. Before he could make a better decision, he drew her into what was meant to be a comforting hug, murmuring adjectives into her sun-warmed hair. "Your paintings are magnificent. Bold. Powerful. Even a total philistine like me wants one."

As his palm slid over the skin bared by the scooped back of her blouse, he sucked in a breath. She felt as silky and smooth as he had anticipated.

She tilted her forehead in so it grazed his shoulder, and spoke into his chest. "Maybe I *am* going crazy. It's not normal to pick up and leave without a word to everyone who cares about you."

It was hard to think straight as he felt the soft press of her breasts against him when she gulped in air. He got a grip on his reeling brain. "That's your uncle trying to make you feel guilty. You needed a second opinion. That's a perfectly rational response to your situation."

"I needed to take sanctuary in Sanctuary," she said, leaning back into his arms to look up at him, her green eyes huge against her pale skin. One tear had painted a glistening path down her cheek. "You see how messed up I am? I can't tell whether I'm crazy or not. Maybe you're right about the artistic temperament."

She looked so small and bereft; he lowered his head to kiss her. He meant to comfort and distract her, but as soon as he touched the heady combination of softness and salt on her lips, he forgot his original purpose. She ran her fingers over his face as though she were trying to learn it by feel alone while her mouth turned hot under his. He buried his hands in her glorious hair, tilting her head so he could angle his mouth harder against hers. She opened to him on a moan, and the tiny sound snapped him out of his insanity. He jerked his head up and gripped her shoulders to set her away from him.

She licked her swollen lips, her eyes glazed with confusion.

"I'm sorry," he said, dragging one hand through his hair. "I was trying to take your mind off your uncle."

"You did." Her voice was husky. "Really well."

"Good. Glad it worked." He felt like an ass. "Let's talk about what you need for your stay here."

"Um, okay," she said, then cleared her throat of a lingering rasp. "We should." She walked over to the desk to seize a pen and pad of paper before propping her hip against the windowsill opposite him. He understood the message. She wanted him to stay at arm's length. "Is there an art-supply store in town?" she asked.

His brain was still filled with the taste of her. "There must be one. We have a lot of artists in the area." He tried to think of what store they patronized, but all that came to him was the image of her red hair spread across a pillow, in particular the one on his bed. He scrubbed his palm against the back of his neck. "Just write down what you want, and I'll figure out where you can get it."

Once he could think straight again.

◆

Julia looked down at the paper to hide the smile curving her lips. If the former mayor couldn't think of a place to buy her supplies, he must be *somewhat* shaken by their kiss. She was. It had started out as an offer and acceptance of comfort, but it had ignited into something entirely different.

She felt the heat climbing up her cheeks as she remembered she had actually moaned out loud.

"I'll need to replenish the minutes on my cell phone. And some clothes. A book to read. An ATM to get cash." She kept talking as she scribbled.

"I only know one women's clothing store, so you should talk to the receptionist here about the clothes. I ought to be able to handle the rest." His fingers tapped at blinding speed against his thigh. "Why don't I draw you a map? You can walk most places, or I'll have the inn call the one taxi in town."

"What if it's already busy?"

"Someone will probably volunteer to give you a ride."

"Are people really that nice here?"

He looked away for a split second. "It's like anyplace else in the world. There are some kind, generous folks, and some folks who take advantage of them. It's just easier to know which is which in a small town."

"I don't want to take advantage of anyone," Julia said, horrified that she might be in the second category.

He made a gesture brushing her comment aside. "You're not the kind of person I was talking about. You just need a little temporary help. Now, let's get going on the map."

She started to hold the tiny pad of paper out to him before she remembered the sketchpad she'd shoved in her duffel. "Wait, I have something better." She dashed into the bedroom and rummaged around until she found it.

When she returned to the living room, he took the book out of her hand before sitting down on the sofa. He flipped it open to the first page, which was a study of a horse's hoof, and whistled with admiration. "I feel like I shouldn't use this paper for something as ordinary as a map."

Julia dropped into the chair next to him. "It's just doodles, sort of like the notes you might take on a legal case. If you turn to the back, there's blank paper."

He glanced up at her. "May I look at some of these first?"

"Sure." Gratification washed through her that he was interested in her rough drawings, especially since he claimed not to like art.

He slowly turned the pages, asking her a question every now and then. When he reached the blank portion of the book, he set it down on his knees. "You can draw anything. I always thought artists sort of specialized, like you and your horses."

She shrugged. "I went to art school, so I got exposed to all kinds of subjects and mediums."

"So you really could paint my portrait and do a darned good job of it." He tossed the pen spinning up into the air and caught it before he drew a few straight lines on the empty page. "All right, here's Washington Street, our main drag."

She watched his hands as he jotted down street names and marked the establishments on them to match the items on her list. He moved with an eye-catching speed and assurance. She began to sense the coiled energy he concealed under his smooth, composed facade.

"That should get the basics taken care of," he said, holding out the pad. "If I pick you up at six thirty, does that give you enough time to collect what you need?"

She glanced at the antique clock on the mantel and nodded.

He pushed up from the couch. "Then I'll leave you to settle in."

She jumped up, wondering how to say good-bye to him. A handshake seemed too formal, while a hug seemed overly casual. And a kiss was too breathtakingly risky. She decided on the safety of formality. Holding out her hand, she said, "Thank you for rescuing me."

He hesitated a split second before he took her hand. "Right. This is a professional relationship." There was an undercurrent of irony in his voice.

"Oh, you mean the..." She waved her free hand in the direction of the window where he had kissed her. "That was just you being kind to a crying woman."

His eyebrows rose, but he didn't disagree with her. She felt a little pang of disappointment. *Well, what did she expect him to say? "I've fallen madly in love with you at first sight"?*

As her uncle would point out, that didn't happen in the real world.

Chapter 6

*B*EFORE SETTING OUT ON HER EXPEDITION INTO TOWN, Julia had taken one look at the claw-footed bathtub and banished the doctors' warnings against baths to take a long, luxurious soak. Her bathroom at home didn't have a tub, since showers were the safer means of bathing for her, so this was the height of indulgence, with a fillip of danger.

Walking the streets of Sanctuary had been another treat, its nineteenth-century storefronts offering a delightful parade of colors and textures. She soaked in as much visual pleasure as she could while she grabbed necessities such as cash, a replenished cell phone, and a book before jogging back to the inn.

Now she twirled her hair up and stabbed a lacquered chopstick through it. Trying too hard. She yanked the chopstick out and let the red curls fall down over the shoulders of her silk top. She hooked long amber dangles in her earlobes and stood back from the mirror to take stock of the full effect.

Not that she had a lot of choices. She'd brought one outfit to wear to the gallery, and this was it. Slim moss-green pants tucked into slouchy russet suede boots. Her top was something she'd bought from a fellow artist: a series of coppery triangles stitched together so they fell from the shoulders to form sleeves and a bodice in an almost sculptural effect.

"The necklace!" she said, rummaging around in her bag to find the silver swoops strung with chunks of amber. Fastening it on, she struck a pose. *Was it too artsy?*

"You never worried about that before you met a certain pressed and tailored lawyer."

She'd thought about Paul the entire time while she bathed and dressed. She'd come to one conclusion: if that kiss led to something more, she would let it. It would be a weekend fling. She'd never had one before, and it seemed like something you should do when you were declaring your independence.

Besides, wasn't that the knight's reward when he rescued the damsel? A little hanky-panky in the castle chamber?

A knock sounded, and she swiped on some shimmering lipstick before jogging into the sitting room to swing open the door.

"Gosh!" she said, taking in the length of Paul's legs wrapped in faded denim and the sinews of his forearms exposed by the rolled-up sleeves of his white button-down shirt.

His smile flashed in the dim hallway. "Much better than hello. 'Gosh' right back at you." His tone was light, but his eyes were intense. He stepped into the room. "Did you figure out the old plumbing?"

"Honestly, no. I took a bath instead of a shower. That tub is practically a swimming pool."

His gaze turned to molten silver, and she somehow knew he was imagining her swimming naked. The idea of a fling became a little too real, making her grab her suede handbag and clutch it to her chest. "Shall we go?" she asked.

"My 'Vette awaits you." He swept an arm out with a slight bow, reminding her of her earlier knightly metaphor.

As she passed him, she left more space than was necessary between them. He fell into step beside her, shortening his stride to match hers.

"Tell me about Claire and her husband," she said to deflect any further fantasizing on either of their parts.

She listened with half an ear as he escorted her to his car and held the door for her. She got the basics: Claire had come back to her hometown of Sanctuary to help out her sister, fallen in love with the local vet, Tim Arbuckle, and stayed, buying in as a partner at the Gallery at Sanctuary. Paul told the story without editorial embellishment, but there was an undercurrent in his voice she couldn't interpret.

"So you knew Claire from school?"

"Yup. We used to tool around together on my motorcycle. It was a weird combination. I was the class screwup, and she was one of the well-behaved, smart kids."

"So she was your girlfriend?"

"No, I was too stupid for that."

"What do you mean?"

He started the Corvette's engine and pulled out of the parking lot. "Claire's pretty special, and I at least had the sense to know that much, but I wasn't interested in a real relationship back then."

"Oh right. Teenage boys and their hormones. I have three stepbrothers, so I know what you mean."

He took his eyes off the road to flick a glance at her. "I've been wondering about an artist who looks pure Irish, is named Castillo, and speaks Spanish with her uncle. What's the family structure there?"

"Complicated. My birth name was Julia O'Malley, but my father left when I was two. Mom thinks he went back to Ireland after their divorce, but she was so pissed off she never bothered to find out for sure. Things worked out for the best, though, because she and my stepfather, Raul Castillo, fell in love and got married." She felt the usual pang of missing her faraway parents. "Papi adopted me, and I took his last name. Carlos is my father's older brother. When my parents moved to Spain ten years ago, I was eighteen and Carlos took over for Papi. He manages my career and a lot of other things for me. He's a very successful accountant, so being my agent is kind of a labor of love. He's a very honorable man and he treats me like his daughter," she added to give her uncle his due.

"That explains a lot."

"A lot of what?"

He steered the sports car through a hairpin curve, its engine growling in low gear as they climbed the narrow mountain road. "Why you've been so sheltered. Three protective stepbrothers. An uncle who's standing in for your parents."

She didn't mention the most compelling reason for her family's protectiveness. She wanted him to see her as whole and competent, not a fragile being who couldn't be trusted to deal with the real world. "You know, it's my own fault."

"What is?"

"This situation. I just wanted to make art, so I let my uncle handle everything else." Julia frowned as her lack of practical experience struck her. Her condition didn't preclude her being involved with the business side of her career. She felt stupid and naive.

"Are you afraid of your uncle?"

Surprise made her glance at Paul. "You mean, physically afraid?"

He nodded, his face tight with concern.

"No. Absolutely not." Her uncle's weapons were more subtle but effective because she cared about him: a headshake of disappointment, a hurt smile, a gesture that said he only wanted to protect her. Just picturing him brought the lingering taste of failure back to her throat.

"That relieves my mind," Paul said.

They rounded a shoulder of the mountain, and low-slanting sunlight splashed through the windshield, making her blink.

"Look left and you'll get a great view of the river," Paul said.

She shaded her eyes with her hand and let out a long "ah" of admiration. Ridges of mountains in varying shades of blue rolled away into the distance, their edges gilded by the low-lying sun. The river wound through the valley below, the water glowing like liquid gold. Her fingers itched for a brush and an array of paints. It would be a challenge to capture this moment of light, which changed even as she watched.

And it would make her uncle happy since it was a landscape, not a terrifying black horse on an abstract background.

She must have made an unhappy sound, because Paul took one hand off the wheel to give her shoulder a quick squeeze. "Does it remind you of home?"

"A little, but I was just thinking about how I would convey the scene on canvas, and how happy it would make Carlos to have me paint something pretty."

"Don't let him poison your pleasure in your work."

She glanced sideways at him. The bone structure of his face seemed to stand out because his jaw was clenched in anger. "Would you let me paint you?" she asked, as her eyes followed the shadows and angles revealed by his emotion.

"What!" The car swerved almost imperceptibly.

"I wasn't kidding when I said you would make a great subject."

He laughed. "Would it tick off your uncle?"

"No, I'd have to paint you nude to do that." She had become so comfortable with him, she forgot to avoid sexual innuendos.

"Now *that* I might agree to, depending on the setting."

She flushed as a sizzle of nerves and excitement surged through her. "I know, walking out of the river, water streaming off you." She was beginning to see it in her mind's eye. "You could have a fish in your hand, as though you'd just caught it, and..."

"Not the setting I was hoping for."

"It could be a really big fish."

"I'm not much of a fisherman. I was thinking of an *indoor* setting."

She sucked in air on a tiny gasp at his implication.

As she cast around for a sophisticated, woman-of-the-world sort of reply, he turned off the road between two stone posts and accelerated onto a paved but winding driveway, saying, "This is the kind of road the 'Vette is built for."

When he took the first corner at a dangerous speed, Julia forgot about his flirting. Her throat tightened in panic, but the low sports car stuck to the road like Velcro. The next curve was gentler so their speed increased, and by the third one, she braced herself in the seat while she hoped he would floor it. "This is fun! Do you ever take your car to a racetrack?"

"Not anymore." His voice was flat, and she wanted to ask why not, since he clearly enjoyed driving. But she could sense his withdrawal, and she didn't want to push him any further away.

As they came out of the trees, a spectacular wood-and-stone house nestled into the hillside just to their right. He drew up to the front door and stopped the car.

"That's a big house," Julia said, feeling overawed.

"Wait till you see its owner."

Chapter 7

*N*OW I UNDERSTAND WHY PEOPLE TAKE HELICOPTERS to eat at the Aerie." Julia picked up her wineglass and leaned back in her chair. "That was the most delicious food I've ever tasted."

"You should take her to dinner there, so she can see the view," Claire said to Paul.

His expression was unreadable in the dim candlelight, but his tone was light. "If she's willing to hang around Sanctuary for another three months, I'd be happy to. It takes at least that long to get a reservation." His eyes went to Tim. "Unless you're a vet."

Tim Arbuckle's laugh rumbled up from his massive chest. He was a giant of a man, and Julia had been relieved when they sat down for dinner because it made him less overwhelming. "I'm pretty sure you have some connections, being a former mayor of the municipality and all."

Julia envied the easy banter between the three friends. Except for her two years at art school, she'd never had a social circle. Most of her classmates headed for New York City or Paris after graduation, so she'd lost touch with them. Especially the ones who were uncomfortable with her condition. On top of that, professional jealousy often ruined friendships.

"Mrs. Bostic was singing Paul's praises as the mayor today," Julia said.

"They tried to talk him into running for the state legislature," Tim said. "I offered to be his campaign manager, but he turned me down."

"Your size would have scared the voters away," Paul said.

"Why didn't you run?" Julia asked.

He twirled his wineglass by its stem. "I guess I subscribe to the axiom that all politics are local, and I wanted to keep mine that way."

Claire muttered something about "your brother" before she stood abruptly and picked up a couple of plates. Paul gave her a sharp look, and she gave it right back. As Tim pushed back his chair, Claire said, "No, no, everyone else relax. I'll just clear enough to bring out dessert."

Julia ignored her and got up. "I'd like to help. I want to get another look at the Salvador Dalí collage you have in the kitchen." Picking up her plate and Paul's, she followed her hostess out of the dining room and stopped in front of the collage. "I love his use of texture in this."

Claire took the plates from Julia and stacked them on the counter. "Dalí was a master of mixed media." Lifting a cardboard bakery box out of the restaurant's cooler, she put it on the counter, pulling out a pair of scissors to cut the string around it.

Julia took a deep breath. "Thank you for looking at my paintings. I really needed a different perspective from someone who was, well, an outsider."

Claire put down the scissors. "I'm honored you came to me."

"I want to ask you one favor." She tried to inject all of her need into her gaze. "Please promise you'll always be honest with me."

"But my opinion is just one person's."

Julia shook her head. "That doesn't matter. I trust you."

Claire went still. "It's strange how life works out," she said, before picking up the scissors to cut the last string around the pastry box. "Back in New York, when your uncle took the wrappings off the first painting I ever saw of yours, I felt this instant sense of connection. It was as if you showed me a better way to look at the world."

"That's a pretty incredible compliment."

Claire spread her hands on the stone countertop and stared down at them. "I've been where you are, not trusting my own judgment." She looked up. "Tim is not my first husband. I was married to the man who owned the gallery your uncle brought your paintings into. My then husband and I disagreed about the merits of your work, and he made me feel as though I had completely lost my ability to appraise art."

"Oh God, I'm so sorry my paintings caused a problem for you!"

Claire shook her head. "Milo was doing everything he could to destroy me. In fact, your painting was the first thing I fought my ex-husband for and won. That was when I started rebuilding myself."

Julia had been listening with growing anger and incredulity. The idea that this dazzling woman had been torn down by a vindictive husband was horrifying. "I'll make sure Milo never gets another of piece of my work to sell."

"That's wonderfully supportive of you, but Milo's gallery went out of business a year ago. I even found it in my heart to be sad for him." A secret little smile played over Claire's mouth, and Julia knew she was thinking about Tim. "He's an unhappy person, and my life has turned out quite well since we parted."

Julia wasn't so charitable. "I would have spray-painted 'Serves you right' across his gallery windows as soon as I heard the news."

❖

Paul was lounging in his chair, lulled into a satisfied stupor by food and wine, when Claire broke the candlelit silence. "Tim, why don't you show Julia the rest of the house while Paul and I clean up?"

"Julia, are you game?" Tim asked, standing up. "Claire picked out all the art, so you should find it interesting."

Paul watched the way Julia's expression blazed with a combination of surprise and delight. She always looked thrilled when someone invited her to do something with them, as though she didn't expect to be included. Claire referred to her as a recluse, yet he saw nothing shy or retiring about this vibrant woman. It seemed even less apt when you considered she had the gumption to drive a rust heap of a car several hundred miles to ask a total stranger to look at her paintings, especially when she thought they might be bad. There had to be some other reason for her seclusion, and he suspected it was her controlling uncle.

"Lead the way," Julia said to Tim, almost leaping out of her chair.

As they walked out of the room with Tim's miniature Doberman dancing around their feet, Paul was struck by the contrast between the big vet and the red-haired wood sprite.

"Do Tim and I look that odd together?" Claire asked, her eyes also on the pair.

"No, because it's clear you were made for each other." He said it without thinking, surprising himself.

She reached out to touch the back of his hand. "Thank you. That means a lot coming from my oldest friend." She propped her elbows on the table and changed the subject. "So what happened at the meeting today?"

He picked up a fork and twirled it through his fingers. "They said I was the obvious choice for the position."

She let out a whoop of excitement. "That's fantastic! Why aren't you happier?"

"I didn't accept it."

"What? Why not?"

"Because there's one significant factor to be ironed out: the location of my new office."

"I thought it was going to be in Charleston. Putting it in the state capital makes sense."

"Well, it turns out they want the project to go beyond West Virginia. They want it to be national in scope."

Her eyes went wide. "That's even more exciting."

He had thought the same thing. In fact, he had started the Pro Bono Project with the idea that it could expand beyond his state's borders. At lunch when ABA president Ben Serra had put down his knife and fork and leaned forward to say, "We want you to take it nationwide," adrenaline had surged through Paul's body so he felt like a racehorse at the starting gate. He was already mentally expanding the scope of his plans when Ben dropped the bombshell that destroyed his euphoria.

"The office would be in DC." Paul spun the spoon so fast it blurred. "For political reasons."

"Oh dear. That's a problem." Her defeated look echoed his own feelings. "There must be some way to work things out for your brother so you can be away during the week at least."

He grimaced. He'd run through every possible scenario, but he could come up with no way to keep tabs on Jimmy while working in DC. "I don't see how. I could have commuted to Charleston every day, but with DC I'd have to stay for the work-week. You know what happened when I took the job in Atlanta. I can't risk it, for Eric's sake."

The thought of his nephew growing up without his father's presence in his life was too heartbreaking to consider.

"Oh, Paul, I'm so sorry. It's such a brilliant idea."

A stab of regret lanced through him, sending the spoon skittering out of his grasp. "It will do a lot of good no matter who runs it."

"And you'll always know you were responsible for it."

"Virtue is its own reward?"

Something in his voice or expression sent Claire on to a new topic. "Well, your virtue was certainly rewarded when you rescued your latest damsel in distress. I never thought I would get to meet the reclusive Julia Castillo."

"Are her new paintings good?" He retrieved the spoon and placed it carefully beside his empty coffee cup. "Or were you just being kind?"

"It would not be kind to tell her they were good if they weren't."

He pushed the glass away and relaxed back in his chair. The suspicion that Claire might have felt sorry for a suffering artist had nagged at him, mostly because he thought the new paintings were so much more interesting than Claire's famous one. Since he was no art expert, he figured he must be wrong.

"It's strange," Claire said, picking up the dessert plates. "She's much younger than I expected based on the emotional depth of her work."

He joined her in collecting dishes. "She's much more Irish than I expected based on her name."

"That too. All that red hair is gorgeous. And I think she's wearing an original Villar. I'd kill for one of those." She sighed with envy.

"A what?"

"Her blouse. I think it's by an artist named Reuben Villar, who occasionally makes one-of-a-kind clothing. He always insists on a photograph of the purchaser to make sure his creation will suit them and vice versa."

"He sounds like a control freak." He stood up and balanced a stack of dirty cups on one forearm.

"Of course he is. He's an artist."

As Paul picked up another pile of dishes, Julia and Tim walked back into the dining room. "Careful! You're going to drop something!" Julia squeaked, diving toward him as he started toward the kitchen.

Tim caught her wrist with a chuckle. "Paul has the manual dexterity of a circus juggler. He's never even lost a butter knife."

"If the lawyer thing doesn't work out, you'd make a terrific busboy," Julia said.

The candlelight gleamed in the strands of her hair, shimmered over the silk of her blouse, and twinkled like dancing imps in her eyes. He nearly dumped all the dishes on the ground so he could wrap himself in the glow surrounding her. "Busboy was my fallback career if I didn't pass the bar exam," he said before he forced himself to follow Claire.

"Or a magician," Claire said as she held the kitchen door for him. "He made money by entertaining at children's birthday parties when he was a teenager," she explained as Julia came in behind him.

Putting down the dishes in his right hand, he dug into his pocket and palmed a quarter. As Julia walked by, he reached behind her ear and pretended to pull the coin out of her curls. "Do you always carry change in your hair?"

She laughed delightedly, and he felt the bitterness of the afternoon's disappointment begin to drain away. He should have known better than to fight the limits of his life.

"That metal sculpture you have in your garden is fantastic," Julia said, as she put the remains of the cake back in its box. "Tim said the local farrier did it. I'd like to talk to him."

"Blake's not big on socializing," Claire said. "Your best bet is to hang around Healing Springs Stables when a horse is due for shoeing. In fact, we should go for a trail ride together. The mountain paths around here are beautiful."

Paul watched in fascination as Julia's skin went from pale cream to delicate pink. "Well, er, that would be nice. Except I don't know how to ride."

❖

The varying expressions of shock on the three faces turned toward her made Julia's flush burn even hotter. She hated to admit this fact about herself. "I never learned."

She was not allowed to.

Her stepfather, a skilled equestrian, had put her on a horse when she was six. She had been excited until the horse moved, and she looked down at the ground whizzing past far below her. Panic closed up her throat so tightly she couldn't breathe, while a cloud of darkness spread over her vision. She woke up cradled against Papi's chest as he frantically called her name while the horse grazed peacefully beside them. No one realized it, but that had been her first seizure.

Although her family believed it was nothing more than a panic attack, when she asked to ride again, Papi refused. He was too traumatized by what he thought he had done to his little stepdaughter to attempt it.

Wanting to please her new daddy, she began to draw the horses she couldn't ride, trying to grind her terror down by understanding them in little pieces: their hooves, their manes, their slender legs and big bodies, their huge, liquid eyes. Then she fell in love with their power and beauty.

A few months later, she was watching the antics of a new foal, her drawing pad balanced on her knees, when the next seizure sent her tumbling off the fence she'd been sitting on. Her uncle found her rolled up in a ball inside the pen, sobbing, as the foal's mother gently snuffled at her.

It was no longer a panic attack. It was epilepsy.

She'd lost count of the times she'd opened her eyes to find the anguished faces of her parents, her uncle, or her stepbrothers hovering over her. No matter how she tried to reassure them, her seizures distressed and terrified them, leading her relatives to cosset her in an effort to avoid another episode.

As she scanned their astonished expressions, she knew she was not going to tell anyone in Sanctuary about the electrical storms that used to wrack her brain. Two years ago, the doctors had agreed to let her stop her antiseizure medication. She'd been fine since then, so there was no need to risk the pity or withdrawal the information always evoked.

"But you paint your horses with such perception!" Claire looked the most flabbergasted.

Julia wanted to shrink down and crawl away under the door. Until she felt the solid warmth of Paul's arm circling her shoulders and pulling her against his side. He ran his palm up and down the silk covering her arm in a gesture of comfort. "It just makes your pictures all the more amazing," he said.

"Of course it does," Claire said, looking horrified. "I'm sorry. I was just so surprised."

"Please, it's fine," Julia said. And it was, as long as Paul offered her the support of his body. "Just embarrassing when you're known as an equine artist."

"You know, you can still hang around Sharon's barn and talk to the farrier," Tim said. "Sharon's an admirer of your paintings too."

"Then I'd like to meet her."

Paul stepped away, and the side of her body that had been pressed against his felt chilled. "I'll take you down there tomorrow," he said.

She felt a surge of gratitude for his matter-of-fact tone, but she didn't want him to babysit her out of a sense of responsibility. It was time for her to stand on her own two feet. "Thanks, but I don't want you to feel no good deed goes unpunished."

"I would hardly call a fifteen-minute drive with a famous artist punishment," he said. His words were light, but he wasn't smiling. She got the sinking feeling she had somehow insulted him.

"A *beautiful* famous artist," Tim interjected into the suddenly tense atmosphere, his eyes holding a twinkle.

When she caught Claire throwing him an approving glance, Julia knew she had put her foot in her mouth. "Well, when you put it that way…"

"Maybe Sharon will find you a whisper horse," Claire said.

"A whisper horse? What does that mean?"

"I'll tell you on the way home," Paul said. "Claire's explanation might make you question her sanity."

Julia's curiosity was piqued when Tim smiled at Claire in a very private way, and said, "We owe a lot to Claire's whisper horse."

Paul came back to Julia's side, taking her elbow with his hand. "We should get going. I have an early meeting tomorrow morning."

Julia said her good-byes with regret. These people made her feel like one of their circle, but they didn't handle her with kid gloves. Her uncle treated her like a hothouse flower that had to be protected from the elements and fed special food. But this flower was expected to grow in a certain direction.

Chapter 8

O KAY, IS A WHISPER HORSE LIKE A HORSE WHISPERER?"
Julia asked as soon as the 'Vette had cleared the first bend
in the Arbuckles' driveway.

"I'll explain, but you're not going to believe it."

"I'm in the mood to believe anything." Julia settled back in
her seat with a contented sigh. "All that good food and wine have
made me very receptive."

"Now that's a good way to get yourself in trouble." Paul's
voice vibrated low and sexy in the dim, enclosed space.

Julia was glad he couldn't see her blush. "You know what I
meant. Whisper horses." Even though her comment had been
innocent, it wasn't far from the truth. She would meet him halfway if he decided to lean across the gearshift and kiss her.

"The owner of Healing Springs Stables, Sharon Sydenstricker..." His voice held a husky rasp, and he paused to clear
it. "Sharon, who is the most grounded human being in most
ways, has this strange idea that every person has a special horse.
Once you find this special horse, you will be overwhelmed by the
desire to whisper all your troubles in its ear. Said whisper horse
will then help you solve all your problems. And everyone lives
happily ever after. In Claire and Tim's case, anyway."

"I don't think that's such a strange idea. Horses are very good
listeners. You can tell what the horse is feeling just by the angle
of its ears."

"I don't discount the effectiveness of talking out your problems. That's part of the reason why people love their dogs and their cats and their birds, and even their lawyers." His tone was wry on the last phrase. "However, Sharon thinks there's one particular horse for each person, and the horse actually helps fix things."

"I'm still willing to go along with the concept because I think it might work psychologically. What about Claire's whisper horse?"

"Claire decided her whisper horse was Willow, a very sick, abused mare who Sharon rescued from a racetrack. Tim was the horse's vet. When Claire was about to leave Sanctuary for good, Willow took a turn for the worse. That forced Claire to stay long enough for Tim to realize what a fool he was to let her go."

"And after that you still don't believe in whisper horses?"

He took his eyes off the road long enough to throw her a sharp look. "Tim would have come to his senses and gone after her."

She sensed a tension in Paul's mood, so she shifted away from the subject of Claire and Tim's love story. "So I guess you don't have a whisper horse?"

He shook his head emphatically.

"Do you know how to ride?"

"I can walk, trot, and canter, but I prefer mechanical horsepower." He patted the car's dashboard. "Sorry we all overreacted when you mentioned you couldn't ride."

"It's not a big deal." That was true, as long as she knew they liked her paintings. She figured they would overlook her other shortcomings, especially if she didn't tell them about the biggest one. "I started drawing horses because I couldn't ride them, as sort of a compensation for disappointing Papi. He's a great horseman."

"I'd say you'd overcompensated," Paul said.

She didn't understand why, but his appreciation of her work meant even more to her than Claire's. Maybe it was because he claimed not to like art, yet his desire to own one of her *Night Mares* had been genuine. She felt like her pictures had changed him in a small way. "You know, I was about to stop painting."

"What!" The car jolted onto the shoulder before he pulled it back onto the asphalt.

"I didn't want to." That was an understatement since art was the only thing she knew how to do. "But I couldn't go back to my old style, and my uncle was telling me not to go forward. So I was stuck."

She felt again the cold, damp suck of the abyss she had stared down into when she thought she would have to give up her work. It was worse than any seizure she'd had.

"Don't ever let another person stop you from doing what you love!" Paul said. "Ever!"

"Okay." Julia didn't know what else to say in the face of such vehemence. "I won't. Ever."

"Sorry for the outburst," Paul said.

"Don't apologize. It's good advice," she said, as she tried to read his face. The country road had no streetlights, and the dashboard's glow was too muted to illuminate his features. Still she got the sense his reaction came from his own experience, not in response to hers. Who had stopped him from doing what he loved?

Julia was drifting in a hazily pleasant dream when a deep male voice came from just beside her ear. "Julia, we're here. Wake up." She didn't quite recognize it, but she liked the sound.

"I don't want to wake up. This is too nice a dream."

Something warm and with an intriguing texture of smooth over hard brushed her cheek as the voice came again. "Julia, we're at the inn."

The inn? Surprise made her open her eyes to see the square white columns of the Traveller Inn. Memory flooded back, and she turned her head to find Paul leaning across the gearshift, his hand poised in the air. He must have run the back of it over her cheek.

The porch light spilled down across the lawn, throwing shadows into all the hollows of his face. She couldn't take her eyes off his lips. They were so close and so perfectly masculine. She wanted to shift her head far enough to touch them with her own mouth, but nerves froze her in her seat.

She forced herself to lift her gaze to his and nearly gasped. His eyes were locked on *her* lips and his intent was crystal clear.

She waited, hoping he would close the distance between them.

He touched her hair, threading his fingers into the strands over her ear, as he leaned closer. She let her eyelids close.

She heard a strangled sound before her hair was released. Stunned, she opened her eyes to watch him leap out of the car and walk around the long hood.

He sidestepped as she shoved the door open. "I guess you're awake now," he said as she got out on her own. "I was going to give you an arm to lean on."

She'd blown it again. If she'd sat still, she'd have his arm wrapped around her, and maybe that would have led to other things. She thought fast. "I'll take the arm anyway. I'm not used to drinking that much wine." She wobbled slightly as she stood.

His arm came around her waist like a warm band of steel. She savored the scent of starch and citrus and man as they climbed the steps to the front porch in slow unison.

He used his free hand to swing the screen door wide and walk her through into the lobby. When she saw a woman sitting behind the reception desk, she reluctantly straightened and stepped out of Paul's encircling arm. She didn't want to start any gossip. A lot of people thought artists had shaky morals.

The clerk, a middle-aged woman with permed brown hair, looked up. "Evening, Ms. Castillo. Paul, good to see you. I hope you had a nice time out."

"Can't complain, Irene," Paul said.

Julia started toward the staircase, expecting Paul to follow.

"I'll pick you up at one tomorrow and take you to the stable," he said, still standing by the desk. "Good night."

Disappointment flooded her. There would be no good-night kiss at her door. "I...thank you. For driving me. And everything else."

He lifted a hand in acknowledgment and walked toward the door.

Julia trudged up the first four steps before she remembered there was a window in the second-floor corridor that looked out onto the front parking lot. She bolted up the rest of the steps and across the hallway. Sidling up to the curtains hanging on the side of the arched casement, she peered downward.

Paul had just reached the edge of the parking lot, ambling along with his hands thrust in his pockets and his head down. The yellowish light made his shirt glow cream and his hair pick up glints of amber. He arrived beside the Corvette and stopped, then pivoted to look back at the inn. Even though he didn't look up, she found herself shrinking back behind the curtain.

He pulled one hand out of his pocket and ran it through his hair in a gesture of indecision. She held her breath. Then he shook his head, and the 'Vette's headlights flashed on as he unlocked the door. He inserted himself into the car and left the lot with a brief squeal of tires.

Back in her room, she paced around the living area, too keyed up to even think about sleeping. If she was at home, she'd go to her studio and work off her pent-up frustration with brushes and paint.

"My sketchpad!" She snatched it up from the table. Even though it was a warm night, she flipped on the switch that lit the gas fire and kicked her boots off before she sank down cross-legged on the couch.

An hour later, she dropped her pencil and flipped through the drawings she'd just finished. One page was a series of faces, all Paul's: one smiling as she remembered him the first time he shook her hand at the roadside; one laughing as he had at dinner; one in proud profile as he surveyed his town from the terrace of the Library Café; and one shadowed as it had been in the car.

Turning the page, she grinned. She had made good on her threat to draw him nude, wading out of a river. Of course, she had to use her imagination about what he looked like without his clothes on, but that wasn't hard. She'd drawn dozens of unclothed male models in her years as an art student. For fun, she had strategically positioned a large trout in his hands to cover his private parts, since she had chosen not to speculate on the size of those.

She turned to the next page, to the single drawing of him with the look in his eyes that said he wanted to kiss her. She had reproduced it as photographically as possible, breaking down her memory into single components: eyes, eyebrows, top lip, bottom lip, sketching each one separately to avoid injecting any emotional interpretation. As she examined it again, she decided she had not misread his intention. For some reason, he had changed his mind.

It had been a long time since she had been kissed by a man… other than Paul's earlier kiss, meant to comfort her, which didn't count. Her current life didn't offer many opportunities, and she was darned if she was going to let such an attractive one slip by.

Chapter 9

$\mathcal{W}$HEN PAUL WALKED INTO THE LOBBY THE NEXT AFTER-
noon, Julia felt intimidated. He was dressed in a pale-
gray suit with a blue shirt and yellow tie, and looked powerful
and out of her reach. Now that they were in his car and he had
taken his jacket off and laid it in the backseat, he seemed more
approachable. But she decided she wanted to get this particular
issue out of the way immediately.

"I ran into Mrs. Bostic downtown this morning," Julia said,
as Paul started the car. She smoothed her hands down her new
short denim skirt. Claire had given her the rundown on the best
clothing stores, and Julia had gone on a shopping spree partly
aimed at changing Paul's mind about kissing her. Unfortunately,
she'd also run into the chatty waitress. "She, um, has decided
we're an item because her sister-in-law is the receptionist and
saw us together last night." She took a quick glance sideways to
gauge his reaction.

A muscle in his face twitched, but she couldn't read his
expression. Was he angry?

"That's what I get for being chivalrous." He twisted around to
check behind him before he backed up, and his glance skimmed
her face. He burst out laughing. "Don't look so worried. I'm a single man with a decent job and all my hair. The ladies of the town
have been trying to marry me off for years."

"Oh, thank goodness." She slumped in the seat and blew out a breath. "I couldn't believe how fast the gossip started. It's kind of ridiculous."

"Gossip is the lifeblood of a small town. Sometimes it can be useful and sometimes it can be hurtful, but you can't stop it. Does it bother you?"

"No, I'm flattered. I've caught the town's most eligible bachelor in my snare."

"Not the *most* eligible. That would be Rodney Loudermilk. He owns the Rhododendron Bank."

"In that case, I'll drop you like a hot potato as soon as I have Rodney in my clutches."

"I have more hair than he does, though."

She smiled and smoothed the sleeve of her new blouse, admiring the feel of the green-and-gold-patterned silk. The blouse was a little too fancy for a visit to the stables, but she'd wanted to try out her new clothes on Paul. "You have some great stores in Sanctuary. I had a wonderful time shopping."

She'd enjoyed just strolling in and out of the medley of distinctive small shops. Some were old-fashioned, with a layer of dust on out-of-the-way shelves that held carved coal animals and hokey hillbilly postcards with yellowed edges. Others showed careful restoration of oak woodwork and freshly painted tin ceilings. Their shelves displayed vivid handmade quilts and artistically labeled local honey. The rich scents of fresh coffee and warm muffins had lured her into the Bean and Biscuit for a quick treat.

"We were voted Coolest Small Town in the USA last year." His voice rang with civic spirit. "Is that pretty blouse from here?"

Julia felt a glow of smug satisfaction. "Bought it this morning." In fact, she had maxed out her credit card to purchase it, since she had already loaded herself up with shopping bags. She tended to do most of her shopping online, so trying things on was a heady experience.

"Let me guess." He did a quick assessment with narrowed eyes. "Annie B's?"

"You're good."

"My mother used to work at the store."

"Your mother lives in Sanctuary?"

"Not anymore. She moved out to Ohio to live with her sister." He spoke with a slight edge that puzzled her. "She's unusual that way. Most folks come to Sanctuary and never leave."

"You make it sound like an episode of *The Twilight Zone*." She deepened her voice to imitate Rod Serling's portentous tone. "Mr. and Mrs. Smith didn't just stop for a home-cooked meal. They stopped for the rest of their lives...in Sanc-tu-ar-y."

He tossed a look in her direction. "Since you've asked me to be your legal advisor, I think we should talk about your uncle."

The change of subject was abrupt; she'd touched a nerve. She sighed. "I bought him a gift this morning."

"That's generous of you, all things considered."

"I still love him as an uncle, even if he's messing with my career. He collects antique weapons, and I saw a Civil War–era sword in a store window."

He coughed and laughed at the same time. "Don't forget to wrap a penny up with it, and have him give it right back to you."

"What do you mean?"

"You don't know the symbolism of a blade as a gift? It means you want to sever the relationship. Unless you exchange money along with it so it becomes a purchase."

"So you don't think I should give him the sword right now?"

"I think I'd like to see his face."

She started to smile. "You know, I would too."

"Back to business. If you confront your uncle, do you think he will tell you the truth?"

"That's a good question." She fiddled with the silver band she wore on her little finger. She thought so, but events might have proved her wrong.

"Would you know if he was lying to you?"

Julia turned to stare at the blur of trees passing by her window. "No, because it seems like he's been lying to me all this time, and I didn't know it. He told me no one would buy my work, when it turns out he wasn't even offering it for sale. Even if he thought it was for the good of my career, he lied to me."

His hand covered the white-knuckled knot of her fingers in her lap. "We all want to trust the people we love. It's a terrible thing when they betray that trust." He gave her hand a quick squeeze and returned his to the steering wheel.

"He nearly destroyed me." Her voice was ragged. "If someone who loves me would do this to me, it feels like there's no one I can trust."

"You can trust me."

The declaration was so simple. She knew it was almost as absurd as Mrs. Bostic having her and Paul marching down the aisle after one day's acquaintance, yet she believed him. Then she realized what he meant. "You're talking about that lawyer-client confidentiality thing."

"No, I mean you can trust me as one human being to another."

She swallowed a couple of times. "That helps."

"We're here," he said, aiming the car between two handsome brick pillars with wrought-iron lamps atop them. On one pillar, a white sign with simple green block letters read "Healing Springs Stables."

"Sharon's a world-class equestrian," Paul said. "People send their horses from all over to train here. Which is why we keep her whole whisper horse idea sort of quiet."

"Horse whispering is considered perfectly legitimate nowadays," Julia pointed out.

"Yes, but this whispering goes from horse to human." They rumbled up a gravel road between immaculately painted white fences. On either side rolling fields were dotted with grazing horses. He neatly slotted the 'Vette in between a green pickup truck and a silver Mercedes SUV. Julia got out, taking with her the recently purchased tote bag containing her sketchpad and pencils. She'd also brought a point-and-shoot camera to capture colors.

And the colors were spectacular. Redbrick barns with bright-white trim. All the varied greens and blues of row after row of mountain ranges receding into the distance. The gloss of horses' coats in every shade from dapple-gray to darkest bay. Even the stable hands contributed to the display, sporting multihued T-shirts that cheered on the WVU Mountaineers or announced the West Virginia State Fair was "bigger and better."

Taking it all in, her fingers twitched with impatience as she followed Paul into the dimness of one of the barns. It felt good to be back with her favorite subjects, like coming home.

"Hey, Taggart, out of my way! You wouldn't want any of this on that pretty suit of yours," a stable hand with a blonde ponytail ribbed as she pushed a wheelbarrow of manure past them. "Sharon's in the office, if that's who you're looking for."

"Thanks, Lynnie. Good to see you!" Paul said in his smooth ex-mayoral way.

The young woman paused. "Hey, did Eric get his horsemanship badge?"

Every angle in Paul's face seemed to soften as a grin of pride spread across it. "He sure did get that badge, thanks to you. He was the youngest scout in his pack to earn it. In fact, they had to make a special exception to give it to him because he's only ten."

"I've never seen a kid so determined to do everything on that list of requirements as fast as he could." Lynnie gave the wheelbarrow a nudge to set it in motion again. "He's something."

"That's Eric, all right. When he gets an idea in his head, he's unstoppable." Paul's grin remained as he led Julia toward the other end of the wide corridor between the stalls.

"Who's Eric?"

"My nephew."

This facet of Paul was unexpected. He seemed so much the urbane man-about-town; she couldn't picture him enjoying an "unstoppable" ten-year-old boy. Yet his expression said he adored the kid. "I didn't know you had a nephew."

"He's my brother's son." His smile vanished, and she wondered what she'd said to wipe it away. "Here we are," Paul said, pushing open a door and waving her through. "Sharon, meet Julia Castillo, your favorite horse painter."

Julia hesitated a moment, feeling shy. Paul gave her an encouraging smile. She stuck her head in to find a red-haired woman sitting with her booted feet propped up on her desk, drinking a diet soda. As Julia came in, Sharon brought her boots down to the floor and stood up, saying, "Well, I'll be. Claire's artist is right here in Sanctuary. Real nice to meet you."

She held out her hand, but Julia was staring, wide-eyed. Sharon looked like a flame-haired Amazon warrior princess. Every inch of six feet, she was solid muscle from the biceps swelling under her polo shirt's sleeves to the cut of her thighs under the snug riding breeches.

Paul gave Julia's elbow a little nudge, making her start and hold out her hand.

Sharon gripped it enthusiastically, saying, "You sure know how to make a horse look like a horse."

Unease speared through Julia. "You may not like my new paintings, then."

"If Claire likes 'em, I figure they're darn good. Have a seat." Sharon sat back down in her desk chair as Paul and Julia took the two wooden chairs across from her. "So you want to use some of my horses as models?"

"I'd love to," Julia said, "but I also want to meet Blake the farrier. I like his sculptures."

"Oh, so you want to talk artist-to-artist like." The horse-woman consulted a computer sitting on the desk. "He's due here on Tuesday."

"Oh no, I wasn't planning to stay that long."

"You look mighty sad about that. Let me show you around to cheer you up. You can draw anything you want to." Once again Sharon straightened to her full, impressive height.

Paul stood too. "Can I join the tour?"

Julia cast an uncertain glance at his business attire. She'd assumed he would introduce her to Sharon and leave. "Don't you need to get back to work?"

"It's my lunch hour," he said.

The mention of lunch made Julia's stomach rumble and reminded her she hadn't eaten anything since grabbing a home-made corn muffin at the inn's breakfast buffet. Carlos believed a regular meal schedule reduced the chance of seizures, so at home she ate like clockwork to avoid his fussing. In the headiness of her newfound freedom, she'd cast that off. She crossed her arms over her waist, but the stable was noisy enough that no one noticed the gurgling.

Sharon kept up a running commentary as she led them through one barn, out to the paddocks, and back into another barn. The stable hands all greeted Paul by name.

"No wonder you got elected mayor. You know everyone!" Julia said.

"I kissed a lot of babies too." He gave her hair a teasing little tug that sent shivers of pleasure waltzing down her spine.

She was so caught up in the deliciousness of the sensation that she paid no attention to the black horse with its head thrust over the stall door. A blur of motion made her turn her head, just as the horse bared its teeth and lunged for her arm. Paul's hand went from her hair to her shoulder in a split second as he clamped her hard against his side and yanked her out of range of the snapping jaws.

"Now who the hell forgot to shut Darkside's cage?" Sharon exclaimed, dodging the vicious teeth as she shoved the horse's head back inside the stall and swung a barred half door closed over the opening. "I'm sorry he nearly tore a strip off your hide. He is the orneriest SOB I have ever met."

Julia stared at the horse through the bars. This was the dark, menacing creature she had been painting over and over again. Excitement shivered through her. "He's my Night Mare," she whispered, trying to make out the black shape in the shadows of his stall.

"He's everybody's nightmare," Sharon said. "Except he's not a mare. He's a stud."

Paul turned her around and took her wrist, pushing up her sleeve so he could check her arm.

The brush of his long fingers over her racing pulse distracted her from the horse. "I'm fine," she said. "He missed me, thanks to you."

"You're wrong about that." His expression was rueful as he pulled out the fabric by her elbow and showed her a sharp-edged hole.

"Wow, I didn't even feel a pull on it."

"He's young, and his teeth are still sharp," Sharon said. "The cage shouldn't have been left open, so I owe you a new shirt."

"No, no, of course you don't. It's my own fault. I've been around horses enough to know I should always be alert."

She had a hard time focusing on anything other than Paul, as he held on to her wrist, absently stroking his fingers across the fragile skin on its underside. She looked up to see him frowning in the direction of Darkside's stall. "You rescued me again," she said. "I'm downright pathetic."

His attention came back to her. "I'd call you dangerous."

"Really?" She felt oddly gratified.

He shook his head. "It wasn't meant as a compliment."

Paul released her wrist and swung into step beside her, putting himself between her and the stall doors. She gave him a look that said she knew what he was doing but she wasn't going to object for the time being.

"Well, that's everything except the foaling shed, and it's empty right now," Sharon said as they reached the opposite end of the barn.

Paul glanced at his watch and turned to Julia. "I have to head back to work. You've got the town taxi's number?"

"I'll drop her off," Sharon volunteered. "There are some errands I need to do in town."

"Do you think you can keep her out of trouble?" he asked.

"Probably not, but, if need be, we can get Dr. Tim to fix her up. I'm pretty sure he'd agree to work on a horse painter, even though she's human."

"All right, but as her lawyer, I should warn you she's very litigious."

"She can sue me for every penny I have because that amounts to about a nickel," Sharon said. "You don't get rich in the horse business."

Paul leaned down to give Julia a quick peck on the cheek. "Watch yourself." He strode out into the sunlight while Julia cupped her palm over the place his lips had touched her skin.

"That Paul," Sharon said. "He's a pip."

"He told me Claire has a whisper horse here." Julia jogged to keep up with Sharon's long-legged pace. "Could I meet her?"

"Sure, her stall's right across from Darkside's. I was hoping some of her calm might rub off on him." Sharon walked back down the barn's center corridor. Darkside's cage was closed, but opposite his door a beautiful bay horse with a black mane poked her head over the door labeled "Willow."

"When she arrived Willow was skin and bones and could barely hold up her head," Sharon said, feeding the horse a carrot. "Now she looks like the Thoroughbred she is. I even use her to start off little kids with riding. They see her and all their fear just evaporates. When you think she'd be dead if two people hadn't spent a lot of love on her..." Sharon shook her head.

Julia stroked the mare's nose, admiring the delicate shape of her head. She found herself gazing into Willow's eyes, deep, velvety wells filled with a spirit of kindness and compassion. As sweet as she looked, Julia felt no urge to talk to the horse. "So how does this whisper horse thing work?"

"It just does." Sharon gave Willow a pat and headed back to her office, with Julia following. "You'll know when you find the right horse to talk to."

Julia picked up her tote bag, thinking of Darkside. She didn't want to tell him things, either. She felt as though it was the other way around: he had something to say to her. After all, he'd already tried to grab her attention. "I'll get out of your hair now, and do some sketching."

Julia walked out of the office, closing her eyes as she drew in the smell of sweet, fresh hay and big, warm animals. She lost herself in the distinctive music of the stable: loud huffs of breath, the clomp of weighted hooves, buckles rattling against water buckets.

"You okay, ma'am?"

Julia's eyes flew open to find a lanky young man standing in front of her with a confused expression on his face. *Had she had an absence seizure?* Her epilepsy hadn't taken the form of blank staring in the past, but maybe her encounter with Darkside had triggered it. "Have I been standing here a long time?"

"No, ma'am," he said, looking puzzled.

"Were my eyes open?"

"Not till just now."

Relief flooded through her. He simply wasn't used to people standing and doing nothing in a barn. "I was enjoying the atmosphere."

"Yes, ma'am." He gave her a tentative smile and continued on with the sack of feed he was carrying.

She gripped the handles of her tote bag as she waited for the flare of anxiety to dissipate. It had been seven years since her last seizure, including the two years since she'd taken her final dose of medication, but she couldn't shake off the sense of dread.

At least there was one fear she could face head-on. She spun on her heel and headed back for the barn where Darkside was stabled. As she stepped outside, her attention was caught by a sudden commotion just inside the other stable's door. Darkside exploded out into the sunlight, his black coat gleaming like watered silk in the sun, his muscles bunched in resistance. The stallion had a groom on each side of his head, the lead lines taut in their hands as they leaned their weight against his plunging.

"Vader warning!" one of the grooms called out. "Evil Jedi coming through."

Julia caught her breath as people and horses scattered while the magnificently foul-tempered animal practically dragged his handlers across the pine bark to a paddock gate. A third stable hand swung the gate open, then latched it behind the stallion. The two grooms counted to three, unhooked their lead lines simultaneously, and bolted for the fence as Darkside bucked twice before he came after them with ears laid back flat against his neck. They slipped safely between the rails just as the stallion snapped at them.

"Better luck next time, Darth-side," one groom said, good-humoredly flipping the bird at the frustrated horse.

The stallion gave an angry whinny and took off across the grass, half galloping and half bucking, his tail streaming out behind him like a banner of war.

Julia trotted over to the paddock fence and peered between the boards. She had seen him in her mind's eye so often, but in the flesh, he was both more and less disturbing than her imaginary Night Mare. The sense of physical power was heightened, but she felt drawn to him rather than afraid.

She propped her hip against a fencepost and bent to her sketchpad, fingers flying as she tried to capture the essence of his motion. It took three circuits of the paddock before Darkside wore himself out and dropped to a trot, his gait fluid and muscular. She continued to scribble furiously, her memory spilling impressions onto the paper.

"What a spectacular creature!" she muttered under her breath as she stuck the pencil behind her ear and flexed her exhausted fingers. Looking up again, she saw the horse peering at her between the boards of the fence, his ears pricked forward. "Yes, I'm admiring you, buddy, even though you ruined my new blouse."

Darkside stomped and shook his head with a short, angry squeal.

"Why are you so grouchy? If I were you, I'd be strutting my stuff in front of all the mares. Do you know how lucky you could be getting?"

A bark of laughter came from behind her as one of the grooms overheard her one-sided conversation. She tossed the woman a smiling wink and turned back to her new model. "You know, if you behave, I might wangle you a carrot."

"I wouldn't get within biting distance of that devil, if I was you," the groom said.

"I can toss it to him," Julia said, stowing her drawing materials in her tote bag. Sharon had shown her where they kept the horse treats, so she headed to the barn to pilfer some.

When she returned, the stallion was still standing by the fence, his large, dark eyes fixed on her. As she came closer, his ears went back and he huffed out a loud breath. "Yeah, yeah, I know. You're the big, bad stud who hates everyone."

She took a quick look around to make sure no one was paying any attention to her before she sidled up to the fence, holding out several pieces of carrot on her flattened palm. She knew she was taking a huge risk, but she wanted to touch this creature from her dreams.

No one yelled at her to stop, so she thrust her hand close enough for Darkside to reach it through the fence. He snorted again and did a threatening drumroll with his hooves. When she didn't move, his ears flicked forward and he sniffed the air above her palm, his wiry whiskers tickling her skin. She stood still, and he threw up his head.

Julia chuckled softly. "You don't know whether I'm crazy or dangerous, do you?"

She and the horse stared at each other. Then Darkside arched his neck and delicately lipped the carrots off her open hand, the velvet of his nose soft against her palm. When she reached up to stroke him, he yanked his head back and bolted across the paddock at a full gallop.

Julia looked around again before she pulled her sketchpad out of her tote and climbed up on the fence enclosing Darkside's paddock. She pretended to be drawing, but she was really keeping an eye on the big animal. She wasn't stupid enough to put herself in harm's way a second time without staying alert.

Darkside's gallop slowed to a trot as he circled back around toward her. She kept her head down and her pencil moving as he pranced closer. He stopped about six feet away, his elegant head high and ears forward.

She kept scribbling as she said, "You're a big chicken, aren't you? Afraid of little tiny old me when I just want to see how strong you feel."

The horse stamped and laid his ears back.

"I have more carrots, but you're not getting any until you let me touch you."

He stretched his neck out and shook his head, making his mane whip through the air.

"Fine, be that way." His nose was getting close to her, and she had a vision of those sharp, young teeth digging into the back of her hand, a hand she needed for her livelihood. "If you bite me, that's it. I'm done with you."

She slid the pencil behind her ear and slowly reached into her back pocket for another bit of carrot, hiding it in her right fist. Sandwiching the sketchbook between her chest and her knees, she leaned forward, stretching out her left hand, open palmed and empty.

For a long moment, horse and artist locked eyes before Julia shifted her gaze to the stallion's ears. As they swiveled forward, she heaved a mental sigh of relief; he didn't intend to knock her off the fence quite yet.

The horse moved one big front hoof forward, just enough to touch her palm with his nose. She curved her fingers up to tickle under his chin. He jerked his head back, but his ears remained pointed toward her, so she stayed on her perch, her hand outstretched.

This time he took two full steps toward her. She could hear him breathing, and she inhaled the warm tang of the sweat he'd worked up with his exertions. Now her entire body was within striking distance of his teeth.

She kept her voice low and humorous as she said, "If you knock me off the fence and stomp all over me, Paul will say 'I told you so.'"

The stallion hesitated another moment before he reached toward her, his breath hot on her bare forearm. His nose traveled right past her hand, to the corner of her sketchbook. She forced herself not to flinch backward. He huffed out a breath and drew his lips back from his teeth to nibble at the paper.

Julia had to bite her lip to keep from laughing out loud in hysterical relief. She let him taste the paper and moved her left hand up to stroke his neck. His ears twitched back and forth, but he continued to snuffle at her pad.

Touching his flexed neck was like smoothing her palm over living marble. His coat was as fine as satin, the muscle beneath stone-solid but warm and vital. "You are a beauty," she breathed.

With a sudden jerk, he ripped off a corner of paper and ground it between his teeth. "Fine, you earned your carrot."

She unfolded the fingers of her right hand by his nose, and he spit out the soggy paper, crunching on the carrot instead. Encouraged, she dared to run her fingers down the long stretch of skull between his eyes and his velvety nose. He nickered as she fluttered her fingers against the soft skin between his nostrils. Then his ears went back and he wheeled on his hind feet to race away.

Julia decided not to push her luck. She clambered down from the rail and shoved the sketchpad and pencil back into her bag. Swinging it onto her shoulder, she turned toward the barn.

Ten feet in front of her, half a dozen stable hands were standing in a semicircle with Sharon right in the center. "Well, that's the damnedest thing I ever did see," Sharon said.

"Plumb crazy is what I'd call it," one groom said, shaking his head as he walked away. "That stud has a mean streak a mile wide. It's a miracle he didn't yank you right off that fence and pound your face into the ground."

Julia noticed a couple of her audience members had pitchforks in their hands. Her eyes widened and went to Sharon's face.

"Yeah, they were ready to use 'em to make Darkside back off, if necessary," Sharon said.

"You called it, though, boss lady," another groom said, letting the tines of her pitchfork rest on the ground. "You said old Darth Darkside was her whisper horse."

"Okay, show's over," Sharon said. "Everyone back to work." She waited for her staff to disperse before she strolled over to Julia. "I know everyone finds their whisper horse, but not in a million years did I think Darkside would be yours. Or anyone else's."

"He's my whisper horse?" Julia was incredulous. She turned to see Darkside slam a back hoof into the fence as a groom walked by, leading another horse. "He's not what I'd call a sympathetic listener."

"Everyone needs their own kind of whisper horse. Your spirit matches his in some way only the two of you know."

Julia understood why Sharon's friends didn't talk much about her theory. However, she couldn't deny the sense she understood Darkside, and he might have something to offer her in return.

"Oh, Lynnie found this in his stall." Sharon pulled something out of her pocket. It was the swatch of material the stallion had ripped out of Julia's sleeve. "You might be able to get it sewn back together somehow."

Julia took the scrap of silk. It hit her that, despite the danger, she hadn't once thought about having a seizure while she was with Darkside. She tucked the fabric into her tote. "Maybe I'll keep it as a souvenir of meeting my whisper horse."

Chapter 10

*P*AUL PUSHED OPEN THE OUTER DOOR TO HIS OFFICE ON the first floor of a 1850s-era Victorian house. His suit jacket was slung over his shoulder on the hook of his index finger, and he had a brown bag holding a deli sandwich in the other hand. As he walked in, his administrative assistant stopped her high-speed keyboarding to look up at him.

"You'll never guess who called," she said, waggling her penciled-in eyebrows.

"Judging by your expression, Verna, someone I wish hadn't."

"Belle Messer."

He groaned.

"The good news is she's given up on auctioning you off as a dinner date at the charity gala next Saturday."

"Then what's the bad news?"

"She pestered me until I said you would donate two hours of legal consultation to the silent auction. And I told her she couldn't buy it for herself this time."

"Did she agree?" The last time he'd spent the two hours fending off the theater fund-raiser's amorous advances.

"Yessir. I think she's given up on you."

"I can only hope. This isn't one of those costume things, is it?"

"Black tie optional, but you do look handsome in that tux of yours." She batted her mascara-thickened eyelashes at him.

"I won't tell Harvey you said that."

"After fifty-two years of marriage, Harvey knows he's the only man for me, so he don't mind if I take a gander when it's worthwhile." She turned back to her keyboard.

Verna Hinkle had been born before anyone had ever heard of a personal computer, yet she had adapted to the new technology without a blink of her big blue eyeliner-ringed eyes. She wasn't afraid of anyone in Sanctuary and guarded his inner-office door with the fierceness of a mother sow, which made her a pearl beyond price.

He sauntered through the inner door, tossed the paper bag on his desk, and neatly draped his jacket over the hanger on the coatrack. Grabbing a bottle of water from the minifridge built into the wall of oak bookcases, he sat at his desk and took a long swallow before he unwrapped the BLT.

He hadn't planned to tour the stables with Julia, but he couldn't tear himself away. Watching her take in the sights at Sharon's had made him see everything differently himself. Her observations turned a bale of hay into a study in textures, while a sleeping barn cat became a series of graceful curves.

The feel of her skin when he touched her wrist had hypnotized him; he couldn't stop stroking the satiny warmth of it. He had nearly kissed her last night in the car. She'd looked so deliciously tousled and sleepy, as though she was already in his bed. But despite the sensuality of her hair and lips, he sensed an undercurrent of innocence that stopped him. He had rescued her, and now he was cast in the role of her protector, not her ravisher.

Claire thought his problem was rescuing too many damsels in distress. His real problem was that he felt responsible for them afterward.

Waking his computer screen from sleep, he scanned down his e-mails, stopping at the one from Ben Serra. It was a request for a phone call.

"Ben, Paul Taggart here. It was a pleasure to talk with you yesterday."

"Glad you called, Paul. I have good news. We have approval to make the Pro Bono Project nationwide right out of the gate. And you're the man we want for the job."

"Are you set on having it based in DC?" Paul asked, knowing the answer.

"We've even got the office space for it. One of the big law firms up here has agreed to give us a whole floor in their office building for well below market rates."

Paul felt the last scrap of hope shrivel up and blow away as Ben went on to describe the floor in enthusiastic detail.

"So you'll consider our offer?" Ben asked, as his catalog of features came to an end.

There was no way he could take the job, but Paul couldn't bring himself to turn it down on the spot. "It's a good one," Paul said. "Let me think about it."

"No one else can do this justice," the other man said. "In fact, I'm not sure anyone else can do it at all."

"I appreciate your confidence in a small-town lawyer," Paul said.

Ben harrumphed. "You and I both know you're hiding your light under a bushel in Sanctuary. You could get a job in a top law firm anywhere."

Paul thanked him and ended the call with a stab of his finger. Balling his sandwich up in the waxed paper, he tossed it in the trash can. His appetite had vanished, and he'd be having dinner at his brother's soon anyway.

Shoving his chair back, he paced over to the tall window looking out onto the ornately trimmed Victorians that lined Court Street. Right now he hated every curlicue of every architectural detail.

Ben was wrong about one thing. He wasn't hiding in Sanctuary. He just couldn't escape.

"Julia! I'm so glad you came by in person instead of calling." Claire's face lit up as she crossed the gallery's main showroom to peck Julia on the cheek. "I have the most amazing idea for your paintings."

When Sharon dropped her at the inn, Julia had found a message from Claire waiting for her. She had changed her damaged shirt and headed for the gallery on foot.

"An amazing idea?" There was something about the enthusiasm in Claire's voice that made Julia uneasy.

Claire led her to a curved cream leather sofa set in the middle of the showroom. Seating herself in a matching chair, Claire leaned forward with her forearms braced on her knees. "I want to have a special by-invitation-only reception for you where we unveil your new work to the art world and thrill our clients with the opportunity to actually meet you. And I want to do it next Friday."

The idea of being the center of attention in a room full of critical strangers made her stomach flip. "Next Friday! That seems really, really soon."

"Well, I want to tie it into something else. We're having a charity gala next Saturday to raise money for the local theater, which means a certain number of my out-of-town customers are planning to be here for the weekend already." Claire smiled, and Julia understood why she was so good at selling expensive art. "I was hoping you might attend the auction and consider donating a drawing. It would bring in extra publicity and add to the theater's coffers."

Julia stopped breathing. Claire wanted her to expose herself to the judgment of an audience not once, but twice? The great black horses of her paintings galloped through her mind with teeth bared and eyes glowing red.

"I've overdone it, haven't I?" Claire said. "I'm just so excited about your new direction. I want to share it with people who will truly appreciate it."

Julia gulped in air. "I, well, I don't think it's a good idea for me to be there." What if she reacted the same way she had at the catastrophic portfolio review in art school? "I've never, you know, mingled with prospective buyers. I'm likely to say something wrong."

"Trust me, you'll charm them just like you've charmed all of us." Julia's panic ratcheted down a notch at the compliment. "Besides, patrons expect artists to be a little odd. It goes with the creative territory." Claire sat back. "And I didn't mean to be pushy about a donation."

"Oh, I'd be happy to donate something." The sketch of Paul walking out of the water flitted through her mind, and she choked on a nervous laugh.

"You have an idea?"

"No, well, maybe something small." She mentally pushed Paul's image away. "But I was only going to stay another couple of days."

"Maybe you'd consider extending your visit?"

Claire's gaze was intent as Julia looked for excuses. "I can't really work in my room at the inn. They might not appreciate the mess."

"Oh, I can find you a temporary studio."

Julia thought of her uncle and the painful conversation she needed to have with him. Maybe putting off their confrontation for another week wouldn't be a bad thing. She might have her emotions under better control so she could approach it as a straightforward business discussion.

She also considered Paul and their one brief, tantalizing kiss. When she thought of leaving without kissing him again, the colors in the paintings around her seemed to go flat.

"If you think it's a good idea..." As soon as she said it, a shudder of nerves racked her. She imagined herself standing in the center of the gallery in a harsh spotlight while well-dressed people holding wineglasses circled her and jeered at her *Night Mares*. As they sniped, her eyesight would darken from the edges inward, and the electrical switch in her brain would flip to seizure mode as she collapsed onto the wide wooden planks of the gallery's floor. "Maybe I shouldn't..." No, she was no longer allowing herself to be imprisoned by her fear. "I'll stay."

Claire clapped her hands and stood up. "I'll get right to work on the guest list and invitations. And setting you up with a studio. Did Paul tell you where to buy supplies?"

Julia nodded. Paul had remembered that the enterprising owner of Hardy's Hardware stocked whatever the local artists asked for.

"Have them delivered here and I'll get them to your studio." Claire bent down and gave her a quick hug. "You're doing me a huge favor. You're going to put the Gallery at Sanctuary on the map."

"What if the art world hates my *Night Mares*? It'll wipe you right off the map again."

"You traveled all the way to Sanctuary because you knew your new paintings were good."

She was right. If Julia hadn't believed in what she was doing, she would have bowed to her uncle's pressure months ago. She nodded and forced her lips into a wavering smile.

Claire gave her an encouraging nod and pulled Julia to her feet.

"We've got a lot to do before next Friday."

❖

As soon as the door swung shut behind Julia, Claire dashed to the desk and spun the chair around to face the computer. As she clicked away with the mouse, she hit a speed-dial button on the phone.

"Hello, sweetheart." Her husband's voice rumbled through the speaker.

"I did it," Claire said. "I got Julia to stay for the reception and the auction."

"She might surprise a few people with her frankness," Tim said.

"Everyone expects artists to be a little different. She'll play right into that, and people will love her." Claire sat back in her chair. "Honestly, I'm more worried she'll overhear a negative comment about her paintings and that will make her question her talent again."

"You'll have to choose the guest list carefully."

She picked up a ballpoint pen, clicking it open and closed. "I will, but part of my strategy involves Paxton Hayes, and you can't control him."

"The blogging art critic? You think he's a pompous ass."

"He's the only person who can stir up interest in Julia's show fast enough. He ought to like these new paintings, since he prefers his art with a dark psychological slant." She dropped the pen and went back to the mouse. "Besides, the most important part of this has nothing to do with the reception."

"It's for Paul?"

"I married a very smart man." Claire's hand went still on the mouse. "I'm worried about Paul. When was the last time you saw him ride his Harley?"

"It's been awhile," Tim admitted. "So you think a week in Julia's company will be enough to cheer him up?"

"Julia's plans might change. I didn't intend to live here, either, and look what happened." Claire's lips curved into a smile. "A big lug of a veterinarian convinced me to stay forever."

Chapter 11

*P*AUL JOGGED UP THE CEMENT STEPS OF HIS BROTHER Jimmy's brick ranch house, carrying two shopping bags. In one was a high-tech compass for his nephew, Eric, while the other held two bottles of gourmet steak sauce.

Ringing the doorbell, he noticed the white wood trim around the door needed repainting. His shoulders sagged under the weight of another disappointment. He'd bought the house for his brother, so Eric wouldn't have to stay even one night in the ratty apartment where Jimmy had been living after his wife threw him out. Evidently, it was too much to ask that Jimmy keep the place up.

The door swung open. "Hey, big brother," Jimmy said. Dressed in a stained apron bearing the slogan "May the forks be with you," he held a spatula in one hand and tongs in the other. His bright-blue eyes were bloodshot, and sweat beaded on his forehead and darkened his blond-streaked hair. "You're right on time."

As Paul stepped into the foyer, a haze of smoke made him cough. "Where's my man Eric?" he said, looking past his brother with the expectation of seeing his nephew hurtling toward him.

"Oh, didn't I tell you? I switched weekends with his mother, so Eric and I can go camping with the Millers next weekend."

Paul forced himself to keep smiling, but the evening stretched before him like a wasteland without the promise of his nephew's lively, rambunctious presence. The agreement Paul had hammered out with Jimmy's ex-wife, Terri, allowed Jimmy to have Eric every Wednesday night and alternate weekends. Paul made sure to visit his brother on those days, both to check up on Jimmy and because he relished his time with his nephew. "I wanted to show him how to use this new compass." He lifted the bag.

Jimmy looked guilty. "Well, at least he can practice with it next weekend."

Paul put his nephew's bag on the hall table and held out the other one. "Thought you might be able to use this."

He had bought the steak sauce at the gourmet shop next door to Annie B's, where he'd gone to ask about a replacement for Julia's ruined blouse. The memory of the malevolent black horse with his lips drawn back from his teeth reaching for Julia's soft, vulnerable arm sent a shudder through him even now. His brother had plopped his cooking implements down on the hall table and was reading the sauce labels, so he hadn't noticed.

Jimmy looked up and waved his hand around to make the smoke swirl in the air. "Probably good you brought these. The steaks could be a mite overdone." He handed the sauce to Paul. "You want to put them on the table?"

Paul went past the kitchen door and into the dining area. The round pine table was already set with ironstone plates that matched the autumn leaf border of the vinyl placemats. The paper napkins were folded into triangles under the forks. Paul placed the bottles in the center of the table with a sinking feeling. If his brother was making such an effort to entertain him, something must be wrong.

"Grab the pitcher of iced tea out of the refrigerator," Jimmy said, as Paul walked into the kitchen, his eyes watering in the thick smoke.

Paul cast a glance at the ceiling to find the smoke detector hanging from its wires with the battery compartment empty.

"Jimbo, if you burn the house down with your cooking, the insurance company won't give me squat without a working smoke detector," he said. His real fear was that Jimmy would drink himself into a stupor, drop a half-smoked cigarette, and go up in flames with the house. Even worse, Eric might be in the house with him, although Jimmy swore he never drank when his son was there.

His brother speared several charcoal-colored slabs of meat onto a platter. "That's just temporary until the smoke clears."

Paul made a mental note to replace the battery himself before he left. Taking the iced tea from the refrigerator, he grabbed a serving bowl filled with chopped-up lettuce, tomatoes, and cucumbers he assumed was their salad before he went back to the dining alcove.

"Here we are! Marinated hanger steak," Jimmy said, setting the mystery meat down on the table with a flourish. "I used some balsamic, some Worcestershire sauce, and a little brown sugar, just like the Internet said."

"So your cable's working again," Paul said. "Did you get my e-mail about the change in your health insurance?" He carried his brother's insurance through his law practice; it was the only way he could persuade the contractor Jimmy worked for to hire a known alcoholic.

"They don't write those things in English," Jimmy said. "Why don't you just tell me where to sign the papers?" He lifted the lid from a casserole dish and steam poured out from the potatoes baked in their jackets. Paul sighed inwardly in relief; his brother knew how to make those because Eric loved them smothered in cheese and bacon bits. Something in the meal would be edible.

"You should know what you're covered for."

"We'll talk about it later." Jimmy grabbed the tongs and put the largest chunk of meat on Paul's plate. "Sit down and enjoy some home cooking. I know you don't get enough of that, being a bachelor without a kid to feed."

Paul sat. "You're right. It's nothing but sandwiches at my desk and takeout pizza." A lie. He often cooked for himself. He'd managed a decent chicken cordon bleu the other night.

Paul sawed at the steak and turned the conversation to a topic they could agree on. "How's Eric doing with his new substitute teacher? What's his name—Voss?"

A look of relief spread over Jimmy's face. "Sounds like he and Eric have come to an understanding. If Eric finishes his test or his in-class exercise before everyone else, he can read his library book quietly at his desk."

"It sounds like Mr. Voss knows what he's doing."

Eric had a quick mind, which meant he spent a lot of time waiting for the other kids to finish their work. If he didn't have something to occupy him, he found creative but disruptive ways to entertain himself.

"Yeah, maybe if we'd had a teacher like him, we would've raised less hell in school," Jimmy said.

"I don't know about raising less hell, but we might have learned something."

"You took in more than you let on."

Paul shook his head, remembering how he'd barely gotten into college. "I was in every remedial class they had at WVU."

"Well, you pulled your shit together for law school."

"Only because I got interested."

"Guess I never found anything that interested me. You know, this peppercorn sauce with brandy and black truffles is right tasty, despite all the fancy stuff in it," Jimmy said, offering one of Paul's gifts.

Paul took the bottle with gratitude, dousing the overcooked beef in the sauce to give it a flavor other than shoe leather. As the two brothers chewed their steaks in a silence that grew longer and longer, Jimmy's eyes began to dance. He swallowed and grabbed his iced tea to take a long drink. Paul was still trying to get to the point of choking down the tough beef when his brother started to laugh.

"Bro, you can spit it out," Jimmy said. "We'll grind our teeth down to nubs if we try to finish this."

With a Herculean effort, Paul forced the bite of steak down his throat. "I was beginning to think I'd need dentures before the age of forty." Jimmy laughed harder, and Paul found himself joining in.

It was like the old days, when he and Jimmy had pulled the best pranks ever seen at the high school and only been caught twice. Of course, Jimmy had charmed his way out of any punishment, while Paul had spent weeks in detention. It had been worth it to see the principal's face when he found the goat on his desk, eating the school budget papers.

That was before his brother had screwed up his marriage, slid into alcoholism, and nearly lost custody of his son.

A buzzer sounded from the kitchen, and Jimmy bolted out of his chair. "Oh shit, I forgot about the apple pie." Reappearing with a steaming pie held between two oven mitts, he said, "Don't look so worried. It's Mrs. Smith's. All I did was heat it up," he said, putting it down on a doubled-up dish towel.

Paul forced a chuckle. "I guess it's vegan night." He speared a baked potato and dropped it on his plate.

"Just trying to keep you healthy," Jimmy said, serving himself a potato. He sliced it in half and shook a liberal dose of salt over it. "So I hear you had a meeting with some bigwig from New York about your pro bono legal project."

The flaky potato turned to ashes in Paul's mouth. He put down his fork and leaned back in the chair. "We discussed how to put together funding from various sources."

"Did he think you could get all the money you need to start it?"

"He's sure of it. The big law firms are already on board. And there are a couple of foundations looking to support an initiative like this." He sounded like an infomercial, but he couldn't make himself speak casually about this.

His pro bono work had kept him sane. A few months after he returned to Sanctuary, he was so tired of wills, real estate closings, and divorces, he called up a classmate who worked at a large corporate firm in Richmond and offered to do research for pro bono cases at a reduced rate. He knew the big firms often struggled to donate the hours the American Bar Association recommended, partly for financial reasons and partly because their lawyers didn't have the right background or experience. His friend had consulted with the firm's senior partners and come back with an enthusiastic acceptance.

Paul found the work satisfying on both an intellectual and gut level; he believed every accused person was entitled to the best legal representation available, and his research gave the defending lawyers tools they wouldn't have otherwise. His reputation spread, and soon he couldn't handle the amount of work offered to him.

So he had come up with the Pro Bono Project, a databank of small-practice lawyers like himself who were willing to do the legwork at reasonable rates. His job as director would be to recruit them, evaluate their qualifications, match them up with the right cases, and monitor the quality of work they were doing, as well as tracking hours and payment.

Now he wouldn't be doing any of that.

Jimmy cut a tablespoon-size chunk of butter and dropped it on his potato. "It must be a pretty good idea if so many people want to pay for it."

"Ben thinks so, and he's the president of the American Bar Association."

Grabbing his glass, Jimmy took a gulp of iced tea. "That's for lawyers all over the whole country?"

Paul nodded.

"I thought you were just going to talk about West Virginia." Jimmy's hand shook, making the ice rattle in his glass as he set it down.

"I did too, but it seems he wants to roll this out on a national level right from the start."

"I guess he wants you to work on it."

"He offered me the job of director."

"That's impressive. My big brother, a director." Jimmy picked up his fork and began to mash the soft butter into his potato. "Where will this project be located?"

"Washington, DC." He knew he was dragging the conclusion of the conversation out unnecessarily, but he wanted to give Jimmy the benefit of the doubt. He always hoped his brother would surprise him.

For a moment Jimmy lifted his eyes from the potato he was mauling, and Paul saw the fear in them. "You remember the promise you made to my ex," Jimmy said in a low voice. "You said you wouldn't leave again so I could be with Eric."

Taking a deep breath, Paul blew it out toward the ceiling. "I remember, and I'll keep it because Eric deserves to have you in his life."

The sear of disappointment when he said the words out loud shocked him. He must have been fooling himself that he might be able to take the job. Jimmy had brought him back to reality.

Shoving his chair back from the table, he picked up his plate. "I'll help you with the dishes."

❖

The drive to his house took seven minutes, even though he forced himself to keep the 'Vette at the speed limit. He pulled in the driveway and killed the engine, but he couldn't get out of the car. A wild restlessness roiled inside him, a rebellion against the ropes of need and guilt his brother tethered him with.

He smacked his hand on the leather-covered steering wheel as he thought of making the phone call to Ben Serra and saying he couldn't accept the position as director of his own goddamned brainchild. The Pro Bono Project was his; he had developed the concept, put together the plan, and outlined how to fund it.

He brought the big engine back to life and backed out of the driveway with a squeal of tires, pointing the car's hood toward the interstate, where he could turn it loose. He hoped a cop had his radar gun on because he was in the mood to outrun anyone who gave chase.

As he rumbled along the main street, he saw the Traveller Inn, and a different sort of restlessness seized him. He swung into the parking lot and leaped out of the car, taking the front steps two at a time.

"Is Ms. Castillo in her room?" he asked the receptionist.

"Let me call up and see." The receptionist reached for her phone.

"It's all right. I'll just go find out for myself." He pivoted on his heel and headed for the stairs.

Rapping on Julia's door, he stood still to listen for movement and was relieved when footsteps creaked across the old floorboards.

"Paul!" She stood in jeans and a fancy printed T-shirt, her feet bare, her hair a red cloud around her shoulders. She had some smudgy black marks on her face. "Is something wrong?" she asked. "You look...strange."

He grimaced comically in an attempt to wipe away whatever expression she found disturbing. "I just need a drink. Care to join me?"

Her face lit up. "Sure. Let me clean up. I've got charcoal all over me."

"Is that what this is?" He stepped in and threaded his fingers into her hair as he rubbed his thumb over a blotch on her cheek. Gratification whipped through him as her eyes went wide and incandescent at his touch. "I think I made it worse," he said, giving her cheek a little brush.

She reached up to touch the smudge, her eyes locked on his. He had to twine his fingers together behind his back to keep from seizing her by the shoulders and backing her onto the couch so he could crush his body against hers.

"Scoot!" he said to keep himself from scaring the bejesus out of her. "I'm thirsty as an opossum in the Sahara Desert."

She cast him a dubious look. "I've never heard that expression before."

"That's because I just made it up."

Laughing, she backed up. "Should I change my clothes?"

He took the opportunity to do a slow scan of the hip-hugging jeans and figure-outlining T-shirt. She flushed and shifted slightly under his gaze, so he lifted his eyes to her face. "Nope, you meet every rule of the Black Bear's dress code. Except for the lack of shoes."

"You enjoyed doing that."

"Damn straight." He felt about ten times better already.

A blast of Willie Nelson hit Julia as she walked ahead of Paul into the Black Bear. Neon beer signs cast a rainbow of colors over the packed-in denizens of the dimly lit bar area. Then Willie was nearly drowned out by the chorus of greetings shouted at her escort.

Paul smiled, nodded, and exchanged gibes, putting a hand at the small of her back to move them through the crowd and toward a larger room filled with booths and tables.

As they broke free of the bar crowd, a waitress walked up to them. "Hey, Paul, honey, you want the usual?"

"You know it, Debbie." He dipped his head so his mouth was beside Julia's ear. "What's your tipple?"

"Er, Budweiser?" It was the only beer she could think of, since she usually drank wine. This didn't look like a chardonnay kind of place.

"Give her a Sam Adams." His breath brushed her ear again. "I have a reputation to uphold."

"There's a two-top in the back room with a Reserved sign on it," the waitress said. "It's all yours."

He saluted his thanks with a touch of his fingers to his forehead and steered Julia between the tables. The press of his palm against her waist made her feel claimed, the possessive gesture sending a shimmer of nerves dancing up her spine. Several people invited them to join their parties, but Paul slid past them with a wave and a joke.

He guided her through a wide arch to a small round table tucked into a corner. He held her chair and then pulled his around to sit close beside her, so their backs were to the room.

"Sorry to crowd you," he said, "but I don't want to make you shout across the table."

"I'm not complaining." In fact, she was contemplating the heat generated by his thigh brushing against hers as he shifted in his chair. "Do they save a table for you every Friday night?"

"No, Debbie just has sympathy for my plight."

"What plight?"

"The curse of having everyone in town feel free to interrupt my conversation with a gorgeous, fascinating woman."

She wasn't used to being flirted with. A little ball of nervousness whirled in her chest. "So where is this extraordinary woman you keep referring to?"

He threw back his head and laughed. Then he draped his arm over the back of her chair and brought his mouth beside her ear again. "She's sitting right beside me, making me wish like hell we were alone instead of in a noisy bar."

"Hey, Paul, I brought you doubles in case I don't get back here anytime soon." The waitress plunked down two frosted mugs and four bottles of Sam Adams.

"You're a treasure, Deb," Paul said, shifting away from Julia so she could breathe again. For a long moment his words and touch had sucked all the oxygen out of her lungs.

Using the neck of a beer bottle to tilt one of the mugs, Paul allowed the cold brew to pour down the inside of the glass without foaming. As the mug filled, he adjusted the angle until the base sat on the table and the liquid stopped just below the lip.

"You've got good hands," she said.

"Sweetheart, you shouldn't feed a man a line like that."

Julia felt a blush creep up her cheeks so she grabbed the mug and took a generous gulp. The crisp tang of the ice-cold beer sliding over her tongue made her close her eyes to savor it.

As she opened them, she glanced sideways. Paul was looking at her, his silvery eyes blazing hot in the dimness of the bar. When their gazes met, he turned away and took a long swig of beer directly from his bottle.

"Taggart, you son of a gun, you owe me a rematch." A barrel-chested man in a plaid flannel shirt and a John Deere baseball cap yanked a chair over to their table, turned it backward, and straddled it. He held a beer bottle in one hand as he rested his crossed arms on the chair's back.

Paul cursed under his breath, and his arm tightened around her back. "Dave, can't you see I have a guest?"

"Evening, ma'am," Dave said, nodding to her pleasantly. "I'm Dave Herndon."

His total lack of concern at Paul's obvious displeasure made her stifle a giggle. She held out her hand. "I'm Julia Castillo."

"Pleasure to meet you." He pumped her hand. When he let go, he shook his own hand slightly. "May I just say that you have a very powerful handshake?"

She smiled.

"Dave," Paul tried again, "Julia and I are having a private conversation."

"Then you shouldn't have come to the Bear." Dave grinned through his scruff of blond beard. "You know I've been waiting for a rematch. Since you haven't been here in weeks, I couldn't let the opportunity slip by."

"Well, that may be how you treat *your* dates, but I'm not leaving Julia alone while I play foosball with a hooligan like you," Paul said. "In fact, that pretty much explains why you don't have any dates."

Dave took a swig of beer. "Good try, but you're not going to get rid of me with insults." He looked at Julia. "Ma'am, did you know that Paul here is the state champeen of foosball and made it all the way to the quarterfinals of nationals?"

She shook her head. Paul's fingers played an irritated tattoo on the back of her chair.

"You ever seen him play?"

An imp of mischief made her say, "No, but I'd like to."

"The pretty lady wants you to play too." Dave pushed his hat farther back with the lip of his beer bottle.

"All right, you've got yourself a rematch," Paul said, tightening his arm around Julia and pulling her upright as he stood.

"Not so fast," Dave said, still sitting. "You said you'd play with a handicap next time, to make it a challenge."

She felt Paul's sigh as his rib cage expanded against hers. "Fine, I won't use the three rod."

"I got a better idea." He looked at Julia. "Ma'am, have you ever played foosball?"

She shook her head, wondering why he cared.

Dave's eyes lit up with sly amusement. "Then she's on your goalie rod."

"Done," Paul said.

"What? That's not fair," she protested, jerking her gaze up to his face. "I don't even know what a goalie rod looks like!"

"You don't have to do anything but stand there with your hand on the handle," Paul said, giving her a reassuring smile. "I'll take care of the rest."

"Pretty sure of yourself, ain't you?" Dave pushed up from his chair.

"Against you? I could win blindfolded with one hand tied behind my back."

She could feel tension vibrating through Paul's body, and his smile had an edge, as though he were anticipating the battle. The easy, polished veneer she'd become accustomed to seemed to melt, and she could glimpse the flash of steel underneath. She might be out of her depth with this man.

He kept his arm around her as he followed Dave into a large room crammed with people competing against each other at various games. Clanging, flashing pinball machines lined one wall, while hissing air hockey platforms commanded the other side. The center of the room was given over to the slam and whack of foosball.

Julia felt a ripple of nerves as they walked to a foosball table set in a flaring circle of light cast by a heavy brass-and-glass light fixture suspended over it on long chains. It was a strange, new situation, and she was part of a grudge match that Paul wanted to win, so she was feeling pressure. She checked the edges of her vision for wavering or blackness before anger at her weakness ripped through her. She wasn't going to have a seizure now.

Dave walked to the table and slapped a dollar on the edge. "I need this table free and clear for one game."

"You play winners like everyone else," one of the combatants at the table said.

"No sir, I got me a rematch against the king of foos," Dave said.

"The king of foos?" Julia said.

Paul gave her waist a little squeeze. "You didn't notice my crown?"

Suddenly, the cry was taken up by the crowd. "Make way for the king of foos! Clear the table!"

The two men grumbled good-naturedly as they vacated the table, their game unfinished.

"Wait! Couldn't I just watch them play for a minute?" Julia asked Paul. "I don't want to do something stupid."

Dave had moved to the opposite side of the table and was rocking the plastic men attached to the shiny silver rods back and forth.

"Give me a minute," Paul said to him before guiding Julia to the end of the table and pointing to the bar closest to the goal with three red men spaced along it. "This is the goalie rod. What I want you to do is just hold it so the middle man stays in the center of the goal. I can handle the rest of the defense with the rod in front of it."

Julia wrapped her hand around the rubber-encased handle and slid the bar back and forth. It moved with a well-oiled weightiness she found pleasing. She tried spinning the players the way Dave was doing and discovered it was harder than it looked.

"Don't move it unless I ask you to dig the ball out of a corner," Paul said. "That way I'll know exactly what I have to protect."

"What happens if we lose?" Julia asked, her knees feeling like jelly.

He pulled her against him in a reassuring hug. "We won't lose."

Releasing her, he shifted a step sideways and put his hands on the two rods farthest away from hers before nodding to Dave. A scuffed-up white ball went rolling across the lacquered green tabletop, and Paul slammed one rod across to send it zinging toward Dave's goal. Dave blocked it with one of his goalies and sent it caroming off a wall toward Paul's goal.

She positioned her rod where Paul had told her to and squeezed her eyes closed as the ball sped closer. She felt the table jerk and heard a smack. Opening her eyes, she saw the ball dancing between the men on the front rod under Paul's control as he set up for a scorching shot on Dave's goal. She was about to cheer when Dave stopped it again.

Pretty soon, she gave up worrying about the ball coming anywhere near her three men. Paul scored three goals in quick succession, so Julia could relax enough to enjoy the speed and confidence with which he shifted his grip from one rod to the other as he passed the ball forward.

She even had time to notice he was overdressed for the bar in his pale-blue button-down shirt, neat khakis, and polished loafers. He'd worn a suit earlier, so she began to speculate about where he had gone between work and showing up at her hotel room. She was starting to think he hadn't planned this trip to the Black Bear ahead of time.

Shouts snapped her out of her reverie. "Heads up, pretty lady!"

The white ball zinged past her stationary goalie and banged into the goal.

"Oh no! It's all my fault." She bit her lip and looked an apology at Paul.

He appeared unconcerned as he reached around her to retrieve the ball. "It's just one goal. Don't change a thing."

"What score wins?"

"First to seven, but you have to win by two goals." He spun the ball through the opening and onto the table.

She stopped staring at him and focused her attention on the game. She knew nothing about strategy but she understood visuals, so she studied how the ball banked off walls and players. She began to see where the ball would go as long as it wasn't intercepted by another player.

Paul scored two more goals, but they were hard fought, as Dave seemed to be bringing his game up a level. A few beads of sweat stood on Paul's forehead. Yet his hands never slowed or faltered.

She saw the ball sneak past Paul's three bar and roll toward the side of the goalmouth. Jerking her rod sideways, she succeeded in changing the ball's path, but it still went into the gaping black hole.

"Nice try," Paul said, giving her a quick smile. "But don't worry about defending. I'll get that goal back."

He flicked the ball into play. Dave got control and slammed it into their goal so fast and hard Julia flinched.

"My fault," Paul said, putting his hand over hers where she clutched the rod with white knuckles. "There was no way to stop that one."

He walloped two goals past his opponent in short order and the game was over.

"Yessss!" she said, pumping her fists in the air. Paul was being pounded on the back by enthusiastic supporters. He winked at her with a wry smile, although his eyes blazed with triumph.

The heat from his gaze spread over her skin and flashed deep inside her. Focusing on him as he played the game—feeling the shift of his body beside hers—made her feel intensely attuned to him.

On the other side of the table, Dave crowed, "I got three goals off him! First time he hasn't shut me out."

"So who's your pretty goalie?" someone shouted to Paul.

"That's our cue to exit," he said, seizing her hand.

She gasped at the touch of his palm against hers. That was all it was, yet she felt a vibration through her entire body.

The crowd began to chant, "Hail, the king of foos! Hail, the king of foos!"

Paul plowed forward, pulling her close in behind him to shelter her. He kept going until they burst out into the cool night air, where the sudden silence seemed almost deafening.

"I should have known better than to go there," he said.

"Are you kidding? We won!" She danced a triumphant jig.

He laughed and pulled her into his arms to dip her in a continuation of the dance. She could feel the waves of energy rolling off him.

"I want to learn how to play foosball," she said, as he set her upright. "Not that I could ever be as amazing as you are."

"If you tell me again I have good hands, I can't answer for the consequences," he said, still holding on to her.

Her eyes flew to his as a flush washed up her cheeks. Watching the swift flex and release of his long fingers on the foosball handles had set her to wondering what it would be like to have all that skill focused on touching her.

"Looking at me like that is even worse than telling me I have good hands," he said. He pulled her around the corner of the building so they were standing in a shadowy alley. Then he slid his fingers along her jaw and into her hair, tilting her face upward as he bent to brush her lips with his.

She closed her eyes to concentrate on the texture of his mouth on her skin as he skimmed over her cheek to nuzzle a sensitive place just below her earlobe. "Oh yes, Paul," she breathed, the ripples of pleasure widening from where he touched to skitter down her neck to her breasts, making her nipples tighten. His contact was featherlight, yet heat bloomed all over her body. "God, yes."

"What are you saying yes to?" he asked, pulling back and looking down at her. His face was in shadows, but she knew what caused the rasp in his voice because she was feeling it too.

"To you. To—" She hesitated, hoping she wasn't misinterpreting what he meant. She swallowed. "To us doing what we both want to...together."

He huffed out a laugh. "I think I understood that. But I'm a lawyer, so I want to spell it out." He moved them both forward a step into the yellowish light cast by the street lamp. He framed her face with his hands and locked his eyes on hers. "I want to make love to you, Julia. Is that what you're agreeing to?"

She nodded, making his hands move with her head.

"Say it again," he grated, the lines of his face taut with controlled desire. "Say yes."

"Yes, I—" She had no chance to finish before he spun her back into the shadows and sandwiched her body between his and the shingles of the Black Bear's wall. His mouth came down on hers as he thrust his hands into the mass of her hair. There was nothing gentle about his touch this time, and instead of a delicate blossom of heat, she felt a bonfire roar to life deep inside her. The pressure of his thighs on hers, the compression of her already aching breasts against his chest, and the feel of his obvious arousal in the vee of her legs made her moan and writhe.

His fingers slid out of her hair and down to her hips, holding her still as he broke from the kiss. She could feel the expansion and contraction of his chest as he dragged in a deep breath. "I didn't mean here," he said with a flash of a smile. "Let's go find a nice comfortable bed."

Chapter 12

*H*E WRAPPED AN ARM AROUND HER WAIST AND LED her to the Corvette where it sat gleaming under a streetlight. As she slid into the leather seat, she gasped out loud. She was so aroused that even that bit of friction made her squirm. He accelerated into a tire-squealing U-turn and sent the sports car hurtling down the country highway back toward town.

"Um, are we going to your place or mine?" She tried to decide which she would prefer.

"Mine." He glanced sideways and shook his head. "No, yours would be better. That way you can kick me out anytime you want to. There's a back stairway we can use so no one knows I'm there."

At first she was disappointed and a little hurt. She wanted to be invited into his home. But then she followed his logic: if things didn't go well or she changed her mind, she was in control. She didn't have to depend on him for a ride back to the hotel. His gallantry made her reach out to touch the back of his hand on the steering wheel. "Lawyers make good dates."

"Well, now that's a unique perspective. My profession is generally considered a negative when it comes to relationships," he said, downshifting as he turned the 'Vette into a side street. "We'll park back here where no one will see the car. I don't want you caught in the gossip mill, since it's already grinding."

"I guess Mrs. Bostic's sister would notice if it sat in the parking lot all night," Julia said.

"I keep meaning to get a minivan for my trysts," he said, killing the engine and swinging out of the driver's seat.

After helping her up out of the car, he bent down for a quick kiss that lingered when she wrapped her hand around his neck. Nervousness was starting to intertwine with her excitement, so she beat it back by plastering her body against his to savor the feel of hard muscle and the scent of starched cotton and warm male.

"This way," he said, breaking the kiss and grabbing her hand. He led her around the inn's rose beds to a side door.

"Do mayors really get the keys to the city?" she whispered.

"No one ever locks anything in Sanctuary." The knob turned in his hand, and he ushered her into a dimly lit entrance hall leading to a narrow staircase. "This comes out in the linen closet upstairs. It's a highlight of the inn's ghost tour," he said, following her up the steps.

She swallowed the laughter bubbling up in her throat as he cracked open the closet door and checked the upper hallway for guests or staff. It was partly tension and partly delight at the silliness of sneaking around.

When he turned and nodded that it was safe, she said softly, "This is so much fun."

He looked startled, and then the brilliant smile she had noticed the first time they met flashed across his face. "I guess it is."

He was still smiling as they slipped through her door. He threw the deadbolt and turned around. The smile was gone. There was nothing in his face but intention and it was all focused on her.

Nervousness nearly swamped her. He wasn't a college boy or a mildly attractive fellow artist, her only two experiences with sex. Paul was a grown man with an intensity and physical presence that both thrilled and scared her. She felt gauche and inexperienced when he looked at her like this.

He moved back, giving her space. None of the hunger left his face, but it was tempered by a tightly held control. "Having second thoughts?"

She looked into those silvery eyes, let her gaze trail down over his wide shoulders to the muscle-roped forearms exposed by his rolled-up sleeves, and finally to the long fingers drumming against his thigh, the only sign he gave of his pent-up impatience. She shook her head.

He approached her slowly, almost as though she were a skittish horse. "I'm not going to run away if you make a sudden movement," she said.

"I'm not so sure. Wood sprites are notoriously shy," he said, running his hands down her arms to twine his fingers with hers.

"Wood sprites?" She liked that.

He tugged her up against him. "It popped into my head on the shoulder of the interstate, and I can't seem to get rid of it."

"It fits right in, because I thought of you as one of those half-god, half-humans who were always running around in the forests of ancient Greece, chasing nymphs."

Now the desire in his eyes was joined by amusement as he stood there, looking down at her, their bodies barely brushing each other. "A demigod? That's a hell of a lot better than the king of foos."

"I don't think so. You earned the crown. The demigod thing is just genetics." She was starting to relax under the influence of his banter. She swayed into him.

That was all the cue he needed. He bent and snaked one arm behind her knees while the other slipped around her shoulders. Scooping her up, he headed for the bedroom. "This is what demigods do when they catch a wood sprite."

She looped her arms around his neck and held on tight as he turned sideways to get through the door. Her weight seemed to offer no challenge. "They generally get in trouble for it, though," she pointed out.

"Some trouble is worth getting into," he said, lowering her so she lay crosswise on the bed, her knees bent over the side and her feet dangling.

He bent and braced a hand on either side of her shoulders, staring down at her almost as though he was debating where to begin. She held her breath, willing him to touch her somewhere, anywhere soon. When he didn't move, she reached up and unfastened the top button of his shirt.

She heard his breath catch, so she went after the next button and the next until his shirt was open to the waist but still tucked into his khakis. She yanked it out and finished her task, pulling it as far down his arms as she could. Then she spread her hands over his bare chest, fascinated by the way his muscles jumped under her palms. Her hands glowed almost white against his warm, olive skin as she traced the curves of his shoulders and biceps. She moved them lower to rest her palms on the cut lines of his flat abdomen, savoring the layered texture of skin over muscle.

The reality of him was so much more beautiful than her drawing.

"There's plenty more to explore," he rasped.

"I think it's your turn." She gave him her best come-hither smile, which probably wasn't necessary considering how fast he pushed her arms upward and jerked her T-shirt over her head.

"You are so worth any trouble I get into," he breathed, finally putting those long, clever fingers to good use as he released the front catch of her bra. All he did was cup his hands over her breasts so his palms just barely pressed against their centers, and a current of arousal flashed down between her legs, making her hips pulse against his thigh.

His mouth came down on hers as his fingers traced circles on her blazingly sensitized nipples. She couldn't keep her body still when he touched her that way, so she held on to the hard curves of his shoulders to keep their mouths together.

He shifted position so he could trail his mouth downward over her throat, along one collarbone, and then over the swell of her breast until his tongue replaced his fingers. The heat and friction and dampness had her arching up so his teeth grazed her bare skin, adding a whole new sensation. "Oh yes, Paul! Please! Yes, there!"

She grabbed fistfuls of the quilted bedspread as he brushed his lips over to the other breast. His fingers teased over the wet skin where his mouth had just played, while the tension between her legs kept coiling tighter and hotter. "Paul, I want...I want to finish," she panted. "Now."

She could feel a vibration against her breast. Was he laughing or moaning? She tilted her head up to see him unsnap and unzip her jeans at lightning speed. He hooked his fingers in the waistband to strip them and her panties off in one swift tug before he knelt between her legs. Oh dear God, he was going to give her an orgasm with his mouth.

"No, with you!" she said, somehow curling her trembling body up far enough to get her hands into his thick, waving hair and pull him upward.

"Are you sure you're ready for that?" he asked, even as his eyes went dark with anticipation.

"So sure."

He nearly sent her through the roof when he gently slid one finger down between her thighs and inside her.

"I guess you're right," he said, making her whimper with pleasure when he lowered his head to kiss her softly where his finger had been. He came to his feet and reached into his trouser pocket, dropping a foil envelope on the bed before he removed his clothes as swiftly as he had hers.

He rolled on the condom and spread her knees apart so he could stand between them. Then he began to slowly, exquisitely enter her as he angled forward onto the bed, coming down onto his forearms so his chest brushed her breasts without crushing them. He kept moving deeper and deeper into her until she felt stretched and filled and gorgeously unsatisfied.

He stopped, and the bed began to vibrate with the shaking of his muscles as he held himself in check.

"You don't have to be so careful." She rolled her hips, seating him even deeper and making them both gasp.

"You don't have to be so impatient," he said, dipping his head to nip at her earlobe. He withdrew as slowly as he had come in and she twisted underneath him, trying to get him to move things along before she blew up in sheer frustration.

"Paul!"

"Demigods like to savor wood sprites," he said, but the cords of his neck stood out in a way that said he was having a hard time curbing his appetite.

"That's what the rest of the night is for." She wrapped her legs around his waist and impaled herself on him.

"Julia! You're going to kill me!" He gave up the struggle and seized her hips, thrusting hard and fast.

She flung her arms up over her head and gave herself to his rhythm as the hot, tight longing deep in her belly wound tighter and tighter. He let go of her hip to flick a finger in just the right spot between them, and her orgasm blasted through her, bowing her up off the bed and digging her heels into his sinewy buttocks. He kept moving, driving her to another climax.

And then he went deep and still for a long moment before he bent backward and shouted his finish at the ceiling.

Julia closed her eyes as he slid out of her and gently shifted her so she was fully on the bed. She wrapped herself around the afterglow still pulsing deep inside her. She heard the whisk of a Kleenex from the box on the table, and then the opposite side of the bed dipped under his weight.

"Asleep already?" His deep voice came from very close, and she pried her eyelids open to find him lying on his side, his head propped on his crooked elbow as he smiled at her.

"Recovering," she murmured, smiling back at him as she ran a finger along one of his strong cheekbones. She uncurled and fell onto her back. "I feel so *good*."

"You look pretty darn good too." He picked up a strand of her hair and brushed it over her breast.

She giggled and gasped at the same time as her nipple reacted to his erotic tickling. Then he dropped the hair and spread his hand over her abdomen, where it burned like a brand against her skin.

"So beautiful," he murmured, flexing his fingers the tiniest bit so she felt their imprint. He stroked over her hipbone and down her thigh, then moved back upward until he feathered a touch along the bottom curve of her breast.

"Try your hardest. I can't move," she said, although in fact everywhere he touched sent ripples of sensual delight dancing over her skin.

For a moment, he let his palm rest on her breast. Then he draped his arm over her waist and pulled her up against him, nestling his face against her neck. She shivered as his breath fanned over her throat.

"Are you cold?" he asked, lifting his head.

"No, no. The temperature is perfect."

Everything was perfect: the weight of his arm claiming her, the warmth of his body snugged up against her side, the bone-melting relaxation following a major orgasm. "I don't know why I didn't do this sooner," she murmured.

"Too much sooner and we wouldn't have known each other's names."

That wasn't what she meant, but she was struck by it. "That's really weird, isn't it? Here we are, stark naked together, and we know virtually nothing about each other." His breathing changed rhythm, and she wondered what that signified. She tucked her chin down to try and see his face, but it was buried in the crazy tangle of her hair.

"Around here I feel like I know too much about everyone."

"Mystery is part of the attraction. Sex is how you find out more." Her eyes were closed, and she was rambling out of a sense of contentment and a desire to have his voice rumble in her ear.

"So what did you find out tonight?" he asked.

"That I got some details in my drawing wrong."

"What drawing is that?"

"The one of you walking out of the river, holding a big fish. Claire asked me to donate it to the charity auction next week."

That got his face out of her hair. "Didn't you say something about it being nude?"

She nodded, knowing her eyes were brimming with amusement.

"You're pulling my leg." He sat up, pulling her with him. "All right, show it to me."

"I wouldn't really donate it," she said, sliding off the bed and padding into the sitting room to retrieve her sketchpad.

He propped himself up on the pillows and enjoyed the view of madly waving red hair tumbling down toward the curve of her rounded bottom. She seemed to have shed her earlier attack of shyness entirely.

Waiting for her, he felt ease soak deep into his body. With Julia, he didn't have to be the responsible brother or the respectable mayor or the do-good lawyer. It was a welcome respite, if a brief one. He couldn't expect someone like Julia Castillo to hang around Sanctuary for long.

She walked back in, already flipping the pages of her pad. Turning the book around, she held it in front of her body as she came across the bed on her knees.

He reached out to take it from her, but she drew back. "Nope. You have to look from the right distance."

"But you're covering up my favorite sculpture."

She blushed adorably. It always surprised him that he could embarrass her. She was so fiercely sure of herself in some ways, and so vulnerable in others. He focused on the drawing, and felt both awe and laughter expanding in his chest.

He was nude all right, shedding water as he strode out of the shallow water. He didn't know how she managed to give his skin the sheen of wetness with just some shading of her pencil. She had idealized his body, making him look like a male model, but the face was definitely his. He wasn't sure he liked the tilt of his head; it held a touch of arrogance. True to her word, she had given him a nice big fish to cover his private parts.

"Is it a bass or a trout?" he asked.

She smacked his shoulder lightly. "Careful, or the drawing will go to the auction."

A moment's recklessness tempted him to tell her to go ahead. Then he thought of the ripples of shock and disapproval that would run through the crowd at the gala. It just wasn't worth it.

He looked up to meet her green eyes and realized she was waiting for his opinion. "You've made me look a lot better than I really do. Except for my face. That's all me. Do I really look that high-and-mighty?"

"Sometimes, but it works for you," she said. She tipped her head and narrowed her eyes as her glance swept down his body. "I don't think I made you look better at all. I need to make a few adjustments, but they'll just add character to the drawing."

Her frank assessment made a certain part of his body stir again. She jerked her gaze back up to his face as another blush swept up her shoulders and neck to brighten her cheeks. She worried her lower lip, and he wondered what she was thinking.

"I'm staying until next weekend," she said, her gaze still on his face. "Claire's giving a reception for my new work Friday night at the gallery. And I'm going to the charity auction. Are you?"

Elation surged through him. He'd been hoping for two more days with her. Now he'd have an entire week.

He would show her the sights of Sanctuary. Maybe seeing it through her fresh eyes would give him a new perspective.

"Well?"

"What?" He had forgotten what she'd asked.

"Are you going to the auction?"

"Yes, and I'm wearing a tux. I hear I look handsome in it."

"Not as handsome as you look in nothing." She waggled her finely arched brows at him.

He pulled the pad out of her hands and tumbled her backward on the bed. After that there wasn't much in the way of conversation for some time.

Chapter 13

*J*ULIA SAT PROPPED UP IN BED, WATCHING PAUL IN THE mirror as he scrubbed at his wet hair with one of the hotel's towels. A slant of early-morning sunshine turned his skin to gold. His unbuttoned khakis sat low on his hips, and he was bare chested. Dropping the towel, he pulled a comb out of his back pocket and lifted his arms to work on the thick, damp waves. It made the muscles of his back shift and flex in ways that sent a yearning to touch him rippling through her fingers.

Yanking the sheet out to wrap around herself, she slid off the bed. She needed to buy a sexy nightgown or two. Her oversize T-shirt didn't cut it now that she had an audience. She tucked the corner of the sheet in and trundled up behind Paul, laying her hands on the moving muscles she'd been watching. "I can't believe I can touch you anywhere I want to," she said, sliding her hands down his warm, satiny back and then around his waist to pull herself flat against him.

He stopped moving, and she felt him take a deep breath. "As long as the privilege goes both ways."

"That's the best thing about it."

He lifted one of her hands and brought it to his mouth, turning the palm inward and tickling her skin with the tip of his tongue. The heat and slickness made her nerves sing, and she tightened her one-armed grip on his midriff.

"Sweetheart, I've got an appointment in twenty minutes." His voice was a register lower than normal. "So you need to hold off on the touching privileges or I won't be able to zip my trousers." She let her hand dip lower to find his burgeoning erection. "I bet it would take less than five minutes to fix that problem."

"You're on."

She crowed with delight as he turned in the curve of her arm.

"Hey, you didn't wear a sheet last night," he said, throwing a disapproving frown at her toga.

"It was dark then. It's daylight now."

She saw his hand move toward the tucked-in corner and all of a sudden the entire sheet was whipped away from her and sent flying. She fought the desire to cover herself with her hands against his devouring gaze.

"I say we can do this in three minutes," he said, placing her arms over his shoulders and sliding his hands down her bottom, to the backs of her knees. His fingers wrapped her legs like steel bands as she went soaring upward, her thighs spread around his hips, her hot, sensitive center pressed against the hard length of his arousal. As soon as they touched, moans tore from both their throats.

Paul let go of one of her legs to haul a condom out of his pocket and hand it to her. She tore the foil with her teeth and leaned back to roll it on him in record time. Lifting her, he eased her down onto his cock and slid his hands around to cup her buttocks. She could feel his fingertips brushing against the private, inner skin he was exposing, and she laced her hands together tightly behind his neck to keep from writhing out of his arms.

Gravity pushed him deep inside her, and his grip opened her to the exquisite friction of his body as he began to thrust. She started to pulse her hips in the same rhythm when he grunted, saying, "We need some resistance." Striding to the wall between the closet and bathroom doors, he spun around to put her back against the striped wallpaper and began moving again. She was pinned firmly between his hard chest and the wall as he thrust harder and withdrew more fully. Her breasts were crushed against him, his fingers dug into her buttocks, and his cock drove into her again and again until the building heat inside her exploded into a supernova of screaming sensation.

She felt him arching and pulsing at the same time. As his climax ebbed, he sagged against her, his dead weight the only thing keeping them from sliding down to the floor in a sated heap. His breath was whistling past her ear in gasps while her heart pounded so hard, she swore she could feel her veins expanding.

He held her there for a long moment before she felt him softening and slipping out of her.

After she unlocked her legs from his waist, he carefully lowered her until her bare feet hit the carpeting. He ran his hands up the sides of her body to cup her face while he leaned in and kissed her with a tenderness that contrasted with the hot, fast sex they'd just had.

"Two minutes, fifty seconds," he said when he ended the kiss.

His smile was crooked, and she reached up to touch one twisted corner of his mouth. "What is it? What's wrong?"

"Not one single thing," he said, enveloping her in his arms so her face was snuggled against his chest and she could no longer see his expression. "You are absolutely perfect."

He was trying to distract her with flattery, but she let the compliment soak in anyway. God knew, she'd been feeling like a failure for long enough. It was good to be appreciated for a change, even if it wasn't for her artistic ability.

"Don't you have an appointment?" she asked when he showed no sign of letting her go.

"They can wait on the porch." But he released her and headed for the bathroom while she retrieved her sheet.

Running water sounded as she nestled into the chaise longue by the window, waiting for him to emerge.

"I'll be done by two so I'll meet you wherever you'll be," he said before a rueful smile crossed his face. "I guess I do get high and mighty at times. I'll meet you, if you want me to."

"I want you to, but I don't know where I'll be. Call me on my cell."

He shrugged on his shirt, buttoning it with the same speed he played foosball. He sat on the end of her chaise and pulled on shoes and socks before he leaned in for a kiss.

"Are you sneaking down the back stairs?" she asked.

"Yes. We'll give the good citizens of Sanctuary some time to get used to seeing us together." He stood and shot his cuffs, even though he wore no jacket. "It's going to be tough keeping my mind on contracts when I know you're sitting here, wrapped in nothing but a sheet."

"Wait till you see what I'm wrapped in tonight." She hoped she could find something good in the local shops.

"Don't torture me. It's hard enough to leave already."

"The sooner you leave, the sooner I can go shopping."

He reached for her mop of hair and gave a strand one of the affectionate tugs she'd come to treasure. "You're a one-woman boost for the local economy, sprite."

Turning on his heel, he strode through the bedroom door. She heard the outer door open and close, and then she stretched luxuriously on the chaise, draping her arms over the padded back and curling her toes into the soft blue velour.

Her body hummed with sensations ranging from a tiny throb where he'd grazed her breast with his teeth last night to the deepest languor of satisfied need. She lay there with her eyes closed, letting memories of their night together spin through her mind.

She had been right to think he would be on a whole different level from her other two partners. Paul knew his way around a woman's body. He was creative and funny and intense and perceptive. He took what he wanted, but he made sure she got so much more.

"Ummmmm," she sighed, stretching again.

She shoved herself upright as a realization flashed through her mind. *She hadn't worried about having a seizure since the moment before the foosball match.*

The only other situations where she completely forgot about her condition were when she was painting in the familiar surroundings of her studio and with Darkside.

She swung her legs off the chaise longue and twirled around the room, reveling in her escape from fear. Paul thought she was perfect. While she was with him, she could convince herself she was too.

She sauntered into the bathroom, plugged the rubber stopper in the bathtub's drain, and turned the taps on full force.

Julia walked into the gallery carrying three shopping bags. She hoped Paul wouldn't mind the local saleswomen being privy to the cut and color of the lace undies he'd be stripping off her.

Claire stood in front of a Len Boggs landscape, talking to a couple dressed in casual clothes that somehow reeked of money. Julia gave her quick smile and took a seat on the big leather couch. She had gotten engrossed in a magazine article on up-and-coming Dutch artists when the sofa bulged slightly under her as another person's weight hit it.

"I found you the perfect place to work," Claire said. "It's right in town so you can walk there. Tim took your supplies over there this morning."

"When can I see it?" Julia swiveled to face Claire, knocking one of the bags off the couch, so a tiny puddle of black silk and lace spilled onto the plank floor.

Claire's eyebrows rose as Julia scooped up the teddy and stuffed it back into the bag. Julia dropped her gaze to fidget with the handles of the shopping bag. "It's for a friend of mine's birthday," she said.

When she found the nerve to look up, Claire was smiling serenely. "I'm sure your, er, friend will enjoy it," she said.

Julia cleared her throat. "I wanted to ask a favor. Well, two favors."

Claire smoothed her hands over her rose linen skirt. "Name them."

"May I invite my uncle to the Friday reception?"

"You can invite anyone you want." Claire frowned. "But you're already jittery about the reception. Won't your uncle's presence add to the pressure?"

"Probably. Definitely. But he's been my agent for my whole career, and I owe it to him to be part of this." Julia had thought about this as she walked between stores this morning. "I also want him to hear what other people say about the work, whether the comments are positive or negative. He needs a different perspective."

"Well, I'll certainly make sure he gets *my* perspective."

Julia was warmed by Claire's fierceness on her behalf. "Which brings me to my other favor. Can you give me some advice on what to wear to the reception and the gala? What is an artist supposed to dress like?"

Claire gave a trill of pure delight. "I need new outfits for the same events, so we'll shop together."

"Really?" She hadn't been shopping with a girlfriend since art school. "Are we going to the mall?"

"Do you want to look like a highly successful artist?"

"Ye-e-es." Julia wasn't sure what she was getting at.

"Then we're going to the Laurels."

"The resort?"

"It's the only place to buy designer clothes within a hundred miles."

"Oh, you meant how much did I want to spend. I'll just have to call the credit card company again. I've kind of overspent my limit on this trip." Guilt cast a shadow over Claire's expression of anticipation, so Julia hurried to say, "It's okay. My bank keeps asking me to please use their card more, so I'm obliging them."

"Get it raised by Monday afternoon. The gallery is closed, and we should get lots of attention at the resort shops since the weekend crowd will have left by then." Claire smiled. "Maybe we can even broker a discount since we're buying in bulk."

———————— ❖ ————————

Julia surveyed her new domain, the former Plants 'N Pages. Empty floor-to-ceiling bookshelves lined the front room's walls while a couch and two overstuffed chairs stood forlornly in a corner. She walked around the end of the bead-board counter separating what had been the bookstore from the greenhouse. The glassed-in back room was empty except for a potting table at one end. It was heavy, but she managed to drag it to the center of the room. Rummaging around in the stack of new art supplies, she found a drop cloth and covered the table with it, arranging her brushes and paints the way she liked them. Finally, she set up the easel and lifted a small blank canvas onto it.

She repositioned the easel to take full advantage of the light and picked up a charcoal pencil to begin sketching in the outlines of her donation for the auction.

Instead of a black horse, Paul's face formed in her mind's eye, and a prickling sense of anticipation danced through her. He would be here in a few hours. She would see his silver-gray eyes darken as she pressed herself against him, feel his hands tangle in her hair, savor the pressure of his lips against her throat. Heat jazzed through her and made it hard to breathe. She gave herself to the daydream, letting her eyelids drift downward.

The electronic notes of her cell phone startled her so much she knocked into the canvas, barely catching it before it toppled off the easel. By the time she had it safely back in place, the call had transferred to voice mail. She checked the caller ID, the pictures in her mind so vivid, she was sure she would see Paul's name on the screen.

It was Carlos.

She felt like someone had upended a bucket of ice water over her head, dousing all the swirling warmth and sensation. She had hoped to put off talking to her uncle for another day, fearing the guilt he could evoke would overshadow her pleasure in Sanctuary.

Then she thought of Paul. Last night she had felt she was his equal. He had been considerate and generous, but he had let her feel the full force of his physical need. And she had found an answering power in herself.

She dialed her uncle back.

"Julia! When are you coming home?" Her uncle's usually slight accent was pronounced, which meant he was upset.

"I'm staying for the week." She decided to forestall any more pointless arguments by issuing her invitation. "I want you to come to a reception for me on Friday here at the Gallery at Sanctuary. Claire Arbuckle is organizing it. You remember her; she used to be Claire Parker. It would mean a lot to me if you were there."

It was true, even if the thought also set her nerves fluttering like a flock of startled pigeons.

"A reception? For what purpose?"

"To show off my new paintings. The *Night Mares*." She stifled the urge to add, *the ones you refused to show anyone.*

"That's not a good idea."

"Claire's very excited about the new direction of my work." It was amazing how difficult it was to contradict him. Her throat was so tight she had to work to force the words through it. "She finds it powerful."

"Perhaps, but it's not the sort of thing people wish to have in their homes, to live with. Even you call them nightmares."

"Come to the reception. See what the patrons and critics say."

"I wish to come up there tomorrow and speak with Mrs. Arbuckle."

"No!" Her throat seemed to have reopened, partly because she didn't want her uncle around to interfere with her fling with Paul. "I need some time."

"Time for what?" Carlos sounded baffled and hurt.

Time to make love to a hot lawyer as often as she could before next Sunday, when she had to go back to her real life. "To…to rest. You know I need that." She winced as she played the card of her condition, but it was the only excuse she could think of that would keep her uncle away.

"Then I will speak with Mrs. Arbuckle by telephone."

"All right, but let me tell her to expect you." She softened her voice. "Remember when Claire took my paintings for her New York gallery? We were both so excited. This is a wonderful way to thank her for believing in my work."

"You feel this is the right way to repay her?"

He had to jab at her with his doubt again. She was almost grateful when a spurt of anger ripped through her. "She and I have total confidence in the *Night Mares.*"

"An hour, and then I will call."

A thought struck her. "Please don't mention my epilepsy to her."

The silence drew out before her uncle spoke again. "I wondered that she would put you in such a stressful situation, given your condition."

She had to convince him not to expose her secret to Claire. "Even if you don't believe I'm cured, you always told me not to share the information with anyone in the art world. Claire is well connected; someone might find out." Not for a moment did Julia believe Claire would reveal a secret she was asked to keep, but Carlos didn't know that.

"And you will come home right after the reception?"

"Two days after it. I promised to donate a painting to a charity auction the following night. Claire thinks my presence will push the painting's value up. It's for a good cause."

Her voice had taken on a pleading note, despite her efforts to sound firm and in control. That's what her uncle could do to her.

"I will stay until Sunday to take you home," Carlos said.

Now he wanted to intrude on her last night with Paul. *How had everything gotten so complicated?* She squared her shoulders and cleared her throat, injecting all the authority she could into her tone. "Thank you, but I've already arranged my transportation home."

"I see." He sounded more sorrowful than mad, which made her feel worse.

She gave him the gallery's phone number and bid him a terse good-bye.

Walking over to the sofa, she flopped onto it, tilting her head over the back and crooking her arm over her eyes as she tried to untangle the threads of the conversation. Her uncle was upset that she discounted his opinion of her *Night Mares*, but he was also genuinely worried the stress of the reception would cause a seizure. His concern was real and it undermined her ability to hold on to her anger. He had hurt her deeply, but he also loved her and it tore at her to cause him pain in return.

She pulled her arm away from her face. With all Carlos's pressuring, she'd almost missed something: when she'd told her uncle not to come to Sanctuary, he'd backed down and shifted to telephoning Claire. She couldn't help feeling a small spurt of triumph. Maybe she just needed to treat Carlos more like Darkside: show strength, hide fear. Except her uncle was far more difficult to handle than the stallion.

Paul walked up the creaky wooden steps of the former Plants 'N Pages. Julia had asked him for a ride out to Healing Springs Stables so she could soak up more artistic inspiration. Peering through the screen door, he saw her in front of an easel, frowning and working a brush through a rag. Her hair was wound up into a lopsided knot, her face was smudged with white paint and charcoal, and all he wanted to do was tackle her onto the ratty velvet couch shoved in a corner of the empty shop.

He cleared his throat as he opened the door. Julia jumped and turned her head, a wide smile banishing the unhappy stare. "Thank God! I have artist's block or something."

In two strides he was behind her, pulling her soft curves against him. He nuzzled his face against her neck. "You smell delicious."

"The only thing I smell like is gesso and turpentine."

"Eau de Artiste," he said, enjoying the feel of her warm body in his arms. "My favorite fragrance."

"Mmm, I'm a fan of Legal Eagle," she said with a shimmy that had him tightening his grip on her waist.

Needing a distraction, he looked over her shoulder at the easel. It held a canvas about two feet by two feet, its surface a bright, unsullied white. He glanced downward to where the legs of the easel stood in a drift of sheets of drawing paper covered with roughed-in drawings of horses. "Tough day at the office, eh?" he said.

She huffed out a breath. "I've never had this problem before. There was always something that wanted to be on the canvas."

He felt tension pulling her away from him. "Maybe your brain is just overloaded with new images." He tried for a deep, seductive tone as he added, "And new sensations."

He cast a thankful glance skyward as she relaxed back into him. "That makes sense," she said. "And there's my biggest distraction. You." She turned and plastered herself against him, wrapping her arms around him and murmuring his name. A quick wash of gratification at her last words was swamped by a stronger reaction to the press of her pliant body against him.

He'd been interested in the couch before, but now he was more focused on the counter. It was closer. He straightened so her feet came off the floor and walked them both over to where he could lift her higher to seat her on the linoleum. She opened her knees and he stepped into the space between her thighs. As he slid his hands up under her T-shirt and circled his thumbs over her already hard nipples, he heard the click of paintbrushes hitting the tile floor. Her head fell back, and he ran his lips up the exposed arch of her throat to take her mouth again.

He felt her fingers at the buttons of his shirt, and then her hands were on his bare chest and his rib cage and his abdomen, her warm, exploratory touch making his erection harder and harder. When she pulsed her hips against him, he passed the point of no return.

Her jeans and panties hit the floor, and he unzipped his fly to roll on a condom in record time. He had just enough brain left to make sure she was ready, although touching her wet heat nearly sent him off. Then he thrust inside her, his hands filled with the delicious curve of her buttocks as he held her at the edge of the counter.

Her fingers dug into his shoulders as she pushed her hips into his thrusts, so he went deep every time. He freed one of his hands to slide his finger down between them so he could add to her sensations.

"Paul! Oh yes, there! Oh please, more!" She went completely still for a long moment, and then she screamed and convulsed around him, her muscles clenching and relaxing, clenching and relaxing.

He gritted his teeth against the urge to finish, waiting until he felt the tension in her body soften slightly. Then he withdrew and surged in once more and joined her in a climax that left his body wrung out and his mind wiped blank.

She slumped against him, her body racked with tiny shudders. He wrapped his arms around her back protectively and savored the aftereffects.

"Paul?" Her breath tickled against his chest.

"Yes, sweetheart?" He kissed the top of her head.

"I think you melted every bone in my body." She shifted in his arms. "Oh dear, I got charcoal on your shirt. I didn't realize my hands were dirty."

"You're welcome to get charcoal on my one and only Armani suit as long as it leads to this."

"So you're not mad?"

Disbelief turned to laughter as it worked its way up his throat. "I walked in here expecting to have a nice chat and instead I get mind-blowing sex. What exactly do I have to be mad about?"

She huffed out a giggle against his bare skin. Incredibly, he could feel a faint stirring between his legs. He decided it was time to put a few inches of distance between them. Gently lowering Julia backward so she lay on the counter, he grabbed a paper towel from the roll on the counter and disposed of the condom. Then he picked up her panties and slipped them up her legs, sliding his hand under her behind and lifting her upward to tug the peach-colored satin into place.

"I love the feel of your hands against my skin."

He froze as her words seemed to stroke down his chest and lower with almost the same impact her fingers had earlier. "If you say things like that, your panties are going to come right back off," he said.

"I wouldn't mind as long as you did all the work." She heaved herself up onto her elbows, her T-shirt still bunched above the lacy bra that matched her panties. He hadn't had time to appreciate her lingerie until now. The color made her skin look even creamier.

"Peaches and cream," he said.

"You like my new undies? I just bought them this morning."

"I like that they don't cover up much." He took another step backward, shoving his hands into his pockets to stop himself from reaching for the swell of her breasts again.

He cursed the streak of chivalry that made him turn away from such blatant temptation. Why couldn't he just be a self-centered jerk and take her up on her offer of a repeat performance? Why did he have to care that she get pleasure from it too?

He pivoted away from her. "You should get dressed before I do something ungentlemanly."

Chapter 14

"WHERE'S DARKSIDE?" JULIA ASKED ONE OF THE GROOMS AS she and Paul walked into the barn hand in hand. She still couldn't believe she had sprawled across a counter in broad daylight, naked from the breasts down while a man she'd known for two days came inside her. When she thought about it rationally, she knew she should be shocked, but it all seemed natural for this new person she'd become in Sanctuary. She had less than a week before she went back to being wrapped in lamb's wool, so she'd better enjoy her liberation, and that included seeing her whisper horse.

"Out in the paddock. He spent the night there because he was such a pain in the a—er, neck that the boss said to leave him."

"Darkside?" Paul frowned. She felt his grip tighten. "What do you want with a horse who tried to tear your arm off?"

"I just want to take some pictures of him." Julia knew he wouldn't approve of her escapade with Darkside yesterday. Hopefully, no one would mention it to him. "He looks just like my *Night Mares*, you know."

"Hey, Julia, Paul! I thought I heard that souped-up gas guzzler you drive come up the road." Sharon strode toward them, wearing her usual outfit of polo shirt, britches, and paddock boots. "Can I get some legal advice since you're here? I just got this contract in from the Laurels. They want me to board a bunch of polo ponies for a match that's being played later this summer. I don't want to sign anything without you taking a gander at it."

Paul hesitated. Julia gently disengaged her hand from his. "You go ahead with Sharon. I'll meet you in her office."

"Don't get too close to Darkside," he warned. "Next time he might get your skin instead of your sleeve."

Julia caught the narrow-eyed look Sharon gave them and hurried to say, "I'll pay attention this time." She couldn't fault him for his protectiveness; after all, only his quick reaction had saved her arm from Darkside's teeth. Still, he wasn't going to keep her from her whisper horse.

She watched Paul and Sharon's well-matched strides as they walked away together. Just as she was about to head for the paddock, Sharon looked back over her shoulder and gave Julia a wink.

"I wonder if she really has a contract," Julia muttered, detouring into the treat room for some carrots. Tucking them in her pocket, she jogged out to the paddock, camera in hand.

To her surprise, a couple of the stable hands greeted her by name. A third one shook his head as he led a big bay past her. "You're that plumb crazy artist. Maybe you can get Darth Horse back in the barn."

Her heartbeat kicked up a notch. *Could she really lead Darkside back to his stall?* It was a crazy idea. She couldn't ride even the most placid teaching horse. Why on earth did she think she could handle a high-strung, temperamental stallion that even experienced horse people couldn't deal with?

Maybe that was why Darkside was her whisper horse: no one would ever expect her to ride him.

"Let's just see what kind of mood he's in," she murmured as she approached the gate. Peering between its rails, she saw the big black horse standing at the opposite side of the paddock, head and tail lifted as he gazed in the direction of the outdoor riding ring. With her eyes she traced the beautiful arch of his neck down to where it met the strong line of his back and along to his muscular hindquarters. His black coat glistened with tints of blue and red in the sun and the breeze swept his tail into a ripple of satin.

For an insane moment, she thought about opening the gate and slipping into the field. Then she thought of how Paul would react, and she climbed up to sit on top of the fence instead. She wanted to photograph Darkside up close, so she had to get his attention.

"Hey, buddy, I've got carrots," she called, keeping her voice low and calm.

He swung his head around and blew out a challenge. Catching sight of her, he laid his ears back and charged across the grass, skidding to a stop just in front of her perch.

She forced herself not to flinch and held out a carrot on her palm. "Want a snack, big guy?"

He stretched his nose toward her, nostrils flaring. Then he jerked back and squealed out a high whinny.

"Tempting, isn't it? But you have to come closer to get it."

Horse and woman stared at each other. Darkside took a step forward and lipped the carrot off her hand.

"Want another one?" She reached into her back pocket. The stallion took another step toward her and snuffled at her knees. She offered the carrot to him. This time he didn't hesitate to take it, his big teeth crunching on the crisp vegetable.

She let out her breath and ran her hand down his glossy neck. He snorted but didn't shy away. Keeping her eye on the telltale angle of his ears, she smoothed his mane and stroked his downy nose.

After bribing him with another carrot, she eased her point-and-shoot camera out of her back pocket, letting him sniff it before she took a shot. He twitched at the electronic noise but didn't bolt. She took several close-ups and put the camera away, deciding she'd better get off the fence before Paul finished with Sharon's contract.

Darkside was standing so calmly she couldn't resist laying her cheek against his for a few seconds as she murmured what a good horse he was. When she drew back, he whickered, and she could almost believe he regretted the absence of her touch.

"Good-bye, handsome," she said, swinging one leg around and down, slotting her foot onto the rail below the top one so one leg was on each side of the fence.

Darkside threw his head up and knocked against her knees. She teetered, pinwheeling her arms to regain her balance, but her position was too precarious, and she felt herself pitching over backward. She willed herself to go limp; Papi had once told her that was the best thing to do when falling off a horse. If you tensed up, you were more likely to get hurt.

She heard a shout, and then she hit something that wasn't the ground. A loud "oof" of expelled air told her she'd landed on a person. When she lifted her head, she found a very angry-looking Paul lying under her, his chest heaving as he sucked in deep breaths.

"Are you all right?" She rolled off of him to make it easier for him to breathe. "I didn't mean to fall on you."

"Are you...totally...insane?" he gasped.

Several shadows fell across them, and Julia looked up to see a ring of concerned faces staring down. She felt a little surge of joy that it wasn't because she'd had a seizure.

"What's going on here?" Sharon asked, striding up to the group. She knelt down. "What happened?"

"I fell off the fence and landed on Paul," Julia said. "I'm okay, but I knocked the wind out of him."

"I'm...fine." He shoved himself into a sitting position. "You... are...certifiable."

"Shhh," Julia said. "Wait until you catch your breath before you yell at me." His usually silvery eyes had gone dark with fury.

"Doesn't look like any bones are broken," Sharon said.

"You deliberately put yourself in harm's way," Paul said, his voice tight, "going near an animal you know is dangerous. What were you thinking?"

"Sharon thinks Darkside is my whisper horse," Julia began.

Paul swung his gaze around to the other woman. "You encouraged her to go near Darkside? She can't even ride."

Sharon didn't blink. "She's got him eating out of her hand. Darnedest thing I've ever seen."

Paul was practically vibrating with anger, and Julia decided she had to intervene. She laid her hand on his chest, where she could feel his heart pounding. "Darkside didn't mean to knock me off the fence. He was just saying good-bye."

"For God's sake, horses don't say good-bye," Paul said.

"I gotta say, I've never seen a man move as fast as you did," Sharon said. "One minute you were standing beside me at the barn door, and the next you were playing landing mat."

"He has good reflexes from foosball," Julia said.

Sharon directed a knowing look at Paul's arm curving around her. "I think he has good motivation."

Paul vaulted to his feet, holding out his hand to Julia with a clear air of command. When she put hers in his grasp, he yanked her off the ground and into his arms. "You scared the hell out of me," he said into her hair. "Don't ever do that again."

She knew what he meant; he wanted her to stay away from Darkside, and she wasn't going to promise that. So she just said, "Mmmph," against the warmth of his chest and hugged him back.

He held her until his heartbeat slowed to its normal pace. As he released her, he stepped back, running both hands through his hair.

"Did I hurt you?" she asked. "I fell right on top of you."

He shook his head, the tension in his face relaxing. "You're just a wood sprite. You barely weigh a thing."

"At least let me make sure your clothing is undamaged." She walked around behind him and winced at the dirt and grass clinging to his shirt and slacks. Without thinking, she began to brush at it, her hands traveling over his back and shoulders before moving down to stroke his tight butt and the hard muscles of his thighs.

"Thanks, but it would be safer if you didn't keep that up," he said, twisting around to catch her hands.

As his fingers closed around her wrists, she shivered with the knowledge that she was poking at a tiger. It was thrilling and a little frightening, but she was determined to enjoy this experience fully. She'd never been involved with anyone like Paul Taggart before; he was protective of her, yes, but he treated her as an adult woman, unlike her family. In fact, he thought she was fascinating.

"Now after dinner tonight is a whole different scenario," he said, his eyes glinting.

"I don't remember being invited," Julia said, enjoying the fact he still held on to her.

"Sweetheart, you are most definitely on the guest list. And it numbers exactly one."

Chapter 15

JULIA FIDGETED WITH THE FRINGE ON HER SAGE-GREEN shawl as Paul drove her to the 1827 House, the nicest restaurant in downtown Sanctuary. After he told her where they were eating dinner, she'd made another flying visit to Annie B's to buy a slim-fitting pleated taffeta sheath in shades of lavender and celadon. It looked like an Impressionist painting, especially when she added a necklace and earrings of glass leaves in varied hues of green. Paul had whistled when he saw her, so she figured it worked for him.

She had wanted to whistle at him too when he walked in her door dressed in a silver-gray suit and pale-mauve shirt. The suit draped over his tall, rangy frame like an elegant glove, and the shirt made his olive skin glow. Unfortunately, she'd never been good at whistling, so she'd settled for a slow scan up and down after which she gave him a long, appreciative kiss. That seemed to work for him too.

"You've gotten very quiet," he said. "What's bothering you?"

"Claire called after you dropped me at the inn. She's set up a phone interview for me with some influential art blogger. It will be good for my show and the auction, but I'm nervous." She hadn't wanted to confess her inexperience to Claire, but nervous was an understatement about how she felt at the prospect of talking to Paxton Hayes. "My uncle has always handled all my publicity. I don't even know what he tells the press."

"We can do some research online," Paul said. "Read the fellow's blog. When is the interview?"

"Two o'clock tomorrow. He has to have time to write the article and post it, so people get interested in the show."

"That doesn't give us much time, but we'll do some role-playing. Although I'm not current on what art bloggers want to know." His smile flashed.

She laid her hand on his forearm, feeling like a drowning person who'd been thrown a lifeline. "Would you really do that with me?"

"As a lawyer, I'm responsible for coaching witnesses on their testimony, so this is just part of the job. Especially since you've retained me."

"Oh right. I keep forgetting I sleep with my legal advisor. Does that reduce the fee?"

"You want me to take it out in trade?" His eyebrows rose as he cast a sideways glance at her. "That could be arranged."

He parked the 'Vette with a flourish and came around the car to help her out. Her high-heeled strappy purple sandals made her teeter on the gravel, and his arm instantly went around her. His hand splayed over the side of her hip, its warmth and strength easily penetrating the thin taffeta.

They strolled along a stone path that wound through beds of fragrant antique roses, showy peonies, and splashy poppies before they reached a stone house with multipaned windows glowing from within and a steady hum of voices wafting through its open front door.

"Paul, my friend, we have a table for you upstairs," the maître d' said as they entered. He collected two menus and led them through the dining room.

From every other table they passed, someone called out a greeting to her escort. As he had at the Black Bear, Paul smiled and nodded and kept propelling her forward with his hand. Only one diner, an older man, actively tried to waylay them, and Paul dodged him with a quip and a brief squeeze of the man's shoulder.

"Thanks, Joe," Paul said, taking the menus as the maître d' held Julia's chair. "It's exactly what I asked for."

"What did you ask for?" Julia asked after Joe left.

"A table in the quietest, darkest corner he had available."

"Embarrassed to be seen with me?"

His smile was rueful. "People forget I'm not the mayor anymore. They want to talk."

"I could tell by our procession through the main dining room."

"Maybe I should have gone with my first instinct, which was dinner at my house." His smile went a little awry. "But I have the right to take a beautiful woman out to a nice restaurant."

She reached across the table and wrapped her fingers around his. "If anyone other than our waiter comes up to the table, I'll be very rude. It doesn't matter if people here don't like me, since I'll be leaving soon."

A strange expression crossed his face. His smile and eyes softened, but there was an almost sad wistfulness about him.

"Joe promised to seat only out-of-towners up here tonight," he said, handing her a menu.

"Good evening, Mr. Taggart. Joe asked me to take care of you tonight." A slim brunette in her thirties, dressed in the waitstaff's uniform of blue shirt, black tie, and black slacks, appeared at their table.

"Since when am I Mr. Taggart to you, Lisa?"

Lisa smiled, her blue eyes sparkling. She was quite beautiful, and Julia felt a twinge of jealousy. "Since you're the customer, and I'm the waitress."

"Lisa, this is Julia Castillo. Julia, Lisa Miller. We went to school together from the third grade on and she married my old drinking buddy Louie."

Julia relaxed at the word *married*. "Do you have any good stories about Paul?"

"You'd have to ask my husband," Lisa said. "He and Paul were always getting called to the principal's office, and I wanted nothing to do with them." Lisa lifted her pad and pen. "No more fraternizing. Pretend I'm just a waitress you don't know."

"Is there anyone in this town he doesn't know?" Julia asked.

Lisa smiled. "That's why he has to pretend. Now how about a cocktail?"

"I think we'll have champagne," Paul said.

"Oh, one piece of good news, and I'll get you our best bottle. Jimmy and Eric are going camping with us after all. Terri was willing to switch weekends."

Paul picked up a spoon and began spinning it through his fingers. "Jimmy gave me the good news yesterday. Eric would have been really disappointed to miss the trip."

"You're invited too," Lisa said. "We've got an extra tent."

He shook his head with what looked like genuine regret. "Wish I could, but I'm committed to the theater auction."

"That's a shame. All the boys love it when you come." Lisa flipped her ponytail back over her shoulder. "All right, no more chatting, I swear."

After she left, Julia looked at Paul. "You go camping with your nephew?"

His eyes glowed with affection. "As often as I can. The last camping trip we took, he got sprayed by a skunk. He said it was the best weekend ever."

"So you slept in a tent with him?" She couldn't wrap her mind around the idea.

"Sure did. Which meant I nearly got sprayed by the skunk too. Eric snuck food into the tent, and the skunk decided he wanted to share. My nephew tried to protect his Doritos and I had to referee."

She enjoyed her mental image of Paul, dressed only in a pair of gym shorts—since that's what her stepbrothers always slept in—standing between a small boy clutching a bag of chips and a glowering skunk. "Sounds like you failed since Eric got sprayed."

"I found out skunks don't speak Latin."

"Latin?"

"When I told the skunk the Doritos were not *bona vacantia*, and therefore he was committing a trespass *de bonis asportatis*, he didn't grasp the concept."

"I sympathize with the skunk."

His grin glimmered in the candlelight. "The Doritos were not ownerless goods and he was committing larceny."

"Seems to me he should have sprayed *you*."

"He didn't want to end up in court. Skunks are notoriously averse to litigation."

Laughter bubbled up her throat. Being with Paul was better than drinking champagne. It felt as though she'd been living in twilight until she journeyed to Sanctuary and found him and her whisper horse.

She sobered at the thought of Darkside. "There's something I need to tell you," she said, fidgeting with one of the empty champagne flutes a busboy had placed on the table.

"You stole those paintings from another artist."

"What! Of course I—oh, you're joking." She scowled at him. "This is serious."

He slid the flute away from her restless fingers.

She lifted an eyebrow at him, since he was the worst offender when it came to twirling dishes. She spread her hands flat on the table. "Sharon was right. Darkside is definitely my whisper horse."

Paul pressed his lips together.

Julia rushed to explain. "I know you think he's dangerous and I'm just asking to be hurt, but it's important for me to figure out why he's in my paintings."

He stared at the small fire guttering in the stone hearth before he brought his eyes back to her. "Do you know why Sharon owns Darkside?"

Julia shook her head.

"Because he put his previous owner in a wheelchair. They were going to destroy the horse, but Sharon—who is as certifiable as you are—offered to take him."

"His old owner must have done something to make him behave that way." Horror at the thought of her magnificent whisper horse being killed had her by the throat.

"He's a killer, Julia."

"No. I've looked in his eyes and there's no darkness, just confusion." She sat forward. "I can help him."

A muscle in Paul's jaw worked. "You have to do what you have to do."

"So you understand."

"No, but I'm not your uncle."

She reached across to tuck her hand in his. "I don't mind when *you* try to protect me. It's kind of sexy."

Julia heaved a sigh of relief as she saw a real smile tilt the corners of Paul's lips. "You say the damnedest things."

She had been expecting him to explode at any minute and had been mentally kicking herself for bringing up Darkside. However, it seemed likely he would find out from someone else, and she didn't want Paul to think she had broken any promises.

Lisa interrupted their conversation to pour the champagne. As Paul raised his glass, his cell phone emitted a series of shrill rising notes.

"Not now," he muttered.

The cell phone sounded again, the notes seeming faster and more urgent. He raked a hand through his hair. "I'm sorry. I have to take this call." Standing, he walked toward an empty alcove of the small dining room with the phone to his ear. As he moved away, she heard him say, "Jimmy?"

He had reacted the minute he heard the ringtone, which meant it had to be someone with a powerful claim on him. Lisa had mentioned his brother, Jimmy, so Julia suspected he was the caller.

After a short conversation, Paul dropped the phone back in his pocket. When he turned, she could see tension in the set of his shoulders and the hard-etched lines of his face. "I'm sorry, but I have to take you back to the inn. There's a family matter that needs dealing with now." His face softened as he looked down at her. "This is not how I wanted our evening to end."

"Is something wrong with your nephew?" she asked, putting her hand in his and letting him pull her to her feet.

"No, Eric's with his mother this weekend, and she lives about a mile outside town, thank God." He didn't offer any further explanation.

"If there's anything I can do to help, I'd like to."

He cupped Julia's face in his hands and leaned down to give her a tender kiss. "We have to go."

As they drove back to the Traveller Inn, Julia noticed his white-knuckled grip on the wheel and the grim set of his mouth. There was no sign of Paul the affable ex-mayor or Paul the charming and passionate lover. This was a man she didn't recognize, and she wished she knew how to call back one of his other selves, because this Paul made her understand how little she really knew him.

He pulled the 'Vette into the parking lot and started to get out. Julia opened her own door before he got around the car and teetered up onto her high heels. "You don't have to worry about me." She stretched up to kiss him. "Go!"

He hesitated a moment before his mouth relaxed into a half smile. "Given the crime rate in Sanctuary, I guess you'll be safe between here and the front door. I…we—" He shook his head. "I'm sorry. This wasn't what I intended." He lifted her hand to press a quick kiss on the palm. Then he strode back around the long hood and disappeared into the car's interior. The headlights flashed once and the Corvette swept around the circular drive-way and out onto the street.

She pulled her stole tighter around her shoulders and wondered about the demons Paul so carefully concealed.

Paul yanked the steering wheel left as an inebriated patron reeled out of Archie's Bar and Games and into the parking lot. Nosing the 'Vette into an empty space, he got out and turned to brace his forearms on the car's cool, hard roof, drawing in and releasing several deep breaths to control the anger and frustration boiling within him.

He kept seeing the bewildered expression on Julia's face. He should have come up with some explanation for his abrupt departure, but he couldn't bring himself to confess his brother was a hopeless drunk. He only had a week with her, and he wanted to keep all the ugliness away for that short period. Baffling her was better than soiling their time with the sordid truth.

Pushing himself away from the car, he straightened the lapels of his jacket before walking to the bar's battered pine door and slamming it open.

The reek of smoke, the thumping bass of the electronic juke-box, and the cacophony of voices raised and slurred by alcohol smacked into him like a fist. This had been his bar of choice in his youth since they accepted his fake ID without a blink. It was here he had honed his foosball game. Now the place made him feel old and tired.

He shouldered his way through the mix of teenagers and farmhands, nodding to the bartender as he approached. "Hey, Vince. Thanks for the phone call."

"He's in the office," Vince said. "He gave me his cell phone to call you."

Paul felt the anger start to build again. His brother had made certain he would come running. He pulled a fifty out of his wallet and held it out to the bartender.

Vince waved it away. "All I did was call you."

Paul slid it across the scarred wooden counter. "Buy your wife a present."

Vince looked at the bill before swiping it up and pocketing it.

Paul nodded and headed for the door that led behind the bar's public rooms. Someone called out his name, but he didn't bother even to lift a hand in greeting. It would be too tempting to start a good old-fashioned bar fight to vent his fury since he couldn't take it out on his brother.

Two strides took him down the cracked brown linoleum of the hallway and to the office door. He turned the knob and stepped inside, closing the door behind him. Jimmy lay sprawled and snoring on a brown-and-orange plaid couch whose springs sagged to the floor. Paul stood looking down at his brother, wondering how the cute, annoying kid who followed him everywhere had become an alcoholic who nearly lost the right to spend time with his own son.

He searched the slack face for signs of the younger brother he'd taught to swing a bat and drive a car, the nervous kid he'd driven to the movies for his first date, the cocky teenager who'd dreamed up some of their best pranks.

All the anger drained from his body, and he slumped into a threadbare red brocade chair beside his brother.

Jimmy might have set out to get Paul's attention, but at least he had chosen a bar where he was least likely to be seen by people who would tell his ex-wife about it.

He reached out to give Jimmy's shoulder a shake. His brother opened his bloodshot blue eyes and blinked at him. "Whah?"

"I'm here to take you home." He stood.

"Paul?" Jimmy pushed himself upright and scrubbed his palms over his face. "What are you doing here?"

Irritation pulsed in his temples, but Paul kept his voice quiet. "You asked Vince to call me because you knew you shouldn't drive home."

"Oh yeah. Vince took my car keys away." His words were indistinct around the edges. "I guess you're pissed at me."

Paul sighed and sat down again. "I thought you were going to your AA meetings."

"I was. I am." Jimmy's shrug sent him listing sideways, and he had to grab the arm of the sofa to right himself. "It was just a bad night."

"Why didn't you call your sponsor? Adam would have helped you."

Another shrug. "He's busy at the Aerie on Saturdays."

"He's made it clear he's available whenever you need him. He wouldn't be your AA sponsor otherwise." Paul knew his words fell on deaf ears, because Jimmy wouldn't have called his sponsor if it had been noon on a Monday. His brother had done this to send a message to Paul: Jimmy needed him to stay here in Sanctuary. Any thoughts he had of leaving should be banished.

Tears slid down his brother's cheeks. "I thought I'd have Eric this weekend, so I didn't plan anything to keep my mind off it." He swiped at his face. "I hear you're dating that famous artist who came to see Claire Arbuckle."

Surprised by his brother's change in topic, Paul nodded.

"You always were a son of a gun with the ladies. So was I."
Jimmy shook his head sadly. "You were with her tonight, weren't
you?"

Knowing how many people had seen them at the 1827 House,
Paul told the truth. "Yes."

Jimmy slammed a fist on the couch. "First your job and now
your love life. I'm screwing up everything for you. I'm a worthless son of a bitch."

"Let's go home."

"You must hate me."

This was familiar territory when Jimmy was drunk. "You're
my brother. I love you. Now let's get out of here."

Jimmy nodded and tried to push himself off the couch. Paul
caught him as he staggered and hooked his brother's arm around
his neck to hold him up. Jimmy smelled like stale smoke, sweat,
and booze. Paul thought of how Julia had smelled when he had
held her earlier. He tried to summon the memory of her fragrance of fresh air and flowers into his nostrils, but it was too
delicate to survive the contrast.

He walked Jimmy down the hall and out the back door. Before
rounding the corner of the building to get to his car, he propped
his brother against the wall and did a quick survey to make sure no
one was there to see them. Jimmy had been doing so much better,
and Paul really didn't want Terri to get wind of this backslide.

Nothing moved except the flashing red-and-blue neon of the
Budweiser sign, so he hustled Jimmy into the 'Vette and quickly
got on the road.

"Oh God," his brother moaned as they rounded a curve. "I'm
going to puke."

Paul hit the button to put down the window. "Do you want
me to pull over?"

"No, the fresh air's good. If I'm going to vomit, I'll lean out.
Don't want to mess up your fancy car."

Jimmy had progressed to his nasty phase.

"I can take it to the car wash tomorrow, but you might be more comfortable if you got the alcohol out of your stomach."

"Nah, I like it there. Makes me feel good, even though I'm a drunken loser. That's what Terri used to call me, you know. Bitch. Not you. Her."

Paul found himself hoping yet again that his brother didn't call his ex-wife a bitch in front of Eric. He'd never heard Jimmy do it, and he'd never seen him drunk in his son's company. Jimmy swore he never touched a drop when he had Eric with him, and Paul was inclined to believe him. His brother loved his son too much to jeopardize his safety or the amount of time he got to spend with him. They made it home without the car needing a wash, and Paul half carried his brother up the front steps. Inside the house he saw the evidence of Jimmy's binge: three beer bottles and a liter of vodka stood empty on the coffee table. A fourth beer was lying on its side, its contents puddled on the table and creating a dark stain on the carpeting. That meant there were at least two more beers hidden somewhere. He would have to hunt for the stash after he put Jimmy to bed.

He got his brother onto his bed, pulling his boots off and tucking a plaid comforter around him. As he leaned down to adjust the pillow under Jimmy's head, his brother's eyes opened and he grabbed Paul's hand. "Swear you won't leave! If I lose Eric, I'll kill myself."

Desolation seared through him as he squeezed Jimmy's hand and said, "I'll be here as long as you need me."

"I'm sorry," Jimmy whispered. His eyelids fluttered closed, and he began to snore like a buzz saw. His grip on Paul's hand loosened, and his arm dropped to hang over the edge of the bed. Paul picked it up and tucked it back under the comforter.

In the living room, he gathered up the bottles and found a plastic bag to haul them out in. He checked all Jimmy's other hiding places, finding the other two beers and several travel-size bottles of Scotch.

Finally he sank down into one of the plastic-covered kitchen chairs, crossing his arms on the table. He put his head down and gave in to despair.

Chapter 16

"I THINK YOU'RE READY," CLAIRE SAID, PUTTING DOWN the legal pad she'd been reading questions from. "I told Paxton you wouldn't answer any questions you didn't feel comfortable with, so don't hesitate to take a pass."

Julia slumped onto the gallery's big couch. "Jeez, you mean there's another question you haven't thought of?"

But even as Claire had peppered her with questions, Julia kept thinking about Paul. He'd called her in the morning, saying he was still tied up and had arranged for Claire to prep her for the interview. His voice had been tight and apologetic. Julia hauled herself upright and locked her eyes on Claire. "Can I ask you a question about Paul?"

"You can ask. I can't promise to answer it."

"That's fair. Last night we were at dinner when he got a phone call. From Jimmy. He said he had to take me back to the inn right away."

Claire's mouth tightened, and she crossed her arms.

Julia hesitated a moment but decided Claire's disapproving stance wasn't directed at her, so she continued. "He looked so... so bleak and unhappy and, well, I hate to see him like that. Is there anything I can do to help him?"

Claire glanced away, staring in the direction of a Len Boggs painting that Julia was pretty sure she wasn't seeing at all. She pursed her lips, and Julia knew she was debating what to share with her. Claire gave an almost imperceptible shake of her head before turning back to Julia. "I can only guess about last night, so I think it's better if you ask Paul."

"I know it wasn't his nephew, Eric, because I asked about him," Julia said, hoping to shake loose some clue. "He really loves his nephew. His face lit up when he talked about Eric."

"I think Paul sees his younger self in Eric, and he wants to keep Eric from making some of the mistakes he did."

Julia wanted to ask what mistakes Paul had made, but she'd thrown enough questions at Claire.

Claire stared down at her pointed red pumps for a moment before she brought her gaze back to Julia. "I can tell you things that are public knowledge. Paul was on track to be partner at a big law firm in Atlanta, until his brother Jimmy's marriage fell apart and he lost custody of Eric. Paul came back to Sanctuary and negotiated joint custody for his brother."

Julia waited, but Claire added nothing further. Julia got the sense the other woman was trying to convey something she wasn't catching on to. "Should I ask Paul about it or not?"

Claire bit her lip. "I don't know."

Julia huffed out a breath of frustration. These hints were almost worse than no information at all. Whatever Jimmy's problem was, it was bad, but she couldn't imagine Paul supporting him if he was doing something illegal or abusing Eric in any way. She needed to figure out a good angle to approach Paul from. Or maybe she should leave it alone, since subtlety was not her strong suit. She forced herself onto another sticky subject. "How did the phone call with my uncle go?"

Claire looked relieved at the change of topic. "He was charming but persistent."

"And?"

Claire's expression turned impish. "I was even more charming and persistent."

"I wish I could have eavesdropped," Julia said, feeling a weight lift from her. She'd been afraid Claire would be cowed or upset by her uncle, but she should have known better. Claire had sold high-priced art in the most competitive city in the world. She took a deep breath and asked the question she dreaded the answer to. "He didn't try to persuade you to keep me away from the show?"

"Well, he expressed some concern about your ability to handle criticism, but I assured him I would run interference on that." Claire turned serious. "Not that I think you need me to. You're as strong a person as I've ever met."

Julia felt a twinge of guilt at the compliment, since she continued to hide an important part of her past from her new friend. However, relief also flowed through her; Carlos had not betrayed her secret.

"It was a pleasure speaking with you too, Paxton," Julia said, forcing a smile because she'd always been told that people could hear it in your voice over the telephone. "I look forward to reading your blog."

She pushed the disconnect button on the gallery's fancy office phone, waited a couple of seconds, then picked up the receiver to make sure there was a dial tone. She didn't want Paxton Hayes overhearing anything he shouldn't.

Now she flopped back into the desk chair, sending it rolling backward as she stared at the ceiling. She half lay there with her legs stretched straight out in front of her and tried to remember if she'd said anything too embarrassing.

There'd been a couple of awkward moments where she'd stammered through an evasive answer, but she'd finally taken Claire's advice and simply said she'd prefer not to respond to certain questions. Not that it stopped Hayes. He would drop the subject but circle back later in the interview, trying to elicit the same information by asking in a different way. He'd caught her the first time.

Maybe her uncle had been doing her a favor by handling all her interviews.

She hauled herself upright. She couldn't let herself slip back into the cocoon she'd allowed her family to spin around her.

The office door swung open and Claire stuck her head in. "How'd it go?"

"Great! Paxton's a charmer."

One of Claire's eyebrows arched. "You must have dialed the wrong number."

"Okay, he's a sneaky manipulator who tried to trap me into saying things I didn't mean. And he succeeded a few times."

"Now I know you got the right person."

Julia grimaced. "The good news is you had almost every question he asked on your list."

Paul followed Claire into the office. Julia's heart did a little stutter step of surprised pleasure when he came straight to her and dropped a kiss on the top of her head. This was the Paul she understood and lusted after. If only she could forget last night's glimpse of a darker side.

The thought shamed her. If she cared about Paul, she had to care about all of him, light and dark. As in her art, one required the other.

"Sorry I wasn't here for the inquisition," he said. Fine lines sketched exhaustion around his eyes, and she wanted to smooth them away. He pulled out a chair from the other side of the desk and flipped it around to face her. "How was it?"

"Exhausting. Exhilarating." Now that the nervous tension had drained away, she realized she meant it. "I felt like we were two foosball players, probing for each other's weaknesses."

He smiled at the foosball analogy. "I'll bet you got the upper hand." He rolled his shoulders tiredly. "I just wanted to check in before I take Eric to the movies."

"With pineapple pizza afterward?" Claire asked.

"It's got all the food groups," Paul said, unfolding himself from the chair.

Claire turned to Julia. "That's why you should never go to Sunday dinner at Jimmy's house."

Julia dutifully laughed, but she would have eaten cardboard if it meant seeing Paul with his trouble-prone nephew.

Paul looked down at her, a shadow of longing crossing his face. "I have an obligation for tonight, but I want you to come to my office tomorrow morning at nine. With the show coming up, we need to discuss your situation with regard to your uncle." He gave her a tired smile. "An office setting can sometimes make difficult matters seem less emotionally charged."

She nodded, trying to hide how bereft she felt at the prospect of spending one of her precious remaining nights without Paul. "I'll walk out with you," she said. "I want to get a little work done on the auction donation before the light goes."

Paul looked surprised, but Claire's eyes lit up. She obviously didn't know about Julia's painter's block here in Sanctuary. "What sort of thing are you working on?" Claire asked.

"Er, a close-up of Darkside." She checked Paul's face but it was unreadable.

"I can see the headline: Local Horse Models for World-Famous Artist," Claire said. "Great publicity."

Julia stood and preceded Paul out of Claire's office.

"Glad to hear you've overcome your painter's block," he said, his voice low and so close she thought she could feel his breath stirring her hair.

"That feng shui you and I did at the studio seems to have made the atmosphere more conducive to creativity," she said, throwing him a sly look as he came up beside her.

She caught the look of puzzlement, then the dawn of realization. "Feng shui, eh? That's a new name for it." He slung his arm around her shoulders. "Does painting Darkside require you to see him in person?"

"Possibly."

He sighed. "Leave it to you to pick the world's most dangerous whisper horse."

Chapter 17

"OOK WHAT PA DID TO MY ROOM," ERIC SAID, LEADING Paul down the hall. "He got the idea from a TV show. It's called penciling."

"You mean stenciling," Paul said, stopping in the doorway. He scanned the newly colorful walls, where soccer balls, horses, campfires, baseball bats, and dogs danced in a kaleidoscopic array. "Your pa did this?"

"Yeah. I got to pick what pictures I wanted and he pen—stenciled them. See, there's a pony, although he's not gray like the one at Sharon's. Maybe Pa can repaint the colors for me."

Paul took a step into the small room, pivoting slowly as he spotted Mario and Luigi from Eric's favorite video game, Harry Potter, hockey skates, and a skunk. He laughed at his brother's reference to the eventful camping trip. "How long did it take him?"

Eric bounced down on his bed, his brow furrowed in thought. "I dunno. A lot of weeks? It took awhile to find the right pictures. It's awesome."

"It sure is," Paul said, sitting beside the boy and considering the amount of work and care that had gone into the project. So Jimmy hadn't painted the outside trim because he'd been busy doing this. Paul felt his frustration with his brother ease.

"Eric? Paul?"

"We're in Eric's room," Paul called out, "admiring the new decorations."

Jimmy appeared in the doorway. "His room needed painting, so I, uh, figured I'd jazz it up a little."

"You could give Martha Stewart a run for her money."

Jimmy made a scoffing sound, but pride shone in his face. "It came out pretty good."

"Pa, could you make the pony gray like Sharon's?" Eric asked.

"Sure," Jimmy said. "I can mix the black and white from the skunk and make gray."

"Pa's a pro at mixing paint," Eric said. "He said he couldn't buy every color under the rainbow, so we figured out how to make colors."

Paul stared at his brother, searching for some outward indication of this new facet of his brother's personality. All he saw was a two-day growth of beard and untrimmed dirty-blond hair.

He tried and failed to picture Jimmy experimenting with various combinations until he came up with all the colors on these walls. Come to think of it, he couldn't imagine him taping stencils up and carefully filling them in, letting each color dry between coats.

"Anyone want ice cream? I got rainbow sprinkles," Jimmy said.

Eric took off like a rocket.

Jimmy shoved his hands in his pockets and stared at his sneakers. "You don't have to babysit me tonight."

Paul levered himself off the bed. "Better safe than sorry." He was still trying to wrap his mind around his brother's unexpected artistic accomplishment.

"Suit yourself." Jimmy spun out of the room while Paul followed more slowly.

When Paul got to the kitchen, his brother had his head in the freezer, rummaging for ice cream. Bowls, spoons, and a bottle of sprinkles sat on the kitchen counter. Jimmy backed out of the freezer, juggling three cartons of ice cream and an ice cream scoop. Paul was pretty sure Jimmy didn't own an ice cream scoop a year ago.

Julia believed a killer horse could change. Maybe it wasn't crazy to believe his brother was changing too.

"This is Verna Hinkle, the best legal secretary in the state of West Virginia."

Julia put her hand out to the woman sitting behind the big oak desk in Paul's reception area. "Nice to meet you, Mrs. Hinkle."

"It's Verna, hon," the woman said, reciprocating with a hand covered in huge, sparkling rings. "A pleasure." She winked at Julia, her thick false eyelashes turning the small gesture into a showpiece of drama.

"Is she typing words or just random letters?" Julia asked in a low voice when Verna turned back to the computer and began keyboarding at blinding speed.

"Whole sentences with nary a mistake," he said, ushering her into his office and closing the door. "Before I hired her she used an IBM Selectric. She said word processing was for the weak fingered, but once I convinced her to give the computer a try, she took to it like a duck to water."

Julia forgot about Verna as she looked around his office. A heavy golden oak desk was centered on a burgundy-and-blue Oriental rug. Two chairs with wooden frames and blue upholstery sat in front of it, a low table between them. Built-in bookcases filled with official-looking legal tomes lined one wall, while sunlight spilled through a large window on the opposite side. A framed print of what had to be Sanctuary in its earlier days hung over the credenza behind his desk.

She was disappointed. The decor evoked a sense of trust and reliability, but it could have been any successful lawyer's office. There was nothing distinctive to Paul in it.

"What's that delicious smell?" she asked, as the waft of something sweet and warm tickled her nostrils.

Paul walked behind her to pick up a tray of muffins from an antique sideboard and offer them to her. "Verna gets them from Tammy's Place on her way in, so they're fresh out of the oven."

She leaned over and inhaled. "I'll bet all your clients try to schedule morning meetings."

"On slow days, I open the window and put the muffins right under it. It never fails to bring in some business."

"Better than chasing ambulances, I guess."

He handed her a china plate to put her muffin on. "Have a seat. How do you like your coffee?"

She plopped down in one of the armchairs and put her muffin on the table between them. "No coffee, thanks."

"How do you survive without caffeine?" Paul poured himself a mug of coffee from the pot on the sideboard.

She bit her lip. In her quest for knowledge about her condition, she'd read caffeine might contribute to seizures, so she'd cut it out of her diet. Her doctors pooh-poohed the idea, but she was willing to try anything to keep the terrifying attacks at bay. "I never got addicted."

Paul surprised her by setting his muffin, his mug, and a bottle of water on the table before he turned the other armchair around to face her and settled into it.

"Aren't you going to sit behind your desk and be lawyerly?" she asked.

Instead of responding with a quip, he looked somber. "Some things are better discussed on the same side of the desk."

"It's Monday," she said with a sigh.

Even with the prospect of an unpleasant decision looming, she couldn't help admiring the way Paul's deep-blue shirt fit over his wide shoulders and tapered along his lean waist, or the drape of his light wool trousers over his long thighs. It was far too easy to picture what was under the fabrics.

"Eat your muffin," he said, nudging her plate toward her. "You're distracting me."

"I'm just sitting here."

"Those green eyes of yours are very eloquent," he said, "and they're saying things I want to hear, but not right now."

"It's your own fault for looking so hot in a suit."

His knuckles went white as he gripped the arms of his chair. "If you're trying to bypass the subject of your uncle, as your legal advisor, I have to tell you such avoidance would be unwise."

"Fine." She broke off a piece of muffin and put it in her mouth.

He sat forward, resting his elbows on his knees and clasping his hands between them. "I understand you love your uncle, and you're grateful to him for managing your career up to this point."

Paul's voice and eyes were kind, and an upswell of tears clogged her throat as an image of her uncle formed in her mind. For a moment, she felt nothing but deep, untainted love for the man who had guided her for so many years. Which made the sense of loss that swamped her at Paul's next words so much worse.

"But you should consider hiring an outside representative, a professional in the field whom you can trust to be objective about your work."

She must have looked distressed, because Paul shifted in his chair and his voice became even gentler. "Julia, your uncle will always see you as a child, no matter how old you are or how successful you become. You need to have an agent who respects your talent and your judgment, and who recognizes you as the mature artist you are. It will be better for your career, and trust me, it will be better for your relationship with your uncle in the long run."

"I don't know if I can do that to him."

Paul looked down at his hands before he raised his gaze back to hers. "He lied to you about the demand for your art, deliberately, and for an extended period of time. Can you continue to work with him, knowing that?"

She turned toward the window, its frame wavering through a haze of unshed tears. "No...I don't know." She blinked and looked back at him. "Maybe if I understood better why."

Paul shook his head. "That will help repair your personal relationship, but you need to separate your family from your work."

"How do I tell him that?"

He sat back. "I'll tell him. One thing lawyers are good at is delivering news people might not want to hear."

"No!" she snapped. "That's how I got in this situation to begin with. I let other people take over the things I didn't want to deal with." She sat up straighter. "If I'm going to fire him as my agent, the news has to come from me."

"If?"

"All right, when." She fidgeted with her water bottle. "I don't know how to find another agent."

"Claire would be able to help with that."

She felt a little jolt of hope. "Do you think Claire would be my agent?"

"Ask her."

"What if she doesn't want to do it?"

"She'll say no and suggest someone else."

Julia sighed. "It sounds so simple when you say it."

"Don't mistake simple for easy. What you have to do will be tough, but it will put your career on the professional footing it deserves. More important, it will remove a significant source of trouble between you and a person you love."

"You're a smart lawyer, Paul Taggart," she said, reaching across the table to touch the back of his hand.

He immediately flipped his hand to clasp hers, his warm grip sending waves of comfort through her. "Just experienced. In my opinion, you and your uncle have a good chance of repairing your relationship because you're handling it sooner rather than later. Some folks let these situations go on until the anger and resentment have built a wall too high and thick to knock down."

"Or the falling debris crushes them underneath it." Julia heard voices beyond the closed office door, reminding her that Paul had real clients who needed his attention. "I've taken up enough of your workday."

He trapped her hand between both of his. "I want to make sure you're comfortable with what we've discussed."

"But you have another appointment. I can hear them out-side."

"That's why I have Verna." He locked his eyes on her face. "How do you feel about this?"

Her fingers tightened around his. "Like I'm about to jump off a cliff into deep water. But I've been letting other people tell me what I should do for too long. Fear forges heavy-duty chains."

"Fear?" His eyebrows drew together. "What are you afraid of?"

Lulled by the honesty of their connection, she'd forgotten he didn't know about her epilepsy. She cast around for an explanation that would satisfy him. "Fear of the unknown, fear of taking a risk, fear of upsetting my family."

It sounded plausible to her, but she could tell Paul wasn't buying it. He continued to search her face, his gaze seeming to bore into her brain in search of the truth she was hiding from him. For a moment she was tempted to confess, but she thought of how that would change their relationship, how he would think of her as someone *less*. She almost shook her head in a refusal to suffer that. Instead she tried to inject a limpid sincerity into her expression as she met his eyes.

His frown deepened, but he let her get away with it. "You have to break some eggs to make an omelet," he said, but she sensed the platitude concealed his skepticism and his questing mind was going to keep at the problem until he solved it...or she left town. If she could keep him at bay until then, it would be enough.

There was a burst of laughter from the reception room, and Julia stood up, bringing Paul with her. "The natives are getting restless."

He stepped around the table and pulled her into his arms. "The natives can wait until I'm sure you're all right," he said, using his thumbs to tilt her head back so he could see her face.

The worry in his eyes nearly undid her. She reached up to cup his cheek.

"I'll call you tonight," he said, turning to kiss her palm with a heat that made promises about what they'd do after he called.

"And send me your bill," she said, dashing out of the office before he could respond.

"Lunch," Verna said, pointing to a brown paper bag on her desk as Paul said good-bye to his last morning client.

"What did you surprise me with today?" he asked.

"Tammy's steak salad with truffle-oil dressing and a side of sweet potato fries."

"Since when did Tammy get so fancy she uses truffle oil?" Paul asked, as he peered into the bag.

"She said a customer brought it to her as a gift and she's gotten real fond of it. Can't abide the stuff myself, but I figured you'd like it." Verna stopped typing. "That little artist girl seems right sweet."

He thought of Julia sprawled on the counter of Plants 'N Pages. "*Sweet* might not be quite the word, but she's a good person. Talented too."

"She likes you."

"And I like her."

"Then why was she about ready to cry when she came out of your office?"

"She has some legal issues involving her family. It upsets her."

Verna eyed him sternly. "That had better be the only reason."

"Jesus, Verna, have I ever—"

"Don't take the Lord's name in vain." She raised a hand to silence any further objections. "No, you treat women real good, but that one's got a sensitive skin, so you need to be extra careful. You don't understand the effect you might have."

"Why do I feel like that isn't a compliment?" Paul swiped the bag off the desk and headed for his office.

"Oh, it's a compliment, hon. You are one heck of a charmer, but I get the feeling she hasn't met up with many of those in her life."

Paul closed the door and frowned across the room. Verna didn't usually comment on the women in his life, and he didn't fool himself into thinking she didn't know about them.

He sat down at his desk and took out the food containers, opening them automatically as he remembered Julia's comment about the chains of fear. The emotion behind it had been too raw for him to believe her vague explanation. Yet her previous denial of any physical fear of her uncle had been genuine. He would bet on that. So she was hiding something else.

He speared a slice of steak out of the salad and put it in his mouth. "Nice work, Tammy," he murmured as the smoky flavor of the truffle oil glided over his tongue. He went after another slice and chewed it as he considered how hard he should push Julia to reveal her secret.

She was his client, so he owed her his best advice, and he needed full disclosure to give that. She was his lover, so he wanted to help her, and he couldn't without knowing what the problem was. However, she didn't want to share it with him, so maybe he should leave it alone. After all, their relationship had a short expiration date. But if she left without resolving whatever she feared, he wouldn't be able to offer any assistance.

He put down his fork. The thought of her absence ruined the exotic savor of the truffles. In fact, the sunlight streaming in through the window seemed to turn gray. Hell, they couldn't even have a long-distance relationship, because he worked all week and couldn't leave his brother on the weekends without breaking the promise Terri had asked of him: to keep Jimmy sober and away from her house. And with a mental apology to Claire, he knew there was no way someone of Julia's caliber would stay in the artistic backwater of Sanctuary.

As the realities of his situation landed on him like a ton of bricks, he decided he might as well call Ben Serra and turn down the directorship of the Pro Bono Project. Better to kill the hope all at once, so he could settle back into his rut without thinking about the might-have-beens.

He pushed his lunch aside and scrolled through his e-mails, hunting for Serra's telephone number.

His intercom buzzed. "Your brother's on the line," Verna said. "Says he'll keep it short."

Paul groaned. The last person he wanted to talk to right now was Jimmy. He picked up the telephone receiver. "Hey, Jimbo. What's up?"

"Paulie, I'm real sorry about Saturday night." Jimmy's voice was pitched low, as though he didn't want anyone to overhear him. "I should have called Adam, not you."

Paul wasn't in the mood to pull punches. "It's not who you called, it's when you called. Next time, call one of us *before* you start drinking."

"Yeah, I know. It's just I got thinking about how I kept you from taking that job, and it made me feel like a worthless shit."

Paul tried to rub the oncoming headache away. "You're not worthless, and I can tell you how I know that. Eric. You've got a great kid there, bro."

"Not because of me."

"I see you with him, and you are one hell of a good dad."

"I don't know." Despite the demurral, Jimmy's voice held a lilt of hope. "Maybe I've gotten better at the parenting thing."

"You were never bad at it, Jimbo. You just had a big problem you let get in the way."

There was silence. Paul waited to see if his brother would explode or just whine in self-justification. For once, Jimmy did neither. "You think I was a good dad back then?"

"When you were sober, yeah, I do." It was true. From the day Eric was born, Jimmy had been crazy about his son, changing diapers, getting up for middle-of-the-night feedings, and beaming as he carried his baby around on his chest at social gatherings. Until he and his wife started having problems, and Jimmy tried to hide from them in a bottle.

Paul didn't hold it against Terri that she'd given up on his brother; she'd just been too young and inexperienced to deal with an alcoholic husband and a young child at the same time. She'd made the best choice she could for herself and Eric. The familiar guilt washed over him; he might have been able to help all three of them if he'd been around.

"I'd do anything for Eric," his brother said.

Except stay sober. Paul scrabbled in his drawer for Tylenol. He knew alcoholism was a disease and his brother was trying to fight it, but right now his sympathy was in short supply. The headache was tightening its grip on his skull.

"Anyway, I wanted to tell you Saturday night won't happen again. I'm going to all my AA meetings from now on. I won't miss a one."

"That's good to hear." Paul meant it.

"Shit, my boss is coming," Jimmy muttered. "Anyway, I called to say I'm sorry. About Saturday. About the job. I gotta go."

The connection went dead.

Paul put the phone down and shifted some papers to get at the pill bottle. As he did, he spotted a drawing Eric had given him last week, a skunk holding a bag of chips. It reminded him of the stencils on Eric's bedroom walls, and he pulled it out and centered it on the desk in front of him.

Jimmy had surprised him twice now. First with the stencils. Now with the phone call. Usually his brother would wait a few days before he cracked a joke about falling off the wagon, and that would be the extent of his acknowledgment of the incident. His apology was something new.

After swallowing two Tylenol, he dialed Adam Bosch's number. Maybe Jimmy's AA sponsor could shed some light on this.

Paul steered the Corvette past the soaring glass entrance to the Aerie and onto the private driveway leading to Adam Bosch's well-hidden home. It was strange to see the restaurant's normally packed parking lot empty, although it allowed him to admire the elegant simplicity of the building Adam had designed and built.

The sound of the 'Vette's big engine was muffled by the dense rhododendron thickets and tall pines lining the curving drive.

As he rounded the last turn, the trees seemed to draw back to reveal a modern house reflecting the same sensibility as the restaurant. It was the first time he'd seen it, since Adam guarded his privacy vigilantly. Paul felt a certain sympathy. Running a famous restaurant was similar to being mayor of a small town: people felt they had the right to your attention 24-7. He had been surprised the man would take on sponsoring Jimmy at AA on top of his business demands.

He parked the car on the sweep of river-stone paving and jogged up the wide front steps. The door opened as soon as he reached it, and Adam Bosch held out his hand. "Nice to see you, Paul. Come in."

"Appreciate your taking the time to see me on your day off," Paul said, shaking hands and noting the chef was dressed entirely in black, as always.

Adam waved him inside. "I always have time for Jimmy's family."

Following Adam out of the foyer and into a high-ceilinged living room, Paul got the impression of clean-lined modern furniture melded with antique art and richly colored rugs. One whole wall was glass and offered a view as spectacular as the one at Claire and Tim's house. Adam led the way to a couple of leather armchairs ranged on either side of a low table. A tray of cheese and fruit, a basket of steaming bread, a pitcher of water, and two glasses waited for them there. "Have a seat. Help yourself," Adam said, as he sat. "It's an occupational hazard, wanting to feed people." Adam filled the two glasses and handed one to Paul. "From the spring behind my house."

Paul took a sip. The water was icy and pure. "Delicious." He drank deeply before setting the glass down.

The chef nodded and waited, his dark eyes unreadable.

"Tell me if I'm asking something you can't answer," Paul said, leaning forward. "I'll understand if there are issues of confidentiality."

"As Jimmy's AA sponsor, I have a certain amount of leeway when sharing information with his family, so I'll give you as much as I can."

Paul locked his fingers together between his knees. "I know Jimmy had a setback on Saturday, because I picked him up at the bar."

Adam's brows drew together. "He didn't call me."

"He used the excuse about Saturday being your busiest night, but he wouldn't have called you anyway. The message was for me."

"What message?"

"That I shouldn't consider accepting an out-of-town job."

The other man cut a chunk of cheese and laid it on a slice of apple. "Try this. The cheese is an Époisses."

Paul didn't want the food, but he couldn't see any polite way to refuse it. So he tossed it in his mouth and chewed. The sheer deliciousness distracted him for a moment. "This is good."

Adam sat back, his elbows resting on the arms of the chair, his fingers steepled. "Were you considering the job or was Jimmy overreacting?"

Paul stared out the window. Something about Adam's question demanded honesty. He looked back to meet the other man's gaze. "I want the job but I wasn't going to accept it."

"Because of Jimmy."

"And Eric."

Adam nodded. "So what do you want to ask me?"

Paul took a deep breath. "Despite his performance on Saturday night, I think Jimmy is making progress. This may sound trivial, but he took a lot of time and trouble to stencil pictures of Eric's favorite things on his bedroom walls. It took patience and discipline and concentration over a period of weeks. That's a side of my brother I've never seen before. And today he apologized for Saturday night's lapse. Another first. He even swore not to miss another AA meeting."

Adam nodded again. For a man who made his living in the hospitality industry, he was surprisingly taciturn. Maybe he used his day off to recharge his conversational batteries. Paul decided the best approach was a direct one. "Here's my question. Is my presence here in Sanctuary a healthy thing for Jimmy or does he use it as a crutch?"

"I'm not qualified to answer that question," Adam said. "You understand I'm a sponsor only because I've been through the twelve-step program and stayed sober for a number of years. I don't have any formal training in therapy or counseling." He took a swallow of water. "However, Jimmy seems committed to being a significant part of his son's life. That's a powerful incentive to stay sober, especially as Eric grows older and is more aware of what condition his father is in."

"Jimmy says he can hold it together during the times he has custody of Eric, but he has to fight harder when he's alone."

"Probably true, but he doesn't have to be alone. He knows that from his AA meetings. Help is always just a phone call away."

"So there's a safety net in place, if he chooses to use it?" Paul hadn't fully understood that until he heard Adam's tone of commitment.

"Absolutely. That's one of AA's promises." The chef shifted slightly. "Alcoholics are manipulative; that's how they hold onto the people who love them in spite of their destructive behavior."

"Are you saying Jimmy is manipulating me? That he doesn't need me to stay here anymore?" Paul didn't mention his agreement with Terri. They had left it open for renegotiation if the situation warranted it.

"That's not something I can confirm."

Paul recognized the care with which the other man was choosing his words. It reminded him of how he sometimes spoke to his clients. There were no guarantees in the law or in life, and Adam was making that clear.

However, he was also giving Paul a new perspective on his brother's behavior. Paul considered Friday night's dinner conversation. Maybe when he thought he was giving his brother a chance to surprise him, he hadn't understood Jimmy's reaction.

He had seen the fear in his brother's eyes, but maybe he didn't know what caused it. He had made an assumption, and Jimmy's behavior on Saturday night seemed to confirm it, so he hadn't probed further. "You've given me some food for thought."

"Now let me give you some real food," Adam said with a half smile. He pushed the plate of cheese closer to Paul.

"I appreciate the offer, but I'll take a rain check." His stomach wasn't real receptive to intake right now.

Chapter 18

JULIA WALKED SLOWLY ALONG THE SIDEWALK, TRYING TO wrap her mind around the idea of firing her uncle. Paul's arguments made sense, but her heart seemed to twist in her chest at the thought. She tried to see through to the other side of the conversation she would be forced to have with Carlos, but she couldn't picture how he would react. Not well, she suspected.

Before she could confront him, she needed the security of having a new agent. Although she knew it was Monday, she quickened her pace as she neared the Gallery at Sanctuary. Sure enough, a Closed sign hung in the door.

Disappointed, she took a moment to admire the Blake Larson sculpture she coveted, starting when she heard locks clicking open.

"What timing!" Claire said, swinging the door wide.

"Isn't the gallery closed today?" Julia said, stepping inside while Claire relocked the door.

"That's why I'm here," Claire said. "Close your eyes."

"Seriously?"

"I want you to get the full effect."

Julia obeyed and felt Claire take a light grip on her wrist to tug her forward. After about ten steps, Claire pulled her to a stop. "All right, you can look."

Julia gasped.

She stood in the center of an open pentagon formed by the freestanding white panels that added hanging space to the gallery. Claire had arranged them so that no matter which way she turned, one of her *Night Mares* galloped toward her.

"It's...it's kind of frightening." Julia spun slowly, eyeing the black horses charging at her. "Are you sure it won't scare the buyers away?"

Claire clapped her hands as satisfaction lit her eyes. "Perfect! Exactly the effect I was trying for."

"Terrifying your patrons is a good sales technique?"

The other woman nodded. "These paintings are meant to evoke strong reactions, so we have to give them the chance to do that. The buyers for these will be excited by the drama, the emotional impact." She did her own slow spin before turning back to Julia. "This is going to make a huge splash in the art world."

Julia's stretched nerves wound tighter. She wasn't sure she wanted to make a huge splash. Maybe Carlos was right; she should stick to the safe stuff.

Claire turned one of the panels on its wheels so the painting faced the back wall. "I'm just going to flip them away from the street so no one can get a sneak preview." Julia spun a second panel in the same direction. Claire seemed excited about her paintings, so it might be a good time to ask her if she would be Julia's agent.

Julia waved toward the now-hidden paintings. "I have more of these at my studio, and my uncle doesn't believe in them," she said. "Would you consider being my dealer?"

Claire looked stunned. "I, well, I—"

"I'll understand if you don't want the job. They're not easy paintings to sell."

Claire scrubbed her palms against the beige twill slacks she was wearing. "It would be an honor to represent your work, but I'm not the person to do it."

Julia frowned. "You think it's good and you sell art."

"It's not that simple. You're a well-established artist, so it's not a question of building up an audience for your work. It's a question of getting the maximum price for it. Your paintings should also be placed in carefully selected museum collections to add to your reputation." Claire spread her hands wide. "Oh, there are so many things your career needs at this point, and I don't move in those circles anymore."

Julia felt a wash of relief. "I don't care about those things. I just want someone to sell my work to people who appreciate it."

"That's not enough for someone with your talent."

"But I trust you."

"There are many reputable dealers I can put you in touch with." Claire's voice sounded a little strangled.

"I don't want reputable. I want someone who will tell me whether the work is worthwhile. Not someone who will sell a painting just because it has my name on it."

"I can't. It would be doing you a disservice."

Frustration made Julia's hands ball into fists. She couldn't force Claire to be her dealer. "Will you think about it?"

Claire sighed. "Yes, although I'll also come up with other recommendations."

Julia uncurled her fingers. "Deal."

Loaded down with shopping bags, Claire walked into her living room to find Tim asleep on the oversize couch with Sprocket nestled on his chest. The little dog lifted his head to acknowledge her presence before laying it back on his paws. Her husband didn't move. She couldn't resist watching the man she loved to distraction as he slumbered unawares. She stood so long letting her eyes roam over him, her arms grew tired and she dropped the bags on the Oriental rug.

Sprocket twitched an ear, and Tim's eyes came open as a slow smile spread over his face. "You're home," he said, as she bent down to brush back a curve of auburn hair from his forehead and kiss him. This disturbed the little dog, who gave her an irritated look before moving to the other end of the sofa.

Her husband took her wrist and tugged her down to sit beside him. "Did you find the perfect dress?"

"I found several perfect outfits, but I only bought two." She ran her palm over his chest, so she felt the vibration of his chuckle.

"How about Julia?"

"She's going to wear the Villar and…you don't want to hear the details, do you?"

"Since I don't know what a Villar is, they won't mean much to me."

"The Villar is the blouse she wore to dinner at our house, an original creation by an artist named Reuben Villar."

Tim's eyes took on the focused look that meant he was exploring his prodigious memory. "The thing that looked like a bunch of triangles sewn together?"

"You are impressive." Claire frowned. "Julia asked me to be her agent."

"I'm not surprised. You believe in her work."

"She's a top-selling artist. A lot of people believe in her work."

"They believe in *selling* her work. Your belief is at a whole different level. She needs that kind of support right now." He pushed himself upright, shifting her to the cushions beside him.

Claire chewed on her lip. "Maybe, but I can't agree in good conscience. The price of her paintings could go into the stratosphere with the right dealer to promote them. Let's face it, Sanctuary is not the center of the art universe, and I'm not going to leave you to jaunt around the world cultivating patrons."

"Well, I always wanted to do some traveling that didn't involve reading papers at scientific conferences. You can cultivate and I'll sightsee."

"What about your practice? You're a busy man, even though you didn't look like it when I walked in."

"Maybe too busy now that I've got a beautiful wife to come home to." His kiss was brief but filled with intent. "I've been thinking about hiring another vet to take on some of the workload." Tim ran one hand up her arm. "You were right on the verge of a high-powered career in connoisseurship when you married me. Representing Julia is the perfect way to get back to that."

Claire climbed onto his lap and twined her arms around his neck. "Hire the vet and let's go traveling together. I don't care about my former career."

"But I do. You live here in Sanctuary because of me."

"That's right. Because you make me deliriously happy and I wouldn't want to be anywhere else." She threaded her fingers into his hair and tried to bring his head down to hers for another kiss.

He resisted, and when Tim resisted there was no budging him. "The feeling's mutual, but I think you should consider Julia's proposition."

"All right, I'll consider it. After you take my clothes off and have mind-blowing sex with me."

All the resistance went right out of him.

Chapter 19

JULIA DROPPED HER SHOPPING BAGS AND FLOPPED BACK-ward onto her bed at the inn. "I had no idea shopping could be so exhausting," she said to the ceiling.

Carlos would have a coronary when he saw the bill. Her personal credit card was maxed out, so she'd had to put it on her business card, the one she used for art supplies. Her uncle paid that bill so he could keep track of the tax deductions, or something like that. Now she would have to take it over, along with all the other business tasks. She found herself looking forward to learning the ins and outs of that side of her art career.

Although they'd chatted nonstop on their shopping expedition, she and Claire had not discussed Julia's need for an agent or Paul's brother, both topics she was burning with curiosity about.

Her cell phone shrilled. Groaning at the effort of finding her purse somewhere among the heap of bags on the floor at her feet, she rolled off the bed and knelt to retrieve it.

"Am I interrupting your painting?" Paul's voice came through the line.

Guilt struck at Julia. "I wish. I haven't painted a stroke all day and I promised Claire something for the auction." She plopped back down on the bed. "All I've done since I left your office is shop."

"You're complaining?"

"You'd be amazed at what hard work it is."

"So are you too tired to go for a spin on my Harley?"

Julia sucked in a breath. "Your Harley is a motorcycle, right?" She was playing for time. Riding a motorcycle was another one of those things a person with epilepsy was strongly advised to avoid. Since the opportunity had never come up before, it hadn't been hard to follow the doctors' restriction. Now she found she wanted to try it. With Paul.

"It's not just a motorcycle. It's a 2002 Harley-Davidson VRSCA V-Rod."

The pride in his voice overcame the last of her qualms. "I just got my second wind. Bring on the Harley hot rod!"

"V-Rod. I'll be there in ten. Wear jeans and boots, if you have them."

Galvanized by the prospect of the new experience, Julia scurried around the room, hanging up her new purchases and changing into her jeans and green cowboy boots. Biker chicks were supposed to wear black leather, but she had to make do with a black silk T-shirt under a gray hoodie. When she glanced in the mirror, she burst out laughing. She looked about as tough as a marshmallow.

She was walking down the stairs when the sound of a powerful engine roared through the front door of the inn. Bursting onto the porch, she saw Paul swing one long leg over the bike to dismount. Like her, he wore jeans, but his were topped by a black leather jacket. He pulled off his helmet and ran his fingers through his thick, dark hair before he turned and saw her.

The way his face lit up made her heart expand to nearly fill her chest. Even she, in all her inexperience, could have no doubt he was happy to see her. She flew down the steps and hurled herself against him. He staggered slightly at the impact as he caught her in his arms. "That's what I call a hello," he said.

She tilted her face up. "Now say hello to me."

He bent her back over his arm nearly to the ground and kissed her on the lips. As he brought her back upright, she felt light-headed and grabbed at his arms to steady herself. A clutch of panic tightened her throat, but she fought it down. It was just the sudden change in altitude that made her dizzy. Nothing more serious.

"You okay?" he asked, the laughter in his eyes fading as he scanned her face.

"Just breathless from your kiss."

He bent to kiss her again, this time slowly and deliberately. When he lifted his head, she was holding on to him because her knees had turned to jelly for a different reason. He looked down at her with heavy-lidded eyes. "Maybe later you'd like to ride something besides my bike."

She felt the blood flushing the skin of her neck and cheeks. "Depends on how good your driving is."

His laugh held a slight rasp as he brushed her cheek with his finger. "Let's get some leather and a helmet on you."

He took her hand and led her toward the gleaming silver motorcycle parked in the circular drive. A study in curves, it dazzled in the bright sunlight. She especially liked the two chrome exhaust pipes that whooshed from front to back, widening as they went. "Wow! It looks like it's going a hundred miles an hour even when it's standing still."

He patted the engine. "One hundred fifteen horsepower at eight thousand, two hundred fifty rpm. This hog can move." The passenger's seat had an extra helmet and jacket strapped to it. Paul freed them and held out the jacket. "From when I was a skinny teenager. It's still going to be too big, but better to have the protection."

She pivoted and slid her arms into it, pulling it around her to zip it. The sleeves fell past her fingertips and she struggled to roll the heavy leather up.

"Let me," he said. She obediently held her arms out, loving the sight of his long fingers deftly coaxing the leather into neat folds.

"Your hands are so beautiful," she said. "I'd like to do some studies of them. See if I can capture the strength under the elegance."

He gave the sleeve a last turn and held his fingers out wide as he examined them. "Can't say I've ever thought of them as anything other than useful." He looked up at her with a wicked grin. "Especially for getting a certain reaction out of my favorite artist."

She fought down her blush this time. "Yeah, they're good at that." Which is why she'd like to have some sketches to take home with her. It would make the memories more real. *Now why'd she have to start thinking about that when she just wanted to enjoy the experience ahead of her?*

She reached for the helmet and gave him a lascivious smile. "I can't wait to feel this baby between my legs."

"Caught in my own trap," Paul said.

He adjusted the helmet and showed her how to climb onto the back of the motorcycle while he held it steady. He settled into the seat in front of her, and she wrapped her arms around his waist and snuggled up against the leather stretched over his back. The front of her thighs fit against the back of his like puzzle pieces. When he kicked on the engine, a flutter of nerves made her lace her fingers tightly together over the flat muscles of his abdomen.

This would be fine. She'd been off her meds for two years without a seizure. But those two years were lived in the carefully controlled environment of her home and studio. She'd never done anything even remotely as dangerous as riding a motorcycle.

If Paul got hurt because she had a seizure and dragged him off the motorcycle, she'd never forgive herself. "Paul! Let me—"

The bike surged forward with a roar that drowned out her request to get off.

She buried her face in his back and forced herself to breathe deeply as Paul guided the motorcycle onto the main street. The speed limit was only thirty-five miles per hour, and he seemed to be sticking to it, so she felt the bands of panic loosen their hold around her chest. She sucked in more air and turned her head so she could see the scenery sliding past. Although Paul's broad shoulders sheltered her from the brunt of the wind, it still whooshed in her ears.

As they passed the last of the Victorian houses on Washington Street, the engine noise ratcheted upward, and she felt the speed increase as well.

It was fine. She was still fine.

The passing scenery became a blur and the wind yanked at the ends of her hair where they emerged from her helmet. She tightened her grip.

The bike tilted left. She felt Paul's body leaning with the motorcycle and tried to follow his lead as he had instructed her, but every instinct in her body screamed to lean right to counteract the disorienting slant. She swallowed a sob of relief when the motorcycle righted itself.

The relief was short-lived as Paul leaned to take the next curve. She felt fear begin to clog her lungs and the old terror claw at her mind.

She couldn't do this over and over again. The stress would bring on a seizure and she would fall off the bike like she had the horse all those years ago...only this time she might drag Paul with her.

The panic ratcheted higher, so she closed her eyes and focused on the feel of Paul's body against hers, the shift of muscles in his shoulders as he guided the heavy vehicle under them, the way he sheltered her from the wind and anything else being thrown at them by the road. This was Paul, the man she had come to trust as an advisor and as a lover.

She felt him lean and this time she went with him, channeling all that trust into her rebellious muscles. The feeling of being melded into one with the man and his powerful machine was like nothing she'd ever experienced. She opened her eyes and laughed out loud in sheer exhilaration.

She had no idea how long they rode, lost as she was in the thrill of speed and trust and risk taking. At some point Paul turned off the highway and wound down a back road before bringing the bike to a grumbling halt in a turnoff area beside the single lane byway.

"Here we are," he said, killing the engine and holding the bike rock steady as she climbed off.

She pulled off her helmet and shook out her hair, the grin she couldn't wipe away still tugging at the corners of her mouth. "That was incredible!"

He unzipped his jacket and lifted off his own helmet. "You're a natural. Once we got past those first couple of curves, I could tell you got into it."

"It was scary at first. If I thought you could have heard me, I would have chickened out and asked to stop. But this is an experience I wouldn't have missed for anything."

He took her helmet from her and pulled her into his arms, the leather of their jackets creaking softly as it rubbed together. "I'm glad I could give it to you." He bent his head and kissed her gently at first, then more intently.

The adrenaline already coursing through her body carried the pleasure in waves. She clutched at the open edges of his jacket and pulled herself inward against his chest, so she could revel in the heat of him. That wasn't enough, so she released his jacket and slid her hands up under his tee, feeling the muscles of his abdomen contract as her palms traveled over them.

His hands slid down to her behind, and he pressed her hips against his as he ended their kiss and tilted his head back, half moaning her name. He stood like that, letting her explore his skin beneath the shirt, as his breathing grew more and more ragged. She skimmed her palms upward to brush over his flat nipples. His grip on her tightened convulsively, so she could feel his erection harden between them. When she came back for another pass, he released her and backed away as he caught one of her wrists. "We need to cool off, and I've got just the place to do it. Come with me."

He turned and tugged her onto a path threading between trees undergirded by dense bushes. The sound of moving water drifted between the leaves as the dirt track tilted sharply downhill. As they burst out of the trees into bright sunlight, a river spread out in front of her, its dark-green water slipping past like glass.

Paul pulled her up onto a huge flat boulder jutting out into the water. "The mighty Limestone River. It may be a tad cold, but I could use that right now." He shrugged out of his jacket and dropped it on the rock before he moved behind her to slip hers off her shoulders.

"What do you mean?"

"Take a swim." He pulled his T-shirt over his head.

"But I don't have a bathing suit." She also wasn't much of a swimmer, since that was one of those things that didn't combine well with epilepsy. She had been allowed to paddle in a swimming pool under the watchful eye of a relative, but their vacations had been planned to avoid oceans—and rivers.

Paul's shirt-tousled hair gave him a rakish look. "You ever hear of skinny-dipping?"

"In broad daylight?"

"Do you see anyone around?"

She followed his sweeping gesture, taking in the tree-lined banks, the sounds of birdcalls, and the ever-present whisper of water.

"You can wear your bra and panties, and it's no different from a bikini."

She took a deep breath as she stalled. The idea of being naked bothered her less than the thought of swimming in moving water. "Don't people around here have boats?"

"Sure they do," he said. "But there's a waterfall just upstream from here that keeps away anyone but extreme kayakers. The next easy put-in for a boat is about half a mile down. I used to come here to drink beer with my buddies when we were under-age. That reminds me, I forgot something."

Julia watched him disappear back into the bushes before she walked to the edge of the rock and looked down. Near the shore, she could see the outlines of water-rounded stones, so it must be fairly shallow there. At the rock's farthest jut, the water was as opaque as milk glass and ran swiftly.

She had trusted Paul on the motorcycle and look how great it had been. He would be with her in the water. Naked. That made up her mind. She toed off her green boots and sat down to yank off her socks.

He reappeared, dangling a plaid blanket in one hand and two long-necked beer bottles in the other. He scrambled down the bank to wedge the beers in a shallow spot in the water. "Mother Nature's refrigerator," he said before climbing onto the rock and snapping the blanket open to cover a section just behind her. "We'll let the sun warm it up for afterward. The swim wasn't in my original plan, so I didn't bring towels." He dropped down beside her to tug off one of his heavy boots. "I see you're getting into the spirit of the occasion."

"I thought about the fact that you'd be naked too."

"When you say things like that, I have to kiss you." He sank one hand into her hair and turned her head toward him, slanting his mouth across hers and tracing the seam of her lips with his tongue.

She twisted to grab at the muscle curving over his bare shoulder. His skin was warm and smooth, and she wanted to feel it against more than just her palm. She whimpered against his lips.

He sat back, and she could see his chest expand and contract with his quickened breath. "Have you ever made love in the water?"

She shook her head.

"Then I'll be your first time," he said, pulling a condom out of his jeans pocket and laying it on the stone.

She glanced down at the foil wrapper. "Will that stay on underwater?"

"With you in nothing but a smile, there's not a chance it will float off." He stood and stripped off his jeans and briefs before reaching down to pull her up beside him. "Let me give you a hand."

He snagged the hem of her T-shirt and dragged it up over her head as she held up her arms. When his eyes alighted on the lacy white bra she wore underneath, they burned even hotter than before. "Maybe we'll leave that on. It will look mighty sexy when it's wet and clinging."

He tossed the T-shirt on the blanket. Then he locked his eyes on hers and set to work on the button at the waist of her jeans. He slid one index finger down between the denim and her skin, making the muscles of her abdomen contract and a pool of heat start to glow low in her belly. He held her gaze as he maneuvered the button out of its hole and slowly dragged the zipper downward, his fingertips grazing the lace of her panties, lower and lower until he was nearly at the vee of her thighs. Her lips parted on something between a gasp and a sigh as he pressed a finger right there before he slipped her jeans down to her ankles. He held out his hand to steady her as she stepped out of them and stood, mesmerized by the slow scan of his silver eyes over her body.

Her gaze drifted down to his erection. Clearly he liked what he saw. "This way," he said, scooping up the condom and turning as he laced his fingers with hers.

"Paul." She stopped. "I just, well, I'm not a strong swimmer."

He laughed. "Sweetheart, what we're going to do doesn't involve much in the way of swimming. We'll stay in the shelter of the rock where the current's weak, and I'll keep you afloat." He lifted her hand to his lips, his eyes glinting over her knuckles. "It's in my best interest to make sure you don't drown."

She started in the direction he'd been leading. Now that Paul knew she needed watching, he'd take care of her.

"Let me go first," he said, as they reached a series of ledges on the edge of the rock.

"Go right ahead. I'm enjoying the rear view," she said, lifting her eyes from where she'd been ogling the play of muscle in his tight buttocks as he walked.

"Stop objectifying me and pay attention to where I'm putting my feet." He deftly stepped from one ledge to the next until his feet were inches from the water's surface before he turned to hold both hands up to her. With his steadying grip, she followed in his footsteps until she stood beside him. She noticed the condom in his hand and realized he didn't have any place to put it. "Why don't you give that to me since you don't have any pockets?"

"And you do?"

She reached for the foil envelope and slipped it under the lace of her bra, using the strap to anchor it.

His eyes went incandescent. "I didn't think you could look any hotter, but that has definitely turned up the temperature."

Gratification zinged through her.

He took the last step into the river, the water hitting him midshin before he turned his back to her. "Why don't you climb aboard, and I'll piggyback you out to deeper water so you don't have to walk on the rocks?"

The mention of deeper water doused some of the excitement surging through her veins. Then he repositioned his arms to allow her to clamber on, and the muscles of his back flexed and shifted under his skin. She wanted to feel that against her breasts so she leaned against him, winding her arms around his neck and giving a little hop to get her legs up. He caught her under the knees and bounced her a little higher, making her already-hardened nipples drag against his shoulder blades.

She hissed as lightning flashed from her breasts straight down to where her thighs were spread against his waist.

Her toes brushed into the water and she squealed. "It's frigid! Aren't you freezing?"

"Not with you wrapped around me."

As the water reached their waists, she shivered with equal parts cold and anticipation. He kept going until the ripples lapped at him midchest, then he released her legs and floated her around him until she was against his front, held there by the slight current still flowing through the pool in the lee of the giant stone. He bent her legs around his waist so his erection was locked between them, pressing hard against her clitoris. She twined her ankles together behind him and pulsed against him, stoking her own pleasure.

"Whoa, take it easy on me. I want to have time to enjoy you being wet, both outside and inside." As he said it, he slid one hand between them, pushing aside the lace covering her crotch so he could slip a finger inside her. "Oh yes, definitely wet on the inside."

She clutched at his shoulders as his stroking sent her arching backward. "That feels...unbelievable."

"Mmm, now let's get you wet on the outside." He sank downward, carrying her with him. She barely had time to suck in a breath before the cold water closed over her head. A jab of fear made her tighten her grip on his shoulders and waist, but she relaxed as she felt his arms envelope her like a living lifejacket. Realizing she had her eyes closed, she forced them open to see his face right in front of her, slightly blurred by the sediment in the water. A school of tiny silver fish skittered past behind his head, and then she was rocketing back toward the surface.

"You dunked me," she sputtered as she released one hand to push back the strands of hair plastered to her face.

"I reckon I did. That's kind of what you do to your girlfriend when you're swimming together."

"Maybe if you're in high school." She gave his bicep a light smack.

"Sweetheart, that's how you make me feel. So I'm going to dunk you again."

He dragged her down. This time as she felt him start to push upward again, she took in a mouthful of water. When they broke the surface, she spouted it right at his forehead.

"Oh ho, you want a fight," he said. "Bring it on."

She noticed he moved into water where she could easily stand before he set her down, and submerged. She tracked him in the semiopaque water, the extraordinary picture he presented as the lean lines of his nude body played against the curves of the river stones arousing her artist's instincts. The olive of his skin, greened slightly by the dark-jade water, made her long for an array of paints to capture the subtle shades of both.

Then he exploded up out of the water with a splash that drenched her and made her blink and spit water. "You are going to pay for that," she said. She couldn't outswim him, so she reached for her only leverage, his erect penis.

He groaned as she closed her fingers hard around him. "You fight dirty, woman."

"We biker chicks do that." She stroked firmly downward, savoring the jerk of his body.

He let her play with him for a few seconds longer, then he stepped in and hooked his fingers into the sides of her panties, sliding them down her thighs and following them underwater until she stepped out of them. As he came back up, his fingers grazed between her legs and she shuddered at the delicious contact. After tossing the ball of wet lace onto a ledge, he plucked the condom from her bra, brushing the back of his hand over her cold-tightened nipple.

A current of pleasure went straight down to her gut, and she gasped.

"Okay, biker chick, let me show you the pleasures of making love in the water." He ripped open the foil and rolled the condom on, flipping the wrapper onto the rock too. Then he lifted her up, dragging her breasts up his chest and the vee of her legs up his erection until she was above it. "Put your legs around me," he commanded.

She opened her thighs and bent her knees around his waist, feeling the head of his penis pressing against her. He wrapped his fingers around her thighs where they joined her buttocks and spread them even farther as he positioned himself. He thrust upward as he let her slide down so he was seated deep inside her.

"Oh dear God!" she moaned as the exquisite ache of arousal was partially slaked by the feeling of him filling her.

"Now lean back and let the water hold you up," he said. "I won't let go of you."

A shimmer of nervousness amplified the sensation of being joined with him so intimately. She slowly eased backward, sliding her grip down his arms until she was perpendicular to him, touching the surface of the water. She felt her hair drift out from her head as the current caught it. The chill of the river water contrasted sharply with the conflagration pulsing between her legs, making her shiver with sensory overload.

"Is it too cold for you?" he asked, concern making him frown.

"No, no. It's just, well, a lot of different feelings all swirling around together."

The shadow on his face vanished. "Then I'll have to give you something to focus on, won't I?"

"That might help." He flexed his hips, and the small movement centered all her attention on the place between her thighs. "Yup," she gasped. "Totally focused now."

"Good." His voice had turned raspy, and she suspected his focus had gotten pretty intense too. "Sweetheart, I've got you, I promise. Let go. You'll float."

"What? Oh." She released her fingers, which were clamped around his wrists, and felt the water cradle her, rocking gently in the wavelets that lapped at her sides. Her arms floated outward as she relaxed into the sense of being anchored and free at the same time.

"That's it," Paul crooned, bending over to suck at first one nipple and then the other. His motion changed the angle where they were joined, sending a tremor through her. The warmth of his mouth seeped through the wet lace of her bra, igniting a slow burn that spread over her skin and sank deep inside her. She expected the water around her to start boiling at any moment.

"Do that again!" She started to arch into him but it tipped her head underwater, so she forced her muscles to relax and do nothing but receive the sensations as he dragged his mouth over the swell of her breasts, up to nip at her neck, down to lap the water from her navel. Trusting him. Letting go.

"Time for this to be removed," he said, flicking the front clasp of her bra open and peeling the cups away from her breasts.

His eyes were hooded as he looked down at her, and she saw the flare of his nostrils as he breathed in sharply. "So beautiful."

He brushed one palm over her bared nipples, making her gasp and writhe. His touch tightened the coiling tension between her legs to the breaking point.

"Paul, please, I need to come now."

"Thought you'd never ask." He took hold of her waist, his thumbs pressed against her hipbones, and began to move, guiding her body in the water so as he thrust forward he brought her in against him. As he withdrew, he pushed her slightly away. The motion sent little crests of water washing gently against her sensitized clitoris, driving her arousal higher and higher without releasing it.

"Oh yes, please. Oh please. Oh please." She begged for her climax, even as she wanted to prolong the extraordinary sensations.

He increased the tempo and ground against her each time they came together. That was all she needed to explode into a screaming, writhing mass of orgasm, the muscles inside her clenching into a hard, tight fist before opening to fling exquisite bursts of pleasure through her body. She wondered why she hadn't swallowed gallons of water in her thrashing before she noticed Paul had slid his hands and forearms under her back to keep her afloat. His cock still filled and moored her to him.

She lay half in the water, half in his arms, as aftershocks danced through her. Once her body quieted, she opened her eyes to find him gazing down at her, his expression a combination of arousal, satisfaction, and tenderness.

"Paul, you didn't finish."

"I don't need to," he said.

"That wouldn't be fair. You worked hard."

"Damn straight," he said, "but I got my reward."

She started to shake her head before remembering she'd get water up her nose. She lifted her hands to his shoulders. "Help me up."

He obliged by tipping her up against his chest while she kept her legs locked around his waist.

"Now take me over to that ledge." She pointed to a shelf of the rock that was almost level with the surface of the water.

He carried her to the stone and eased her bare behind onto it. She unhooked her ankles, sliding her knees up onto his hips and leaning back against the boulder so her pelvis was tilted up for him. He started to pull out but she clamped her knees in hard. "No, do it here."

She could feel his erection swell, but he looked torn. "Are you sure you're ready?" He framed her face with his hands, scanning it.

"Born ready," she whispered, turning her face to give his thumb a playful bite.

His restraint evaporated at that. He whipped his hands down to her hips and angled them to his satisfaction before he let go to brace his hands on the rock above her. He withdrew almost completely before slamming back into her, his eyes locked on the place where their bodies came together. He dropped one hand to feather his fingers through her pubic hair. "Ah, I love the color of this. It glows as brightly as the rest of you."

His finger slid lower and she jerked in surprise as her body reacted with a leap of pleasure.

"Oh, I see," he said, gently massaging the sensitive spot. He moved his finger in rhythm with his thrusting hips until his control snapped and he clamped his hands around her thighs and pounded into his own orgasm. He shouted her name so loudly, it echoed back from across the river. As he pulsed against her, her inner muscles fired once more, sending her sighing into a climax of rippling, delicate shudders.

Her strength sapped, she melted back against the warm, smooth rock as her eyes fluttered closed. She felt Paul slip out of her and heard some splashing before a warm touch brushed the outside of her thighs and a weight settled on her shoulder. She slitted her eyes open to see him braced over her on his forearms as his head rested on her shoulder.

"You think you can drive the bike home, sweetheart?" he mumbled against her shoulder. "You've wrung me dry."

"Wimp. I had two orgasms. You only had one."

"That was not an orgasm. It was a nuclear blast."

She felt a smile of satisfaction tug at her lips. She might not be experienced, but she could sure as heck improvise.

She felt the huff of his breath against her damp skin and shivered.

He lifted his head and grabbed her wrists to tug her upright. "Let's get you out of this cold water and onto a nice warm blanket."

"I'm really not cold."

"You will be soon." He lifted her off the ledge and let her down into the water, taking her hand to lead her back to the natural stairway up the boulder. He scooped up her panties and the condom foil on the way past.

"Oh no, my bra!" Julia said, feeling around her bare back at the reminder she had been wearing her fancy new lingerie when she stepped into the water.

Paul put up a hand to shade his eyes as he scanned downriver. "I think I see it. Take these." He pushed the panties and foil in her hand and launched himself toward a fleck of white bobbing along the shore.

"Paul! Don't worry about it!" she called, but he was in full pursuit and either didn't hear her or chose not to listen. She contented herself with watching the beautiful play of muscles in his shoulders and back as he stroked hard to outpace the current.

He caught the white spot and yodeled in triumph, waving it above his head before he dove into the water and fought his way back upstream. As he reached the pool, he stood up so the water streamed down his chest, which heaved with his exertions. "You look just like my drawing, only better," she said, letting her gaze linger on the hard-cut lines of his abdomen and the lean sinews of his thighs.

With a mischievous smirk, he spread the bra between his hands and held it across his groin in the same position as the fish in her sketch.

She laughed as she splashed over to him and ran her hands down his chest, following the rivulets of water. "You're so beautiful."

His breathing seemed to stop. "That's my line."

"Men can be beautiful too."

He seized her hand and kissed it. "Your fingers are going all pruney." He towed her toward the boulder and helped her up to the flat top, his touch lingering on her hips and behind as he boosted her up.

She laid her bra and panties out in the sun while Paul pulled on his briefs and jeans. As she picked up her jeans, he reached out to grab the denim. "Wood sprites don't wear clothes when they're in the wild."

"You're dressed."

"Because I'm half-human, remember?"

His gaze turned to molten silver as it skimmed down her body, making her feel wanton and daring. She dropped her jeans and lay down on the blanket, stretching her arms over her head and pointing her toes as she basked in the heat of his eyes.

He stood over her, scanning up and down her body, his chest rising and falling as though he'd been racing the river for her bra again.

"I'd pay every penny I have for a picture of you like this." His voice had the texture of gravel.

"Maybe I could paint a self-portrait." She arched up, wanting his hands to follow his gaze.

He dropped onto the blanket beside her and rested his hand on her stomach, gently pushing her downward. "Stop, temptress."

"Why?" Her skin tingled deliciously where his palm lay against it.

He shifted away. "Because...oh hell, I don't know. Because you need a break."

"Mmm, don't they say there's no rest for the wicked?" He didn't answer so she rolled her head sideways to see him staring across the water, his beautiful back curved as he draped his arms over his jeans-clad knees. His bare feet were long and elegant like his hands, and his hair glinted with droplets of river water. The image burned into her mind's eye as her eyelids drifted closed.

Not until he heard her breathing go deep and even did Paul allow himself to turn his gaze back to the infinitely desirable woman lying beside him. He had nearly gone up in flames when she stretched her satin-smooth body out on the coarse red-plaid blanket and offered herself to him. He wouldn't have been able to withstand one more come-hither glance from her before he yanked her legs wide apart to feast on her and then bury himself inside that wet, welcoming heat.

He was like a horny teenager around her.

Despite her delicious sensuality, he knew she was inexperienced. For God's sake, she'd told him so, but he would have known anyway. He needed to rein in his nearly insatiable appetite for her.

Truth was he wanted to experience everything he could with her before she disappeared from his life as suddenly as she'd entered it. The last thought sent a shudder through him, and he pushed it away, dwelling instead on the delight she took in the firsts he'd shown her.

Her first foosball game. Her first motorcycle ride. Her first time making love in the water.

What worried him was that he was no longer satisfied with being the first one to show her these things. Now he wanted to be the only one.

And he couldn't. He couldn't ask someone with her talent and potential to move to a place he himself could barely tolerate. He let his eyes drift over the gleaming copper hair drying in waves against the blanket, tracing down her arms to the slender fingers that held such genius. Her eyelids hid clear green eyes that saw the world in colors and shapes he never imagined.

Once the art patrons got an eyeful of her *Night Mares*, she would have that world at her feet. An actual physical pain made him wince as he realized he would not be there to see her reaction to New York and Paris and all the new places she would go.

Because he knew Julia was done with letting her family confine her. Her uncle thought she was going to meekly return to North Carolina after the show, but Carlos was wrong. She had broken those chains by coming to Sanctuary, and no one was going to be able to fasten them on her again.

He dragged his gaze away from Julia and pinned it to a river birch slanting over the water on the opposite bank as he remembered his conversation with Adam Bosch. The man could out-lawyer a lawyer when it came to being cagey about Jimmy's chances of staying on the wagon.

But Bosch had tried to tell him something about manipulation. That was the part he kept replaying in his mind. Maybe he needed to have a heart-to-heart with his brother. In his bitterness and frustration, he hadn't given Jimmy a chance to talk. He just shut down when his brother started spinning what Paul saw as his bullshit.

Maybe it wasn't bullshit anymore.

A pulse of hope coursed through Paul until Eric's face rose up in his mind.

It didn't matter what Jimmy promised. If Paul left Sanctuary to follow his own selfish desires and something happened to Eric, he would never forgive himself.

Paul picked up a small stone and hurled it as far across the river as he could.

Chapter 20

A JAB OF DISCOMFORT IN HER HIP SENT JULIA'S EYELIDS fluttering open to find Paul glaring across the river, his face set in the bleak lines she remembered from Saturday night. She shifted away from the protrusion of rock she'd rolled onto in her sleep and examined him with an artist's eye. From the defeated curve of his back to the slump of his shoulders to the locked muscles of his jaw, everything spoke of a deep-seated despair. If she had to paint hopelessness, she would use Paul as a model.

She frowned as she considered his thriving legal practice, his close relationship with his nephew, and the vehicular toys he clearly enjoyed. He had wonderful friends in Claire and Tim, and the respect of an entire town.

Heck, she and he had just made love, and she was pretty sure he'd enjoyed it as much as she had.

So why would this man who seemed to have so much look like he had no hope of happiness in the world? His sadness tore at her.

"Paul, are you all right?" she asked softly.

He started and turned toward her. She could see the effort it took for him to paste a smile on his face. "Never better." He leaned down to drop a light kiss on her lips.

Sudden self-consciousness made her pull the edge of the blanket over herself as she pushed up to a sitting position. "What were you thinking about just now?"

"Are you cold?" His eyes dark with concern, he flipped the other side of the plaid wool over to wrap it around her.

"No, just a little too naked."

His smile was genuine this time. "There's no such thing as too naked when it comes to you."

"You're not going to tell me, are you?"

"It went clean out of my head when I kissed you." He folded his legs under him and stood. "How about a nice cold one?"

"Cold what?" She recognized deflection when she saw it.

"Beer, sweetheart." He climbed down and snagged the two bottles out of the water, holding them up to show her.

"Should you drink and drive?" she asked, as he returned and twisted off both caps.

He handed her a bottle before dropping down beside her, his bare shoulder brushing against hers. "If I can't handle one beer, I shouldn't be riding a hog."

He clinked his bottle against hers before tilting his head back to take a long swallow. She admired the line of his throat before taking a sip of her own beer. The river water had chilled it to the perfect temperature and she purred at the deliciousness of the first taste.

"Nothing like a cold beer and a hot babe," Paul said, his wink inviting her to laugh at his political incorrectness.

"I was thinking the same about a hot guy." She leaned into him to get another dose of skin-to-skin contact. An imp of mischief made her press her bottle against his bare chest.

He yelped and grabbed her wrist to pull it away. He looked down at her with a devilish glint in his eyes. "That's dangerous provocation from a woman wearing nothing more than a blanket. When I think of all the places I could put this bottle..." He let his gaze wander down her cocooned body.

Which made heat bloom over her skin under the scratchy wool. She went from being self-conscious about her state of undress to wishing he would touch every inch of her body.

Deciding to take advantage of her newfound boldness in order to distract him from his revenge, she released her hold on the edges of the blanket. As it fell away, she leaned back on her elbows. "Do your worst."

Instead of pouncing on her as she had hoped, he groaned her name and shifted away, lifting the beer to his lips and gulping down the rest of the bottle. Baffled and a little hurt, she sat back up and stretched out a hand to lay it against his back. "What is it?"

He jerked at her touch and she dropped her hand. "Did I do something wrong?"

"No, sweetheart, I did," he said, staring across the river again. He turned back to her with a smile so sad it made her chest hurt. "You're so close to perfect I can't find a fault."

Tears burned behind her eyes and she blinked hard. If only he knew.

"We'd better get going. You'll catch a chill once the sun starts going down."

Leaping to his feet, he bustled around, scooping up her now-dry lingerie and handing it to her before he finished dressing.

She tried to think of a way to stop all the activity so she could drag the truth out of him, but his smooth, implacable facade was back in place. Anything she said would just slide off it. So she followed him up the path to the motorcycle, exchanging nothing more than pleasantries. She strapped on the helmet and climbed on behind him, pressing up against the sun-warmed leather covering his back.

As they roared along, she tried to savor the wind and speed and sense of being melded into one piece with Paul and his Harley, but her mind kept stumbling over the fact that her week in Sanctuary was blowing by faster than the scenery.

As she contemplated returning to her home, the image sprouted metal bars on the doors and windows, sending a shudder of revulsion through her.

She didn't hate her home or her family. Maybe she felt a little smothered sometimes, but she understood their concern for her. It came from love.

She just didn't want to leave the fascinating man whose waist she had her arms wrapped around. Anywhere she went without Paul was going to seem bleak.

So why not extend her stay in Sanctuary past the gala? Carlos couldn't force her to go home. She could afford the inn and she had a free studio for now.

Would Paul want her to stay? If he did, for how long?

Julia faced the fact that she didn't know much about how this sort of relationship worked. Paul was firmly settled here with his practice and his family and his strong connection to the town, so she would be the one moving, if it came to that. The idea didn't conjure up any monsters.

But she would have to tell him the truth about herself at some point. She clutched harder at his waist.

Not yet. She wanted him to think she was perfect just a little longer.

The next morning, Julia settled into the heavy oak chair, rolling it forward so she could reach the mouse. When Paul had kissed her good-bye after a night in her bed, he'd advised her not to read Paxton's blog until Claire vetted it. But both he and Claire underestimated her toughness when it came to her work.

The inn's computer stood on a massive antique lawyer's desk strewn with papers and brochures, lit by an old brass library lamp. The sleek lines of the large-screen monitor with its plastic base looked like a spaceship that had landed in a Victorian parlor. The office was empty and quiet. She wasn't sure if someone had instructed the staff to give her privacy or whether they were all busy elsewhere.

She wound her hair into a bun and took a deep breath before she clicked on the Internet icon. The blog loaded quickly. Evidently, state-of-the-art equipment wasn't considered an impediment to historic atmosphere.

Paxton Hayes didn't feel the need for a catchy title for his blog; it was called simply "Paxton Hayes on Art."

Julia Castillo Goes to the Dark Side was his headline. She chuckled at his unintentional double meaning.

Popular equine artist Julia Castillo has resurfaced with a new style, one that appears to have more depth and interest than her pleasantly bucolic earlier work.

"Ouch!" She wasn't happy about the condescending description of her older paintings, but it didn't destroy her, either. Maybe it was because she'd left that period behind, or maybe she had more confidence in herself, thanks to her new friends in Sanctuary.

The new work, which Castillo calls her "Night Mares," offers psychological layering and a disturbing power that was absent from the idyllic landscapes she has created up until now. While this critic has always acknowledged its technical virtuosity, the painter's earlier work invited no further analysis.

"And here I thought you were an art critic, not a psychiatrist." Julia was starting to enjoy herself. The man was so pretentiously nasty it was impossible to take him seriously.

Hayes briefly recapped her career up to this point, inserting photos of Claire's treasured painting and a couple of others that were especially well-known. There were references to pastoral pleasantness and her youth with an implication of immaturity, all subtle denigrations of the work, but it bounced off her new-found armor.

She frowned at his discussion of the run-up in prices of her work since the supply had been cut off two years ago. Hayes speculated about it being a deliberate ploy to create pent-up demand for her new and different style. He chose to ignore the carefully crafted explanation she and Claire had come up with: that she didn't want to bring her new work to the market until she was satisfied with its quality.

"Jerk," she said, but more in irritation than anger.

He quoted her a couple of times, accurately but out of context, so she came across as a combination of naive and airheaded. She skimmed through those.

Finally she got to the all-important paragraph.

Those interested in Castillo's new work will have the opportunity to reach their own conclusions this Friday when the Gallery at Sanctuary will show five of the "Night Mares." Despite the gallery's remote location among the Appalachian Mountains of West Virginia, this blogger confesses to having his curiosity piqued and plans to attend.

Julia whooped in triumph. Not only was Hayes coming, he had announced it to the entire art world!

"Everything okay?" Lyle Lee, one of the inn's two owners, poked his head in the office door.

Julia knew she was grinning like an idiot. "I've been insulted up, down, and sideways, but the jerk is coming to my show."

The man raised his eyebrows. "He must be an important jerk."

"He's influential in the circles we needed to reach on short notice." She stood up, mentally congratulating herself on being unaffected by Hayes's criticisms.

Julia's cell phone vibrated in her jeans pocket. "Excuse me, that must be Claire," she said, pulling out the phone and putting it to her ear as she walked to a secluded corner of the lobby. "It worked!"

"Julia! Why did you speak to Paxton Hayes?" Her uncle's voice was taut with anger. "I agreed to this show of yours because it was in a country gallery no one would hear of. Now word of it will be spread all over the place."

Just like that, her balloon of confidence deflated. She thought Carlos was finally allowing her to make her own decisions, but he was just humoring her because he thought the show wouldn't matter. His words pushed her back into the well of insecurity he'd dug over the past two years. She felt apologies rising up in her throat.

Her uncle didn't give her a chance to speak. "This is a catastrophe. I cannot come today, but I will be there tomorrow to speak with Ms. Parker—"

"Arbuckle," Julia corrected with petty satisfaction. "There is no point to your coming before Friday."

"We must decide how to control this mess," Carlos said. "We'll find a reason to cancel the show."

Julia thought of Claire's carefully laid plans for the exhibit and forced herself to speak with conviction. "Paxton Hayes is coming. There's no way we're canceling."

He muttered an unflattering epithet about Hayes in Spanish. "He called your paintings 'bucolic' and 'pleasant.' He knows nothing about what is good art."

Her uncle's partisanship lit a tiny glow of affection inside her. Even if Carlos didn't like her *Night Mares*, he wasn't going to allow Paxton Hayes to attack her work. "Thanks, Tío," she said softly.

Her uncle sighed. "*Mi querida*, you must come home with me tomorrow. You cannot be exposed to what might happen."

"What? No!" Every fiber of Julia's body shrieked a refusal. She needed more time with Paul. She had to figure out whether he wanted her to stay or not. "I'm not walking out on the show. People are counting on me."

"We will discuss it tomorrow, face-to-face," he said. "I am only trying to protect you, Julia."

"And I love you for it, but the time when I needed that has passed." She hung up and slumped onto a hard wooden bench set beside the wall. It didn't matter what she said, because Carlos refused to believe her. She slammed a fist into the bench as tears of frustration burned in her eyes.

Another thought made her sit up straight in horror. *Would Carlos try to use her epilepsy as leverage to convince Claire to cancel the show?*

Chapter 21

*A*s Julia's brain reeled at the possibility, her phone pinged, signaling a voice mail. Her hands shook slightly as she punched the buttons to play it. It was Claire, her voice vibrating with excitement as she conveyed the good news about Hayes's promised attendance and dismissed the rest of the blog as not worth reading. "He's a pretentious ass, but we already knew that."

Julia frowned. Why did everyone think she was so fragile she couldn't handle a bad review? Yes, she had driven all the way to Sanctuary to get a second opinion on her new paintings, but that seemed more pigheaded than feeble to her.

She stared down at the phone in her hand. Claire deserved an excited, congratulatory return phone call for the coup she had pulled off, but Carlos had destroyed Julia's jubilant mood.

She forced the muscles at the corners of her mouth upward and dialed the phone. "Claire, you're a genius."

"Did you read it?" Claire sounded worried.

Julia shoved down a spark of irritation. "Yes, and he's a jerk, but he walked right into our trap."

"It really wasn't bad for Paxton," Claire said, her relief sounding clearly through the phone. "Not everyone considers 'bucolic' and 'pastoral' undesirable qualities in a painting."

"He sure makes them sound repulsive, though."

"You'll have to talk to him at the show, but I don't think he'll have the nerve to be quite as awful face-to-face."

"Paxton Hayes doesn't scare me." It was her uncle she didn't know what to do about. She chewed on her lip before she decided she had to warn Claire. "My uncle Carlos saw the blog too."

There was a pause. "How did he feel about it?"

"He's coming here tomorrow." Julia felt reduced to the status of a wayward child.

"What is he planning to do?" Claire sounded puzzled.

"He wants to talk you into canceling the show. Failing that, he wants to drag me home with him." Julia kept her tone light. "He wasn't happy about Paxton Hayes attending."

"I guess you and your uncle lock horns frequently," Claire said.

Gratification warmed Julia at Claire's assumption that she had the strength to stand up to her uncle. "I felt I should warn you, in case he goes to the gallery first." Julia hesitated. Should she risk making Claire suspicious that she was trying to hide something? She just couldn't bear the thought of Paul hearing about her epilepsy from someone other than herself. "I know I can trust you to keep what he tells you in the heat of the moment confidential."

"Of course you can." The puzzled note was back in Claire's voice but she continued, "Don't worry about your uncle. We'll convert him, just like we did Paxton."

"If anyone can do it, it's you," Julia said before she thanked Claire for all of her efforts and hung up.

She dropped the phone on the wooden bench with a bang and stared in front of her at the wall hung with antique farm implements. The surface part of her brain traced the curves and lines of the metal and wood shapes, but her focus was on the impending collision of her two worlds.

As long as Carlos was several hundred miles away in North Carolina, her courage burned bright and strong. The minute he threatened to come here, all that shiny new bravado shriveled up and blew away like ashes. Dread swelled into a lump in her stomach. What would her new and treasured friends think of her when they saw her in relation to her overpowering uncle? Would they think more or less of her for standing up to someone she owed so much to?

What if he informed them she couldn't handle all this publicity and pressure because of her epilepsy? They would all agree with him and tiptoe around her as though she were a bomb that could explode at any time.

She pictured Claire's brown eyes going soft with pity and Tim treating her with all the medical kindness her doctors always showed.

And Paul. He would believe he had endangered her by taking her on his motorcycle and making love to her in a river. He would be angry with her for not warning him about the possible consequences, and she couldn't blame him.

Even worse, he would refuse to do any of those things with her again. He would treat her like a china doll, not like a living, breathing woman. He would treat her like Carlos did.

She clamped her hands on either side of her head. She could barely draw a breath into her lungs and her vision began to blur. Oh dear God, she wasn't going to have a seizure here in the lobby of the inn. That would be the ultimate humiliation.

It wasn't a seizure.

It was the pain of loss, a gut-punching, oxygen-depriving, throat-closing agony she'd never felt with such intensity before. When she was a teenager and her mother and stepfather moved to Spain, she'd been sad and lonely, but the relationship between her and her parents had not altered in any profound way, so she hadn't felt this wrenching grief.

This would be a game changer for Paul.

Her phone trilled, its vibrate function making it clatter and dance like a live thing on the wooden bench.

She picked it up to check the caller ID. Paul. She couldn't talk to him right now, not with her emotions roiling so close to the surface. He would know she was upset and keep asking his lawyer questions until he found out why.

What she needed right now was the comfort of a paintbrush in her hand. She stood and waited for Paul's call to go to voice mail before she turned off the phone and tucked it into her jeans pocket. She knew he had a busy day at work, so he wouldn't have time to pester her until lunchtime. By then she should have regained enough control to hide things from him again.

Julia stuck her brush behind her ear and stepped back from the canvas as she considered her work.

She'd walked into the makeshift studio, taken one look at the start of her painting of Darkside, and removed it from the easel. She wasn't in the mood for fine, detailed work.

Hoisting a blank canvas onto the easel, she began squeezing paints onto her palette, not bothering to do a rough sketch first. She could already see what she wanted on the clean surface.

She'd worked for two hours in a white heat, spilling her vision onto the canvas, turning the morning's emotions into fuel for her creativity.

It was done. Well, maybe except for a few dabs of titanium white or cobalt blue here and there.

She'd painted Paul straddling his motorcycle, his helmet in the crook of one arm. He looked out of the picture, right at the observer, his face alight with an invitation to join him on an adventure, his smile flashing with warmth and intimacy, his silver-gray eyes holding just a trace of sexual heat.

She nodded and lifted the painting off the easel, turning its back outward before she leaned it carefully against one of the empty bookcases to dry. This creation was meant for her eyes only. It was the way she wanted to remember him.

She decided it was time to return Paul's phone call.

"I'm sorry, I was working and had the phone turned off, so I didn't get your voice mail until just now." Julia winced. She hated telling him lies, even minor ones, especially when she'd checked her missed calls to discover he'd called four more times.

"As long as you're not sobbing into your pillow because of what that asshole Paxton Hayes said, it's all good." His words were light but his voice held undertones of anger and worry.

She forced a chuckle. "He's coming to the show, so nothing else matters."

"You don't sound like yourself. Are you still at Plants 'N Pages?"

"Don't upset Verna by canceling an appointment to come over here."

"She'd be more upset if she thought I'd left you alone when you needed a friend."

She should be annoyed with him for thinking she couldn't handle the art critic's remarks, but the sound of his deep voice just made her wish he was there in the room with her. She wanted to press herself against his long, lean body and kiss him until they were both senseless. That was the drawback of spending two hours focused on capturing Paul's body in a painting; it got her all hot and bothered. "I was leaning more toward needing a lover," she said.

"Damn, my next appointment is here," he growled. "I'll be shoving the last client out the door by four, so I'll pick you up then."

"Thank you for worrying about me. Even if you don't need to, it makes me feel...cared for."

"Never doubt it, sweetheart."

She hung up, shaken. Oh dear God, she'd almost said *loved*. That would have sent Paul running for the hills.

It should send her fleeing in the same direction. In her experience, being loved had become synonymous with being smothered and coddled and not allowed to live fully. Paul's brand of caring offered the opposite. He took pleasure in expanding her horizons, in challenging her.

But that was because he didn't know about her weakness. She had seen how people responded to that.

She jumped as her phone rang again. It was Carlos, and she had no intention of talking to him again today. She waited for the ping of the voice mail arriving before she brought the phone to her ear. "Julia, this is your uncle." And he sounded annoyed. "I have gone to considerable trouble to rearrange my schedule to arrive in Sanctuary at noon and will expect to see you at the Traveller Inn. I understand they serve lunch there so we will eat together."

"If it was so much trouble, you shouldn't come," she muttered.

She walked back to the easel and lifted the Darkside painting onto it. She stood back and examined it, trying to decide what part to work on first. She'd sketched in Darkside's head with a focus on the horse's eye. You could see his ears and part of his cheek and neck, but the rest bled off the edges of the canvas. She had challenged herself to catch the liquid depths of his eye and the silken texture of his glossy coat as it stretched over muscle and bone. It required a totally different technique from her nearly abstract *Night Mares*.

After a couple of minutes, she shook her head and walked to the front window to watch the people and cars pass.

A sense that this was the last day of her idyll in Sanctuary built in her mind. Carlos would arrive tomorrow and blast the gutsy, adventurous image she'd somehow created to smithereens. Paul and Claire and Tim would see her as the fragile, reclusive invalid her uncle believed her to be.

"So I'd better gather some rosebuds before Carlos says the thorns are too dangerous for me," she said, turning back to recap her paint tubes.

It was time to visit her whisper horse.

Chapter 22

*Y*OU PAID GOOD MONEY FOR A TAXI TO COME SEE DARK-side?" The lanky young stable hand shook his head in disbelief. "That horse ain't worth spending a red cent on. I don't know why Ms. Sydenstricker keeps him around, eating his head off and kicking up nothing but trouble. Anyway, he's in the north paddock over yonder."

"Thanks," Julia said, jogging in the direction he pointed. She'd stopped to collect some carrots before discovering Darkside's stall was empty.

She burst out of the barn into bright sunlight and blinked a few times, trying to figure out which way was north. It turned out all she had to do was follow the cursing to locate her horse.

"Goddamned devil horse, get your butt out of the way of the gate!" One of the hands was trying to maneuver an empty water bucket into the paddock. Darkside was having none of it. "I don't care if you die of thirst, but the boss lady says you gotta have some water."

"Here, I'll do it," Julia said, holding her hand out for the bucket.

"No, ma'am," the man said, shaking his head. "This horse'd kill you as soon as look at you."

"He's my whisper horse, so I'll be okay."

"You're trying to pull ole George's leg, ain't you? I know what Ms. Sydenstricker believes about whisper horses. Not that I hold truck with that nonsense, but Darth Vader there ain't nobody's whisper nothing."

"Darkside and I understand each other," Julia said. "Let me give it a try."

She gave the handle of the bucket a gentle tug, and George relinquished his grip on it with obvious reluctance. "Well, if you put the bucket by the fence, I'll run a hose into it," he said.

"I'm Julia Castillo." Julia held out her hand. "Just in case you need to tell Ms. Sydenstricker who the crazy lady with Darkside is."

"You that famous painter?" George gave her hand a brief shake.

"Yes," she said, throwing humility to the winds. "Could you just open the gate for me and I'll slip in?"

"If you die, I guess your paintings will be worth more." With that observation, he pushed the gate open a crack.

Darkside squealed angrily from the other side of the slats as she slid through the opening. "Hey, buddy, it's me, and I've got carrots, so don't kick me in the head just yet."

George swung the gate shut behind her. "I'll leave it on the latch in case you need to get out fast. Just chain it up when you leave."

"Got it," she said, sidling sideways with the bucket as she kept an eye on Darkside. The giant black horse had his ears flat against his head while his nostrils flared wide with each audible breath. He looked magnificent in his rage, like a knight's charger ready to gallop into battle.

"Are you afraid of a bucket, buddy?" she asked in the teasing tone he seemed to respond to. "What a chicken!"

He stamped a huge hoof but his ears swiveled forward a couple of times. Julia settled the bucket against the fence and turned her back on it as she pulled a carrot out of her back pocket. "Okay, you get a treat for not killing me when I came through the gate."

The horse snorted as she held out her flattened hand. For a moment, the muscles in his shoulder bunched and she wondered if he was going to lash out at her. Then his ears came forward, and he stretched out his head to swipe the carrot off her palm. As he crunched on it, she pulled another out of her pocket and sidled closer.

Darkside whickered and calmly ate the second carrot before he took a step forward to snuffle at her jeans pocket.

Julia laughed in sheer relief as she used his halter to pull his head away from her behind. "Don't be so forward," she said, stroking the powerful curve of his satiny neck.

"Is it okay if I turn the water on, ma'am?" George asked. "I don't want to scare him while you're so close up. Although he does seem to have a fondness for you."

"Go ahead. I'll keep his attention away from it."

Darkside's head came up when the first drops of water spattered into the metal bucket, but George knew his business, increasing the flow of water so gradually the horse quickly lost interest.

She spent a few minutes just stroking him, making admiring noises about his beauty and strength and brilliance. She could swear the horse arched his neck and preened.

"No one's told you what a great guy you are in a long time, have they, buddy? So you've gotten grumpier and grumpier. Who can blame you? We all need positive feedback in our lives. I certainly learned that the hard way."

Julia glanced around. George had finished filling the water bucket and vanished. No one else knew she was in the paddock with Darkside. She'd told Paul that Darkside just needed someone to show him how to behave normally. Now was her chance.

She wrapped her fingers around the leather of his halter and gave a little tug. "Walk with me, buddy."

The big horse seemed to consider the idea for a long moment before he stepped forward in the direction she was facing. A spurt of triumph rose in her chest as he plodded along beside her, his head bobbing comfortably by her shoulder. They walked side by side around the entire paddock before she turned him around to walk the other way.

"See, this is nice and companionable," she said, as they made a circuit in the opposite direction.

She led him to the middle of the paddock and walked him through several figure eights. Then she stood in front of him, her hands on either side of his halter, and backed him up, all the while telling him what a fine, smart, handsome fellow he was.

"So you do know how to behave!" she said, feeding him two carrot bits before laying her cheek against his and winding her arms around his neck.

She stayed there, absorbing the living warmth and latent power of the huge creature as he stood still, allowing a puny human to keep him there. She heard his heart pumping, his lungs drawing in air, his tail swishing at flies, and a crazy idea formed in her mind.

She let him go and stepped back to look into his eyes.

"When was the last time someone rode you?"

"Honey, you told me flat out you don't know how to ride, and Darkside ain't exactly a starter horse." Sharon stood in the middle of her office and looked at Julia like she had two heads. "Hell, I haven't tried to ride him since he bucked me off six months ago. It's not worth the bruises."

"I was just in the paddock with him," Julia said, winding her hands together almost in a prayer. "He let me lead him around in circles and figure eights and even back him up."

"I know. George told me."

"George was watching?"

"He knew he'd better keep an eye on the devil horse."

Julia crossed her arms. "He's *not* a devil horse. He's just not used to being good."

Sharon crossed her arms in response. "Look, I may be soft-hearted about horses but I'm not crazy. Darkside is more than a handful for an experienced rider. There is no way I'm putting a beginner up on his back. Can you imagine what Taggart would say to me?" She shook her head.

The mention of Paul only increased Julia's sense of urgency. She put her hand on Sharon's forearm. "My uncle arrives tomorrow, and he's more protective than Paul. If I don't do this now, I'll never have another chance and Darkside won't, either." She sensed a softening in Sharon. "You wouldn't have brought the horse here if you didn't believe he could be redeemed. Let me help him."

She didn't mention that Darkside would be helping her at the same time. It was time to face her Night Mare. The cause of her epilepsy. If she didn't, she would never really believe she was cured.

Julia kept talking. "You'll be right there the whole time, leading him, no faster than a walk. I'll just sit quiet as mouse on his back." Sharon started to shake her head again, and Julia injected every ounce of pleading she could muster into her voice. "Please!"

Sharon sighed. "Since I believe in whisper horses, I reckon I have to believe he won't hurt you. Not deliberately anyhow." She grabbed a pair of gloves off her desk and strode toward the door. Julia skipped along beside her as Sharon found George and told him to bring Darkside's saddle and bridle to the paddock.

"You lookin' to get dumped again?" the groom asked his boss.

"I'm lookin' to get some tack out to the paddock without any smart-ass comments from you," Sharon said.

George harrumphed and headed for the tack room.

"Okay, here are the rules," Sharon said as she walked toward the paddock. "Well, there's one rule: I make the rules. You do whatever I say without question."

Julia's heartbeat was already accelerating with nerves. "Whatever you say goes."

"Remember that when you get up on Darkside and everything's going smoothly and you decide you want to gallop."

Julia's breath hitched. "Gallop? I might be rash, but I'm not suicidal."

"Could have fooled me," Sharon muttered under her breath as they approached the paddock gate.

"Sharon, did Darkside really cripple his previous owner?"

"I guess Paul told you that. Yeah, he did, but I knew that son of a bitch Earl Samms and I'm willing to bet he deserved it. Earl abused his horses to make them afraid of him. He liked the feeling of power when a big, strong Thoroughbred would back away from him in terror. It worked until he met up with a horse who didn't believe in backing away." Sharon reached the gate and stopped.

"So what happened?"

"According to the groom who saw it, Earl went into Darkside's stall with a whip, saying he was going to teach the horse a lesson. He thought he had Darkside tied up tight enough to keep him still while he beat him, but that stud is strong to begin with and anger added power to those big muscles." Sharon's eyes were on the stallion where he stood in the paddock and her tone was admiring. "He broke both the ropes Earl used on him and stomped the hell out of his abuser."

"So he was just defending himself," Julia said.

"Only reason Earl's alive is the fool groom risked his own life by going into the stall and dragging him out," Sharon said. "At least Earl sold all his horses so he can't torture them anymore."

"What would have happened to Darkside if you hadn't taken him?"

"Well, Earl wanted to shoot him. The groom got word to me, and I offered five hundred dollars for the horse. The only thing Earl liked better than abusing his horses was money, so he sold Darkside to me instead of destroying him."

The image of Darkside's glorious body lying lifeless on the ground tightened a fist around Julia's heart. "Thank you for saving him. I know he hasn't seemed very grateful, but I am."

"I'd about thrown in the towel on Darth Horse here, but then you came along. Goes to show you should never give up on something you think is worthwhile."

George walked up with a saddle on one hip and a bridle slung over his shoulder. "Changed your mind about riding the devil horse?"

"No," Julia said. "I'm more determined than ever."

The groom did a double take. "*You're* going to ride him?"

Julia lifted her chin. "He's my whisper horse."

George looked dubious but asked, "Who's tackin' him up? Me or you?"

"I'll take care of the saddle," Sharon said, hefting it onto her own hip. "I'll help Julia with the bridle."

"You want me to come in and hold him?" the groom offered, as he passed the bridle to Julia.

"No, we're good," Sharon said, unlatching the gate and holding it as Julia slipped through. "Just hang around outside the gate for when Julia needs a leg up, will you?"

At the opposite end of the paddock, Darkside threw his head up and whinnied before he trotted toward them, his tail swishing with temper and curiosity.

"Was George the groom who worked for Earl?" Julia whispered, never taking her eyes off the stallion.

"How'd you guess?"

"He's less afraid of Darkside than your other hands. I figured he might remember how Darkside was before Earl mistreated him."

"Yeah, when Earl sold all his horses, George was out of a job, so I hired him on here. He worked out better than the horse," Sharon said.

Julia choked on a nervous giggle. Darkside was almost upon them and his back looked very far off the ground from where she was standing. His hooves kicked up little puffs of dust as they struck the earth, reminding her of his weight and power.

"Howdy, big fella." Sharon reached into her pocket and offered him a carrot bit. The horse took it off her palm without hesitation. "Now that's a first," Sharon said. "Usually he has to dance around and try to scare me before he'll eat."

"I've gotten him addicted to carrots," Julia said, giving her whisper horse a treat too before she reached up to stroke his nose. She looked into his large, liquid eye and found no malice there. "Hey, buddy. Feel like having a rider today?" As usual, Darkside sniffed at her back pockets, and she laughed. "Males are all the same."

Sharon snorted. "Ain't it the truth? Here, snap this lead line onto his halter and hold him for me while I get the saddle on."

Julia followed her instructions and stood by Darkside's head, scratching behind his elegantly pointed ears to distract him. "How does he feel about being saddled?"

"No worse than about anything else, which could mean anywhere between ornery and furious. I'd bet Earl never tacked him up, so he doesn't associate the saddle with being hurt." Sharon slid the saddle into place so smoothly the horse didn't seem to notice. She walked around his head to ease the girth down and back again to buckle it up. "He may not like it when I start to tighten it up."

Julia decided food was the best distraction. "Hey, boy, you want another carrot?"

Darkside grunted when Sharon pulled the girth tight, but otherwise he didn't object.

"Now's the hard part," Sharon said as she came up beside Julia. "He's head shy. Not surprising the way Earl whipped him."

Julia sucked in a deep breath. "Okay, tell me what to do."

"First put the reins over his head so they're around his neck. That way we have something to hold him with when you take the halter off."

Julia gave Darkside's halter a tug to lower his head and lifted the reins over his ears, letting them slide down his glossy neck. Sharon brought them together in a close loop and held on. "Now unbuckle the halter and ease it off."

As she unbuckled the strap of the halter, Julia took another deep breath. Once she took this off, the only thing controlling Darkside would be the loop of reins and the horse's goodwill. As the halter slipped off, Darkside stretched out his neck and shook his head, his long, coarse mane whipping Julia in the face.

"Hey, careful with the flying horsehair there." She blinked to clear the haze of involuntary tears.

"Now take the headstall in your right hand and the bit in your left and see if Darkside will let you slip the bit in his mouth while you get the bridle over his ears."

Julia got her hands positioned and lifted the bridle toward Darkside's head. He squealed and threw his head up, the whites of his eyes showing. "Easy, boy," she said, lowering the bridle. "That didn't go well."

She transferred the bridle to one hand and reached out to stroke the horse's soft nose. Darkside shook his head hard before he let her touch him. "Okay, buddy, you don't like leather around your head. How about if we start with the bit and pretend the rest of the bridle isn't there?"

She stepped in close so her back was to his chest, her shoulder nearly under his chin. Letting the top of the bridle dangle, she used two hands to bring the bit up to his lips. He squealed again and danced backward, making Sharon jog with him as she struggled to keep a hold on the reins. For a moment, Julia had a terrible vision of her whisper horse bolting with the saddle flapping on his back, adding to his terror. She nearly called off the whole crazy project. But she thought of how Darkside's fear isolated him and knew she had to do everything she could to help him conquer it.

She put the bridle in her right hand and walked to where Sharon had managed to bring him to a standstill. He watched her, his ears flicking back and forth. She came right up to him and rested her forehead on his for a moment before straightening. "Listen, you've had some bad things happen to you, but you have to leave them behind."

As she spoke, she brought the bridle up and simply stroked his head with the bunched leather.

"The bridle's in my hand now, buddy, and you know my hand would never hurt you."

She switched it to her left hand and stroked the other side of his head with it.

"See, it's just a few leather straps. Nothing to be afraid of when your friend is holding it."

Darkside's ears stayed forward and Julia brought the bit to his lips, pushing gently until he opened his mouth so she could slip it in. Ever so slowly, she brought the headstall up where he could see it and kept going until she could ease first one ear and then the other through it. She buckled the throatlatch and sagged in relief.

"Good job," Sharon said quietly, as she released the reins and came forward to hold Darkside's head. "George, we can use your help now."

The groom was inside the gate before Julia even realized he'd opened it. Darkside seemed to grow so large he blocked out the sun. The saddle on his back looked ten feet above the ground. She closed her eyes against the vision and counted to five as she drew in a breath, another five as she held it, and a final five as she let it out and opened her eyes. She unclenched the fists she hadn't realized she'd made and scrubbed her sweating palms on her jeans.

"Ready, ma'am?" George had run the stirrups down to the bottom of their leathers and stood with his fingers laced together, waiting for her to put her knee in so he could help her up.

She'd dealt with Darkside's fear. Now she had to deal with her own.

She nodded and stepped up to the side of the horse, stretching up to grasp the saddle as she'd seen her father and uncle do countless times. She fitted her knee in the groom's hands and jumped upward. Propelled by George's surprisingly strong grip, she found herself lying across Darkside's back with barely any effort on her part. She scrambled around to swing her right leg over to the other side and sat upright as the big horse did a dance step under her.

"Whoa, boy, steady," Sharon said, her voice both commanding and soothing.

George slotted Julia's left foot, in its green cowboy boot, into the stirrup before she leaned down to hold the other iron to get her right foot settled.

She straightened and gathered up the reins in both hands, in imitation of the many times she'd watched various family members ride.

"Here, hold them like this," Sharon said, showing her how to thread the leather straps through her fingers.

George checked the girth to make sure it was still tight.

"I'm going to lead you around the paddock the first time, all right?" Sharon asked.

Julia dragged her gaze away from the ground so far below her and looked at Sharon. The other woman's expression went from questioning to concerned. "You okay, hon? You look a mite pale."

Julia tried to swallow so she could speak but her throat muscles were locked up tight. She forced herself to take a deep breath and nodded.

"You got Darkside bridled," Sharon said. "Maybe that's enough for today."

Julia shook her head, sucking in another breath before she croaked, "My uncle comes tomorrow."

"Yeah, but I'm more afraid of Paul suing my ass if you faint dead away and fall off."

The very real possibility of that occurring almost persuaded Julia to follow Sharon's suggestion.

But she wasn't riding just any horse. She'd been seeing Darkside in her mind and spilling him onto her canvases for months. She watched his elegantly curved ears doing a ballet as he listened to first Sharon's voice and then hers. He stood patiently, waiting for her to stop allowing her past to cast its long shadows of fear.

He'd overcome his past enough to accept her inept fumblings with his bridle. She needed to follow his lead.

She cleared her throat. "I want to ride."

"You got it, hon." Sharon pivoted forward and clipped the lead line on Darkside's bridle. "Okay, big guy, let's take it slow."

Julia felt the horse shift his weight and suddenly surge forward. Something between a sob and a gasp came out of her throat, and she hoped Sharon couldn't hear the cowardly sound. She managed not to drop the reins as she grabbed for Darkside's mane and twisted her fingers into it.

Her mind spun in a disjointed kaleidoscope: the creak of leather, the thud of hooves, the flex and push of huge muscles, the boards of the fence sliding past with the occasional vertical punctuation of a post, the metronomic bob of Darkside's head, Sharon's crown of red hair floating along beside his shoulder.

And then it all settled into place as she relaxed and let her body move with the horse, feeling the connection strengthen with each long stride he took. She watched his ears turning forward to see what was coming and backward to see what she wanted to do about it. She let go of his mane and felt the messages traveling back and forth through the reins.

"I'm riding a horse," she said, the realization hitting her. She felt a knot deep inside her begin to loosen. "I'm riding a horse."

"In fact, you're riding the devil horse."

"I'm riding Darkside," Julia said, blinking as tears streaked down her cheeks. She leaned forward to bury her face in his mane. "Thank you so much, buddy," she murmured to him.

"You've got an audience," Sharon said.

Julia sat up and glanced around. Sure enough, every hand in the place had found some task that needed doing right outside the paddock. A few didn't even bother to pretend to be busy, resting their elbows on the fence and watching.

The instructions her father used to shout at her stepbrothers sounded in her mind. *Heels down. Elbows in. Back straight.* She tried to follow them all. Somehow she transmitted something to Darkside in the process, because his head came up and his pace seemed to increase.

"Easy there," Sharon said, pulling the big horse back. "Let's keep it to a walk."

They came around to the gate. Sharon unhooked the lead line and stepped away from Darkside's head. "He's all yours, hon."

Darkside hesitated, and Julia clucked at him the way she'd heard her father do. The horse started walking again, following the fence line as though he was in a show ring.

Everything was fine until a rabbit bolted across the paddock ten feet in front of them. The horse stopped abruptly and threw his head up, slamming Julia against his neck. She grabbed at his mane to steady herself and dropped one side of the reins.

"Hey, buddy, easy. It's just a little bitty bunny," she said, as she felt his muscles bunch underneath her. She knew she couldn't control him with the reins or her legs, so she used her voice. "You could squish him like a bug with just one hoof."

She stroked his shoulder and murmured teasing words as he snorted and danced. She wished she could retrieve the flapping rein so he didn't catch one of his hooves in it.

Finally, she could sense him relaxing. His breath no longer came out in loud, audible puffs. She gingerly leaned down over his shoulder and snagged the loose rein, gathering it into her hand and turning him back toward Sharon.

His walk was noticeably faster than before, but she let him set the pace, heaving a sigh of relief as Sharon stepped forward to halt their progress.

"You did good," she said. "I was figuring out what I was going to say to Paul when you got tossed, but you got Darkside back under control."

"Under control?" Julia gave a shaky laugh. "All I did was embarrass him into not running from a tiny little rabbit."

"If you can embarrass this pain-in-the-ass stud, you're a better horsewoman than I am," Sharon said.

Julia made a moue of disbelief. "I think I'd better take some lessons before you turn me loose again." She patted Darkside's shoulder. "I got a little ahead of myself."

"Maybe. You want to take another turn around on the lead line?"

Julia nodded. "If you don't mind. It's so amazing to me that I'm sitting on a great, big horse and not—" She stopped herself just before she said *having a seizure.*

"Not what?" Sharon asked.

"Er, not terrified." Julia's heart squeezed at the near miss.

"Well, it's downright sensible to be terrified of Darkside, but there's no reason to be afraid of most horses. I can put you up on a nice quiet ride for your next lesson."

"No, I need to ride my whisper horse," Julia said. She had so little time left with him.

"Lord knows he can use the exercise and the socialization. I don't think I'll be putting any of my other lessons up on him, though."

Sharon led them once more around the paddock before Julia felt too guilty about pulling her away from her busy day and asked to stop.

She swung her right leg back over the saddle and braced her body weight on her arms as she kicked her left foot out of the stirrup. George caught her around the waist and helped ease her downward to the faraway ground, where her knees promptly collapsed under her.

"Happens all the time," the groom said, grabbing her elbow to support her. "You ain't used those muscles for riding before."

"I wasn't on the horse for that long," Julia said, feeling her blush go atomic. She knew it was mostly the aftermath of sheer nerves. "I feel like such a wimp."

Sharon chuckled. "George, I guess you're going to have to handle the tack."

Julia wobbled over to the fence and braced herself on it. She gave him an apologetic smile. "I'm sorry to add to your work."

"Happy to do it after seeing the devil horse walking around as quiet as a lead pony at the track," the groom said, already running the stirrups up their leathers.

Julia's knees had gone from jelly to rubber, so she pushed off the fence and managed to stagger through the gate Sharon had opened. As she came out into the open space behind the barn, several hands nodded to her. She nodded back.

A young man carrying a water bucket walked past her and said, "Nice job, ma'am."

Paul's friend Lynnie came up and shook her hand. "You got a way with horses."

"Just the one," Julia said. "He's my whisper horse."

"So Sharon's got you believing that stuff." Lynnie walked away, shaking her head.

"Not me," Sharon said. "Darkside's got her believing it."

Chapter 23

*E*RIC'S MAMA IS ON LINE ONE," VERNA ANNOUNCED through the intercom.

Terri only called if there was a problem, so Paul fought down a touch of worry as he excused himself to the client sitting in front of his desk. He picked up the receiver and walked over to the window, lowering his voice. "Is everything all right with Eric?"

"Eric's fine, but his babysitter's sick, so I need someone to pick him up from school and keep him until I get home from work. Jimmy's on a job where there's no cell phone reception, so I figured I'd give you a try."

He glanced at his watch. He had twenty minutes before he'd have to leave. "Sure, I'll take care of it."

An idea was forming in Paul's mind, bringing a smile with it. "Call my cell before you come to pick him up. I might be taking him to visit a friend of mine."

"You're a good uncle."

"You're a good mother." He meant it.

Paul hung up and came back to the desk to fill Verna in. He'd been called on for last-minute Eric duty before and usually brought his nephew back to the office. Verna loved having a youngster to spoil. He wrapped up his appointment right on time and headed out the door.

Parking across from the school, he leaned against the Corvette until he saw Eric race out the school's front door. He crossed the street and planted himself in the flow of kids.

"Uncle Paul! Did you bring the 'Vette?" Eric's small face lit up like a Christmas tree. "Can you drive by the school so I can wave to all my friends?"

"Nice to see you too, and Gina has the flu but she should be fine in a few days," Paul said, giving his nephew a head noogie to further muss his unruly brown hair.

Eric shrugged. "You didn't look all serious, so I figured nothing really bad had happened to Gina."

"It's still polite to pretend to care."

"I'll pretend the next time, I promise."

Paul laughed as he escorted his nephew to the car, slinging the boy's backpack into the rear seat before Eric scrambled into the front. "Would you like to meet a friend of mine who's an artist?"

"Like Pa?"

"Kind of like that." Paul smiled at the comparison.

"Sounds cool."

Eric made him cruise by the school at five miles an hour while he lorded it over his friends in their mothers' minivans. As they passed the last clot of children, Eric pulled his head and arm back inside the car and said, "That was cool."

"New favorite word?"

"Huh?"

"Never mind." Paul punched the in-car telephone on. "You want to say it?"

"Yes, please!"

"The name is Julia."

"Ju-li-a!" Eric shouted. "Dialing Julia," he recited along with the car's electronic voice.

The phone rang repeatedly before a distracted voice said, "Hello? Paul?"

"Eric and I are in the neighborhood and thought we'd come see you. Are you in your studio?"

"Um, yes. Come on over. I'd love to see Eric...and you too, of course."

Paul hit the disconnect button. "No stealing my girlfriend, okay?"

"I can't help it if girls like me. They just do."

"It's the curse of the Taggart men."

Eric sighed. "Yeah, it's kind of a pain, especially when two of 'em like you at the same time. They can get mean."

"A life lesson you're lucky you've learned young, my boy."

He pulled up in front of Julia's temporary studio and turned off the engine. "Take it easy on her. She might get overwhelmed by all this Taggart charm in one room."

Paul raced Eric to the front door, catching him before he barged through the unlatched screen door. Paul peered into the interior. "Julia?"

She appeared from the dimness, her flaming red hair piled into a messy bun with two paintbrushes speared through it, a huge man's shirt splattered with paint hanging off her shoulders. She looked good enough to eat. He managed to restrain himself sufficiently to give her a chaste kiss on the lips and an only mildly lascivious squeeze of her nicely rounded behind. She smirked up at him and stepped in close to give his groin a return squeeze under cover of her billowing shirt.

"Nice way to say hello," he said, as every nerve in his body surged on a spike of lust.

"I'd do better if we didn't have a chaperone," she said, cutting her gaze over to the counter where they'd made love before.

He cleared his throat and introduced his nephew. "So Eric wants to see an artist like his father at work."

"Your dad's an artist?"

"He painted really cool pictures on my bedroom walls with stencils. Do you use stencils?" Eric wandered toward the easel in the glass room.

"No, I'm more of a freestyle type myself," Julia said without a tremor in her voice.

"Yeah, me too," Eric said. He stopped in front of the partially finished painting of Darkside. "It's the big mean horse from Ms. Sydenstricker's."

Paul strolled up to look more closely at the painting. He draped his arm around Julia's shoulders, just because he couldn't stop himself from touching her. He gave Eric credit for recognizing the horse; he wasn't sure he would have, given how close the perspective was and how little was painted. In fact, he didn't notice a whole lot of progress since the last time he'd seen the picture. Maybe Julia had artist's block again.

"Is the work going all right?" he asked.

Her green eyes went wide as she looked up at him. "Why do you ask?"

"Well, I know you were struggling a couple of days ago."

He felt her shoulders relax. "I seem to be past that now, thank God. This just requires a lot of small, careful brushstrokes, so it doesn't go so quickly. Which is a problem since the auction's in three days."

"You could always offer it as it is and promise to finish it later. That might intrigue prospective bidders, sort of like buying a surprise package."

"I like surprises," Eric said, his voice coming from the front room. "Hey, Miss Julia, could you draw a picture of me too? Except I want to be driving the 'Vette, not a motorcycle."

Julia's shoulders went rigid under his arm. "Oh no," she said under her breath.

"What is it?" he asked, lowering his head in an effort to read her expression.

She averted her face. "Um, just a quick painting I did for myself. Not for anyone to see." She raised her voice for Eric's benefit. "Sure, I can draw you. Come over here in the light, and I'll grab a fresh sheet of paper."

"Uncle Paul, you look really good in her picture," Eric said, as he trotted up to them. "Like you're having fun."

Julia blew out a breath and slid from under his arm. "You might as well see it."

She went to the front room and came back with a square canvas in her hands, its back to him. "Close your eyes," she said.

"Bend down and I'll cover them," Eric said gleefully.

Paul squatted obediently while his nephew came around behind him to put his palms over his eyes. "When was the last time you washed those grubby paws?" Paul asked.

"This morning after I peed."

Paul groaned and heard a chuckle from Julia.

"Okay, Eric, let him look."

His nephew removed his hands, and Paul straightened before taking in the painting now displayed on the easel in front of him.

It was himself, only not the way he was anymore. This was his old self, the one who felt free to go off on any adventure that beckoned. The one who flirted with women for the sheer fun of it. The one who bought a motorcycle because no one was relying on him to keep their life out of the crapper.

This was how Julia saw him. Either he had fooled her or she wanted to believe this was her lover. A lover and an adventurer rather than the embittered ex-mayor of a small town in the sticks.

Julia waited for Paul to say something, but he stood frozen, his expression blank. He must hate it, and he was stalling so he could think of something polite to say. "It's just for me," she repeated. "You don't have to worry I'll show it to anyone else."

"Christ," he said hoarsely. "I want you to show it to the world."

She swung back to look at the painting. It was a pale, flat version of the man standing in front of it. "It's just a quick study. The motorcycle needs a lot of filling in and the shoulders are not quite in proportion."

"You've made me look"—he made a frustrated gesture as though he couldn't come up with the right words—"ready to roar off into the sunset at a moment's notice."

"Aren't you?" she asked, turning back to him to catch the flash of torment that contorted his mouth. She glanced down to see Eric watching his uncle with a question in his clear blue eyes. "He's a swashbuckler, isn't he, Eric?"

Paul's gaze dropped to his nephew. She saw the effort it took him to turn his grimace into the semblance of a smile. "That's me. King of the road."

Relief washed over the child's face. "Will you leave your hog to me in your will?"

Julia gasped, but Paul chuckled and ruffled Eric's hair. "Motorcycles are dangerous. You can have my 'Vette. Now sit down and get your picture painted."

"I'm going to just draw it for now," Julia said, grabbing a pad and a pencil before she sat on a rickety wooden chair.

Eric dragged a stool over from the counter and climbed up on it.

"Can you scoot around so you're sideways?" Julia asked. "Now look at me." She did a quick scan of the child's face, working out proportions and angles, before her pencil began to move across the paper. In her peripheral vision, she saw Paul walk to the rear of the building to stand with his back to them as he stared out through the dirty glass to the weedy garden behind.

As she sketched, she tried to unravel his reaction. She'd expected amusement or a little smug preening, maybe even annoyance that she'd presumed to take his likeness without his permission. She had not anticipated the raw pain she'd seen in his eyes.

The last thing she wanted to do was stir up trouble since she knew she would be in hot water for riding Darkside. Not to mention what revelations her uncle might make.

She sighed as she blocked in the Corvette's sleek lines and drew Eric's elbow hanging out the open window. "You can move now. I'm just going to add some shading."

Eric leaped off the stool and came around to peer over her shoulder. "Cool! Uncle Paul, look! She made me the driver."

The little boy raced over to grab his uncle's hand and pull him back to Julia. As they approached, she looked up to gauge Paul's emotional barometer. The pain was gone, but he moved as though it took every ounce of his will to make the effort. She reversed the sketchpad and held it up for him to see.

"That's the mighty power of the artist," Paul said. "She can make dreams look real."

"Eric will be in the driver's seat before you know it."

She decided this might be a good time to bring up her afternoon's adventure. Paul couldn't yell at her too much in front of Eric, and he might get over some of his anger before they were alone. Of course, he might be angrier at her for setting a bad example for his nephew. She was damned if she did and damned if she didn't. "Speaking of being in the driver's seat, I have some great news."

Two expectant male faces turned toward her and she was struck by the sense that she was seeing the same person at two different ages.

"I went riding this afternoon."

Eric was unimpressed since he didn't know about her past, but he said a polite, "Cool."

Paul, however, shed his listlessness as his eyes lit with genuine triumph. He leaned down to kiss her cheek and remained at her eye level as he said, "Congratulations! How'd it go?"

"Pretty well, all things considered." Julia took a deep breath. "I rode Darkside."

Paul straightened abruptly, his face tight with anger. "Between you and Sharon, you haven't got the sense God gave a squirrel when it comes to that horse."

Eric's eyes went round. "You rode the devil horse?" He slapped his hand over his mouth as his gaze shifted to his uncle.

"You just have to know how to handle him," she said, her gaze on Paul.

Paul didn't care about his nephew's brush with blasphemy. His fingers were drumming at high speed against his leg, and fury was rolling off him like the heat from asphalt on an August afternoon. "Don't get any ideas, Eric," he snapped. "Darkside is off-limits."

"Yes, sir." Eric knew better than to argue with his uncle in this state.

"There's a reason I rode Darkside. Carlos is coming here tomorrow. It was now or never."

"Never would be good."

"Paul, he's my Night Mare and my whisper horse. He's the one I was meant to ride. Once Carlos arrives..." Julia shrugged. It was impossible to explain how her uncle could control her with a word or a look. Even she didn't understand how she had allowed him to become so powerful. She supposed it was a combination of love and a desire to please him, a habit that went back to her younger days, one she'd never been able to break free of before.

Paul made a wordless sound of frustration. Julia understood he was holding back what he really wanted to say and mentally thanked Eric for acting as a buffer.

A cell phone beeped and Paul pulled his out of his pocket, tapping the screen to read the text message. "Change of plans. Your dad is going to pick you up at my office," he said to Eric. "We'd better get going."

Julia opened her mouth to point out Eric's father could just as easily come to her studio, but Paul's expression was too forbidding. She closed her mouth and carefully tore the drawing of Eric off her pad. "Maybe you can hang this up alongside your dad's stenciling."

Eric took the paper, looked at it, and handed it back to her. "Since you're famous, would you please sign it?"

Julia wrote her name carefully and legibly before she scrawled a flourish under it. "I keep forgetting I'm famous."

"Really?" Eric said, his brow wrinkled. "Isn't that kind of opposite? I mean, if you're famous, everyone knows about you so you should too."

"You're a smart kid," Julia said, holding out the drawing again.

"Smarter than some adults," Paul muttered.

"Cool," Eric said. "Are you going to give Uncle Paul his picture?"

"No, that one's for me to take home."

"You're leaving?" Eric asked.

"In a few days." And Carlos was coming tomorrow. Regret clogged her throat as she realized how little time she had in Sanctuary.

"Wow, I'm glad I got this before you left," Eric said.

Julia stood up and shook hands with the boy before she looked at Paul uncertainly. Should she kiss him good-bye? It seemed ridiculous not to, but he didn't look like he'd welcome it.

"I'll see you later?" she said, shoving her hands in her jeans pockets because she didn't know what else to do with them.

"Count on it." He took her shoulders in a less than gentle grip and kissed her on the lips. As he pulled away, she got a good look at the temper still burning in his eyes.

At least she had gotten the truth out before he heard it from someone else. He ought to give her credit for that. However, as she noted the way he stalked out the door, she decided she should just be grateful she hadn't added that particular fuel to the flames.

As soon as the screen door slammed behind them, she walked back to the painting of Paul, stopping to look at it as she recalled his reaction. No matter how she tilted her head, she still couldn't see what had upset him so much. Shrugging, she took it off the easel and propped it against the counter. In its place she put the Darkside canvas and felt her spirits soar again.

She had ridden a horse.

Chapter 24

"ERIC'S PA IS HERE," VERNA ANNOUNCED THROUGH THE intercom.

Paul followed Eric's dash out of his office and into the reception area. His brother stood in front of Verna's desk, laughing as he threw his arms open to catch his son. Jimmy still wore his dirty work clothes and heavy construction boots, but he looked more like the brother Paul had once known than the defeated alcoholic he'd become.

"Hey, Jimbo," Paul said. "You didn't have to come rushing home. Verna's always glad to have Eric's company. Of course, once she's done feeding him sweets, he may not have any teeth left."

"Eric knows two pieces of candy are the limit," Verna said. "Then he has to switch to apples."

Jimmy smiled at his son, his blue eyes striking in contrast to the tan he had acquired since he started working construction. "I'll make sure he has one when we get home."

Eric made a face.

"I know you're busy," Jimmy said, holding out his hand to Paul and pulling him into a brief embrace, "but I just wanted to say thanks. I don't know what I'd do without you, bro."

"You'd do fine," Paul said, surprised by his brother's demonstrativeness. He gave Jimmy an affectionate pound on the back before he released him. "It's always a treat to see Eric."

The smile faded from Jimmy's face. "A lot of people talk the talk," he said, "but you walk the walk too. I just want you to know I appreciate that." He turned back to his son. "Okay, buddy, let's get out of Uncle Paul's hair so he can bill some hours."

Paul watched them as they exited, Eric carrying Julia's drawing as carefully as a ten-year-old could while describing his encounter with Julia to his father. Jimmy's arm was around Eric's thin shoulders again, and the love between the two of them practically glowed like a halo.

His job was to keep it that way.

The roar of a motorcycle engine shattered Julia's concentration. She stepped back from her painting as footsteps sounded on the front porch of her studio. The screen door creaked open and Paul strode in, dressed in jeans and leather.

"Hello, sweetheart," he said, coming around the counter to bend her over his arm for a soul-searing kiss.

She took fistfuls of his leather jacket and tilted her head back so he could run his mouth down her neck. When he grazed her skin with just the edge of his teeth, she shivered as the sensation rippled outward from his touch.

"Gosh," she said, as he righted her, "that wasn't what I expected. You're not mad anymore?"

His expression darkened slightly. "It's not my place."

"You were mad before."

Although he didn't release his hold, he looked away. "Your life and mine are different, and you can live yours any way you see fit."

Julia wasn't sure she liked the sound of that. The overprotective Paul made her feel connected to him. This Paul seemed to be distancing himself. She gestured to the painting, just to see if she could provoke him. "What do you think? I was inspired by my first horseback ride and found new depths to add."

He pivoted, keeping one arm around her waist. "Hmm. My expert appraisal is that it's pretty damn good. You've given him that adolescent combination of insecurity and bravado."

She studied the half-finished painting, looking for what Paul saw. It was there in the angle of Darkside's ear and the gleam in his eye. She'd also conveyed the fragility of his skull under his smooth coat. It added a touch of vulnerability.

"That's what I understood about him today," she said. "He's not sure what he's supposed to do so he acts out to cover it up. I can't wait to ride him again." She was so pleased by Paul's perception she forgot about trying to strike a spark of anger.

Until she felt him stiffen and regretted her last words. Then he drew in a deep breath. "As long as I don't have to watch."

Leaning away to look up at him, she said, "When did the aliens kidnap Paul and put a pod person in his place?"

He gave her a tight smile. "You want to go for a ride on the hog?"

"Oh yeah," she said. "Just let me clean my brushes." She gathered up her supplies and carried them to the bathroom to give them a speedy scrub.

When she emerged, Paul was standing at the back window as he had earlier. For all his devil-may-care facade, his posture was leaden. She dropped the brushes with a clatter, and he started.

"Ready?" he asked, coming back toward her. Paul plucked the paintbrushes she'd forgotten about out of her hair, sending it tumbling around her shoulders. "Biker chicks let the wind blow back their hair," he said, combing the fingers of one hand through the mass of tangles. One snagged him, and he carefully worked it out before taking her hand and towing her out the door. "I brought the jacket for you for a farewell ride."

"Farewell?" A pang of alarm seared through her. *Was he saying good-bye to her already?*

"I'm donating the bike to the charity auction," he said. "It's time to hang up my helmet."

Relief made her nearly giddy until the full import of what he said sank in. Somehow she knew this had something to do with her painting of him. "It's my fault, isn't it?"

"What gave you that idea?" he said, holding up the jacket for her to slip her arms into. "I was going to sell it, but your painting made me think of using it as a fund-raiser. It's for a good cause."

She couldn't see his face, but she knew he was lying in some way. "But you and the Harley just go together." She made a gesture of frustration. "I don't know what I did, but I'm sorry."

"Sweetheart, you haven't done anything except show me a good time," he said. "Now let's ride."

She snugged herself up against his back as she had before, already mourning the fact she would never do this again. She swallowed hard to move the lump out of her throat.

The big engine yowled as he peeled out. He was riding less gently than the first time. She wasn't afraid, but the sense that he was deliberately pulling away from her persisted. His anger at her ride on Darkside hadn't dissipated; he had simply redirected it in some way.

They sped onto the highway and headed out of the town. As they passed the entrance to the interstate and kept going on the winding, hilly local route, she understood that he wanted the curves, to really feel his bike on this last joyride before he handed it over to the auction. It was sort of like the way she felt about leaving Darkside. She let the wind and the speed and the noise wrap around her like a comforter she was snuggled under with no one but Paul.

He slowed and turned onto a dirt track, bouncing along at low speed through a field dotted with bushes. The track climbed gradually until they came out on a ridge overlooking the ribbon of river far below. Paul killed the engine and swung off the bike, taking her hand to help her down.

"Where are we?" she asked, lifting off her helmet and shaking out her hair.

He put both helmets on the seat. "The family farm."

"I didn't know you came from farmers."

"My cousin owns it. I used to come up here when I was a kid."

"I can see why you'd like it now," she said, surveying the view of soft-blue mountain ridges and deep-green river valley, "but kids aren't usually into scenery."

He half turned and gestured toward a large tree. "That's a good climbing tree. I'd go up as high as I could. Higher every time, just to push myself. When I thought I could get away with it, I'd bring my father's binoculars with me. I wasn't supposed to borrow them." The remembered rebellion lit his face. "I got whipped a couple of times for that. Of course, if he'd known where I took them, I'd have gotten worse."

"What were you looking at with the binoculars?"

"Where I would go when I grew up."

Julia brought her gaze back to her companion. He was staring straight out, past the river, past the mountains, into the future as he had seen it in his childhood. So he had longed to get away, yet here he was, back where he had started. "How far did you go?"

He lost the long stare. "University of Virginia Law School. A law firm in Atlanta. It seemed far enough."

"How long were you away?"

"Seven years. Then my brother got divorced."

"That's what brought you back?"

He shrugged. "More or less."

He seemed in the mood to talk, so she pushed. "Why?"

"It's not really my story to tell."

"How is it not your story?" Frustrated, she took hold of his jacket and gave it a shake.

He covered his hand with hers. "It involves Jimmy and Eric and Eric's mother."

She yanked at his jacket again. "I'm not going to go around town spilling it to everyone I see. I'm not even going to be in Sanctuary that much longer."

"Why do you want to know so badly?"

Just like a lawyer to answer a question with a harder question. She released his jacket and tried to disengage her hand from his. His grip tightened, so she couldn't escape. *Keep it true but simple.* "I want to understand you."

"Huh." He seemed stymied by that, and she felt a certain triumph at rendering Paul Taggart speechless. "Oh, what the hell. It's not like the entire town doesn't know most of it anyway." He pulled her over to a fallen tree trunk, stopping to look at it a moment. "This tree was standing the last time I was here."

He handed her onto it and settled down beside her, stretching his long legs out and crossing them at the ankles of his heavy leather boots. He thrust his hands into his jacket pockets and looked straight ahead. "My brother, Jimmy, was twenty-two when he got Terri pregnant, so he did the honorable thing and married her. I don't know if they loved each other or not, but they didn't hate each other. They were just too young, I guess. Terri was only nineteen."

"That is pretty young to have a baby."

"I was graduating law school when Eric was born. I came home for the christening before I headed off to Atlanta to the partner-track job waiting for me."

Julia wanted to touch him to offer comfort, but he'd put his hands off-limits and stroking his thigh seemed too sexual. She braced her palms on the tree trunk on either side of her hips.

"Jimmy had a good job at Walmart and was climbing his way toward management when he got fired. He won't say why, and the Walmart people say it's a personnel matter and therefore confidential."

"Do you have any theories?"

"It had something to do with a woman who worked there too," Paul said with a shrug. "The best light I can put on it is he tried to protect someone from sexual harassment and lost the battle."

"Chivalry runs in the Taggart genes. I'd still be stranded beside the interstate if it didn't."

He glanced down at her with a half smile. "Sometimes good deeds pay dividends." His gaze swung away. "Mostly though, they don't go unpunished. Anyway, losing that job did something to him. He drank up all the money Terri made cleaning houses. Couldn't hold any new job. Picked fights in bars and ended up in jail.

"Finally, he came home drunk one night and backhanded her across the face when she called him on it. She told him to leave and never come back. The only thing good I can say about the situation is he didn't argue with her, he just went. He knew he'd crossed the line."

He pulled his hands out of his pockets and locked them together. Julia covered his intertwined fingers with her hand. He let her.

"Long story short, Terri divorced Jimmy, and the judge gave her full custody of Eric. Whatever his faults—and he has many—my brother loves his son, so it was killing him not to be able to spend time with Eric, especially since they live in the same town. The drinking got worse."

"So you came home."

He nodded. "I negotiated a deal with Terri. I would stay in Sanctuary and act as the guarantor of Jimmy's good behavior if she would agree to joint custody."

It was Julia's turn to stare off into the distance as she took in the magnitude of what Paul had done for his brother and his nephew.

He'd given up his dreams.

"So the night you had to leave after dinner..." Julia began.

"Jimmy got drunk at a bar and I had to go pick him up." Paul looked down at their hands. "He's been going to Alcoholics Anonymous, and I thought he was making progress." He blew out a breath. "Truth is that was partly my fault."

"Your fault?"

He turned one hand up to give hers a squeeze before he dropped his palms to his thighs. "I got a job offer in DC. He wanted to make sure I didn't take it."

"What was the job in DC?" Something Claire had said nagged at her. Something about Paul having a great idea people were interested in.

"Not worth talking about." He uncrossed his legs and drew his feet in. "So that's my story."

"You did an incredible thing for your brother. And for Eric."

He shook his head. "I've been lucky to be a part of Eric's life. I forgot to say thank you for today. He couldn't wait to show his father his portrait by the famous artist."

She decided not to point out he'd been too angry to express his gratitude earlier. "I keep thinking that's what you must have been like at age ten." She raised her eyes to his, trying to communicate some of the emotion roiling around inside her.

"You don't have to look at me like that," he said, chucking her under the chin. "I'm not fishing for sympathy."

Julia was still trying to fit all the things she knew about Paul into this new framework. "If your brother's in AA, doesn't he have a chance of getting better?"

He laced his fingers with hers. "You may believe that whisper horse of yours can be turned into a model citizen, but it's my experience that people don't change in significant ways. I want Eric to have his father, so I have to be around to make sure Jimmy stays on the straight and narrow."

"You're a good brother."

"You're not the only person who's said something like that to me today. But it doesn't change anything." He raised her hand to his mouth and kissed the back of it, his silver eyes going hot over their joined hands. "Let's go back to my place and I'll give you a tour."

Pulling her up and against him, he ran his hands under her shirt and up her back, so she could feel his touch on her bare skin. He lowered his mouth slowly to hers as he opened the catch of her bra and slipped around to tease her nipples to hard peaks. Her body responded before her mind could catch up to the abrupt change of his mood.

He deepened the kiss, his tongue touching hers, and she arched into him, her hands twined into his hair as much to hold herself up as to feel its strong texture. She moaned when his hands skimmed down and around her rib cage to slip under her jeans and knead her buttocks with a powerful, erotic grip. His revelations were forgotten as heat went zinging down between her legs. "Oh God, yes! Lift me up!"

"Easy, sweetheart. We've got the rest of the day."

"It's not enough," Julia said, using her grip on his hair to hold his mouth to hers. "Carlos comes tomorrow."

He squeezed her butt one more time before he slid his hands upward to retrieve the two ends of her bra and deftly refasten it. "Carpe diem."

"I know what that means, and it's not legal Latin."

She felt rejected. *Why didn't he ask her to stay in Sanctuary?*

Chapter 25

ULIA TRIED TO SAVOR THE SWIFT RUSH OF THEIR RIDE
back to town, but her body was jittery with arousal and
her mind kept running through Paul's story. The enormity of his
sacrifice took her breath away. She understood he had powerful obligations in Sanctuary, so he couldn't think only of himself when it came to the future. He couldn't leave, but that didn't
mean she couldn't stay. Yet he seemed to be pulling away from
her, not trying to keep her here. Was he too proud to ask her to
remain? Did she need to make the offer first?

She was out of her depth here.

"You can unlatch your arms now," Paul said over his shoulder, as they turned and rumbled into a driveway. "I think you
may have cracked a few ribs in the last couple of miles."

Julia yanked her arms away, noticing her muscles were shaking with fatigue. "I'm sorry. I didn't realize I was squeezing so
tight."

"I slowed down in case I was making you nervous, but it
didn't seem to loosen you up." He held the bike as she clambered
down. "Is everything all right?"

Was that her opening? Should she say something now? She
glanced around the quiet neighborhood where dusk was just
drifting in and golden light bloomed in house windows. No, this
conversation needed to be more private.

Something caught her attention and she focused on the house they stood in front of. It was Victorian but had a distinctive shape and design. "Is this an old train station?" she asked, noting the simple but elegant crisscrossed gingerbread decoration under the peak of the entrance gable.

He nodded, his eyes on his home. "I rented it originally and then it grew on me. It used to be right in town, but they moved it when the train stopped running. You can still see the ticket window inside." He walked to the attached garage and keyed in a code, making the door rise so he could wheel the big bike in.

She followed him, skimming her palm along the sleek lines of the black Corvette crouching in the dim light, as the garage door clanked down again. The car looked sexy, ominous, and fast, reminding her of her first sight of it on the gravel shoulder of the interstate. When she stopped to admire the long, elegant hood, Paul came up behind her, wrapping his arms around her waist. His voice rumbled past her ear. "I'm picturing how your bare skin would look against the shiny black paint."

She sucked in a gasp as she wondered what it would feel like to lie naked on the hood of the car with Paul's silver eyes locked on her. "Wouldn't it dent the car?"

He made a strangled sound. "That would be one repair I wouldn't mind paying for."

She turned in his arms and pulled his head down. He came willingly, locking his mouth on hers. Her body caught fire and she opened her legs so his thigh pushed between them, the friction making her throw her head back and moan. "Oh dear God, yes!"

"Ah, Julia," he breathed against her throat as he dragged his lips down the skin bared by the neckline of her shirt. She worked her hands up between them and ripped the shirt off over her head. He understood the invitation and ran his tongue along the lace edge of her bra before he closed his mouth on the hard, sensitive nipple.

She rocked her pelvis against his thigh as she nearly came just from the heat and moisture of his mouth soaking through the fabric. "Oh please, take it off," she begged, wanting his lips against her skin.

He released her to unhook the bra. Yanking the straps down her arms to drop onto the cement floor, he lifted her breasts with his hands, bending to suck at them, first one and then the other. She threaded her fingers into his thick hair and held on as wave after wave of sensation rolled from her breasts downward to pool deep between her legs. As she felt the pressure building inside her, she drew his head upward. "I'm ready. Now."

His eyes blazed. "All right. Let's go inside."

"No. Here. On the car."

She unzipped her jeans and yanked them and her panties down to her ankles while she toed off her loafers. As his gaze was drawn to her body, she retreated until the backs of her knees hit the 'Vette's bumper, and she thudded down less than gracefully on the hood. She got one heel onto the bumper and scooted herself up enough to recline on her elbows.

Paul stood like a statue, his gaze devouring her as she lowered herself onto the curving metal, her eyes never leaving his face. The car's surface was unyielding but smooth, the feel of it on her bare skin erotic and charged.

"Do you know what you look like?" His voice had dropped an octave and taken on the rasp of sandpaper.

She shook her head, kept speechless by the scorch of his attention.

"Every man's fantasy." He stood several moments longer, his eyes tracing a path she could nearly feel over her body. Then he was between her legs, spreading them as he braced a knee on the bumper and lowered his head to kiss her inner thigh. "I want to feast on you."

He blew a waft of breath against her that brought her arching up to his mouth. For a moment she felt the graze of his lips before he skimmed his hands down behind her knees and pulled them upward, bracing his shoulders between them. Now she was spread open to his eyes and his mouth. Her eyelids fluttered closed and she splayed her hands over the satiny metal as he drove her into a delirium of sensation with his lips, tongue, and an occasional graze of his teeth.

Her mind filled with flares of pleasure and escalating need until she heard herself begging him to let her finish. He slid one finger inside her as he flicked his thumb in exactly the right place. Her orgasm exploded, sending her internal muscles into a clench so hard she screamed and bowed up off the car, carrying his weight upward with her. He flicked his thumb again and sent another contraction ripping through her. After that, she lost track of how many waves broke over her until she sprawled limply across the hood, tiny rills of pleasure eddying through her wherever Paul feathered his fingers along her bare skin.

She summoned enough strength to force her eyes open. He bent over her, one hand braced on the hood beside her hip, while he ran the other one over her body, his gaze following its progress. When his touch moved up to her cheek, she saw the arousal still white-hot in his eyes. "Paul." It came out as a croak, so she cleared her throat and tried again. "It's your turn."

He shook his head. "You just gave me something I'll never forget. I don't need anything else."

She got herself up onto her elbows. "Are you trying to tell me that bulge in your jeans is your wallet?"

He gave her hair a tug. "You can barely move. I'll carry you into the house."

He took one of her hands and started to pull her upright, but she resisted, putting her free hand on his chest to keep him from scooping her up. "Don't you want to have me on the Corvette?" She dropped her voice to a husky purr.

"Sweetheart, I want to have you everywhere I see you. Now let's get you up to my bed where we can be comfortable."

For a moment, Julia forgot the seductress act as the compliment sent a different kind of pleasure singing through her. "I don't want to be comfortable. I want you to come inside me on the hood of your car. Hard."

She snapped open his belt buckle, then tore the button of his jeans from its hole and yanked the zipper down. He caught her hands in one of his and pushed her chin up with the other. The cords of muscle in his neck were taut, but his touch was gentle. "Are you sure you're ready, sweetheart?"

In answer, she pulled her hands from his grasp and freed his cock from his briefs, giving it a hard stroke between her palms.

His breath hissed in as his hips jerked forward, and she knew she had him. "Give me the condom," she said.

The foil envelope appeared in his hand as if by magic. As she opened it, he whipped his shirt up over his head, revealing the stretch of smooth olive skin over the defined geometry of muscle. She rolled the condom down his erection and reached toward the undulation of his bared abdomen.

"No." His voice grated harshly. "If you touch me again, I won't last. Lie back."

She lowered herself onto the metal, squirming slightly as her heated skin touched its cool surface.

He slid his hands under her bottom, easing her closer to him. Then he stepped between her thighs, the denim of his jeans brushing her inner thighs. She gasped as the touch sent her nerve endings pirouetting along the edge between pleasure and overload.

He locked his thumbs around her hips, lifting her, and then in one stroke he was inside her. She felt the scuff of his jeans on her skin, the curl of his fingers into her behind, and the pressure of his cock pushing deep within her. "Oh yes," she said. "Oh yes."

He pulled back and thrust into her again, his breathing harsh, his grip turning to iron. "Sweetheart, I can't hold on any longer."

"Don't hold on." She pulsed her hips against him. "Let go. Take me with you."

The sound that came from him was primal. He yanked her right to the edge of the hood, lifting her hips so he could drive even more deeply into her. As his rhythm quickened, her body shifted from satiety to wanting again. She could feel the fist of arousal squeezing tighter and tighter inside her, until he ground his hips against her and she convulsed around him, screaming his name.

She took him over the edge with her. She felt the pump of his climax and heard her own name echo against the walls of the garage as he shouted it.

For a long moment, he stood like that, holding her lifted against him as his erection softened and the aftershocks trembled through her. Then he slipped out of her and lowered her hips so her knees hung over the hood and her heels grazed the bumper.

He blew out a long breath and brought his gaze to hers. His eyes glinted in the dim light with some emotion she couldn't read. He bent at the waist and laid his forearms on either side of her, bringing his forehead down to rest on her shoulder. "Julia." His voice vibrated into her bones.

"Yes?"

"Just Julia. There's no room for anything else right now."

She lay still, listening to Paul's breathing slow, a delicious lassitude wrapping itself around her body. Her heart was singing at his words. If this didn't make him ask her to stay, nothing would.

Her stomach growled so loudly she jumped.

Paul lifted his head. "When was the last time you ate?"

Julia thought back but couldn't remember any meal after the corn muffin she'd had for breakfast. "This morning?"

He stood and pulled her up to a sitting position. She put her hand to her head as a wave of dizziness swept over her.

"Let's get you fed before you faint on me," Paul said, concern shadowing his face. He gathered their clothes in one hand before he swept her off the car and against his side with the other.

He swung open the interior door and walked her through it. Embarrassment flared as her dizziness faded. "You can let go. It was just sitting up so suddenly that made me woozy."

He loosened his hold and watched her carefully before he nodded. "You can use the downstairs bathroom to wash up while I rustle up something to eat. It's through the hall on the right." He held out her clothing.

Julia followed his directions, closing the door and pulling on her clothes. As she turned to the sink, she caught sight of herself in the mirror and shrieked.

Paul must have sprinted because he was at the door almost immediately. "What is it? I'm coming in." He eased the door open.

"My hair!" she wailed, holding up the mass of red tangles in both fists. "Please tell me you have a brush."

He braced his hand on the doorjamb and leaned his forehead against it. "You scared the bejesus out of me."

"Sorry, but it will take me hours to undo this." She tried to work her fingers through a snarl but it refused to budge.

"In that case, we'll work on it later. Together."

"I don't want you having to look at this across the dinner table," Julia said. "It'll give you indigestion."

"Sweetheart, you give me indigestion in so many other ways. Your hair is the least of my worries." A smile glinted in his eyes.

"Try not to look in the mirror while you're washing so I don't have another heart attack." He gave her an affectionate pat on the behind before he turned and left, closing the door behind him.

A few minutes later, Julia was perched on a high stool at the kitchen counter, nibbling on cheese and chopping three colors of peppers for some Italian concoction Paul was whipping up. "I had no idea you were a gourmet cook," she said.

"It's that or eat out every night."

"I'm pretty sure the single ladies in town would be delighted to bring dinner over for you."

He picked up a bottle of olive oil, flipped it end over end in the air, and caught it in his other hand before he twisted off the cap and poured it in a frying pan. "That happened a few times. I didn't mind the food; it was the strings attached."

"I can imagine. Even if you're not Rodney Loudermilk, you're still pretty eligible."

He chuckled as he walked over to ruffle her hair before he scooped up the pepper bits. "The ones looking for a commitment weren't the worst."

"What do you mean?"

"A couple of them were married."

"Woo-hoo!" Julia cackled. "They just wanted you for your body. Not that I blame them."

Paul didn't comment as he scattered the vegetables in the sizzling oil and shook the pan.

They bantered back and forth through the rest of the food preparation. Julia knew they were deliberately keeping it light and superficial, but every time they came near each other, there was always a touch. It kept the physical awareness between them simmering as hotly as his frying pan.

Finally the chicken Marsala was ready, and they sat at a table topped with rich green and brown tiles. Julia had set out thick golden plates with borders that picked up the green of the table. Paul clearly cared about the aesthetics of his home, which pleased her.

He shook out a deep-green napkin and laid it on his lap. "*Mangia!*" he commanded.

"*¡Buen provecho!*" she said, repeating her family's traditional comment as she dug into the deliciously scented food. Putting the first bite of chicken in her mouth, she closed her eyes at the burst of flavors on her tongue.

"Hunger is the best sauce," he said dryly. She noticed, however, that he was devouring his own food with gusto. After a few minutes of silence as they enjoyed their meal, he put his utensils down. "Your Spanish reminded me of the other bombshell you dropped this afternoon. Are you ready for your uncle?"

Surprise made her swallow badly, and she had to gulp a few swallows of water before she could speak. She should have known Paul wouldn't forget that. "I know exactly what I'm going to do with him." She'd been considering it while she'd painted. "After lunch, I'm going to take him to the gallery to see how Claire will show my *Night Mares*, and then I'm going to take him to my riding lesson."

Paul gave a short bark of laughter. "I see you don't intend to ease him into the situation."

"You can't ease Carlos. He's like a bull in a ring, and I'm not going to let him run over me this time."

"What about lunch? What do you plan to say to him then?"

That was the one vulnerability in her scheme. She had to fire him before she could demonstrate her strength and independence. It would be worse if she tried to delay the lunch; he was very set on regular mealtimes. She cut another piece of chicken, put it in her mouth, chewed, and swallowed before she said, "I'll have to break the news to him that he's fired. He can't come to the show thinking he's still in charge of my career."

"Would you like me to join you? Maybe I can wave a red flag so he charges at me instead."

She dropped her fork and reached across the table to cover his hand with hers. "Always ready to come to my rescue." However, she wasn't going to risk Carlos revealing her secret in an effort to bring Paul around to his point of view. She let go of Paul's hand and sat back. "I have to face him myself."

Paul pleated his napkin into an elaborate geometric shape and stood it up beside his plate. "Julia, you're in a tough situation, and I'm an experienced mediator. Let me help you."

She wanted to accept his offer so badly, it made her ache. Her eyes brimmed as she balanced the comfort of having Paul by her side against the danger of Carlos spilling her secret. She imagined the look on Paul's face when he heard about her epilepsy, and her decision was made. Shaking her head, she picked up her fork again. She wasn't going to risk him pitying her. "It's like riding Darkside. No one can do it for me."

She saw Paul's jaw tighten, but he said nothing as he picked up a hunk of bread and ripped off a piece to dip in the Marsala sauce. She lifted her water glass and drank, watching him over the rim. He tore off another slice of bread with more ferocity than was necessary. His reaction made her happy. He might be annoyed, but he also was engaged with her again. It was much better than this afternoon's attitude of laissez-faire. "I like it when you get mad at me."

He looked up from his plate. His eyebrows were still drawn together in a frown but one corner of his mouth kicked upward. "Does that mean you go out of your way to provoke me?"

"No, that comes naturally," she said, going back to her chicken.

He snorted in agreement. "Why do you like it? Make-up sex?"

Chewing, she shook her head. He leaned back in his chair, twirling his knife as he waited for her to swallow. "It shows you care," she said.

The glinting amusement in his eyes died, and he put the knife down. "Trust me, sweetheart, I care."

Two hours later Julia snuggled herself up against Paul in his big sleigh bed. "I've never had sex like this before."

"I'm not sure what you mean by that."

She felt a blush creep up her neck to her cheeks. "I mean this intense, this, I don't know, *sexy*." She realized she sounded like an idiot so she made it worse. "You've probably had lots of great sex, but I haven't."

"I've never had sex like this, either."

She lifted her head to look at him. "Really? This is unusual for you too?"

"God help me, yes," he said, and pulled her closer so she couldn't see his expression. He held her so tightly she could barely breathe, but she didn't complain, understanding that whatever emotion had him in its grip was powerful. Some primitive part of her reveled in being able to affect him so strongly. She could feel the quiver of tension in his arms, hear the deep breaths he was drawing in and expelling as he fought for control.

"What's wrong?" she asked, her lips brushing his skin.

His arms relaxed so she could breathe. "I've got an armful of gorgeous, naked woman. What could be wrong?"

"For a lawyer, you're a pretty bad liar."

"After two orgasms, you're going to insult me and my profession? I call that ungrateful."

"I call it the truth." She knew it wouldn't do any good to push him. He would just slide past any question he didn't want to answer with a joke and a smile. Besides, she didn't want to ruin what might be their last night together.

She thought she'd pushed too hard when he shifted her gently away from him and got out of bed. "I'll be right back," he said, disappearing into his bathroom.

Julia frowned when he returned with a wooden-handled brush. "Is that for something kinky?"

"It's for your hair," he said, stacking two pillows against the backboard before he slid into the bed beside her. "I promised I'd help you untangle it."

"Oh right," she said, the little clutch of anxiety dispelled. "I think it's hopeless."

"I have very good hands." He flexed his long fingers.

"No argument with that."

He settled her so her head rested on the quilt covering his abdomen and her hair spread upward over his chest. "I'll try not to yank too hard."

"I'll brace myself." In fact, all she felt was a deliciously sensuous tingle skimming over her scalp as his deft fingers sifted through the strands of her hair. Her eyelids drifted closed. "Mmmmmm. Feels so good."

"You're enjoying having your hair pulled?"

"It's like a massage, only better because my hair will look good at the end."

Paul chuckled as he worked out a knot in the mass of red. He spread the disentangled strands over his palm and smoothed them with the brush, admiring the glint of gold among the auburn. Once it was glistening like silk, he moved it away from the still-snarled part.

Between knots, he indulged himself by letting his gaze trace the bare curve of Julia's spine down to where the quilt draped over her hips. The weight of her head pressed comfortably on his mid-section while her bare shoulder brushed his hip. Contentment washed through him like the warm water of a Caribbean island. It was a sensation he wasn't accustomed to.

"Mmmmm," she purred again.

Maybe after she left, he should get himself a cat. He'd heard they could induce something close to this mood in other people. He was dubious, though, since not even other women had ever made him feel like this before.

She sat up abruptly, jerking the snarl he'd been working on out of his hands. "Ouch!" she yelped as she clutched the quilt to her chest with one hand and rubbed her scalp with the other.

"You have to warn me when you're going to move. I had my fingers woven into a tangle."

"I figured that out."

She looked cute and disgruntled with half her hair flowing over her shoulder like a satin curtain while the other half resembled a poorly constructed bird's nest. A smile lifted his lips.

Her answering smile was tentative and brief. Warning bells went off in his brain.

She eyed him for a long moment before she took a deep breath. "Why don't I stay?" she blurted out. "There's no reason I shouldn't. I mean, the sex is fantastic and we enjoy being together, so why should we stop now?" A blush turned her neck and cheeks a deep rose. "If things change between us, we can end it."

For a selfish moment he thought of a whole procession of days with Julia in his bed, her flaming hair spread across his pillow or his chest like a banner, her green eyes lit by laughter or dazed with arousal, her smooth, creamy skin warm under his hands. The word *yes* nearly forced its way between his lips.

How could he explain to her that he would never want to end it, so it was kinder to do it now?

He thrust a hand through his hair, trying to formulate a response that wouldn't hurt her. "You've got places to go and people to meet way beyond Sanctuary, West Virginia."

She squared her beautiful, bare shoulders. "I can do that later. I want to spend more time with you now."

"Sometimes it's better to quit while you're ahead."

He saw her flinch and felt like a heel, but he had to nip this idea in the bud.

"The sex is still great so we're still ahead," she said, before she gave what she undoubtedly thought was a worldly shrug. "When it isn't great anymore, we'll say good-bye."

He would have laughed if he didn't feel like his heart was being ripped out of his chest. "Sweetheart, the reason the sex is incredible is because of our feelings. Neither you nor I are the kind of people who find casual sex satisfying. There's something more between us."

"Exactly!" She pounced on his words like a terrier on a rat. "Let's see where it takes us."

He braced his hands on the mattress to shove himself fully upright against the pillows. She was sinking the talons of regret deeper and deeper into his flesh. "It will only make the inevitable that much worse."

Her lower lip quivered and she sank her teeth into it.

"That came out wrong." He stretched out to take her hand, thinking of the skill that lay in the fingers he held. "What I meant is I can't leave here because of my brother and Eric. You need to leave because your talent demands the scope of the entire world." He rubbed his thumb over the back of her hand. "As it is, I hate the thought of you leaving after I've known you only ten days. How do you think we'll both feel after six months or a year?"

A sob wrenched itself from her throat. He had to consciously restrain himself from pulling her into his arms and telling her he didn't mean any of it.

"M-maybe I won't want to leave after a year. Or two years. Maybe I'll decide to stay. I can paint anywhere."

"Have you ever been to New York?"

Triumph flared in her eyes. "Yes."

"How old were you?"

Her shoulders slumped. "Eleven. But I've been to Madrid to visit my parents several times since they moved."

"What was it like to be there?"

"Thrilling. Inspiring. It gave me new ideas about color and composition." Resignation laced her voice as she told him the truth.

Her honesty nearly undermined his self-control. She could have lied and said she found it dirty and noisy, but she'd refused. He'd never admired another person so much in his life. "You did me the honor of telling me the truth. I owe you the same." He released her hand and fisted his in the bedclothes. "Much as I want to, if I agreed to let you stay, I would hate myself. It would poison our relationship sooner or later."

She shook her head vehemently. "I don't believe that. If we—" She stopped and slid him a look he couldn't read. "If we fell in love with each other, neither one of us would care where we lived."

He felt as though someone had slammed him against a brick wall. *She thought she was in love with him.* Then he got slammed a second time, even harder, as he faced a reality he had been shoving away: *he was head over ass in love with her.* "Holy shit," he muttered.

"What?"

He took a deep breath. "You said you hadn't had much experience with sex, so you may be confusing a really good orgasm with something more."

"I'm not that stupid," she said, her body rigid at the insult.

"Hear me out," he said, holding up a hand. "I have a fair amount of experience; I know how to make you feel things you haven't felt before. It might color your view of me, make you think I'm something I'm not."

"I think you're a good lover," she said. "And a good man. Are you going to disagree with either of those?"

Her eyes were hazed with tears again, which made it hard for him to think straight. "I'll take the fifth."

"I'm capable of making my own decisions and living with the consequences," she said. "It won't ruin my life if our relationship doesn't work out."

But it would ruin his. Was he just being a coward?

She didn't wait for a response. "I'm tired of everyone assuming I'm some fragile flower who has to be protected from the realities of life. If I never feel pain, how will I understand joy? How can I be honest as an artist if I go on living this overprotected half-life?" She scrambled off the bed, dragging the duvet with her and gesturing wildly with her free hand. "Hurt me, Paul. At least you'll be treating me like an adult."

Pushed beyond his limit, he snapped. "Did you ever consider it might hurt me?"

Her hand fluttered downward. "What?"

He swung his feet to the floor and stalked around the bed to look down at her. "I'm not made of stone. How do you think I'll feel when you decide to leave?"

Her eyes were huge with shock. "But you're so...so confident and...and popular. Even married women want to sleep with you."

He just barely stopped himself from taking her shoulders and giving her a good shake. Instead he sat on the bed so their faces were nearly level. "Sweetheart, do you really have no idea how extraordinary you are?"

"I'm not," she whispered, a strange, stricken look in her eyes.

"Yes, you are. And I'm not talking just about your artistic talent. I'm talking about the essential Julia." He grazed a fingertip over the swell of her breast where her heart lay. "You are a breath of fresh air, a woman with grit and integrity. And you're sexy as hell." His smile went a little crooked, but he was trying to steer the discussion to safer ground for both of them. "Losing all that won't be easy for me."

She plunked down on the bed beside him. "I didn't look at it that way. I mean, it never occurred to me that you would"—she waved her hand vaguely—"feel like that if we got involved and I left." She twisted to look up at him. "That sounds selfish, but it's more I don't think of myself as being especially important in your life."

If it had been any other woman, he would have suspected her of fishing for reassurance, but Julia didn't fish. That she believed she meant nothing more to him than a passing fling nearly gutted him. The problem was if he told her the truth about how important she was to him, she would refuse to leave.

He dropped his hand to her thigh and gave it a squeeze. He thought about all those times he'd held onto his smiling mask during town council meetings and tried to convince himself this was no different. "You're the first world-famous artist I've ever made love to," he said, cringing inside at the caddish words, "so I'd say you were significant."

He expected some indication he'd hurt her, but she just kept looking at him, her striking green eyes clear of tears or accusation. "We don't have to stop seeing each other now, do we? Just because we had this conversation?"

"I—" He was nonplussed. He'd figured she would be either so angry or so distressed she would refuse to have anything further to do with him. As it dawned on him she was offering the precious gift of four more days in her company, a grin tugged at the corners of his mouth. He intended to relish every minute he could with her. "No, we don't have to stop. In fact, stopping sounds like a really bad idea."

A look of relief skittered over her face. "Good, because I was afraid I'd messed up the rest of our time together."

He grabbed her shoulders and fell backward on the bed, pulling her down with him as happiness coursed through his body. He was going to cram the next ninety-six hours as full as he could with memories of this incredible woman. He rolled them over, bracing his weight on his elbows as he lowered his head to kiss her.

Starting now.

Chapter 26

*J*ULIA PULLED THE PLUG ON THE BIG TUB AND SLOSHED TO her feet. After a long soak to take out some of the soreness from last night's activities with Paul, she felt energized and ready to carry out her plan of action.

Grabbing a thick white towel from the brass rack, she stepped out onto the bath mat and buffed herself dry before heading to the bedroom to dress. She'd chosen her outfit carefully: the tailored beige trousers, narrow brown leather belt, and moss-green silk blouse said "serious businesswoman." In a gesture of individuality, her cowboy boots peeked out from underneath the neat cuffs of her pants. She smoothed the hair Paul had so carefully and deliciously untangled into a tidy ponytail.

She made a face at herself in the mirror, just to prove the person underneath was still Julia Castillo. "Time to take over the world."

She pivoted on her boot heel and strode out the door of her room. She was meeting Claire at the gallery in fifteen minutes for step one of her plan to convince Paul and Carlos she could manage her own life.

As she walked toward the Gallery at Sanctuary, a few aches and twinges lingered, reminding her of the tumultuous night she'd spent with Paul. She'd nearly made a mess of things with her outburst about staying for the sex. It had seemed like a good approach as she had lain basking in the afterglow of the Corvette caper. Men were supposed to be susceptible at times like that, and Paul was all male, but he had that annoying and endearing protective streak.

He had nearly convinced her with his nonsense about how much it would hurt him if she left, but then she realized he was playing the role of white knight again, worrying about her feelings. He didn't understand it would be much worse for her if she didn't stay. If it didn't work out between them, at least they would have given it their best shot.

Not to mention the joy of spending weeks and months with Paul while they explored the possibilities of their relationship. In fact, she hoped it would stretch into a lifetime.

All she needed to do was prove to everyone she could handle whatever real life threw at her.

Julia flung open the door to the gallery. Claire was seated at the glass-topped desk, staring at her computer screen. She swiveled the chair to face Julia, a smile lighting her face. "The acceptances are pouring in. I'm doubling the wine order and adding more trays of hors d'oeuvres. This is going to be a major event in the art world."

Julia dropped onto the big cream couch as her knees went wobbly. Her focus was so entirely consumed by Paul, she had forgotten about her upcoming public trial by fire. "That's great." Her voice squeaked slightly and she cleared her throat.

"Don't look so terrified," Claire said, rising from her desk to join Julia on the couch. "These people are coming because they already admire your talent."

Carlos's harsh evaluations of her *Night Mares* swarmed like spiders through her mind. "But this style is so different. If they like my previous work, they won't like this."

"Give my clients some credit," Claire said, her tone firm but kind. "They're sophisticated connoisseurs. They expect artists to grow and change."

"If you're sure…" Julia heard the tentativeness in her voice and hated it. She straightened her spine and lifted her chin. "I believe you." No more letting her uncle get into her head. "I wanted to ask you two things. First, could you set up the paintings the way you're going to display them for the show before Carlos arrives?"

"Are you sure that's a good idea? From what you tell me, the strong emotional content is what bothers your uncle. Maybe we should downplay that."

Julia shook her head. "I want him to feel the impact full strength." She wanted him to understand that she had come into her own as an artist and as a human being.

"Consider it done. When does Carlos arrive?"

"Noon, but we're having lunch first so I'll bring him by at about one thirty. Thank you." Julia nodded before she locked her gaze on Claire's. "I'll be telling my uncle he's no longer my agent. So I wondered if you'd given further consideration to taking his place. Don't feel obligated, but I'd like to know going into the discussion."

She expected Claire to look away and refuse. Instead delight lit her brown eyes. "I would be honored to be your agent. I didn't mention it because I wasn't sure if you were having second thoughts with your uncle coming."

A weight she hadn't realized she was carrying slid off Julia's shoulders. "Yes!" she exclaimed, doing a little fist pump.

Claire glanced down at her hands before looking back at Julia. "You did me a favor."

"I did?"

"Turns out Tim wants to come along on my business trips." Claire's face glowed with excitement. "Keep this under your hat, but he plans to hire another vet to ease his workload."

"Glad I could help," Julia said. Would Paul be able to come with her on business trips? How tied was he to his brother and nephew? It didn't change her feelings about staying, but it would be thrilling to have Paul by her side in a new place. She yanked her mind back to practical matters. "Do we need an agreement or can we just shake hands?" She stuck out her hand toward Claire.

The other woman took it in both of hers and gave it a firm squeeze. "I'm sure Paul will insist on a legal document, but a handshake is good enough for me."

Just like that, Julia had a new agent. "This feels good," she said, as a sense of control poured through her. She needed someone outside her family to be involved with her art.

"We'll drink a toast to our new partnership at the show," Claire said. "I've ordered very good wine so our patrons will feel less pain when writing the checks."

She winked and Julia laughed. So far her plan was right on track. She pushed up to her feet. "Shall I give you a hand with the paintings?"

Claire rose but waved away her offer of assistance. "It's easy to roll the panels around. You go brace yourself for your uncle's arrival."

On an impulse, Julia threw her arms around the other woman. Claire looked surprised, but she responded with a return hug almost immediately.

"This is going to be a great partnership," Julia said, releasing her new agent.

Now she just had to break the news to her uncle.

An hour later, she stood on the front porch of the Traveller Inn, jiggling from one foot to the other as she watched a black sedan swing around the front circle. The driver leaped out of the car but before he could get to the back door, it opened and her uncle emerged. He wore a gray pinstriped suit, a pale-blue shirt, and a red tie.

"In full intimidation mode," she muttered under her breath as she walked down the shallow stone steps to greet him. The image of Darkside bucking and tearing around his paddock before he took a carrot from her hand flashed through her mind. She'd been able to tame an untamable horse; surely she could handle her uncle.

He said something to the driver before turning toward her. She was surprised to find that he looked smaller than she remembered, and the silver threads in his dark hair seemed more noticeable.

His face lit up as he opened his arms. "*Mi querida*, it is so good to see you."

She walked into them, breathing in the lemon-and-sage scent of his cologne. The strength and familiarity of his embrace were reassuring, and for a moment she clung to him. No matter what had happened in their recent past, he was still the man she thought of almost as a father.

"I've missed you," she murmured next to his ear.

"Then why have you stayed away so long?" he asked, holding her away from him and giving her a small, exasperated shake.

"I've been gone all of six days," she said, with a smile.

"And every one of those days I lived in fear."

The will to smile vanished. "That's unnecessary, Tío. I'm no longer a child."

"You will always be my *sobrinita*." He slipped his arm around her waist and steered her up the steps. "Tell me about this inn. Do you know when it was built?"

She recognized the tactics: he'd realized his error and was withdrawing behind his charm to regroup. "Pre–Civil War," she said. "The owner can tell you the details."

Her uncle continued his flow of observations as they were seated in the cozy dining room. "That is a Henry repeating rifle!" he said, his voice tinged with excitement.

Julia followed his gaze to see a long gun hanging on the wall over a print of a battle. The rifle had a polished wooden stock and brass fittings.

The innkeeper emerged from the kitchen. "That rifle belonged to my great-grandfather," Lyle explained. "He always said it kept him alive through the war."

"That weapon is a true masterpiece," Carlos said.

Julia felt her temper spark at the word. Her uncle considered an old gun a masterpiece but thought her *Night Mares* were too awful to let anyone see. She leaned forward. "After lunch, I want to show you where my paintings will be exhibited."

A line formed between Carlos's eyebrows but he nodded before he opened his menu. "What do you recommend?"

"Their corn muffins," she said with a faint smile. "I've never eaten anything but breakfast here."

The line deepened as he frowned. "You know how important it is for you to eat regular meals."

"This isn't the only restaurant in town." Guilt made her defensive; she knew eating at regular intervals was something her doctors had recommended to help control her epilepsy. In her newfound freedom, she'd let that particular safeguard slip.

Carlos made a disapproving sound but turned back to the menu. The waitress approached, her pen poised.

"Rainbow trout for both of us," Carlos said, closing the leather folder. "And lemonade."

"Actually, I'd like the crab cakes," Julia said, choosing a dish at random. She had planned to order the trout until her uncle presumed to speak for her. "With a side salad. And sparkling water."

"Yes, ma'am," the waitress said, scribbling rapidly.

As soon as she collected the menus and left, Carlos said, "But trout has always been your favorite."

"I've broadened my horizons." Julia shook out the linen napkin and laid it across her lap. "There's a business matter I need to discuss with you."

He held up his hand. "I apologize for withholding those paintings from the market. It is possible I misjudged their artistic merit, but I did what I thought was best for your career. And for you."

Julia forced herself not to spew forth the hurt and sense of betrayal his actions had caused her. She took in a breath, counted to five, and let it out before she spoke. "Did you really show them to any dealers, or was it just your opinion they would damage my reputation?"

"Of course I showed them to dealers!" His nostrils flared and an angry flush washed up his cheeks. "I did not like the paintings myself, but I would not be so unprofessional as to make an artistic judgment on my own. I consulted several experts before I made the decision to keep them private."

"Who did you consult?"

He unclenched his fists to drum his fingers on the table. "First I took them to Raymond Ballantine. He said he couldn't sell them."

Raymond's gallery was in Hickory, North Carolina. Carlos had persuaded him to take three of Julia's horse paintings on consignment when she was still in art school. Much to everyone's surprise and delight, the pictures had sold in a week. It reminded Julia of all she owed her uncle when it came to building her career.

However, her uncle was well aware that Raymond's clientele was very regional. The tourists went there to buy furniture, not art, so it wasn't the right place for her *Night Mares*.

"I'm not surprised," Julia said, hanging onto her temper by a thread.

Her uncle shrugged dismissively. "I did not expect him to have buyers for the paintings; his patrons are not of the level you have reached. However, I respect his opinion on art. I also took several to Richard Cruz and Eva Mady in Asheville, both of whom are very well-known. Neither was enthusiastic."

That smarted. Asheville had a fairly sophisticated art scene.

"They asked if I would reduce the prices to encourage new buyers and I of course refused. The paintings were still by Julia Castillo." Indignation rang in his voice and Julia felt her anger diminish. Her uncle might not like her black horses, but he wasn't going to devalue them. "I wonder now if they simply did not have buyers who were able to afford your work as it grew more valuable." He shook his head. "I may have misread their reactions."

It was quite an admission from her proud, confident uncle, and a little more of her hurt drained away. "Why didn't you show them to Claire? You knew she was passionate about my work."

"Because she was no longer in New York. You do not think she can sell your paintings here in this *aldea*." He waved his hand around to indicate the smallness of Sanctuary. The fact that he used the Spanish word for village told Julia he was upset; he prided himself on his English vocabulary.

She'd been right about his easy acquiescence to the art exhibit at Claire's gallery; he thought it would go unnoticed by the larger art community.

He leaned toward her, lowering his voice. "I was not going to hide your work in a third-rate gallery. It deserves the proper respect."

"Claire's gallery is highly respected," Julia said, her temper flashing at the disparagement of her friend's business. "Paxton Hayes is coming here."

"Mr. Hayes is coming because Julia Castillo's work will be on display," Carlos said, sitting back with his arms crossed, an arrogant tilt to his head.

She didn't know whether to be gratified or ticked off. He clearly held her work in high esteem, yet he did nothing but criticize it in private. At least he hadn't lied to her when he told her dealers didn't want the new paintings. Perhaps his choice of dealers was questionable, but he had tried to get a cross section. He didn't believe in the work himself, so he'd given up too easily.

She was trying to decide how to explain the devastation his lack of faith in her had caused when he uncrossed his arms. "*Mi* Julia, I am concerned about the art exhibition. Paxton Hayes is not a supporter of your work, you know. He can be very...cutting. It might be upsetting to you."

"Upsetting?" Julia was afraid she knew where he was going with this.

Her uncle shifted in his chair. "You will be in a room full of critical strangers, with strong lighting and a certain level of chaos. It will be stressful." He shifted again. "You might have a seizure."

Julia crushed the napkin in her fists. "I don't have seizures anymore. The doctors confirmed it. I'm cured."

"No, the doctors believe you might be cured because you have not had a seizure. But that is because we keep you safe and away from anything that might provoke one."

Now he was jabbing at her most vulnerable point. She had been wrapped in a protective cocoon for several years. Did she only *appear* to be cured? "Do you know what I've done in the last six days, Tío? I've driven myself three hundred miles in a car that broke down on the side of the interstate three miles from my destination. I've ridden on a motorcycle twice. I've swum in a river." That was stretching the truth but she wasn't going to tell him what she'd really done in the river. "I've taken long, hot baths. And"—she tossed her ponytail back over her shoulder— "I've ridden a horse."

He sat silent until her last statement when his eyes widened. "*Dios mío*, is that true?"

She nodded. "I have another riding lesson scheduled for this afternoon. I thought you might come."

"I—" Carlos shook his head. "I don't know whether to be alarmed or joyful."

"Joyful." She managed to unclench one hand and reached across the table to lay it over his. "I was nervous, but I never felt as though I was going to have a seizure."

"Raul will want to know about your riding. He always wanted you to have the same pleasure in horses that he did," her uncle said, referring to his brother, her stepfather. "Perhaps *he* will feel joyful. As for me, I am concerned."

Julia realized that seeing her on Darkside wouldn't ease his concern. Maybe taking him to the stable was a mistake.

"Ma'am?" The waitress hovered beside her with the plate of crab cakes, blocked by Julia's arm from putting it down in front of her.

"Oh, sorry." Julia squeezed her uncle's hand before she removed hers. As she sat silent while the waitress fussed around the table, all the pieces of her conversation with her uncle rearranged themselves into a revelation.

If he hadn't driven her out of her comfortable bubble, she wouldn't have done any of the things she'd just listed for him.

"Can I get you anything else?" the waitress asked.

Carlos shook his head with a smile, and she went on to another table.

"It had to happen," Julia said, almost light-headed at the insight.

"What do you mean?" Her uncle looked up from his plate.

"I needed to grow, but not just in my art. In my life. My *Night Mares* are all about fear. No wonder you hated them. But my fear was holding me back, and I had to pull it out of me and trap it on the canvas." She knew she sounded delirious. "You did me a huge favor, Tío. You forced me out into the world."

"I don't know what you're talking about. The last thing I wanted was for you to take off in an untrustworthy car without any word of where you were going."

She locked her gaze with his, willing him to understand. "When I started to change the style of my work, you told me you didn't like it. I wasn't sure I liked it, either, but I knew I couldn't go back to what I had been doing. I had to keep going in the direction I had started. As the paintings got darker, you liked them less and less, but to me, they were becoming better, stronger." She waved her arms around, trying to pluck the right word from the air. "They came from a place inside me that I'd never visited before, a place I needed to explore."

"A place of nightmares," her uncle said. "Not a place art patrons want to visit."

Julia shook her head. "I was wrong to call them *Night Mares*. They're about taking risks, about facing the unknown. That's not a bad dream. That's real life."

"They are not beautiful like your other work."

"They have a different kind of beauty, one that comes from power." Her eyes burned with tears as she remembered the days of despair when she had to force herself to go to her studio. The times when the thought of painting another pretty pastoral landscape made it impossible for her to even pick up a paintbrush. "It was a terrible time for me, Tío, when you didn't believe in my work. I nearly stopped painting."

Carlos's fork clattered onto his plate. "You have a brilliant talent. It would be a terrible crime to stop using it."

"I think it would have killed me," Julia said simply.

Her uncle rubbed at his chest. "I never intended...you should have told me."

"I tried, but I felt so beaten down and alone."

Carlos lowered his head. "I never wished to cause you such pain. You are the daughter of my heart." He shrugged in regret. "I am terribly sorry, *mi niña*. I do not deserve it, but can you forgive me?"

She reached across the table and touched the back of his hand, her smile tremulous. "Of course I can. I love you very much, but I am not a *niña* anymore. That's the problem. It's been so easy to let you take care of me, but it's not healthy for either of us. If you hadn't threatened the one thing I can't live without, I never would have realized that."

"I was trying to protect you." Carlos shook his head. "You are fragile."

"No, I'm not." She sat up straight in her chair and thought of fighting through her panic on the back of Paul's motorcycle, of facing down Darkside when he tried to intimidate her with a thousand pounds of out-of-control horse. "I've learned that about myself."

Her uncle shook his head again. "You have not had to watch the child you love crash to the ground, her body convulsing, her limbs flailing, and know you cannot do anything to help her in her torment."

"No, I haven't," Julia said, seeing his genuine anguish in the tic of a muscle in his cheek. "But neither have you for seven years."

"It is hard to banish those images from my mind."

"For my sake, will you try?"

He made a restless gesture with his hand. "I will do my best."

"Good," Julia said, giving a decisive nod. She'd walloped Carlos with some pretty emotional stuff and he seemed to have heard her. Now came the hardest part. She spilled it out in one long rush. "This situation has shown me the necessity of putting my career on a more businesslike footing. I appreciate everything you have done to build my reputation as an artist, but I need to look outside the family now. Claire Arbuckle has agreed to be my agent."

She waited, her hands clenched around the wadded-up napkin in her lap.

Carlos rocked back in his chair. "I see. This is my punishment."

"No, it's business. Nothing more or less."

She expected an explosion, but he merely picked up his fork and calmly took a bite of trout. "If you hire Mrs. Arbuckle, you must tell her about your condition," he said, after he swallowed.

She stabbed a crab cake and shredded a piece from it. "I see no reason why it's necessary."

"She must keep you out of situations like Friday night."

Julia put down her fork. "You're missing the point. I *want* to be in situations like the reception." She took a deep breath and reminded herself to make this a *business* discussion. "I've reached a point in my career where I need to broaden my customer base. As you pointed out, my current work might not appeal to previous buyers. Claire Arbuckle has contacts in New York City so she can put my paintings in front of an audience more accustomed to edgier art."

"I thought I was protecting your reputation, not limiting your customers," her uncle said. Her plan to distract him from her epilepsy had worked. "Mrs. Arbuckle simply wants to make money from what you have given her now. It will sell because of the popularity of your older work, but she does not care about the long-term view of your career as I do."

His implication that her *Night Mares* were not good enough still stung. Then she remembered Paul's reaction the first time he'd seen her painting; it had given him a good wallop. He'd wanted it and he claimed never to have wanted a work of art before. Her chin angled higher. "Mrs. Arbuckle understands I have to move forward in my work."

"Then perhaps it is best I don't represent you." He flaked off another bite of trout.

Her mouth nearly fell open. *That was it?* He was taking his dismissal that calmly?

"Fortunately, I have invested your earnings carefully so you will never be without resources."

He must be desperate if he was invoking the gods of financial ruin. She spoke softly, trying to project the love she felt for him across the table and into his heart. "Let's go back to being family, not partners."

"We have been both for years."

"I love you, Tío. Don't let business drive a wedge between us."

Carlos put his fork down and raised his napkin to his lips. When he looked at her again, she saw hurt in his eyes. "You mean this, *mi querida?*"

She nodded, tears welling. She hated to cause him pain, but it was better to make a clean break now than to let it fester.

"Your paintings hang in the homes and offices of governors and movie stars and CEOs," he said, drawing himself up in his chair. "Why you feel that is not good enough I don't understand."

The tears spilled down her cheeks. "I—"

He waved his hand for silence. "I love you as a father loves a daughter, and I understand that children must rebel sometimes. So I will step aside."

"This will be better, I swear," Julia said, nearly choking on the lump in her throat.

"You know she will charge you forty percent commission?" he said, giving her a mock warning look. "I worked for only twenty-five."

Her laugh was shaky, but it was a laugh. She and Carlos would be all right.

"Verna, can you give me a lift to my house?" Paul said, as he closed the door after his last client before lunch.

"That fancy car of yours break down in the parking lot or something?" his secretary asked. She opened the bottom drawer of her desk and hauled out a purse the size of an overnight bag, ornamented with silver fringe and rhinestones. "Course I can give you a lift."

"Thanks, and the 'Vette is running fine."

She didn't ask why he needed the ride in that case, just walked out the door he held for her and waited while he locked up. It was one of the things he valued about her; she knew when not to probe.

Fifteen minutes later, he stood in his garage with the door open, stowing the cover for the Harley in one of the bike's storage compartments. He shrugged out of his suit coat and folded it into another compartment. He took his helmet and leather jacket off the hook on the wall and slipped both on.

Running his palm over the curve of the fairing, he let his eyes drift along the sweep of the exhaust pipes. It was a beautiful machine, and someone else needed to own it now.

He kicked in the stand and straddled the seat as he started the engine. For a moment he just stood there, feeling the power vibrate deep in his bones. Then he gunned it and peeled out of the garage with a squeal of tires.

Minutes later he turned into an alley stretching behind the block of buildings that included the theater. Parking the bike by the stage door, he removed the helmet and rapped loudly, hoping someone in the office would hear him.

The door swung open and an older man poked his head out. "Paul Taggart, as I live and breathe. What brings you to our back door?"

Paul waved at the motorcycle. "I brought in my auction donation, Lester. Is Belle here?"

"She sure is, but the auction's not till Saturday." Lester opened the door wider to let him in. "Don't you want to keep ridin' it for a few more days?"

Paul followed him along a dimly lit hallway. "Belle wants to put it on display in the lobby to drum up interest."

They walked into an office whose walls were plastered with brightly colored posters of plays the theater had produced in the past, some classics, some written by local talent. "Belle, Paul's brought his Harley for you."

The tiny woman behind the desk practically leaped from behind it. "Aren't you a generous donor? Letting us have your precious motorcycle early!" She clasped her hands to her breast and raised her eyes to what would have been the sky had they been outdoors. Her short, straight hair was bleached almost white except for the ends, which were dyed a deep teal. "I've already had Vincent set up a spotlight in the lobby to make it positively gleam. Can you two big strong men roll it in there for me?"

Paul held out the helmet and the leather coat. "You can add these to my donation."

She accepted the two articles of clothing as though they were the crown jewels, widening her eyes in admiration. "Maybe you could autograph the helmet," she said. "Mayor Paul Taggart."

"I'm not the mayor anymore," Paul said. "And nobody wants my signature except as a witness to their will."

"You're too modest, but I won't pester you."

"That's a first," Lester muttered under his breath. Paul gave him a wink as they followed Belle back down the hallway.

The two men wrestled the big bike into place under Belle's supervision. The chrome gleamed in the artfully placed spotlight, and Paul felt a jab of regret. The Harley had been his dream since he was a teenager. He took his suit jacket from the storage compartment, sliding his arms into it and settling it on his shoulders.

"Ah, I know what this needs to make it the perfect display," Belle said, trotting back to her office. She returned with the helmet and jacket. "We'll create the sense that you'll be back at any minute to roar off into the sunset."

When Belle draped the leather jacket over the seat and positioned the empty helmet atop it, Paul turned on his heel and headed for the door.

"Hope it fetches a good price," he said over his shoulder.

As the door swung shut behind him, Belle looked at Lester and then at her artistic arrangement. "What did I do wrong?"

Lester just shook his head knowingly. "A man and his hog. It's not something you'd understand."

Chapter 27

"M R. CASTILLO, IT'S A PLEASURE TO SEE YOU AGAIN."
Claire greeted them as they came through the
front door of the gallery, her hand held out, a serene smile on her
beautiful face. Julia envied her such composure in the presence
of Carlos.

Her uncle shook Claire's hand. "The pleasure is mine, Mrs.
Arbuckle," he said. "I understand you are helping my niece introduce her new work to the art world."

"Yes, her *Night Mares* are extraordinarily powerful, so I'm
excited about seeing their impact on our patrons. We have several influential critics attending the exhibition as well."

"Paxton Hayes. You are brave women, both of you, to solicit
his opinion." Carlos smiled as he said it, and Julia let out her
breath. She should have known he would be civil to Claire. After
all, this was business, and Carlos was a businessman through
and through.

Except when it came to protecting her. She was beginning
to comprehend the depth of his commitment to her well-being,
even if she didn't agree with the results.

"I wanted my uncle to see how you're going to display the
paintings," Julia said, feeling she needed to assert her presence
in the exchange. "It plays up the strengths of the *Night Mares*."

"Thank you," Claire said, looking as pleased as if she'd never
heard Julia's approval before. She turned to stand beside Carlos,

gesturing as she set the scene. "It will be evening, of course, so the illumination from the windows will be minimal. All the other paintings will be removed from the walls and the lights will be concentrated on Julia's art. Our guests will enter where you did and be directed into the circle of paintings. I want their experience to be immediate and undiluted by other people's comments." She smiled and gestured toward the entrance between the panels. "Shall we?"

Julia stepped forward with her uncle. She wanted to see his reaction to Claire's display. As they came into the space, a *Night Mare* charged directly toward her. She ignored it and slid her gaze to her uncle's face. He walked to the center of the arrangement and pivoted slowly. After a complete circle, he nodded once. "I understand your vision now. This will be a success."

Julia wanted to know whose vision he understood, hers or Claire's. However, he was already asking how the paintings would be priced. She had to settle for the satisfaction of hearing Carlos say the exhibit would be successful.

As her gaze skittered around the display, one painting caught her attention, the one Paul had admired. She'd offered it to him in payment for rescuing her and he'd turned it down. "Claire," she said, interrupting the conversation, "I don't want to sell this one. I'll get one of the others shipped up here to replace it."

"I can facilitate that," Carlos surprised her by saying.

Claire's eyes lit up. "How many more do you have?"

"Worthy of a public exhibit? Maybe three."

"That's marvelous. We can add all of them to the show."

"You can return home with me to choose the ones you want," Carlos said to Julia.

He thought he had set a neat trap, but she wasn't falling into it. She shook her head. "There are things I need to finish up here. If you photograph the remaining *Night Mares* and e-mail me the images, I can tell you which ones I want."

Her uncle bowed his head in agreement and a subtle acknowledgment that she had won that round.

"Now it's time for my riding lesson," Julia said.

Julia took Carlos back to the inn so she could change. She left him talking to Lyle about the antique rifle while she ran upstairs to throw on jeans and a white cotton blouse. As she walked to the door, she noticed the Civil War sword she'd bought for her uncle, wrapped in brown paper and propped up beside the mantel in her suite's sitting room. Maybe this was a good time to give it to him, as a sort of peace offering. She smiled at the irony and picked up the weapon. Remembering Paul's comment about the blade's symbolism, she rummaged around in her purse for a penny and slipped it into her jeans pocket.

She found her uncle in the now-empty dining room with Lyle, inspecting a print of a battle fought near Sanctuary. The innkeeper smiled and excused himself when he saw Julia approaching. She hid the package behind her back with one hand and held out the penny to Carlos with the other. "I have something for you, but you have to buy it from me."

Her uncle sent her a baffled look before he took the penny, standing with it in his hand.

"Give it back to me now," she said, holding out her hand palm up, just the way she did when she fed carrots to Darkside.

He laid the penny on her palm with the same dubious expression, and she brought the sword around to present to him. "I found this in an antique store here and thought of you," she said. She'd had to ask Claire to vouch for the check she used to purchase it, since the weapon was expensive and she didn't want to put it on her credit card.

Carlos took it in both hands, saying, "But you were angry with me."

"More sad than angry, and you are still the uncle I love."

Relief chased the confusion from his face and he gave a little bow. "Thank you. From my heart."

"Open it!"

He placed it on a heavy oak sideboard and carefully peeled the tape off, unfolding the paper from around her gift. The sword lay gleaming against the dull brown wrapping, its brass hilt and iron sheath showing the unmistakable patina of over a century's age. "It's a light cavalry saber from 1860," Julia said, reciting what the proprietor of the store had told her.

Carlos touched the hilt. "This is a gift of great generosity." His voice had a hitch in it and he blinked several times.

"You deserve it. Do you like it?" His profile was to her, and Julia couldn't read his expression. She was worried he might already have something similar in his collection.

He turned and she thought she saw the sheen of tears in his eyes before he swept her into a bear hug. "It is perfect, *mi querida.* Like you."

They held each other for a long moment, her uncle's arms wrapped around her so tightly it was hard to breathe. Julia knew this was her uncle's way of communicating his regret and his love for her without the words he found so hard to say.

He released her and dashed the back of one hand against his eyes. "But why did we need to exchange a penny?"

"My lawyer says the gift of a blade is symbolic; it means you wish to sever the relationship, which is the opposite of what I wanted the sword to do. So I couldn't give it to you as a present. You had to buy it from me." She kissed him on the cheek. "We should go."

He rewrapped the saber with painstaking care and carried it outside to the sleek sedan he'd hired for the day, carefully supervising as the driver stowed it in the trunk. Once she and Carlos were settled in the back, her uncle said, "You mentioned a lawyer."

Julia didn't want to discuss Paul with her uncle. "I needed someone to draw up the agreement between Claire and me for the exhibition." It was partially true.

"There are many kinds of lawyers, not all of them good."

Julia waved an airy dismissal. "Oh, mine's the best lawyer in town, a former two-term mayor."

"Humph, a politician. Perhaps I should examine the agreement he drew up." He was frowning and tapping his finger on the armrest between them.

She put her hand over his to still it. "Tío, this is *my* business now."

He grunted but allowed her to change the subject to Sharon's many equestrian accomplishments, including her Olympic gold medal. She hoped he would be so dazzled he would believe Sharon could teach a total beginner to control Darkside in six days. She didn't mention she'd only ridden the stallion once, at a walk, with a lead line.

"Ms. Sydenstricker is not aware of your epilepsy?" her uncle asked, as the tires crunched over the gravel in the parking lot at Healing Springs Stables.

Julia glared at him as she gestured toward the driver and hissed, "No, and I don't want her or anyone else here to know."

Carlos had the grace to look guilty, and she knew he hadn't considered the driver's presence. He didn't apologize but he did drop the subject.

She exploded out of the car, nearly bowling over the driver when she flung open the door he was attempting to hold for her. "Sorry," she muttered, giving the man a grimace of a smile and hoping professional drivers had a code of confidentiality similar to lawyers and priests.

Her uncle came around to stand beside her and survey the immaculately maintained buildings and fences with obvious approval. "Your friend keeps her place well."

"She's a pro," Julia said, starting toward the indoor riding ring.

When Julia had explained she was bringing her uncle, Sharon insisted on a controlled environment. "It's bad enough to have Taggart breathing fire about you riding Darkside. I don't need a family member on my back too. I'll have him tacked up and ready so we keep it simple."

"What about his bridle?" Julia asked, remembering their previous difficulties.

"I'll take care of it."

Now she was glad Sharon had the foresight to give her uncle only the briefest glimpse of her mount before she got on him. As they passed through the barn, several stable hands greeted Julia. "Back for another joyride on Darth Horse?" one asked.

"I like to push my luck," she said.

Carlos turned to her with a question in his eyes. Julia shrugged. "Stable humor."

Their feet sank into the deep, cushiony mixture of sand and sawdust as they walked through the big open door of the indoor riding ring. Shafts of sunshine speared from high windows onto the ring's dark surface, motes of dust dancing in them. Julia blinked a few times as her eyes adjusted to the change in light level. Then she saw Darkside standing on the other side of the ring, Sharon holding his head.

He looked…unhappy. That was the only word for it. His back was bunched up under the saddle, and he kept shifting from one hoof to another as though he couldn't get comfortable. She forgot all about her uncle as she jogged across the ring to soothe him.

"What is it, buddy?" she said while she ran her hand down his neck. It felt tense too.

She looked at Sharon.

"We had a little disagreement about the bridle," Sharon said.

"So he's grumpy. You might want to rethink your timing."

Carlos walked up, his face like a thundercloud. "This is the horse you are learning to ride on?"

Darkside threw up his head at the angry tone. Sharon staggered slightly as she hung onto the bridle.

"Easy, boy," Julia said, taking the reins from the other woman and leaning her forehead against Darkside's. "I'm here. We're going to have a ride together."

"You cannot ride this horse," Carlos said, planting his feet apart. "He is a stallion."

"He's my whisper horse," Julia said, keeping her voice neutral and soothing. "We understand each other."

"What are you talking about?" Carlos hovered, clearly wanting to separate her from the horse but afraid to set off the big creature with Julia so near him.

"Julia and Darkside have a special bond," Sharon said. "They help each other out. That's what a whisper horse is about."

Carlos spun to face Sharon. Julia watched in astonishment as her usually imperturbable uncle flushed and took a step back from the tall horsewoman. "My apologies," he said as he held out his hand. "I am Carlos Castillo."

"Sharon Sydenstricker," she said easily, giving his hand a firm shake.

"You are the owner here," he said, gesturing around the building. "It is very impressive."

"It's right nice of you to say so."

"You are also an accomplished horsewoman. My niece is honored to be instructed by you."

Darkside nudged Julia in the shoulder. "Maybe I should get started with my lesson."

"I reckon so," Sharon said, taking the reins from Julia to slip them over Darkside's head. "Grab that helmet from the post. We'll use the mounting block over there."

Julia fitted the helmet on her head as she followed Sharon to the wooden platform. Her uncle stood frozen where he was.

Even with the added height of the mounting block, Julia had to hurl herself upward to get onto Darkside's back. As she settled herself into the saddle, the tense arch of Darkside's back seemed to relax underneath her. She told herself she was imagining things, but then Sharon said, "He's feeling better already, just having you on him."

"Are you sure?"

"Hon, I might lie to you about whether your jeans make you look fat, but I'd never lie about a horse."

A surge of confidence swept through Julia as she fitted her feet into the stirrups and positioned her hands on the reins. Sharon checked the girth and stepped back. "Take him around clockwise."

Julia's confidence ebbed as she looked around the huge echoing space. "What about the lead line?"

"You want your uncle to see you on a lead line?" Sharon gave her knee a pat. "You'll be fine in here. No rabbits."

Julia straightened her back and sucked in a deep breath before she clucked to Darkside. The big horse moved out instantly, heading for the track worn along the perimeter of the ring. Julia's heart sang as she felt her body meld with her whisper horse's. This was the joy Papi had tried to give her with that first riding lesson. Until the epilepsy had ruined it.

She felt panic touch her throat with cold fingers. Her body tensed, and Darkside's ears swiveled back as his pace increased. "It's okay, buddy, take it easy. My past just tried to grab me, but you're going to help me outrun it. Except not literally, so slow down."

As soon as she stopped speaking, Darkside's ears swiveled forward and he dropped back into a smooth walk. "Phew!" Julia said, blowing a lock of hair up off her forehead.

As she came around the corner and started down the long side of the ring, she tried to read her uncle's reaction.

His shoulders were rigidly squared, but he gave her a faint smile. Self-consciousness had her checking that her heels were down, her elbows tucked in at her sides, her knees steady against the saddle skirt. Having an audience containing one of the most important people in her life seemed unfair when this was only her second time on a horse.

"The hell with Carlos!" she said, as realization dawned. "I'm here for you, buddy." She transferred the reins to one hand and leaned forward to stroke Darkside's strong, gleaming neck. "We're going to learn together. You need to know how to be a normal horse, and I need to figure out how to ride you."

The next pass by her gallery, she flashed a brilliant smile. Her uncle gave her a little salute, his posture more relaxed. It buoyed up her spirits even further, and she turned her concentration to exploring how best to communicate with her whisper horse. She watched the beautiful, eloquent movement of his ears, let her body shift with the bunch and reach of his powerful muscles, and felt the signals traveling along the reins. All her other concerns faded into the back of her mind.

Half an hour later, Sharon slipped into the ring and waited for her. "You're going to be mighty saddle sore if you don't stop now."

Sharon walked over to the mounting block beside her. "Be careful, hon. Your muscles may not hold you up at first."

Julia swung her right leg over the back of the saddle and slid slowly down to the wooden platform. When her boots touched it, she felt her knees begin to buckle.

"You okay?" Sharon asked.

"Give me a second and I will be." She sent all her willpower to her thighs, commanding them to keep her upright. Taking a breath, she released the saddle. A slight sag and then she was standing on her own.

Now she just had to walk down three shallow steps. As she lowered her foot to the first one, muscles she didn't know she needed screamed at the unaccustomed use. Once she was on the level, it wasn't so bad, except she felt the disorienting sensation of being unusually low to the ground.

She wobbled around to Darkside's head and ran her fingers under the straps of the bridle, scratching where she thought it might itch. He reciprocated by rubbing his head up and down her chest, nearly knocking her over. "Hey, save that for when I don't have legs made out of rubber." She looked up at Sharon. "I understand why you do what you do."

The other woman nodded. "Wait till you take him over a jump."

Julia laughed in disbelief.

"It won't be long before you'll be begging me to do it. But we won't advertise that to your uncle." Sharon jerked her head in his direction.

Forcing her legs to move in a semblance of normalcy, Julia walked over to where he stood. "What did you think?"

"A beginner does not belong on that horse, but you handled him well." He nodded in approval.

From her uncle, it was high praise.

Sharon led Darkside up to them. Carlos reached out to run a hand over the horse's shoulder. "He's a magnificent creature. Do you breed him?"

"I haven't but I may now," Sharon said. "I worried about his temperament before he met Julia."

Julia grinned. "I have a soothing effect on difficult personalities."

Sharon gave a little choke of laughter. "I'm going to take him back to his stall for a good rubdown."

"Wait," Julia said, wrapping her arms around Darkside's neck so she could speak into his ear. "Thanks for a good ride, buddy. I owe you a carrot." She gave him a pat and turned to her uncle. "Shall we go back to the inn so I can get cleaned up?"

"I will drop you off there, and then I must return home."

"You're leaving?" Carlos kept knocking her off balance.

"I believe that is your preference."

"I—" She swallowed. "As long as you come back Friday. I want you at my exhibition."

"Wild horses would not keep me from it." He gave her an impish smile. "You planned today well, *mi querida*. My eyes are opened."

Another soak in a hot bath eased the new aches and pains created by her ride. As soon as she was dry, she texted Paul: "Carlos vanquished and in retreat back to NC. What time will you be free?"

The answer came back almost instantly: "Two hours. Where will you be?"

"The studio." She wasn't lying when she said she needed to make some progress on her auction donation. Julia wiggled into snug jeans and a T-shirt before brushing her damp hair into neat waves and leaving it down over her shoulders to dry. Grabbing her cell phone, she skipped down the steps of the inn.

As she strolled along the streets of Sanctuary, she soaked up the unusual combination of paint colors on one Victorian and a quirky shingle pattern on another, the warm patina of antique handmade brick, and the pattern of light and shade under a tulip poplar. The town seemed to glow with the same satisfaction she felt.

Her relationship with Carlos was on a whole new footing. If her uncle was still hurt by the change, he had chosen not to reveal it, and she was grateful to him for that. For all her sense of betrayal, she loved him deeply and hated to cause him pain. There would probably be occasional skirmishes going forward, but she believed her uncle respected her right to make her own decisions now.

Her next hurdle—and it was a much higher and wider one—was Paul's conviction that Sanctuary would somehow stifle her career. He couldn't make her leave, of course, but she knew what a towering wall of easy, inconsequential cordiality he could raise between them. If he decided their relationship should end for her own good, he would slip right out of her fingers.

Her calm evaporated, and she banged open the screen door of her studio. "Stubborn, do-gooding man!" she huffed as she thrust her arms into the sleeves of her paint-splattered overshirt.

Stalking over to the easel where Darkside's portrait sat, she felt a stab of panic. The auction was two days away and the painting had a long way to go before it was finished. Seizing her paints, she began squeezing colors onto the palette and shoved all thoughts of anything but a huge, troubled black horse out of her mind.

"Did you say Carlos Castillo wants to see me?" Paul said into the telephone receiver, not sure he'd heard Verna correctly.

"That's right," she confirmed. "No appointment, but…"

"I'll be right there." Paul stood and went to the coatrack to retrieve his suit jacket. He shrugged into it and straightened his tie before he pulled open the door. Striding into the reception area, he spotted a trim older man of medium height, his dark hair salted with silver strands. "Mr. Castillo? Paul Taggart. It's a pleasure to meet you." He offered his hand.

Carlos took it in a firm grip and gave him a courteous smile. "I appreciate your willingness to meet with me when I have no appointment."

"Of course, sir," Paul said, escorting him into his office and closing the door. "I'm a friend of your niece's."

"Ah, I thought you were her lawyer," the older man said, as he settled into the chair Paul indicated. Paul took the chair beside him, turning it to make the arrangement friendly.

"Contrary to popular belief, lawyers are capable of friendship," Paul said, giving Carlos a rueful smile as an invitation to share the joke. He was treading carefully since he had no idea what Julia had told her uncle about him or why her uncle had chosen to come here.

Carlos did not return the smile, and Paul could see why Julia found him intimidating. The man wore his well-tailored suit with all the authority of a Fortune 500 CEO.

"Julia tells me you have drawn up the agreement for her new agent, Claire Arbuckle," Carlos said. "I wish to see it."

"Well, sir, I'd like to help you out, but there's the matter of attorney-client confidentiality." He kept his tone light to rob his words of any offense. He also hid his surprise, since no such agreement yet existed.

"But I am her uncle and stand in loco parentis to her." The other man's voice was even but held an undercurrent of command.

Paul nodded. "Julia has spoken of you with great respect and affection. However, she is my client, so I cannot breach my professional responsibility to her." He knew he was stretching it to call Julia a client since they'd never had any formal arrangement, but it made a convenient excuse.

"Have you ever drawn up such an agreement before?"

"Yes, sir. There are several local artists whom Mrs. Arbuckle represents. I handled all of their agreements." Paul tamped down his irritation at having his competence questioned.

Carlos leaned forward, his hands on the arms of the chair. "None of them are of the same caliber as my niece. She is an artist with an international reputation, which will only continue to grow. Her situation requires a sophisticated, airtight contract."

As his temper began to simmer, Paul reminded himself that Julia had just fired her uncle, so he was probably feeling cranky and hurt. This was his way of compensating. His voice was calm as he said, "Believe me, I have Julia's best interests very much at heart. I can draw on several resources at large law firms known for representing clients in the arts, if necessary." He decided not to let Carlos get away with his veiled insults entirely. "May I add that I have known Mrs. Arbuckle for many years and can vouch she is a person of the highest integrity."

"In your profession, I am sure you have noticed integrity can be overwhelmed by large amounts of money."

"Sometimes even by small amounts," Paul said, working hard to keep the edge out of his voice. However, he'd had about enough. "Mr. Castillo, I understand your concern, but this is between Julia and myself."

Carlos sat back in his chair and simply looked at Paul, his expression giving nothing away. "Are you the reason Julia has refused to come home?"

Paul hadn't seen that coming. "Why would you ask me that?"

The other man's gaze never wavered. "A little conversation here, a little conversation there, and the pieces begin to fit together."

Paul just barely stopped himself from rolling his eyes in exasperation at the impossibility of privacy in a small town. "I haven't asked Julia to stay here."

Carlos snorted, a surprisingly inelegant sound from such a controlled man. "My niece has developed a mind of her own recently. I don't think it would matter whether you asked her or not."

Paul was surprised into giving him a nod of agreement. "Very true, sir."

"I wanted to meet you for myself," Carlos said, standing up.

Paul leaped to his feet as well. "And I you."

For a long moment, they measured each other. Carlos nodded. "Now we have met." He held his hand out to Paul. "Julia is the daughter of my heart. Remember that."

When Paul shook the older man's hand, Carlos exerted just enough pressure to make sure Paul understood his warning.

"I'll keep it in mind," Paul said, his tone casual, his smile nonchalant. He respected the man's concern for Julia, but he was damned if he was going to kowtow to it.

"Will you be at my niece's exhibition on Friday?" Carlos asked as they walked to the door.

"I'm looking forward to it."

"Good. She may need our help," Carlos said, turning to go.

"Where is this adventure taking place?" Julia asked, as Paul gunned the 'Vette up the hill leading out of the town.

"You'll know when we get there." Without taking his eyes off the road, he reached over and took her hand, twining his fingers with hers and bringing it back to rest on the console between them.

"I guess I'm dressed all right," Julia said, eyeing his faded jeans and West Virginia University T-shirt with some relief.

This time he glanced sideways, his gaze sliding quickly down her body. An appreciative gleam sparked in his eyes. "Since you insist on wearing clothes, you're dressed just fine." His expression turned serious. "Your uncle came to my office."

"What! I didn't even tell him your name," Julia said.

"You didn't need to. This is Sanctuary."

Carlos must have weaseled it out of his hired driver. "Does Carlos...what did you talk about?" She couldn't quite bring herself to ask if her uncle knew they were lovers.

"Yes, he knows we're together."

"Oh." She realized she had tightened her grip on his hand and forced her fingers to relax. "Um, what exactly did he say?" She couldn't imagine Carlos asking Paul if he was sleeping with her.

"He wanted to know if I was the reason you refused to come home."

"How did you answer that?"

"It didn't matter, because it became apparent he already knew." He threw her a quick glance. "He came because he wanted to put me on notice to behave."

Julia grimaced. "I'm sorry. It's none of his business." Her uncle meant well, but it was humiliating to have him meddle in her love life. She needed to make sure he understood that was as off-limits as her professional life.

"Truth be told, I wanted to meet him." He gave her hand a light squeeze. "It's not a bad thing to have someone care so much about you."

"Just suffocating at times."

"How did he take being fired?"

"Well, he threatened me with the loss of my reputation and total financial ruin. Neither one worries me."

"That's my Julia." Paul gave her a quick flash of a smile. "Did he admit to lying about showing your work to dealers?"

"He didn't lie. He just showed it to dealers who couldn't handle the edgier style." She sighed. "He didn't believe in it enough to explore new markets."

"I'm sorry. I know that was rough on you." He lifted her hand to give it a gentle kiss. "At least your uncle seems to have accepted the inevitable, because he wanted to make sure I wrote up an airtight contract between you and Claire."

Julia groaned.

"Don't worry, I stuck up for Claire." Paul slotted the car into a space on the street and turned to her. "You've had a hard day, sweetheart. Are you sure you don't want to go back to the inn and rest?"

"Not a chance. Distract me."

"You got it."

Julia looked out her window to discover they were parked in front of the Black Bear. She was little disappointed since he'd promised her an adventure.

Her door opened, and Paul pulled her up from the car's low seat. Slinging his arm around her shoulders, he guided her through the Bear's front door, past the sparse Wednesday night crowd, to a closed door off the side of the main seating area. He reached forward and threw open the door with a flourish.

The room was small and empty except for a foosball table positioned in the center and a couple of chairs set around a small round table in the far corner.

"I'm going to teach you to play my favorite game," Paul said.

Excitement raced through Julia. She wanted to be able to share this with him. She walked to the table and put her hands on two of the rods. "Show me what to do."

For the next hour and a half, he had her practice rod technique, execute carom shots, dance the ball from man to man, and explicate strategy. All the while awareness simmered between them as he stood behind her, his hands over hers on the grips, demonstrating a play. Or he faced her across the table, his hands flashing from grip to grip, his face lit with passion for the game he loved.

As he complimented her on a tricky bank shot, certainty flooded through her like molten steel.

There was no way on earth she was ever leaving this man.

Chapter 28

I NEED A BEER," PAUL SAID, SENDING TWO RODS INTO A
blurring spin before he stepped away from the table.

Julia swiped the back of her wrist across her forehead. "This
is hard work."

"You're a natural. Must be your visual ability. You understand angles better than a lot of experienced players. And you've
got strong hands."

"Years of holding palettes and paintbrushes." Julia braced
her hands on the edge of the table and leaned on them. "You're a
tough teacher."

"I want to make sure you've got a firm grasp of the basics."
He opened the door and held up two fingers to someone she
couldn't see. "That way you won't get into bad habits when I'm
not around."

Julia understood. This was a gift he wanted to give her before
she went off to the glitter of international fame.

"You got quiet all of a sudden." He came up behind her and
wound his arms around her waist, nuzzling his lips against the
side of her neck.

"My electrolytes are depleted. I need that beer." His breath
blew warm against her skin, sending wavelets of pleasure cascad-
ing down her spine. She crossed her arms over his, wanting to
stay wrapped in him like this forever.

"I'd say get a room, but you have one." The waitress gave Julia a wink as she bustled over to the round table and set down two mugs and two bottles. "Lock the door behind me, will ya? The Black Bear is a family bar." She chuckled as she pulled the door closed.

Paul slid one arm out from under Julia's and pulled her toward the table. "Let's get you some electrolytes, otherwise known as Sam Adams."

Julia let him settle her and himself in the chairs. She grabbed the bottle before he could pour it into a mug and tilted it back for a long, hard swallow of beer, like the cowboys in movies before they slammed through the saloon doors to shoot it out in the street.

She put her bottle down on the table with a *thunk*. "I'm not leaving."

He'd been lounging back, his chair balanced on two legs, watching her with an admiring gleam in his eyes. Now his chair's front legs banged onto the floor. "I'm not sure what you mean."

"Sometimes you're such a lawyer," she said. "I mean I want to stay here with you."

"We've had this conversation already." His fingertips beat against the table.

"No, we had a different one. Because I didn't tell you the truth."

His fingers stilled.

She rotated her beer bottle in her hands, not sure if she should look him in the eye or if it would be better not to see his reaction. She lifted her eyes to his. She could read nothing; his mask was in place. She summoned up the courage to keep watching him. "I love you. Not because you give me great orgasms, but because of who you are. If you make me leave, I'll be miserable, no matter what city you think I should drag myself off to in the name of my career."

He surged out of his chair and walked over to the foosball table, smacking the goalie rod so it bounced across the playing surface. "How do I spell this out for you? I don't want you here." She felt as though the rod had slammed into her own chest. "Why not?" She tried to make her voice strong, but failed entirely. He rounded on her. "Because I can't leave. How do you think I'll feel when I can't go with you to celebrate your opening in Paris or London or wherever? What about traveling to find new inspiration for your art? You'd have to go alone while I'd be back here in Sanctuary, pretending I wasn't missing you and worrying about you every second of the day." He paced back and forth in front of her. "You'll be growing and absorbing new things and I'll be stagnating here. One day you'll come home and wonder what the hell you're doing with this ignorant, unsophisticated hick."

"That won't happen," she whispered.

"The hell it won't." He dropped back into his chair.

"Maybe you're not giving your brother enough credit."

"What my brother has can't be fixed. You don't understand what it's like to live with an incurable disease."

How wrong he was about that.

"As long as Eric is here, I am my brother's keeper."

"Have you asked Jimmy what he thinks?"

"He got drunk when he thought I might take a job in Washington. That's all the answer I need."

"Are you sure that's why he did it? Maybe he felt guilty about you not taking the job because of him."

Anger flared in his eyes. "You don't know what you're talking about."

She braced herself. "I know what it's like to have people assume I need to be protected without asking me. Your brother went through a very tough period, and you came home to help him with it. You're still seeing him as he was then. It might be time for both of you to look at it from a different perspective."

Couldn't Paul see how similar he was to Carlos? No, because she was still withholding an important element of her life from him.

"I'm not your uncle, if that's what you're thinking." It was uncanny how he'd read her mind. "My situation is entirely different."

She wrestled with herself, trying to summon the courage to tell him about her epilepsy. Every time she began to form the words, her throat closed up. Paul already thought she needed protecting from herself. How much worse would it be if he knew there was a reason for Carlos's constant concern?

"Will you talk to your brother? If not for your sake, then for mine?" She attempted an appeal to his chivalrous side.

He looked away. "I spoke to his AA sponsor. He painted a pretty bleak picture." He brought his gaze back to hers and his tone softened. "You need to be realistic about this."

Panic hit her as she realized he was determined to sacrifice both of them for his brother. She stood up. "Look at Darkside. Everyone gave up on him except Sharon. She knew he just needed someone to believe in him. Maybe your brother needs you to believe in him."

His face hardened to stone. "Are you accusing me of encouraging my brother to drink?"

"Of course not." She put her hands out as though to push his question away. She was making a huge mess of this. "I just want to find a way for us to be together."

"Sometimes life doesn't give you a way," Paul said.

"It doesn't matter that I love you?" She offered her heart once more, hoping he wouldn't rip it out of her chest.

He dropped his hand into his lap. "You don't know that."

"If you're going to reject me, at least don't patronize me." She tried to whip up some anger to give herself the strength to survive the rest of the conversation. "I'm very clear on my feelings for you."

"I'm not rejecting you." She thought she heard a rasp of pain in his voice.

"What do you call it?"

"Self-preservation."

"Oh, don't give me that crap." She couldn't believe he was back to trying to convince her he was protecting himself, not her. "Just take me back to the inn. I'm too ticked off to talk to you any more tonight."

The look he gave her killed her rant. It was filled with longing and regret, pain and resignation, and she could swear something that looked like it might be what she hoped for. Then he said, "Sweetheart, we won't ever talk about this again."

Julia hovered inside the front door of the inn until the Corvette growled away. The ride home had been silent and excruciating as she kept her gaze away from the one place she wanted to look: Paul's face. She'd told him to stay in the car and, infuriatingly, he'd done as she asked.

As the engine noise faded into the quiet night, she jogged back down the steps and onto the sidewalk, striding along the quiet main street of Sanctuary, her tears giving the streetlamps halos. The headlights of a cruising car caught her in their glare, and she turned toward a dimly lit window display in one of the closed stores, swiping at the wetness on her cheeks.

Arguing with Paul was like running head-on into that plate glass window. She hurled herself against his conviction that he knew better and bounced off, rubbing her head at the pain of the impact. How could she break the damned glass and get through to him?

She knew how: tell him about her epilepsy. Maybe he would pity her, but at least he would understand she wasn't the perfect woman he kept holding her up as. He'd see her as flawed, as weak, as someone who needed his protection.

"No!" She slapped the glass with her open palms, the impact stinging.

Playing the pity card was out. She'd worked too damned hard to tear off Carlos's suffocating cocoon.

She started walking again, turning down the street to her temporary studio. She leaped up the three porch steps and slammed open the door. Light from the neighboring houses filtered through the glass walls at the back of the room so she could see her painting of Darkside on its easel. In the dimness, his gaze looked uncertain, confused.

She mashed the light switches to see if the impression lingered when the picture was better lit. "That's not right," she said, frowning. Darkside had never been uncertain. He'd been willing to pay the price to keep his spirit from being broken. There was strength in his anger.

She understood and she was going to stay pissed off as long as she could. Because the alternative was to believe Paul didn't want her or her love.

Whirling, she stomped over to the counter to pick up her palette and brushes. By the time she was done, Darkside was going to be the scariest horse in the world of art.

Chapter 29

"J ULIA?"

A woman's soft voice tugged Julia out of her dream-infested sleep. Her eyelids felt so heavy, she could only manage to open them to slits. She tried to lift her head but yelped as neck muscles that were contorted in an uncomfortable position spasmed. A blanket of misery weighed her down even though she was too groggy to remember why.

"I'm here," she croaked, realizing she was huddled on the derelict sofa in her studio. She connected the voice with Claire and struggled to push herself upright.

"Oh my God, are you all right? What happened?" Claire knelt in front of her, her face set in lines of concern.

Julia kneaded the knot of discomfort in her shoulder. "I painted all night and was too tired to walk back to the inn. What time is it?"

Claire slid onto the couch beside her. "A little after ten. I've gotten a few worried phone calls. Where's your cell phone?"

"It might be in the garbage can." She'd turned it off and tossed it there to keep herself from waiting for a call that wouldn't come. Now she remembered why she felt so awful. "Did Carlos call you?"

"And Paul."

His name sent a jagged edge of pain ripping through her. "He has some nerve worrying about me."

Claire's gaze turned soft. "He practically begged me to find you."

"We had a disagreement."

"Hmm. Verna told me he looked like someone dragged him through the woods backwards, and you look like, well, it's hard to describe."

"That bad?"

Claire smiled. "Your eyelids are red and swollen. You have paint pretty much everywhere, including your eyebrows, and I wouldn't want to be the one who has to untangle your hair."

That sent another jab through Julia as she remembered the feel of Paul's fingers gently working the snarls out of her hair. She hitched in a breath as she absorbed the blow. Changing the subject seemed like a good idea. "What did Carlos want?"

There was a moment of silence before Claire answered. "To let you know the extra paintings you requested are on the way here." She scanned Julia's face. "I've known Paul for years, and he has a protective streak a mile wide. Whatever he did, I'm sure he didn't mean to hurt you."

Julia shook her head, trying to retrieve some of the anger she'd felt the night before. Maybe she'd poured it all out onto the canvas. Her gaze strayed to the easel, and she sat up straight.

Darkside glared out at the world with a ferocity she thought would make most viewers take a step backward.

Claire followed the direction of her glance and gasped. "That's how you see your whisper horse?"

"One side of him. It's his anger that gave him the strength to survive in a bad situation." Satisfaction warmed Julia as she took in the changes she'd made to her work.

Claire stood and walked over to the painting, stopping a few feet away. She stood silent for several moments, and Julia could see the connoisseur in her stance and focus. "I see it now. You've layered the anger over the vulnerability. He's using the anger but not defined by it. There's a yearning underneath." Claire turned back to Julia. "He wants to be loved, like all of us."

Julia felt her defenses disintegrate into dust. She dropped her head into her hands as a sob racked her body.

"I'm so sorry." Claire sat down beside her and drew her into a hug. Julia leaned against her friend. "I feel like an idiot."

"Why?"

"Because I've known Paul for all of ten days, and I feel this horrible about leaving him."

"Don't leave him then."

Julia lifted her head to see something like hope flit across Claire's face. "I'm trying. He's not cooperating."

"That's interesting, because Paul once commented that Tim couldn't force me to leave Sanctuary."

"Tim tried?" Julia pulled away from Claire and used the corner of her smock to wipe her nose.

"He had what he thought were good reasons."

"So does Paul. He's just wrong."

Claire laughed and covered Julia's hands with hers. "You're exactly what Paul needs. You remind him of the person he used to be. I hope you won't give up."

Julia thought of Paul turning away as she told him she loved him. Her shoulders sagged. "I'm running out of ammunition."

"Then you need to reload. Go see your whisper horse. That's what I did when Tim got difficult."

"It's hard to picture your husband as anything other than madly in love with you," Julia said, thinking back to the dinner party where she'd envied the way they looked at each other across the table.

"Oh, he was madly in love with me back then." Claire stood. "He just couldn't handle it."

Claire had driven her back to the inn, and after one glance in the car's rearview mirror, Julia had been glad she did. It had taken over an hour, but she was finally free of paint and her hair waved in a smooth, civilized fashion. Now she prowled around the table where her cell phone sat, also cleaned up after its sojourn in the trash.

Did she have the courage to invite Paul to see her ride Darkside?

It was the last way she could think of to shock him into believing she could handle herself and her life.

But could she? Exhaustion and despair surrounded her like a fog, not the best condition in which to deal with a high-strung horse. Being rejected again might just destroy her.

Deciding she didn't want to feel like this any longer, she swiped at the phone, barely catching it as it spun off the table. Punching the speed dial for his office, she indulged in a moment of cowardice.

"Hi, Verna, it's Julia Castillo. Do you know what time Paul will be finished with work today?"

"He's running 'em through quick, mostly likely because he's surly as a bear. I'd say he'll be done around three thirty."

"Would you ask him to meet me then at Healing Springs Stables? Tell him it's important."

"He should be done with his appointment in about ten minutes. You want to ask him yourself?"

"No, no, I can't. I'm, er, going to be in a meeting the rest of the day." Julia smacked herself on the forehead for not thinking of a better excuse. What she intended to do was take a long nap.

"I guess there's a reason for his bad attitude," Verna said. "I'll make sure he gets to the stable. Don't you worry about that, hon."

Paul complained about everyone in a small town knowing your business, but Julia liked having allies.

❖

"You want to ride outdoors without me even being in the paddock with you?" Sharon bent her head and rubbed her hand across the back of her neck as she considered Julia's request. "That's mighty risky."

"Paul's coming to watch," Julia said.

Sharon's head came up. "You tryin' to prove something?"

Julia nodded.

"Well, Taggart will probably rip me a new one, but I guess I understand a thing or two about proving yourself." She glanced at her watch before she turned and headed toward the tack room. "We got about forty minutes before he's due. Let's get the kinks worked out of Darkside before then. He's in his usual paddock. You go tell him what's up while I get the tack."

Julia peeled off for the paddock. She loved that Sharon expected her to explain what she needed to the horse. They both believed Darkside would help her out if he understood.

The stallion was trotting in circles at the far end of the field as he watched a horse being schooled in the paddock next to him. The beauty of his movements made her stop so she could savor the way his muscles rippled under the dark satin of his coat. After a long moment of admiration, Julia slipped inside the gate and started toward him across the springy grass. Darkside's head swung around, and he whinnied shrilly before hurling himself into a series of stiff-legged bucks that brought him closer and closer to her.

"Hey, buddy, it's me," she called, freezing in place. Maybe she had overestimated her influence over him. She fumbled in her pocket as his big hooves pounded the turf like a boxer hitting a punching bag. "I've got carrots."

He kept coming, over a thousand pounds of muscle and bone she had no way to stop. She held out the puny bit of carrot, feeling like a lunatic. "You want a treat?"

He planted his front feet and skidded to a halt inches away from her outstretched hand. After blowing out a couple of loud breaths, he lowered his head and delicately lipped the carrot off her palm.

As the adrenaline drained away, her knees nearly buckled under her. She wrapped her arms around his neck as much to hold herself up as to thank him. "I should have trusted you, shouldn't I?" she crooned in his ear as he went through his usual exploration of her pockets. "You were just playing with me."

Suddenly, tears were streaming down her cheeks and she buried her face in his neck, letting her weight fall against his chest and shoulder. He was so solid and warm; she felt as though his strength was being transferred to her own body, where it hummed with almost electric energy. She clung to him, soaking up the power and comfort of the huge creature.

"You let me know when you're ready." Sharon's voice came from outside the fence, pitched low and calm so as not to disturb the stallion.

Julia surreptitiously dried her wet cheeks on Darkside's coat. She unlocked her arms from him and walked around to look him in the eyes before she touched her forehead against his. "I need your help here, buddy. You have to give me the ride of my life today because I'm going to have a very important spectator. You do this for me, and I'll be staying here to feed you carrots for the rest of your days." She stepped back and took his head between her hands. "You got that?"

Darkside didn't do anything as hokey as nodding his head, but she felt the understanding between them.

Between the two of them, the stallion was tacked up in record time. Sharon threw her up on his back and checked the girth and the stirrups twice. "I guess you're good to go," she said. "Remember what I told you about using your leg signals. And there's no shame in grabbing a handful of mane if you need to."

"I appreciate your letting me do this against your better judgment," Julia said, sensing Sharon's reluctance to let her go off on her own.

"Just take it slow." The other woman gave Darkside a pat on the shoulder and walked back to the gate.

Julia closed her eyes for a moment, letting her weight settle deep into the saddle. Now all that power and muscle was beneath her, controlled by two slender strips of leather and the pressure of her legs. She opened her eyes and squeezed her knees lightly.

In an instant, they were in motion, the horse's powerful strides eating up the ground as she guided him toward the rail. As he turned obediently onto the path that ran around the perimeter of the paddock, exhilaration fizzed through her veins.

She could ride.

After a couple of circuits, Sharon began calling out helpful suggestions from her perch on the paddock fence. Julia turned Darkside through figure eights and backed him up without any trouble.

"Someone trained that horse right before Earl got hold of him," Sharon said. "You want to try a trot?"

"Don't I have to practice posting first?" Julia knew she had to rise and fall with the horse's gait. Her stepfather appeared to do it effortlessly, but she didn't fool herself into thinking it was easy.

"Nah. It'll come natural once he starts moving. Just let his motion push you up, then sit back down."

Julia tightened the reins and gave Darkside another squeeze with her legs. Suddenly, she was bouncing all over his back, her teeth banging together with every step the horse took. His ears swiveled toward her as though asking what the heck was going on back there.

"Up. Down. Up. Down," Sharon chanted in time with Darkside's hoofbeats.

Julia flexed and released her knees, trying to keep up with her instructor's voice, and then it happened. She found the rhythm. "I'm doing it. I'm posting!"

They trotted around the paddock twice before Sharon told her to drop to a walk. "Otherwise your muscles will start screaming."

Julia signaled Darkside to slow down and leaned forward to pat him on the shoulder as they approached Sharon. "I never thought I'd be able to trot on a horse." She nearly bit her tongue as she realized what she'd said. Luckily Sharon didn't read anything more into it than a beginner's nervousness.

"That horse has a trot smooth as satin," Sharon said. "Course it took all I had to keep him from turning it into a flat-out run when I rode him. For you, he's acting like a school pony." Julia couldn't help the proud tilt of her chin. She was riding a horse who gave trouble to a gold-medal equestrian.

As she left Sharon behind, Julia relaxed into the now-familiar motion of Darkside's athletic stride. She couldn't help wondering what it would be like to experience the surge and power of those muscles at a full gallop. He was a racehorse, after all, bred for the thrill of competition. He must miss it. She patted him again. "You're going to have to wait awhile for that, buddy."

They came around the corner of the path to head back toward Sharon's perch, and Julia glanced up to find another figure beside her, one whose tall, lean silhouette she recognized instantly. Her breath caught in her throat and she stiffened, making Darkside pick up his pace. "Easy, boy," she said absently.

In her excitement about trotting, she'd forgotten the real purpose of this riding lesson. She tried to slow down Darkside to give herself time to think, but the big horse wasn't amenable to shortening his stride. Giving up on that, she scanned the man standing beside Sharon, trying to read his mood from his posture before she could see his face.

He was wearing a white shirt, the sleeves rolled up to his elbows, pale-gray slacks, and black loafers, so it looked like he'd come straight from the office. He stood outside the fence, his forearms crossed on the top rail, while one toe was slotted between two lower rails. He seemed to be looking directly at her, so she straightened her back, tucked in her elbows, and pushed down her heels. Not that she thought Paul cared about her form on horseback. His concern had always been for her safety.

As she got closer, he turned his head to say something to Sharon, but she couldn't distinguish the words above the thud of hooves and creak of saddle leather. The deep timbre of his voice sent a shudder of awareness through her. Sharon replied, and Paul turned back to watch her approach.

She pulled Darkside to a halt in front of her audience. "Thanks for coming, Paul," she said, her voice squeaking slightly. She cleared her throat. "I wanted you to see how well Darkside and I are getting along."

His silver gaze was shuttered, giving away nothing. "You and he look good together." A flicker of hope warmed her before Paul continued. "Maybe you can talk Sharon into selling him, so you can take him home with you."

She flinched and her reaction set Darkside sidling sideways. Somehow she focused her attention on the horse enough to bring him to a stop again. It gave her time to absorb the very deliberate blow Paul had dealt her.

Maybe he was angry because she'd dragged him out to the stables without an explanation. Or because she was on Darkside's back. Or both. But it was unlike him to lash out. Even Sharon was eyeing him with surprise.

"I don't think Sharon wants to give him up." The prospect of losing both Paul and her whisper horse was what had kept her awake and painting the night before. She decided to give herself time to think. "I just learned to post."

Signaling Darkside to move, she urged him into a trot and began posting. Sharon called out something about diagonals, but Julia was too lost in the misery of Paul's comment to pay attention.

Why had she thought it was a good idea to force him to watch her ride a horse he thought was dangerous?

Sharon's words about Darkside behaving like a school pony for her drifted into her memory. A spine-steeling rush of confidence snapped her out of her funk. Even if it made him mad, Paul needed to see her in control of something powerful, something risky. She needed him to see her that way.

Out of nowhere, a deer sailed gracefully over the fence and landed in the paddock. Darkside shied hard right, and Julia pitched out of the saddle to the left, her back scraping against the fence before she walloped into the ground, knocking the air out of her with an "oof." She lay staring up at the sky, trying to suck oxygen into her deprived lungs. A string of curses and the pounding of hooves sounded distantly in her ears before Paul's face appeared in her vision.

"Julia! Julia, are you all right? Can you see me? What hurts?"

She felt the frantic but featherlight brush of his fingers down her body as she opened and closed her mouth like a beached fish. No words came out, just a few ragged gasps.

"Jesus!" He fumbled in his back pocket. "I'm calling nine-one-one."

She rolled her head from side to side, trying to stop him. "I...I'm..." she gasped again, "fine...no...air..."

He ignored her as he pushed the buttons on his cell phone and held it to his ear. After a few seconds, he pulled it away and looked down at it with a scowl. "Goddamn it, there's no reception here." He turned his head and shouted, "Sharon, can you get someone to call an ambulance from your office?"

The spasm in her diaphragm eased and she managed to draw a shallow breath. "Don't call. Just got the wind knocked out of me." She wasn't actually sure of that, since her focus had been on breathing and preventing his phone call. Now she tried to test her arms and legs with subtle movements so he wouldn't notice. Much to her relief, no sharp jabs of pain resulted from her efforts. She struggled up onto her elbows.

"Don't move," he snapped. "You might be injured and not realize it." His voice was rough but he cradled her head and shoulders gently, easing her back onto the ground.

She stayed down but grabbed his wrist and shook it. "No ambulance. I'm not hurt. Don't embarrass me."

"Embarrassing you is the least of my concerns," he said.

Sharon's face appeared opposite Paul's. "Where does it hurt, hon?"

"In my pride," Julia said, her voice still wispy.

The worry left Sharon's eyes as she sat back on her heels. "You've got grit."

"But no sense," Paul said. "I want you to move one limb at a time. Slowly and carefully."

Deciding she'd offered him enough provocation already, Julia obeyed. Satisfied, he slid his arm under her shoulders and helped her sit up, removing her riding helmet and probing her scalp for lumps.

"I shouldn't have worried about your skull because it's so damned thick," he muttered.

A giggle escaped her, and she heard Sharon choke. No answering smile lightened Paul's stormy expression as he pushed off the ground and rose to tower over her. "I have to go. Sharon, I'm counting on you to make sure she has no lasting damage."

With that he turned and walked away, his gait stiff and angry.

"Guess that backfired," Julia said, clasping the hand Sharon offered her and standing up.

"Maybe. Maybe not." Sharon watched Paul slam the gate shut, making Darkside dance away and yank at the reins tying him to the fence. "You got a pretty strong reaction out of him."

"Yeah." Julia sighed. "But it was the wrong one. He's right back to thinking I don't know what's good for me."

"Maybe he says that, but it's not what he's thinking."

Julia gingerly explored the sore spots in her back. "What do you mean?"

"He couldn't take his eyes off you while you rode Darkside. It was like you were some kind of goddess, come down from Mount Olympus. That's how he looked at you."

Julia smiled sadly as she remembered Paul calling her a wood sprite. "Then I went and fell off my pedestal."

Her ploy had been a mistake right from the beginning. Instead of seeing her as strong and independent, Paul saw her as foolhardy and willful. Riding Darkside worked with Carlos because he didn't know the horse's history. Paul understood the size of the risk she was taking. Which should make him realize she was willing to take the risk of loving him. He accused her of having a thick skull, but his stubbornness equaled hers and then some.

Julia picked up her helmet and fitted it back on her head. "There's one thing I know about falling off a horse."

"What's that?"

"You have to get right back on."

Paul wrenched the wheel of the Corvette hard right, sending the car skidding onto the gravel shoulder. He shoved the gearshift into park and bolted out of the car. It was close but he reached the weedy verge before he bent over and threw up.

"Goddamned fish sandwich," he muttered, his hands braced on his knees as he waited for the surge of nausea to subside.

But that wasn't the culprit. It was terror, pure and simple. The terror of watching the huge black stallion toss Julia against the fence like a rag doll before he tore off around the field bucking and kicking, the metal shoes on his hooves flashing in the sun. All Paul could think of as he raced across the paddock toward Julia's motionless body was Darkside's previous owner in a wheelchair. He heaved again, although nothing came up.

If he thought about it rationally, he knew Darkside had behaved like any normal horse when startled. The stallion had jerked sideways, and Julia, being an inexperienced rider, hadn't been prepared. She had simply fallen off and the fence had been in the way.

He moaned as the image repeated itself in his mind. At least he didn't retch again. Straightening, he swung open the passenger door and grabbed the bottle of water he always carried, rinsing and spitting to clear the nasty taste from his mouth.

His stomach lurched, so he closed the door and leaned against it with the cool bottle pressed against his aching forehead.

This whole situation was his fault; he had indulged himself in an affair with a woman he knew would leave him in her dust. He would nurse a memory so brilliant and vivid, no other woman would ever be able to measure up. But he could live with that. Welcomed it even, knowing how badly he'd screwed up.

What had kept him tossing all night was the expression on Julia's face when he'd told her he didn't want her here. How he had found the strength of will to force those words out of his mouth he would never understand. When he saw the terrible hurt in her green eyes, he'd nearly told her the truth: that he wanted to lock his arms around her and keep her with him in Sanctuary forever. Instead he had taken her brave, honest declaration of love, thrown it on the ground, and ground it into the dirt with his heel.

Another image shimmered through his brain. His Julia looking so tiny atop the massive black horse, her hair flaming in the sunshine, her face lit with excitement as she said, "I just learned to post." The moment was burned into his memory along with the emotions roiling inside his chest: awe, fear, and a love that took his breath away. *Julia* took his breath away: her courage, her passion, her generosity. God, she was magnificent.

And he had to let her go.

His gut clenched so hard, he dropped the water bottle and doubled over. He stayed that way until the wave of overwhelming pain passed. Then, feeling like an old man, he bent down gingerly to retrieve the plastic bottle.

Pulling in several long breaths, Paul got his stomach under control. He glanced at his watch and realized he was going to be late arriving at Jimmy's house. His brother had asked him to come by for some unspecified reason. The timing stank big-time, since Jimmy was the reason he was in this pain. No, that wasn't fair to his brother; Paul knew what his responsibilities were. He had just chosen to push them to the back of his mind until he had to face the consequences.

Right now he wanted to get on his Harley and ride until he drove into the Pacific Ocean. Oh yeah, he couldn't do that because he'd donated his hog to the charity gala.

Today was truly the day from hell. And it wasn't going to improve at Jimmy's.

He shoved himself away from the car and walked around to the driver's door, swinging it open and levering himself inside. Taking the mountain curves too fast was the only outlet he could allow himself, but he was still half an hour late pulling up at Jimmy's door.

"Sorry I'm late, Jim," Paul said, as his brother opened the front door. Light from the low-hanging late afternoon sun illuminated the trim, and Paul noticed it had been freshly painted.

"No problem, bro," Jimmy said, waving Paul in. "Want some iced tea?"

What he wanted was an entire bottle of Scotch, but if Jimmy had one, he wouldn't confess to it. "Sure."

As his brother collected glasses from a cabinet and a filled pitcher from the refrigerator, Paul realized Jimmy's hair was newly trimmed. He glanced around the room with startled attention. No dirty dishes moldered in the sink. The stove top was scrubbed clean.

"Is Eric coming over later?" Paul asked.

Jimmy looked up from pouring the tea. "No, he's at Terri's. Why?" "Just wondered."

"He's got a half day of school tomorrow, so we're heading out to the state forest tomorrow at lunchtime for our camping trip." Jimmy's blue eyes blazed with anticipation.

"You taking any Doritos?"

Jimmy laughed as he handed Paul his glass. "I'm strictly enforcing the no-food-in-the-tent rule. I got no interest in meeting a skunk in my skivvies."

"Good move," Paul said, following his brother into the living room.

"Have a seat," Jimmy said, waving Paul to the couch while he sat on the edge of the recliner. He scooted a coaster over to the corner of the coffee table and set his glass on it.

Paul sank onto the burgundy cushions and wondered what the hell was going on. His brother had never used a coaster before in his life. He'd also never walked into the living room without turning on the television.

Jimmy set his elbows on his knees. He cleared his throat but his voice still came out low and raspy. "I've been thinking a lot since Saturday. About Saturday and before that." He laced his fingers together and cracked his knuckles. "One of the things you're supposed to do in AA is make amends to the people you've hurt with your drinking."

Paul started to interrupt, but Jimmy stopped him. "You're one of them. You've given up a hell of a lot for me. And then I go and repay you by doing something stupid like I did Saturday."

Paul let his brother take the time he needed.

"I got scared last week," Jimmy said, looking down. "Real scared because of your job offer. I know Terri made you swear not to leave me alone even when Eric wasn't staying with me, because she was afraid I'd go over to her house and get violent. I was scared you'd take the job and she'd move away with Eric to put distance between her and me."

A couple of tears spilled onto Jimmy's cheeks and he scrubbed them away with the back of his hand.

"Jim, you know I wouldn't do that," Paul said, feeling the usual exasperated frustration rubbing at him like sandpaper.

Jimmy nodded and swallowed hard before he said. "Yeah, but Saturday I lost it and I tried to drown the fear in booze. I didn't even want it, but I kept drinking because I couldn't face the idea of a life without Eric."

Paul felt his mouth twist into a grimace of understanding. *Hadn't he just felt the same way about a future without Julia?*

Jimmy lifted his eyes and looked at Paul straight on. "I called Adam on Tuesday and went to talk to him. We've talked a lot since then. I understand something really important now. You are not responsible for keeping Eric in my life. I am. If I don't love my son enough to stay sober even when he's not around, then I don't love him enough. Period."

Paul sat forward as his brother said the words he'd always hoped to hear.

"I've made a commitment to myself and to Terri and most importantly to Eric, although he doesn't know it," Jimmy said. "I will stay sober for the rest of my life, one day at a time, because I love my son down to the bottom of my soul."

Conviction rang in Jimmy's voice, and Paul felt a tightness in his throat.

"I told you about making amends, so I went to see Terri." Jimmy picked up his glass and took a sip of tea. "I told her how sorry I was about what I'd done to her and our family." He looked at Paul over the top of the glass. "I asked her to release you from your promise."

Paul was afraid to hear Terri's answer. "It's not a promise; it's a legal document."

Jimmy ignored him. "After we talked for a long time, she said she'd be willing to consider it as long as I keep going to the AA meetings." Jimmy dropped his gaze, his throat working. "She thinks I'm being a good dad to Eric nowadays."

Paul had to swipe at his own cheeks to dry them. His brother had finally found the strength to be a worthy father to Eric.

His brother straightened abruptly to look Paul in the eye. "I'm going to earn your way out of that promise to Terri, I swear. I'm going to make sure you're free to live your own life again."

Paul felt something like hope unfurl in his chest. His brother might have a long road to walk, but at last he was taking the first real steps. Paul stood and walked over to him. "Jimmy, you've made me proud." He opened his arms, and Jimmy rose and stepped into the embrace. Paul hugged him hard. "Real proud."

Chapter 30

*J*ULIA HELD THE EDGES OF DARKSIDE'S PORTRAIT GINGERLY
as she jabbed her elbow against the buzzer. Claire had
closed the Gallery at Sanctuary for the day to get ready for the
exhibition that evening, so the front door was locked. Belle
Messer, the gala auction organizer, had persuaded Claire to
exhibit the portrait tonight to drum up interest in the gala and
perhaps entice some big spenders to attend.

The door swung open, and Tim Arbuckle towered over her.
"Let me give you a hand with that," he said in his rumble of a
voice.

"Thanks but it's still got some wet spots. Just point me to an
easel." She'd gone over to her studio that morning to put some
finishing touches on the painting, adding her signature in bright
turquoise blue so any prospective bidders could see it clearly.

Tim led the way to an easel set at an angle in one corner of
the gallery. "Claire wants it here in the lights, away from everything else. Displayed like a rare and precious gem, she said."

Claire's description brought some welcome warmth to the
fog of desolation surrounding her. Julia gave Tim a grateful smile
and eased the canvas onto the stand.

As she stepped back, Tim crossed his arms and planted himself in front of the portrait. The strong lights brought up a tint of
auburn in the hair curving onto his forehead. Julia wished she
were staying longer so she could paint the big man as a gift to

Claire. He pursed his lips in a low whistle. "This painting has layers on layers. You need to study it to understand them all."

She shouldn't have been surprised; Tim was married to a very sophisticated art dealer. But she hadn't expected such perception from a man who seemed so straightforwardly a country veterinarian.

Something of her reaction must have shown in her face because Claire laughed as she came up to slip her hand through the crook of Tim's elbow. "He fooled me too when I first met him. He's a collector of equine art, so one of your *Night Mares* just might find its way into his collection. Not that I will show any favoritism."

"The only reason she married me was to get her favorite Castillo painting back," Tim said, his eyes glinting with mischief.

The love enveloping the two of them made Julia ache, so she turned toward the *Night Mares.* "You opened up the space more when you added the new ones," she said, sweeping her hand around the circle of panels. "It looks great."

"And we can get more people into the exhibit at the same time," Claire said.

"Let me move that last chair and then I have to go vaccinate the Cruikshanks' new cows," Tim said, dropping a kiss on the top of his wife's head. He picked up a leather armchair like it was a paper cutout and strode off down the back hallway with it.

Claire tugged Julia over to the couch, which was now positioned near the desk. "Tell me what's happened," she said, pulling Julia down beside her on the cushion.

Julia knew she looked like hell. She'd passed up dinner the night before because her stomach had tied itself in a knot that refused to unravel. This morning, the smell of pancakes and bacon had twisted the knot tighter.

She'd spent the sleepless night drawing Paul's face over and over and over again, trying to empty him out of her mind and onto the paper. She'd awakened this morning on the sofa, a snowstorm of torn pages blanketing the floor around her.

"I love Paul," she said to Claire, "but he doesn't feel the same way."

Concern shadowed Claire's brown eyes. "I think you're wrong. He just has a very complicated set of responsibilities."

"He told me." Julia swallowed hard. She had also decided she wouldn't cry over him anymore, but that was proving difficult. "I'm not asking him to shirk them. He's the one who thinks he can't do both."

Claire frowned and looked away. "I was afraid of that."

"I know you're old friends and you're worried about him," Julia said. "I threw everything I could at him, but I can't break through that wall he's put up. He doesn't love me enough to let me in." It was the conclusion she'd reluctantly reached after her long night of reliving every moment of their time together.

Claire sighed. "I really thought…" She shook her head.

"I feel like I've swallowed a gallon of brush cleaner, but I'll never regret loving Paul," Julia said, wobbling up off the divan. "Now I've got to get the painting over to his office. Verna told me he has a fifteen-minute opening right before lunch."

Claire stood and enveloped her in a hug. "I hope you can get him to keep it."

"That's why I want witnesses."

They walked down the hallway to a room filled with artwork neatly slotted into wooden racks. "I got my framer to do a rush job on it so Paul can hang it immediately." Julia started to stammer a thanks, but Claire waved her into silence. She pulled out a big bubble-wrapped canvas and lowered it to the floor. "How are you going to get this there?"

"Carry it."

"On foot? It's pretty big and unwieldy."

"More witnesses. And I'm used to carrying big canvases around." Julia took a breath and met Claire's eyes straight on. After the woman's kindness in having the painting framed, Julia felt even guiltier about what she was about to say. "I know I promised to stay for the auction tomorrow, but do you think I could decline? My uncle is flying home Saturday morning and I thought I'd go with him. I don't think it will hurt the bidding all that much if I'm not at the gala."

Claire's eyes brimmed with understanding. "Of course you can go home. I'll deal with Belle. You've done more than enough."

Julia nodded in gratitude. Bending her knees, she grabbed the two handles the framer had considerately attached to the picture's wrapping on one side. "As long as I don't run into a high wind, this won't be too hard to carry," she said, as she straightened with the painting held against her right hip. It topped her head by a couple of feet and reached to the middle of her shins.

"There's no question people will notice you," Claire said.

"That's my plan." She'd learned the power of social pressure from Paul himself. If everyone knew she'd given this to Paul, he would have a hard time returning it.

Hefting it to a slightly more comfortable position, Julia followed Claire to the front door and maneuvered the painting through it. She was grateful for the bubble wrap as she banged one corner into the doorjamb as she turned. This was going to be a little harder than she anticipated.

Setting off toward Paul's office, she kept watch for pedestrians, flower tubs, benches, and lampposts, all of which populated the sidewalks of Sanctuary. A glimpse of a particularly abundant tub of purple and yellow petunias lit by late-morning sunshine stirred her with its simple but lavish beauty. She drank in the sound of tires on pavement, greetings called to acquaintances, and during a lull in traffic, the trill of a robin perched in one of the linden trees lining the street.

Several men across a range of ages offered to give her a hand with her burden, reminding her of the friendliness she'd come to cherish here. People in Sanctuary might know each other's business, but they also pitched in when that business got sticky. She thought of Verna, who was aiding and abetting this little escapade with relish. Isolated as she'd been at home, it surprised and delighted her when someone she barely knew lined up beside her to help.

She needed to carry the painting herself, but she let everyone know where she was going with it. That information earned a few approving winks and nods, which brought an ache to her throat. She didn't explain this was a farewell gift.

It took a couple of rest stops but she finally made it to the Victorian house where Paul worked. She clumped up the steps and put her package down to swing open the heavy oak-and-glass door. Edging the painting through the opening, she leaned it against the banister of the staircase as she closed the door behind her. When she turned, Verna was gesturing her into Paul's reception area.

"You are a sight for sore eyes," Verna said, helping her guide the big canvas through the doorway. "His last appointment canceled, and I've been keeping him busy with finding old documents on the computer."

"It's heavier than I thought, so I had to rest once or twice." Julia propped the canvas against some chairs.

Verna eyed the painting, which seemed to take up half the room. Julia frowned as she realized she'd only seen the *Night Mare* in her large studio at home or a wide-open gallery space. Maybe the scale was too big for any place Paul had to hang it.

She couldn't worry about that now.

"Verna, do you really need the Snedegars' divorce papers right—" Paul stopped in the door to his office as his gaze met Julia's. Something flared in his eyes and then the mayoral smile closed the shutter on all emotion.

"If it's not my favorite artist." He walked over and gave her a kiss on the cheek. "Did you stop by to look over the contract with Claire? Verna, can you print that out for me?" He turned away a little too quickly to be convincing in his unconcern.

Julia closed her eyes to brace herself against the yearning response of her body to the all-too-brief touch of his lips. She swallowed and opened her eyes again. The back of his pale-blue shirt stretched across his shoulders as he leaned over Verna's desk. Shoulders whose skin and muscle and bone she had explored with her fingers, even raked her nails over in moments of passion. She tucked her fingers into her palms to keep herself from skimming them over the warmth of his body one more time.

This was harder than she expected.

"Here you go," Paul said, holding a stapled document out to her. He had to lean forward slightly to bridge the distance between them. As soon as she grasped the papers, he took another step backward. Glancing at his watch, he said, "I guess we could take a quick pass through it now." His gaze went past her and narrowed. "What the—?"

She took a certain pleasure in knowing he'd just noticed the giant painting in the room. It meant he'd been focused entirely on her. "It's the *Night Mare* you admired. I'm giving it to you."

The easy smile slipped slightly as his jaw muscles went rigid. "I seem to remember telling you I couldn't accept such a valuable gift."

"I carried it all the way over here by myself and I'm not carrying it back."

He glanced at Verna, who sat behind her desk, not even pretending to work. "I imagine I can find someone with a pickup truck to take it back."

Unlike Paul, Julia didn't care what Verna heard. She squared her shoulders and locked her gaze with his. "Don't reject this gift too."

He flinched. "Maybe we should discuss this in my office." He swept his hand toward the open door in a command she decided to obey.

She preceded him into the room, hearing the door click shut behind her. He kept his back to her as he walked to the other side of the desk. When he turned, his mask fell away. "I'm no art collector. What the hell will I do with something that valuable?"

"Remember me when you look at it." His stony refusal tore at her.

He rested his fists on the desktop and leaned forward, his voice low and sibilant. "Your memory is burned into every cell of my body."

"Oh." The words seemed flattering, but he said it as though he regretted the fact.

He collapsed into his chair. "I'll keep the painting but please leave now."

"I have to tell you one more thing." She perched on the edge of the chair closest to his desk.

He lifted his head as though it weighed a ton. The fingers of his left hand beat a near-silent tattoo on the blotter.

She cleared her throat. "I didn't want you to know this about me, but I owe you the truth."

"Sweetheart, you don't owe me anything. Quite the opposite."

"I owe you this." She twined her hands together in her lap. "My uncle had a reason for being so overprotective. It's why I'd never learned to ride a horse. Or ridden a motorcycle or swum in a river."

Paul's fingers stilled.

"I had epilepsy." She said it carefully to make sure it was in the past tense. She couldn't look at Paul yet, so she stared at the shape her hands made. "The first time Papi put me on a horse, I had a seizure and fell off. He caught me so I wasn't hurt, but he never wanted to risk it again. So I drew horses instead." She hazarded a glance at Paul. His face gave away nothing.

"You say you *had* epilepsy." His enunciation was as careful as hers. "Does that mean you no longer have it?"

"It's not a question with a yes or no answer. I haven't had a seizure in seven years. Two years ago my doctors allowed me to stop taking my antiseizure medication." She faltered to a stop.

"So are you cured?"

"As long as I don't have another seizure I am. Many people grow out of epilepsy if it develops when they're children. I seem to be one of them."

"Seem?"

She shrugged. She wasn't going to lie to him. "I believe I'm cured."

He folded his hands together on his desk. "Why didn't you tell me?"

"Because you would have treated me differently."

"You're damned right I would have. Do you realize how dangerous—" The volume of his voice rose until he cut himself off. "Of course you do," he said levelly. "You deliberately withheld the information."

Despite her resolution, Julia felt tears burn in her eyes. "I didn't tell you because you wouldn't have taken me riding on your motorcycle or to the river or—"

"Jesus Christ!" He surged to his feet, sending his chair slamming into the wall. "How do you think I would have felt if you'd gotten hurt? Or worse?"

The tears spilled down her cheeks and she dashed them away with her wrist. "I wanted you to see me as a normal person."

"There's nothing normal about you. I've been saying that all along." He stalked over to the window.

She fought down the sob threatening to tear out of her throat. "Maybe I'd better go."

He turned, his arms crossed. "I've been telling you that for days. You don't belong here."

She wiped her eyes one last time and stood up, her head high. "I don't regret anything I've done."

"Wish I could say the same. I could have hurt you several times over. When I think about the hazardous situations I put you in…"

"I'm sorry you feel that way, but I had a chance to leave my past behind and I took it." She risked a quick glance at his face. His jaw was clenched tight and a vein pulsed at his temple.

She retreated to the door, stopping as she put her hand on the doorknob. Keeping her eyes on the wood panel in front of her, she said, "Will you still come to the reception tonight?"

"I'll be there." His words were as sharp as broken glass.

She nodded and opened the door. Verna swiveled her chair around, but Julia held up her hand in a silent plea.

"You go on then, hon," Verna said. "It's none of my business what happened in there."

Julia got herself out the front door and down the steps before the sobs broke through.

She'd feared his pity, but she hadn't been prepared for his anger.

Chapter 31

$\mathcal{P}$AUL RAN A YELLOW LIGHT RIGHT IN FRONT OF A TOWN
police car. The cop waved and let him pass. Terri had
just called to say Eric was in the hospital after some sort of serious accident involving bees. She was on her way from her job, but
Paul was closer so he'd volunteered to offer backup to his brother.

Slamming the 'Vette into a parking space, Paul raced
through the doors to the emergency room and strode straight
to the admittance counter. For once he blessed living in a small
town because he knew the woman behind the desk. "Afternoon,
Iris. Can you tell me where my nephew, Eric, is?"

She scanned the computer screen. "Room F. Go through
those doors, and take a left." She looked back up. "He's going
to be okay. No anaphylactic shock, no trouble breathing. Dr.
Bhattacharya's treating the bee stings now."

"Much obliged," he said, some of his fear draining away.

He walked through the doors and down the corridor, reading the signs beside the doorways. As he approached Room F,
Jimmy's voice carried clearly to his ears. Paul slowed to listen. "I
had tweezers in the first-aid kit so I got Lisa to pull the stingers
out while I drove here. I told her to clean the welts with the sani-
tary wipes and put some ice on them."

"I couldn't have treated him better myself," a voice with a
faint British accent said. Dr. Bhattacharya.

"I took a first-aid course before we went camping last year," Jimmy said. "I even bought an EpiPen, but I told Lisa not to use it unless Eric had trouble breathing."

Paul stopped. *Jimmy had studied first aid?* This was news to him.

"Has Eric ever had an allergic reaction to bee stings?" the doctor asked.

"Nah, just the usual. But he stirred up a nest this time and got stung pretty bad, so I figured I'd better bring him here."

"Ow! Sorry, ma'am, but that hurt," Eric said, and Paul smiled and leaned against the wall, his head cocked. His nephew's voice sounded strong and slightly irritated.

"My apologies," Dr. Bhattacharya said, "but I have to count the number of stings, just for our records."

"There's about a million," Eric said. "And they itch."

Dr. Bhattacharya chuckled. "You're getting an intravenous antihistamine for that. You've already had the epinephrine injection, so I'm going to take you off oxygen. However, we're going to keep you here at the hospital overnight, just for observation."

"You mean I can't go back camping?" Eric's voice sagged with disappointment.

"We'll find another weekend to go," Jimmy said.

The last of Paul's worry ebbed. If Eric was ready to get back to his tent, he couldn't be feeling too bad.

The doctor gave a few more instructions and left the room, heading for Paul. He pushed off the wall. "Dr. Bhattacharya, I'm Paul Taggart, Eric's uncle."

"Of course," she said.

"I overheard what you said in there." He nodded toward the room. "Just tell me what the prognosis is."

"Eric's father knew exactly how to treat the stings, so there shouldn't be any infection. I'm keeping the child overnight because the swelling and discomfort may worsen, and we can handle that better here. If there hadn't been 'a million' stings," she smiled, "I'd send him home now."

"That's a relief."

The doctor continued past him and Paul ambled into Room F, his brain working furiously to process this new perspective on his brother.

Jimmy jumped up from the chair beside the bed. "Paul! You didn't have to come."

"I know. You've got this under control." Paul held his brother's gaze to let him know he meant it. "But Terri was worried, so I said I'd check in." He reached out and ruffled his nephew's hair. "First a skunk and now a swarm of bees. Maybe you should give up camping."

"No way!" Eric said. Paul winced inwardly as he saw the masses of angry red welts clustered on the boy's skinny limbs. "I won't get into bees again because now I know what they sound like."

"He heard a weird noise and decided to go find out what it was without telling anyone," Jimmy said, subsiding into the chair. "Next thing I know he's hollering that he's being attacked. I've never run so fast in my life."

Paul dropped a hand on his brother's shoulder. "Good thing you were a sprinter in high school."

"I'm out of training," Jimmy said. "It felt like it took forever to get to Eric."

Paul gave Jimmy's shoulder a squeeze before he dropped his hand. "Next thing we know he'll be bringing a bear cub back to camp with its angry mama in full pursuit."

"Pa says never to get between a cub and its mama," Eric said. "You'll get eaten."

"Your pa knows what he's talking about," Paul agreed. "Well, bub, looks like you're going to live, so I'm going back to work."

Jimmy looked up in surprise. "You're not staying?"

"You don't need me," Paul said, the truth of his statement nearly making him light-headed.

The two brothers looked at each other in silence. Jimmy straightened in his chair. "I guess you're right about that," he said, his blue eyes lit with pride.

Paul walked out of the emergency room doors into the sunshine and inhaled deeply, filling his lungs with the soft summer air. He felt so light he might just float away, swimming through the puffs of white cloud above him.

His nearly overwhelming impulse was to find Julia. He had to tell her she was right to believe people—and horses—could change.

Since she'd been right about that, he was going to trust her about being cured of epilepsy too. Of course, he was still going to be careful. He shook his head. That was exactly why she'd refused to tell him about her condition. He grimaced as he realized she would never give up riding Darkside. That would be his private cross to bear.

As he walked slowly to his car, head down, hands shoved into his pockets, he remembered the disaster of their last meeting. When she said the word *seizure*, guilt and horror at what might have happened to her had overwhelmed all rational thought. All he could think of were the fast and furious motorcycle rides he'd taken her on, and the guilt had made him turn ugly.

She'd been right about how he would have treated her if he'd known about the epilepsy. He would have wrapped her in cotton wool just like her uncle did. Hell, he still wanted to. So he had to change. Even more important, he had to convince her he could.

Chapter 32

HERE, YOU LOOK FABULOUS," CLAIRE SAID, PUTTING down the makeup brush and adjusting one of the jeweled chopsticks holding Julia's loose bun in place. "Take a look." She gestured toward a large mosaic frame that contained geometric pieces of silvered glass held in place by lead strips.

Julia walked over to the art mirror and planted herself in front of it. The shimmering copper-colored triangles of her Villar blouse fell over slim-fitting brown suede slacks. Her feet and calves were encased in the fantastically expensive embroidered chocolate-brown boots from the Laurels. She wore her chunky amber earrings and necklace on their swoops of silver along with a wide silver cuff Claire had loaned her. With her hair swirled up on top of her head and the slightly dramatic makeup job Claire had given her, she had to admit she looked like a successful artist.

A miserably unhappy successful artist.

She stuck her chin up and squared her shoulders. People she cared about had worked very hard to make this reception happen and she was not going to let them down by moping. Forcing the muscles in the corners of her mouth upward, she turned back to Claire. "Look out, Paxton Hayes."

"Just remember our strategy for handling him and you'll be fine."

Davis Honaker, Claire's partner in the gallery, bustled into the office. In his white linen suit, he was the archetype of a southern gentleman. He rubbed his hands together. "The bar's set up, the canapés are arranged, and Darlene's by the door with the guest list. She's a little grumpy because I made her spit out her chewing gum."

Claire stood up, smoothing her palms over her black satin trousers. The sleeves of her turquoise silk blouse fluttered as she moved. "I'll get the music started."

Julia narrowed her eyes as she realized Claire might be nervous too. She was trying to think of something reassuring to say when Tim walked in, wearing a charcoal-gray suit that had obviously been tailored for his big frame. Julia's mouth nearly fell open as she took in the transformation. She watched husband and wife's eyes meet and stopped worrying about Claire. The other woman had all the support she needed.

"Sorry I'm late," Tim said, kissing his wife on the forehead. "I had an emergency surgery on a golden who ate a pair of socks."

Julia choked on a nervous laugh and Tim swung around to look at her. He gave her one of those slow, warm smiles that made her understand why Claire had fallen for him. "You look mighty fine," he said. "Just the way I picture an artist about to take the art world by storm."

"Where is everyone?" Sharon's voice boomed down the hallway.

"Back here in the office," Claire called, "but it's getting a bit cozy. We'll come out there."

The group moved into the gallery. Julia got a quick look at the bar gleaming with glassware and colored bottles, where one black-clad server deftly pulled a cork while his five colleagues chatted quietly. Sharon strode up to her, dressed in dark pants and a white silk blouse, a large, brightly patterned scarf draped over her shoulders. "I've got something I need to tell you," she said, taking Julia's elbow and steering her into the corner near Darkside's portrait.

Sharon paused as the painting caught her eye. "Now that's a right good picture of Darth Horse." She turned back to Julia. "Which brings me to my reason for coming early. I want you to have him. If you're going back to North Carolina, I'll ship him down to you."

Julia was flabbergasted at Sharon's generosity. "But he's a Thoroughbred stallion. He's very valuable."

Sharon shook her head. "He's not worth a plugged nickel without your influence. Although if you'd let me breed him to a couple of my mares, I'd be right grateful. Now that I'm sure his meanness wasn't born in him, I think he might have some pretty good potential as a sire."

"I'm accepting your offer only because he's my whisper horse and I need him as much as he needs me," Julia said, tears blurring her vision. "But I'll find some way to repay you."

"Hon, you repaid me by turning that horse around. I hate to see a good animal ruined by a bad human."

The elegant sound of classical music swelled through the room, interrupting their conversation.

"Sorry," Claire said, as the music's volume decreased. She stepped away from the bar and walked toward Julia. "While I have everyone's attention, I'd just like to remind you all to enjoy yourselves. Yes, we are hoping to sell Julia's paintings, but this is not really about business. It's a celebration of the growth of an artist whose work I have loved for a long time. Now I've come to love the artist herself too." Claire held out her hand to pull Julia into a hug. "I can't wait to share both with people who will appreciate them."

"You and Sharon are trying to make my mascara run," Julia said gruffly as the others cheered and applauded.

Davis consulted his watch with a flourish. "It's showtime. Darlene, you may unlock the door."

Disappointment dragged at Julia. Neither Paul nor Carlos was here. She did the chin-up, shoulders-back routine again as the first guests strolled through the door.

"Let's get into position," Claire said, walking to the place where people would turn to enter the circle of paintings. "Kate and Randall, so nice of you to come down from New York. I'd like you to meet Julia Castillo, one of my favorite artists, as you know."

Julia smiled and shook hands with one well-dressed art patron after another. Some were familiar with her previous work and complimented her on it; others were being introduced to her *Night Mares* without prior acquaintance. The experience of being the artist of the moment was not unpleasant, although she was beginning to wish she had forced down some food before she came. Her stomach was growling noticeably, and a hunger head-ache lurked behind her forehead.

"Your uncle's here. He must have come in the back door," Claire said, smiling and nodding in the direction of the bar. "Why don't you go see him while I take care of the latecomers?"

Julia skirted the outside of the panels to reach Carlos, who stood chatting with two women. He wore another of his power suits, this one with a burgundy shirt and black-and-gray striped tie. His companions, both of whom were young and attractive, were laughing delightedly. A little smile tugged at her lips; Carlos was an accomplished flirt.

"Hello, Tío," she said, greeting him with an air kiss on each cheek.

"*Mi* Julia!" He swept her into a warm hug, which she returned heartily as a rush of love for the man swept through her. He held her away by her shoulders. "Your show is a triumph. I have been eavesdropping on the conversations around me. I am a wrong-headed old man."

"Wrongheaded maybe, but not old," she said, smiling.

He excused himself from his company and walked her over to a quiet corner. "I see you here, surrounded by people who respect and admire you, looking so beautiful, and I understand I have hidden you away for too long."

Julia shook her head. "You gave me time to prepare for this. I wasn't ready before."

"So now I must step back and let others carry you into the future." He gestured around the crowded gallery. "I am proud to have been part of it."

"You're still part of it, part of me," Julia said, touching the spot over her heart. "As exciting as all this is, I kept wondering where you were. I wanted to share it with you." And despite all their problems, with Paul, but he must have decided he couldn't bear to see her after all.

Carlos cupped her face between his hands. "You are a good girl, *mi querida*. And a great artist, of course," he added with a twinkle in his eyes.

"Mr. Castillo, a pleasure to see you," Claire said, offering her hand to Carlos. Julia watched in amusement as he raised it to his lips and Claire looked coy. She recovered quickly, saying to Julia, "Paxton Hayes just arrived. He's in the circle of *Night Mares* now."

Julia tried to peer through the crowd. "Does he look like his blog photo?"

"If you add ten years and glasses," Claire said. "He's very tall and thin."

"Let me guess. He's wearing black," Julia said.

"He'd be drummed out of the society of New York art critics if he wasn't. Ah, there he is, headed for Darkside's portrait. Might as well go hear his verdict." Claire headed toward the scarecrow of a man standing in front of the single painting.

Julia followed, running through the possible scenarios she and Claire had discussed. Neither one of them expected Hayes to tell them what he really thought, but Claire wanted to feed him certain information and hope it made its way into his blog.

Just before they reached him, Claire halted and put her mouth next to Julia's ear. "You should know that three of your paintings have sold already. I'm reserving one for Tim now that everyone else has had their chance to make an offer. And several people have given Belle sealed bids for the auction of Darkside's portrait tomorrow night."

Elation flared, temporarily banishing the misery of Paul's absence. She savored the knowledge that her crazy last-ditch pilgrimage to Sanctuary had been justified. She pumped her fist.

Claire's musical laugh rang out. "Exactly."

The sound brought Paxton Hayes's head around, and Claire put her hand on Julia's back to move her toward the critic. "Paxton, you and Julia have already met by telephone, so you don't really need an introduction."

"Still, it is an honor to shake such a talented hand," Paxton said, surprising Julia with a firm, warm grip.

"Thank you for traveling here on such short notice," Julia said.

"So, I have to ask," he said, "are all of these paintings the same horse?"

"Yes and no." Claire had predicted this question and told her to be honest, even if it sounded farfetched.

He raised an eyebrow.

"The horse in the *Night Mares* came from in here." She tapped her temple and wished she hadn't, as it set her headache throbbing harder. "It kept coming at me and coming at me, so I kept painting it. Then I came here and found my *Night Mare* in the flesh. Turns out he's a stallion, but *Night Stud* didn't sound quite right."

Hayes's lips thinned into an almost smile. He nodded toward Darkside. "So this is the real horse."

"Up close and personal."

"Interesting story," he murmured, his eyes on the portrait. "The *Night Mares* are all about power and fear. This one is subtle." He turned back to Julia. "Quite a range."

"Thank you," she said, although she wasn't clear if it was a compliment or not.

A rise in the volume of conversation made all three of them glance toward the front of the room. Julia gasped when she saw Paul cleaving through the crowd, headed straight toward her. As he passed, people looked him up and down and turned back to their companions to comment. She understood their agitation because he was dressed in his leather motorcycle jacket, faded jeans, and heavy black boots. He carried two helmets and another leather jacket. He paid no attention to the disturbance behind him, his eyes never leaving her face.

The room tilted, and the voices faded to a murmur. She fought against it, locking her gaze on Paul like a lifeline, but she felt her knees begin to buckle as blackness closed over her.

Paul shoved a tall, thin man out of the way and caught Julia just before her head would have banged onto the floor.

"Julia!" Carlos pushed through the crowd and knelt on the other side of his niece's limp body. He tried to take her out of Paul's arms, but the younger man held on as he lowered her gently to the floor. Carlos pushed at his hands, saying, "She has—"

"Fainted," Paul interrupted, giving Carlos a level stare before he lifted Julia's head and slipped the folded leather jacket under it.

"No, she's having a—"

"Spell of low blood sugar." Paul stopped him again, this time with a scowl.

Carlos met Paul's gaze before he nodded, having received the message at last. "It is best if you put her on her side."

Paul eased her over, making sure her arms and legs were in comfortable positions.

Carlos fell silent and sat back on his heels, while Claire knelt to help Paul unhook the heavy necklace from around Julia's throat.

"I don't think she ate anything today," Claire murmured. "She said her stomach was upset. And she's been working late to finish the painting of Darkside."

Carlos tsked. "She knows she has to take care of herself."

"You can't trust these artistic types to remember to keep a normal schedule," Paul said, casting a fierce glare at Julia's uncle to make sure he stayed silent about Julia's secret. He pulled the chopsticks out of Julia's bun and loosened it, his fingers gently stroking the silk of her hair.

Claire stood to shoo away the guests who had gathered around Julia's limp form, assuring them, "She'll be fine. In the excitement of getting ready for tonight she forgot to eat."

Paul watched for the expansion and contraction of Julia's chest as he laid his fingers over the pulse on her wrist. It was regular, if not strong. She wasn't convulsing or having muscle spasms. All he could do was wait and wonder if it was a bad omen that she had blacked out at the sight of him.

It seemed like an eternity, but according to his watch, it was only a minute and forty-five seconds before her eyelids fluttered open. She blinked several times and turned her head to look up at him. "You came." She frowned. "But why are you dressed like that?"

"It doesn't matter. Just lie still." He beckoned to the tall man he'd nearly knocked down. "Could you ask one of the servers for some orange juice?"

"Julia, how do you feel?" Carlos asked.

"Like an idiot," she said. "It's not what you think, Tío. I should have eaten something."

"You don't know that," her uncle said.

"If she says she fainted from hunger, that's what happened," Paul said. "She's been standing up all night too." Not that he was entirely convinced, but he had to trust Julia to know her own body.

A young woman appeared with a glass of orange juice on a silver tray. Paul helped Julia into a sitting position and held the glass to her lips. She took the glass out of his hand and drank several swallows. Her stomach growled so loudly she clamped her free hand over it.

Paul gave her a smile. "Keep drinking."

She gulped down the rest of the juice, and he was relieved to see color returning to her cheeks. Carlos must have felt the same way, because he nodded to Paul.

"Is she going to be all right?" the tall man leaned down to ask.

"As soon as we get some food in her."

The man straightened and turned away, saying, "Interesting company she keeps."

Carlos coughed.

"I'm going to take you back to the office," Paul said, removing the glass from Julia's hand. "Mr. Castillo, will you round up some food?"

Julia tried to get her feet under her, but Paul slipped one arm behind her knees and surged upward with her in his arms. She squawked and squirmed. "I can walk."

"Maybe, but this is safer. Hold still."

Having her warm body pressed against him and her hair spilling over his arm made him want to walk out the back door and keep going. As he turned them both sideways through the doorway to the office, he allowed himself to lower his lips to the top of her head, brushing the waves lightly and inhaling the exquisite scent of her. An overlay of exotic perfume, an undernote of turpentine, and just Julia. To think, a few hours ago he'd believed he'd never get to touch her again.

He laid her on the couch, propping a pillow under her head before he sat down beside her.

She grabbed his jacket and pulled herself up to a sitting position facing him. "Why are you wearing those clothes?"

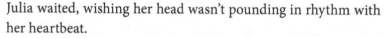

Julia waited, wishing her head wasn't pounding in rhythm with her heartbeat.

"I came to take you on a motorcycle ride." He was smiling at her in a strange way.

"You donated your motorcycle to the gala."

"I bought it back."

"Why?" She was hoping against hope.

He picked up a strand of her hair and wrapped it around his finger. "Remember you told me Darkside could change? And my brother could change? Well, I needed the motorcycle to convince you I could change."

The door opened to admit Claire and Carlos, laden down with plates and glasses of juice. Julia growled in frustration. Paul winked and gave her hair one of the teasing tugs she loved so much. He let them fuss over her for a minute and then firmly ushered them back out, saying she would eat better with less distraction.

"I'm not eating until you finish," she said, as he picked up a plate piled with hors d'oeuvres and brought it over to her.

"Okay," he said, sitting down beside her and putting the plate on the end table. Her astonishment must have shown on her face because he said, "You see, I've changed."

She was going to explode if he didn't tell her what she wanted to hear. She grabbed the lapels of his jacket and shook them, making the leather creak. "Get to the point."

His half smile evaporated, and she wondered if her hope was misplaced. She felt better when he took her hand and laced their fingers together.

"You told me I had to give Darkside and my brother a chance to be better people, or horses...you know what I mean."

There was no sign of the smooth-talking former mayor now.

"I watched you ride that stallion and it took my breath away. You'd transformed him into the horse"—he shot her a humorous look—"he was meant to be. When he threw you, it felt like a betrayal of all that trust you'd given him."

"He didn't throw me. I fell off."

He took a deep breath. "Right. He shied like any horse would. He wasn't trying to hurt you."

She nodded and squeezed his hand in approval. He looked at her, his face tight with the strain of whatever emotions he was reining in. "Today Eric ended up in the emergency room because he tangled with a swarm of bees and got multiple stings."

"Oh no!" she gasped. "Is he okay?"

"He's fine. Just itchy," he added with a reminiscent smile. "Terri called me to ride to the rescue, but when I got there, Jimmy had already handled it. Better than I could, because he'd taken a first-aid course before their last camping trip. I'm not saying he doesn't have serious issues to deal with, but he's got a powerful reason to fix them. I'm just in the way."

Julia touched his cheek. "Never."

He turned his head to kiss her palm. "There are still some things to work out, but my brother doesn't need a keeper anymore."

Her heart leaped, but he didn't pull her into his arms and declare his undying love.

"I was a real asshole yesterday," he said, "and I owe you an apology…"

"I'm not interested in apologies," she said.

"But—"

"Maybe later."

He sat silent a moment before saying, "I brought the bike to prove I was done trying to make your decisions for you. If you say you're cured of the epilepsy, then we're going out on the hog. If you think that devil horse will let you control him, then I'll pick you up when you fall off."

He stopped and scanned her face, his silver-gray eyes dark with uncertainty. "And if you're crazy enough to want to stay here in Sanctuary with me, then I hope like hell you'll do it. Because if you don't, I'm going to camp out on your doorstep in North Carolina until you change your mind."

Now he pulled her into his arms, crushing her against him and murmuring into her hair, "I love you so much it nearly rips my heart out. Give me a second chance."

Love and relief and exhaustion sent cascades of tears down her cheeks, and she burrowed into him. "I'll give you all the chances you want," she said, slipping her arms underneath his jacket so she could feel the heat of his body.

He unwrapped one of his arms to tilt her face up. "You're crying," he said with a frown.

"I thought I'd never see you again after tonight, and now, well, I hope—" She faltered to a stop because she'd been about to say she would get to spend the rest of her life with him.

"Now you're stuck with me forever," he finished for her before he brought his mouth down on hers, touching her lips gently at first but increasing the intensity as she responded. His hands began to move over her body, stroking the satiny fabric of her blouse so it slid sensually against her skin. She guided one of his hands to her breast.

He lifted his head, his breathing audible. "There's a whole gallery full of people out there."

"I know, so let's get out of here." She wanted to be naked and wrapped in his arms so she could obliterate all the wretchedness of the last few days. "On your hog."

He hesitated and her elation took a dive.

"I have to ask you this," he said, a line of worry between his brows. "Did you really faint from hunger or were you just saying that for your uncle's benefit?"

"It was really from not eating," Julia said, understanding his need to know. "It was completely different from a seizure."

He nodded and reached for the filled plate. "I trust you to know, but we're not going until you've eaten."

She could see the worry in his eyes and loved him all the more for overcoming it to accept her word. She wanted to fly through the night with him, the wind blocking out everything except the two of them together. She shoved two miniquiches in her mouth. "Orange juice," she mumbled as she tried to swallow the oversize bite.

He fetched her the glass as she stuffed in two more canapés. She washed them down with a slug of juice and licked her fingers, making his eyes go dark and hungry. "I know what you're thinking and I like it," she said.

He stood and held out his hand. "Let's ride."

Claire had been hovering near the hallway leading to her office. She couldn't leave the reception, but she was concerned about Julia's health. Julia's uncle had taken up a position just inside the hall, so when she saw him turn toward the office door, she hurried to join him.

She heaved a sigh of relief when Julia emerged beside Paul, her face radiant.

"*Mi* Julia, you are recovered?" Carlos said, the lines in his forehead smoothing away.

"Completely, Tío." She let go of Paul and threw her arms around her uncle for a quick hug. "I was just too nervous to eat."

Paul met Claire's gaze. He was wearing his old devil-may-care grin and her heart leaped with joy for him. "Can you spare Julia for the rest of the reception?" he asked. "We have someplace we need to be."

Claire smiled in answer to his as she nodded and shooed them back down the hall. "Go now before anyone sees you!"

She watched them disappear out the back door with a sense of satisfaction. Tim strolled up just as the roar of a motorcycle engine filtered through the hum of conversation. "Sounds like your plan worked," he said, slipping his arm around her waist.

"My plans always work," Claire said with serene self-confidence as she gave her husband's ribs a light squeeze. She noticed Julia's uncle still gazing toward the back door and started to say something reassuring when Belle came bustling up, a fistful of envelopes in her hand.

"These are the written bids for the Castillo painting for tomorrow night," she said. "You vouched for most of these folks, but there are a couple I wanted to check with you."

Claire waited as Belle consulted her notes. "Virgil Hofstatter?"

"Yes, he's a client from my New York days."

"How about Sandra Barron?"

"A noted collector from Texas."

"Then there was this weedy-looking fellow with an unusual name who claimed you knew him. Here it is. Paxton Hayes."

Belle looked up to find the normally controlled, dignified Claire Parker seize her husband's hands and swing him into a victory dance.

Epilogue

One Year Later

THE CHANDELIERS IN THE BALLROOM AT THE Laurels sparkled over the tables of elegantly dressed guests. Julia fidgeted with one of her long, dangling earrings until Claire leaned over the empty chair between them. "Did I tell you another painting sold in Milan? The gallerist called today, demanding more. She wants you and Paul to come back for another reception next year."

"I'm pretty sure she's more interested in Paul than me," Julia said, remembering how the woman had ogled him.

"I'm sure she's more interested in the money she makes from selling your work."

"Where did Uncle Paul go?" Eric piped up from across the table, pulling at his already crooked necktie.

"To talk to the man who hired him," Jimmy said.

"His boss?" Eric asked.

"Not exactly," Julia said. "Uncle Paul is his own boss. He runs the whole Pro Bono Project."

"That's why he goes to Washington all the time," Eric said. "I've been to see the space shuttle with him. And the Spy Museum. It was cool."

"Don't forget the Capitol building and the White House," Jimmy reminded him.

"They were okay."

"I thought they were boring," Julia teased. She'd been on that particular expedition with them.

Eric shrugged. "Maybe a little."

"Good evening," a man's voice boomed through the ballroom.

"Oh great, another speech," Eric muttered. He'd been excited about coming to a grown-up dinner for Uncle Paul, but there had been one speech too many for him.

Jimmy shushed him with a glint of sympathy in his eyes. Everyone at the table turned in their chairs to face the raised podium. The man at the microphone had gray hair and wore a tuxedo. His glasses flashed in the lights as he looked around the room.

Julia barely spared him a glance. Her gaze was focused on the tall, dark-haired man standing slightly behind the speaker, looking sexy as hell in his well-tailored tux. The man she'd fallen more and more in love with every day she'd spent with him over the last twelve months.

"I'm Ben Serra, and I'd like to tell you a little bit about Paul Taggart, the man who both imagined and brought to life the Pro Bono Project. First, you should know that he threatened to resign if I did this."

Polite laughter filled the room, but it wasn't far from the truth. Paul had objected strenuously to being honored tonight, only capitulating because Ben promised to make it a fund-raiser. All of the guests had paid far more than their gourmet meal had cost because they believed in Paul's creation. But they also wanted to meet its charismatic director.

"As you know, the project has been up and running less than a year, yet it has handled seven times as many cases as we originally planned for. Only the tireless efforts of the man standing next to me made this possible. He's a master recruiter, a fair taskmaster, and an exacting judge of quality. He's just not good at taking a compliment."

Julia chortled under her breath because although Paul flashed a good-natured smile, she could see his fingers drumming against his thigh.

"There's no plaque or crystal bowl because I was afraid he might wing them at me"—Ben paused to let the laughter die down—"but no one deserves one more than Paul Taggart, director of the Pro Bono Project."

Paul shook hands with Ben and stepped up to the podium to enthusiastic applause. He lifted a hand for silence. "Ben deserves as much credit as I do. He's the one who found the project a home and the money to succeed. That's the real reason there's no crystal bowl; he didn't want to waste any of our hard-earned funding on it."

The audience chuckled.

"There's another person here who deserves an imaginary crystal bowl. She's the extraordinary woman who convinced me I could be an agent of change in my world."

Julia's eyes brimmed with tears as he swept his gaze over the crowd and locked it on her.

"Julia Castillo, would you please stand up and give these nice folks a wave?" he said, another smile flashing across his striking face.

"Now I'm going to kill him," she said, rising and nodding to the crowd's applause. She could hear murmurs of "famous artist" and "paints black horses" from the table next to her.

She sat down and Claire touched her shoulder. "He knows how much he owes you," she murmured.

Julia shook her head. Paul was the extraordinary one; his work literally saved people's lives.

He finished by explaining the mission of the Pro Bono Project with a passion that brought the crowd to their feet for a standing ovation.

Eric looked around, his eyes wide. "These people really liked his speech."

"Hard to believe," Tim said, a glint of mischief in his eyes as he clapped.

Claire elbowed her husband. "I won't take you back to Milan if you don't behave."

He leaned down to whisper something in her ear. Julia saw a blush climb up her cheeks as she said, "All right, you can come with me."

Paul wove between the tables, stopping to shake a hand here or kiss a cheek there, as he headed back in their direction.

"God, I love a man in a tux," Julia murmured, her eyes following him.

"Tell me about it," Claire said, running her hand up Tim's lapel.

"That's the only reason we wear 'em," Tim said, capturing his wife's hand and bringing it to his lips.

Paul strode up and fell into his chair, snaking his arm around Julia's shoulders.

"You knocked them dead," Julia said, giving his thigh a squeeze. "But I'm going to make you pay for bringing me into it."

"I look forward to it," he said, his eyes going hot. He blew out a breath and faced the rest of the table. "I told Ben no more speeches for a month."

"You know you love having all those people hanging on your every word," Jimmy said.

"Since you were once our mayor, I'd think making speeches would be second nature to you," Tim joined in.

"I liked your speech, Uncle Paul," Eric said.

Paul's face softened as he looked toward his nephew. "You did?"

"Yeah, it was short."

Paul rocked back in his chair with a shout of laughter as the rest of the table guffawed. Once he stopped laughing he looked at his watch. "I'm officially off duty, and I have better things to do than be abused by my nearest and dearest. You ready to go, sweetheart?"

Julia nodded and everyone called out their good-byes. Paul retrieved their helmets and her leather jacket from the coat check and soon they were roaring down the highway toward home, the silk of her evening trousers rippling in the wind. She snuggled up against him, enjoying the fine wool of his tux against her cheek.

She felt him slow and lean into a right turn off the road. Peering around his shoulder, she saw the gates of Healing Springs Stables lit by the bike's headlight. Why in the world was Paul bringing her here at eleven o'clock at night?

He slowed down as they approached the barns, keeping the engine sound to a low grumble. He parked and cut the motor.

"What are we doing here?" Julia asked, as he helped her off the Harley.

"Visiting Darkside." He put her helmet on the bike's seat.

"At this hour?"

"He's your horse. You can visit him anytime you want to." He took her hand and started toward the stable. "Besides, I kept you in DC for two weeks straight. He needs more quality time with you."

"These shoes were not made for walking anywhere but a luxury hotel," she said, as she wobbled over the gravel on her four-inch heels.

"Up you go then." He dropped her hand to scoop her off her feet.

She wound her arms around his neck. "Much better but I still want to know why we're trespassing at Sharon's."

"You ask too many questions." He stopped to lower his head and kiss her long and intensely. She subsided against his chest and let him take her wherever he wanted to without comment.

"Hey there, Darth." Paul's voice rumbled through his chest. He still referred to Darkside as the devil horse, but it had taken on a certain tone of affection. He lowered Julia's feet to the ground and steadied her.

The stable lights were dimmed for nighttime, but Darkside's coat caught a gleam as he arched his neck over the stall door and whickered sleepily. "Hey, buddy," she said, running her hand up to scratch behind his ears. "Sorry to wake you up."

Willow's head appeared over her stall door. "You too, Willow," Julia said. She turned back to Paul. "Okay, now that we've wakened every horse in Sharon's barn, what are we here for?"

He took a breath. "At the banquet, I called myself an agent of change, but the truth is you're the real transformer. You've changed a lot of lives for the better, and none more than mine and this guy's." He smoothed a hand down Darkside's nose. "So we came up with a joint proposal for you."

Joy flooded her. "A proposal?"

Paul took both her hands in his and sank onto one knee on the pine bark, his expression solemn. "We both want you to marry me."

"Yes, yes, oh yes!" She yanked at his hands to get him to stand up. She wanted to wrap herself around him so he could feel her happiness and love.

"You just made Darkside a very happy horse," he said, before he gave her a kiss that seared her soul with its tenderness and passion.

As he pulled away, he reached behind her ear and brought out a ring, its stones flashing even in the low light. She laughed in delight.

"May I?" he asked, holding out his other hand.

She put her palm on his, savoring the warm strength of his long fingers as he slid the ring on. "It's a horseshoe," she said. "With black diamonds."

"Darth insisted."

"I love you so much," she said, feeling as though there wasn't enough room for her heart inside her rib cage.

He locked his arms around her and smiled. "I've loved you since I saw you standing beside a broken-down old car looking like a disgruntled wood sprite."

She shook her head. "You tried your darnedest to drive right by me."

"But I couldn't. I thought I was there to rescue you, but you're the one who saved me." His smile was replaced by a look of love so powerful she felt it in her bones. He lowered his mouth to hers.

As Paul's hands began to move over her body, focusing her attention on the swirl of heat and pleasure he knew so well how to evoke, she felt an insistent tug on the back of her jacket.

Pulling away from Paul, she turned to find Darkside nibbling at the leather. She laughed as she eased the hem of the jacket out of his mouth and stroked his nose. "Don't worry, buddy, I said yes."

"He just wants to make sure," Paul said, "because I promised him a lifetime supply of horse treats if he could convince you to marry me."

Julia wound her arms around Paul's neck and locked her body against his. "I'm convinced."

Discussion Questions for Country Roads

1) Julia's relationship with her uncle, Carlos, is complicated because she loves him but chafes against his overprotectiveness. Where is the line between protecting someone and controlling them? Do you think Carlos crossed it?

2) Paul also wants to protect Julia but does so without curtailing her freedom. Is this because he did not see her when she was affected by epilepsy? Do you think he would act differently toward her if she still had seizures?

3) Darkside plays a major role in giving Julia the confidence she needs to present her art to the world, stand up to her uncle, and fight for Paul's love. How can an animal, especially one that can be dangerous, help people work through their problems? Have you ever felt an animal helped you through a difficult time?

4) Julia's art changes throughout the book. How did each of her paintings reflect the events in her life? Do you see the *Night Mares* as sinister figures or as something different?

5) In *Take Me Home*, the first book in the Whisper Horse series, Claire Arbuckle is a principal character. She also plays an important role in *Country Roads*. Does including a familiar character

help tie the books together? Would you like to see Julia and Paul play a part in the next book?

6) Julia grew up feeling fragile and damaged because of the way her family treated her. Despite many instances of courage and independence on her part, it is hard for her to believe she is strong until those around her see her as such. What affects our self-image? Is it dependent on other people's opinions or do we determine it? Do you have something you believe is special about yourself, as Julia believed her art was?

7) Paul remains in Sanctuary to take care of his alcoholic brother, Jimmy. Do you consider it noble or foolish for Paul to sacrifice his own happiness for the sake of Jimmy's? If Jimmy hadn't had his son, Eric, do you think Paul still would have stayed?

8) The town of Sanctuary, West Virginia, is an important part of the story in *Country Roads*. What other books have you read in which the setting plays a strong role in the book? Do you have a favorite kind of setting?

MUSIC OF THE NIGHT
Detective Anna Salazar must resist the seduction of Maestro
Nicholas Vranos and his music to die for.

"Smart, sexy, and deeply emotional." —Barbara Bretton, *USA
Today* bestselling author

Acknowledgments

I COULD NOT WRITE MY BOOKS WITHOUT THE HELP OF family, friends, and colleagues. You all make my creative life richer and more satisfying. Many, many thanks to:

Kelli Martin, my editor, who champions my books and makes me feel valued as an author;

Jane Dystel and Miriam Goderich, my agents, who never cease to amaze me with their professionalism and support;

The author relations team at Montlake, who are helpful, knowledgeable, and just plain nice;

Andrea Hurst, my developmental editor, who makes every book she touches better;

Tara Doernberg and Deb Taber, my copy editors, and Toisan Craigg and Sara Brady, my proofreaders, who allow me to sleep at night;

Miriam Allenson, Cathy Greenfeder, and Lisa Verge Higgins, my critique group, whose wise and judicious reading of my work makes it infinitely stronger;

Rebecca Theodorou, English major extraordinaire, who developed the thoughtful, provocative discussion questions for this book;

Patti Anderson, my exercise guru, who helps me take care of myself in so many ways;

Clemente Brakel, Bruce Funderburke, and Mary McElroy, my friends and treasured resources, who have the answers when Google doesn't;

Brodie and Rocky, my whisper dogs, who keep me healthy by taking me on long walks; and

Jeff, Rebecca, and Loukas, my family, whose love is my anchor and my joy.

About the Author

Photo by Phil Cantor, 2003

Although she now lives in the suburbs of New Jersey, Nancy Herkness was born and raised in the mountains of West Virginia. A graduate of Princeton University, she majored in English literature and creative writing. Her senior thesis was a volume of original poetry.

Her contemporary romances have won several awards, including the Golden Leaf, the Gayle Wilson Award of Excellence, and the Aspen Gold.

She enjoys vacations to exotic locales (like Niagara Falls and Philadelphia, PA) and shares those with readers on "From the Garret," her own personal blog. She loves animals, having grown up with five dogs, three cats, a pony, and various wild creatures the cats brought home. She has phobias about driving across bridges and flying.

Nancy lives in a Victorian house with her husband and two mismatched dogs and cheers loudly for the New Jersey Devils hockey team.

To read excerpts, enter her contest, or find out about upcoming releases, please visit Nancy's website: www.NancyHerkness.com.